Travelling the world and hunting out antiques has given Andrew Harding a broad insight into the unravelling of the human mind. His fascination with the paranormal, supernatural and also crime have inspired him to cross boundaries and write this series of books.

The people who have crossed his path have covered such a broad spectrum that he's realised that anything is possible, and that there are no barriers to the depravity that could be hidden beneath the surface.

THE HYBRID SERIES:
CRITICAL MOMENTS

To Russell Blake
A thriller writer, with an extraordinary talent.

You don't have to give me your time, but you give it, willingly
and I'll be forever grateful to you, for the help you
continue to give me, as a new author.
Thank you, Russell.

Blake, our new genius wordsmith.
The powerful pull of his descriptive
penmanship is indefatigable and compelling.

http://RussellBlake.com

Bibliography of his work:

Fatal Exchange
Geronimo Breach
Zero Sum trilogy of Wall Street Thrillers
The Voynich Cipher
The Delphi Chronicle
How to sell a Gazillion ebooks in no time
(even if drunk, high, or incarcerated)
An Angel with Fur
The King of Swords
Night of the Assassin

Andrew Harding

THE HYBRID SERIES: CRITICAL MOMENTS

AUSTIN & MACAULEY

Cover art by Louisa Taylor

A CIP catalogue record for this title is available from the British Library.

ISBN 978 1 84963 107 5

www.austinmacauley.com

First Published (2012)
Austin & Macauley Publishers Ltd.
25 Canada Square
Canary Wharf
London
E14 5LB

Printed & Bound in Great Britain

This book contains descriptions of scenes of an explicit sexual nature which are suitable for adults only. The contents are not suitable for readers under eighteen years of age.

Acknowledgements

First and foremost

Austin &Macauley for believing in me and making a writer's dream come true.

My sister, Gerry, who has patiently listened to all my thoughts and read some of the hairy bits. I had her toes curling most of the time.

Finally to you John, for listening to my rampage about my book and being so supportive and enthusiastic. The knowledge you imparted was invaluable.
Thank you.

[www.honeysucklerose.co.uk]

Chapter 1

I pushed through the people with Harvey; they were gathering around the body on the pavement. Sitting; huddled into a ball beside it was a girl, woman; I wasn't sure yet.

"Could you all stand back please and give us some room. There's nothing to see. Get on your way, now?" Harvey stared at them, until some of them moved, but you always have a few who ignore you. He took out his warrant card, "I'll have you taken to the station, if you don't move on." They reluctantly moved; more were filling the spaces they left. Harvey stood away from me and the girl with his back to the crowd, giving me some space.

The rain was hammering down; Harvey pulled his phone out and asked where his team were. I suppose the rush hour has stopped them getting here, as quickly as us; coming from a different direction.

"I believe it was you who rang us; can you tell me who you are, please?"

I looked at the girl. *Why can't she look at me? Sitting on the wet pavement with her back to the wall; I don't understand her.* Her head was resting on her knees; looking straight ahead. The rain soaking her hair and running in little rivers down on to her thin clothes.

She called us, why the fuck won't she look at me?

I turned my attention to the body on the floor, beside her. It was a man. His hair stuck to his neck in clumps, because of the rain and the gap between them, dribbling blood from two small wounds.

"Harvey, look at this." He sat on his haunches in front of the body and looked to where I was pointing.

"Jesus Alli, that's a bite." He kept his voice low. "I'll ring Hillary and warn her what's coming in." We both stood up and looked at the girl, huddled beside the body of the man, touching the top of his head with her thigh.

"What's your name?" She didn't move, let alone, look at us. I bent over and touched her hand, wrapped around her knees. She flinched.

Harvey, she's petrified.

I can feel it Alli; try again?

"What's your name? You called us. I'm Alli and this is Harvey; we're here to help you."

She looked at me now. "You can't help me, so leave me alone."

Do you think she'll come with us, so we can talk to her Alli?

I'll try to read her mind. Whatever she's hiding is buried really deep, give me a minute.

I squatted down in front of her and took both of her hands in mine. She tried to pull away, staring at me but I held them firmly and she stopped pulling.

"I'm psychic. I can see you're the same as us." Her eyes bulged. "We'd like to talk to you."

"Don't bullshit me!" she screamed in my face.

"It's not bullshit, you are the same as us." *She doesn't believe it, Harvey.*

"You can stop talking in your heads. I can hear everything you're saying."

"And you say you're not?" I threw straight back at her.

"I'm Detective Inspector Burgess. Look, we need to talk to you either in a cafe somewhere or down at the station, it's up to you." She looked worried now. I heard cars screech to a halt.

Harvey forced his way through the crowds to his two detectives, who were just getting out of their car.

"Andy, wait for the doctor. Jamie, get Uniform to clear all these people out of here. We're taking her over the road to the cafe, she's bricking it about something and Alli can't read her yet. She may open up a bit, away from the body."

"Okay, Sir. Shall I get Socco down here?"

"I don't think they'll get much, it's been raining for hours but call them out Jamie."

"Will do, Sir." He ran over to the nearest Uniform Officer.

Harvey turned back to me and pushed his way through the onlookers. "We'll take her over there," he sat on his haunches in front of the girl. "We're taking you to the cafe over the road. Come on, you look like you could do with a hot drink."

"I tried to help, I wasn't strong enough." Harvey stood up, "Come and tell us out of the rain, you'll catch your death out here."

She looked at me. "Is he trying to be funny."

"No love, he's trying to be kind; you're completely missing the point."

"I'm sorry." I put my hand out for hers and helped her up, she was shaking like a leaf and soaked to her skin. Her bare arms looked white in the gloom of the storm. Andy came to stand with the body as we walked away.

We hurried her across the road to the cafe and sat at the back, not succeeding at staying away from anyone. A girl came over and asked what we wanted. I ordered three teas and took my jacket off to put over her shoulders. She only had a T-shirt and jeans on and should've been shivering, if she wasn't a Hybrid.

She'd had her arms crossed over her body until we sat down. It was obvious she had no underwear on and a few of the men in the cafe were staring at her.

"Thank you. Sorry I'll get it soaked inside."

"Put your arms in the sleeves, I don't care if it gets wet, it's okay." Harvey was trying to read her mind.

"What's your name?" She just stared at me for a moment.

"I don't know what it is, that's why I couldn't answer you before. I know what I am; I don't know who I am."

"How did you phone us? It doesn't look like you have a phone on you now or did you use a call box."

"I grabbed a man's trouser leg and screamed for a phone. He could see I needed help and let me use his. He hurried off, after I gave it back."

"Do you know who the dead man was?" Harvey asked her gently.

A tear ran down her cheek and I gave her a tissue from my bag.

"Thank you. His name is Olli and he found me hiding in a shed six months ago; he's looked out for me ever since. I can't believe he's dead."

"What the hell happened?" Harvey asked her.

She looked at Harvey. "A huge man came over and started rowing with him, over something really stupid. I'd never seen him before, we've only been in this town for a couple of days. We were in a derelict house, keeping out of the rain and two policemen moved us on. That's why I haven't got a coat on. They wouldn't let me take it. Our rucksacks are still there with all our belongings in."

"Did these policemen have uniforms on?" Harvey asked.

"No, they said they were plain clothed policemen and they're moving all tramps out of town."

"You're the cleanest tramp I've ever seen," I said to her. "Were you sleeping rough?"

The tea was put on the table. Harvey gave her a fiver and said keep the change, to hurry her away from us.

"Not really, we always did for maybe a couple of nights before we found ourselves a flat but we've always worked and moved about. Olli never liked staying in one place for too long, he had itchy feet."

"Was he the same as you?"

She smiled, shook her head and lowered her voice. "No, he wished he was many times. He always said when he ages he'll look like a perv, being with someone so young. He made a joke of it but I know he was serious."

"How did an argument turn into him being killed? I'm sorry to keep pressing you, I need to know if we're going to catch whoever did this."

She looked at Harvey again, "From the way the big man kept yelling about something that happened a while ago, I'm sure he thought he was someone else."

"Can you remember anything he was saying?"

"He kept saying, last month, I told you not to do it. I was screaming and trying to pull him off so I missed a lot of it."

"There's a bite on your friend's neck," Harvey whispered.

She stared at Harvey. "What do you mean a bite, he's never been bitten." Harvey looked towards the door, Jamie was hurrying, to speak to him.

"What is it Jamie?" Harvey could see he was confused about something.

"Sir, this is weird. The doctor says he's not dead, he's got a heartbeat."

Harvey got up to leave with Jamie. "Stay here with her, Alli."

and headed for the door. The other customers were wondering what the hell was going on. I stared at them and they lost interest.

"I want to go and see him."

I put my hand over hers. "He'll come back as soon as he knows for sure. He can see how much you care about him."

She looked at my hand. "Bloody hell, they're real aren't they."

"Yes, I'm married to Harvey. We got wed four months ago. Harvey runs the murder squad. That's why we were called out to this."

"Are you in the police, too?"

"Almost a year now. I was taken on by them because I read minds and see the dead. It's very handy in his line of work."

"He's not come back, they must have made a mistake." Silent tears were rolling down her face. I put my arm around her shoulder and gave her a hug.

The door opened and her eyes shot up, to see who was coming in. Harvey walked towards us and sat down. The man we thought was dead, stood before us soaking wet.

"Olli!" she yelled. I stood up to let her out of the corner. He flung his arms around her shoulders and kissed her. I sat beside Harvey and they took the bench, opposite. Harvey waited a few minutes before he asked him anything.

"Olli, do you understand what's happened to you?"

"Not really, everything went black and then I started to feel things like the pavement and the rain hitting my face. When I opened my eyes, someone had a stethoscope on my chest, listening to my heart."

"Can you remember where your belongings are?" Harvey asked him.

"Yes, two streets away, where a whole row of houses are boarded up and we were in the only one boarded opposite. The front door was already open."

"I know it, we'll get your stuff and you're coming home with us. I'm sure Alli won't mind you using the cottage that was left to her, by our dear friend, when she died."

Harvey looked at me. "You know I won't Harvey."

Olli looked at us both. "Why are you helping us? We're just drifters,"

"Everyone needs a helping hand at some point in their lives and this is your time," Harvey answered him. Olli looked stunned. I got up and let Harvey out.

"Come on, you could do with a bath and dry clothes, you both look like drowned rats." The girl giggled at me. "What are we going to call you?"

"I've always called her Gina, I think it suits her," Olli told us.

"Gina it is from now on. Are you ready?" I swept my hand to the door, and they got up to follow us out of the cafe. The rain was very fine now and we got in Harvey's car, to pick up their stuff.

Harvey went into the building with Olli, to help him get their things and their bags had been ransacked. Olli was pissed off; their clothes were strewn all over. They picked them up and stuffed them into the rucksacks.

"The bastards that made you move on must have watched you come in here with your gear. Forget it. We have plenty of clothes and we'll get you more over the next couple of days."

"I don't understand why you're helping us like this."

"We've both been in your position and someone helped us in the past; like I said it's your time, let's go."

Harvey parked the car outside our house and we took them into Jenny's cottage next door, to show them around.

"It's not very modern but she was eighty-two when she died. If you want to stay we'll change the furniture for you, it won't be a problem."

"We haven't any money for rent until I get a job."

"We didn't ask you for rent, we don't want any." They both looked astonished.

"After you've got changed, come to the big house next door. I'm ordering a curry, if you both eat it?"

They smiled. Harvey opened a drawer in the kitchen and took out a bunch of keys. "Here are the keys for this house and so you don't worry, Jenny died in hospital. Some people are a bit weird about that sort of thing."

"I can't believe how kind you two are." Gina looked like she was going to cry.

"I told Olli; we've both been in your position. I'll order for an hour's time, if you're ready before that just come round, we'll have a drink."

The bell on the front door rang. I opened it and asked them in. They looked shocked at the house, their eyes were everywhere.

"Come in, make yourselves at home. There's no standing on ceremony here. What do you both drink?" Harvey asked them.

"We drink wine when we've got money Harvey; red wine," Olli answered.

"That's what we mainly drink, sit down and relax." They both sat on one of the sofas very close together. Harvey went down to the cellar.

"This house is incredible. I've never seen furniture like this before Alli."

"Harvey looked for all this years ago, long before I met him."

"He doesn't look old enough; did he buy it from his pram?" Olli joked.

I smiled at him. "You'll understand things when we've talked to you, after we've eaten. Just remember this; we've been where you are now and had help from others. We're passing on the favour we were once given."

Harvey brought them a glass of wine each and went back for ours.

"Thanks Harvey." I raised my glass. "To new friendships and new beginnings." I toasted them. They both looked gobsmacked.

"Drink up," Harvey coaxed, "Your lives change from this point on; that's if you want it to."

The bell rang and Harvey hurried to pay for the takeaway. As he walked back through the sitting room, towards the kitchen, he said, "Come and help yourselves." I followed him and they came into the kitchen staring at everything.

"Bloody hell; I've never seen a kitchen like this," Gina said. "Not that I can remember, anyway."

"If you stay I'll get one fitted, just as nice as this, next door." Harvey was opening all the cartons. "Have anything you want; dive in. We'll throw anything that's left; don't be shy." They picked up plates and gathered what they wanted.

"We eat off the big coffee table in the sitting room. The

dining room is a bit formal for a chat." Gina looked at me, smiled and picked up her cutlery.

I cleared all the plates, loaded the dishwasher and joined them.

Olli was the first to speak. "The meal was great, thank you. Please don't think I'm being rude, but why us?" Harvey smiled at both of them and started explaining.

"I run the murder squad at the local nick and Alli works with me. She reads minds, sees the dead everywhere and can dig inside someone's head to find out what we need to know, to solve the cases we get. Today, Gina phoned 999 for help as you'd been attacked. When we got there, you were dead as far as both of us were concerned." Olli's face showed total shock.

"I was even going to ring the pathologist, to tell her what was coming in. You've been bitten the same as us."

"What the hell are you saying?"

Gina touched his hand, "Listen Olli, he'll explain it all to you."

He stared at her, "Am I the same as you?" She nodded. A smile broke out on his face, "This is fucking brilliant." He gave her a cuddle.

"Sorry Alli, I got a bit carried away and swear a lot I'm afraid."

"You should fit in here perfectly then." Harvey was laughing at me.

His mobile rang, "Sorry, I have to get this." He listened and said, "You bugger Jo, I thought we were getting called out. I was going to ring Hillary today and things changed, slightly." He listened again. "Come round and you'll see for yourself, I'm not telling you, okay; see you soon." He hung up. "They'll be here soon. Sorry; Jo works with us and Hillary is a pathologist. They're a gay couple; you don't have any hang-ups about that, do you?"

"Gay, straight; it doesn't bother us. We both know what we want."

"Hillary is human and would love to be in your position now Olli; once they've been told I think the subject should be dropped."

"I agree; I know how that feels Harvey. It didn't sit well with me."

"What work do you look for, Olli?"

"Anything to do with cars; mechanic is my first choice but I've done delivery driving. I haven't got an HGV licence but I wouldn't want to be away from Gina, now we've found each other."

"I know exactly what you mean by that," Harvey squeezed my hand.

"They're outside; I'll let them in."

As I left the room, Harvey said, "Who needs a doorbell, when you can read minds." I heard laughing behind me.

"Come on you two, I'm getting bloody wet standing here?" They came running up the path and I stood back to let them in.

"What's the big secret he couldn't tell Jo over the phone?" Hillary asked. I put my finger across my lips and walked into the sitting room. They followed right behind me.

Harvey got up to do the introductions and went for more wine.

"This fucking weather is driving me mad. You get a day off and it pisses down," Jo said to no one in particular.

Harvey walked back in with wine for them. "And you were worried about swearing; Olli." That set us off laughing and everyone relaxed.

"What were you going to ring me about today, Harvey? I didn't get what Jo meant about things changing."

"We were called out because Olli had been attacked and was dead, but had a bite on his neck. About an hour later he was kissing Gina, again."

"Lucky bugger," was all Hillary said. We could see the tears in her eyes. Jo put her arms around her.

"Come on, we'll give them a bit of space. Does anyone fancy a swim?"

Olli looked at Gina. "We haven't got costumes."

I giggled. "Nor have we." Harvey got up and followed me through the kitchen. I opened the double doors and flicked the light switches.

The pool was flooded with light. I dropped my clothes with Harvey's and we dived in. Gina and Olli were looking from the door and smiled at each other. It didn't take long for them to strip and jump in. A few minutes later Jo dived in and Hillary used the steps. I did a few lengths on the bottom and above me, Harvey was trying to catch up on the top; ploughing through the water.

Olli and Gina watched us and couldn't stop smiling. I caught sight of Jo and Hillary laughing and carrying on; disappointment buried once more.

I came up for air and dragged Harvey to the bottom where we made love for ages. We've both been able to stay down for much longer than we used to and have it to twenty-five minutes, now. When we came up the look on their faces was priceless.

"They're both fish. They pretend they're Hybrids, but they lie," Jo said when she saw their faces.

"Can you do it Jo?" Gina asked.

"Christ no, I'd bloody drown. That was stupid I can't die. Put it this way, I haven't tried." Hillary was behind her, jumped up and planted her hands on Jo's shoulders and pushed her under. Jo swam away from her hands, down to the bottom and back up.

"I'm changing that; maybe I could with practice," she put her arms around Hillary and they floated with their feet kicking to the other end of the pool to make out.

I got out, hurried to the cupboard in the corner and pulled out tons of towels for everyone. I wrapped one around my body and another for my hair. When I was putting the coffee on I felt Harvey's arms around me.

"How are you Mrs Burgess?"

I pressed my body into his, "I'm very happy Mr Burgess, and you."

He squeezed me tight, "Ready and waiting Mrs Burgess."

Pack it in you two, you've got guests.

"Did you see that parrot flying around Mrs Burgess?" We could hear Jo and Hillary laughing in our heads.

I filled the cafetière and got coffee cups out. Gina and Olli came through from the pool, wrapped in towels.

"I never expected that Alli, this is a different world than we've been used to." I smiled at him. "And good taste in music, what more could a man want."

"That's Harvey playing his guitar," Olli was shocked and left Gina to go and see for himself.

"Do you need a hand with anything, Alli?"

"The only thing I want from you is to know if you're sticking around, Gina. We've all had a nomadic life of sorts, even Hillary; put down some roots. The house next door is yours for as long as you want it. We don't bond easily with humans, apart from life partners and you have friends here. All four of us like you both, I'm sure you've felt it." I went to the pool room door, "Come on, stop shagging, the coffee's made."

Gina was laughing when I turned back to her, "I want to stay. If Olli gets a job I think he will, too."

"We'll have to work on that, won't we?" I carried the coffee through just as Harvey came to the end of some music. My towel slipped as I put the tray down.

"Sorry," I dragged it back up.

"Don't be sorry, Alli." Gina came over, "Can I see your back? I noticed it in the pool but didn't see it properly." I faced away from Olli and let the towel drop down my back. "Alli it's beautiful. I don't know how any of you dared get as much done as you have."

Jo and Hillary came in. Jo only wears a towel around her bottom half. She has no boobs and was covered in tribal tattoos, like Harvey. Her shoulders were broad and she'd been weight training recently. Her physique was as good as his and we think nothing of it.

"Blood hell Jo, you look like a guy!" Gina put her hand to her mouth, "I'm so sorry Jo, it just fell out of my mouth."

Jo started laughing, "Not another one with Alli's disease." That set us all off. We fell about, laughing.

"Gina, you've made my fucking day," Jo said. "I couldn't give a shit how much I've spent in that gym now." Gina giggled and Olli cuddled her with a huge grin on his face.

"I think I ought to pour this coffee before it turns solid." I picked up the coffee and poured.

Hillary and Jo left about an hour later. Hillary has to have more sleep than me and we talked about more serious things.

"Gina, what did you feed off? I'm only asking, because I buy blood for us. Alli used to go out to feed before we got together."

"This is the bit I'm not sure about," Olli admitted and his face showed it.

Gina told us, "Olli never saw me feed, I wouldn't let him. I was ashamed of it, if you want the truth. Small animals, deer mainly."

"You must be fast if you catch deer. I do the speed thing but Alli hasn't had to and has never tried it. We drink ours in the shower and wait for the feelings to hit and then the change."

"What the hell is that!" Olli asked, now very unsure what he'd got himself into.

Harvey smiled at him and explained. "The feelings hit and you're as randy as fuck, to put it bluntly. The change is different and that happens when we get aroused or really annoyed about anything. We look different and couldn't afford to change in public. We find it difficult sometimes at work, especially if kids are murdered. Don't be worried about it when you feed. Let it happen as we revert to type at that time and it heightens everything. You'll enjoy it, I can promise you that. I'll supply you with blood as you wouldn't find many deer running around here, Gina." She giggled at him.

"How did you manage feeding on your own, Gina? That must have been really frustrating for you," I asked. *Maybe I shouldn't.*

"It's alright Alli. I don't feel embarrassed in front of you two because we're the same I suppose. I used to hide and masturbate, and it drove me nuts at times."

"I told you I should've been with you."

"I'd have probably shagged you to death, Olli. It was hard enough hiding the fact I change when we made love. Now you know why I insisted on having the light off."

"What a way to go though." He flung his arms out and fell on the empty seat beside him with a huge sigh. We started laughing.

"I'm making tea. That coffee was too strong,"

"I'm having more wine Alli and I think these two will help me drink it as their hands didn't shoot up for tea."

"I have to find a job pretty quickly because we can't keep taking off you both." Olli looked upset.

"Listen, the pair of you. I've been playing the stock market for the last fifty years or…" He didn't get another word out.

"What the fuck are you talking about, Harvey; you're not old." Olli was really confused.

"Let me explain. Alli and I were bitten when we were kids and aged normally up to a certain date. For Alli it was twenty-two but she's been stuck there for the last fourteen years. I got to twenty-four and have been there for over a hundred years."

They made no sound because their mouths were open.

"You're catching flies," I called.

Gina started giggling and elbowed Olli. "That's fuckin incredible. It doesn't show you're alright."

"Another witty bugger in our midst. I have enough trouble with Jo," Harvey was grinning at him. "I'll get more wine and continue."

I made my tea and carried it in. "Who plays the piano?" Gina was looking at it.

"Oh, it's me," and sat down on a floor cushion.

"Play it Alli, for me." Harvey came in with three glasses of wine. How could I say no? I love him. I took a sip of my tea and walked to the piano. I sat down and started playing something I'd heard on the classical channel on the radio. We were driving into work so I didn't hear all of it.

"Why have you stopped, Alli?"

"That was all I heard on the radio. We don't work far from here, Gina."

"Please play the music you played last night for me." Harvey came over and stood behind me to listen. I went through the whole piece and at the end of it he kissed my neck.

"Thank you, I loved that. Your tea is getting cold." We sat on the other sofa and Harvey cuddled me as I drank my tea.

Gina and Olli finished kissing. "Sorry, that music got to us. You play really well Alli, it was beautiful."

"Thank you Gina but I think Harvey takes the biscuit for music."

"Olli loves the guitar but I love to hear a piano. Do you ever play together?"

"Sometimes; I'd like to hear you again Harvey. I missed most of your playing earlier." He squeezed me and got up for his guitar.

He played my favourite track of Chris Rea's and I closed my eyes and just listened. It did something to my head and always made me really horny. Harvey knew exactly what it was doing to me and played it over and over, changing it slightly so it sounded like one piece of music. I kept my eyes closed when he finished. Olli and Gina thought I was asleep and said they ought to go. Harvey took them upstairs, gave them enough blood for tonight and they left us. I heard the door close and waited for Harvey's first touch.

Chapter 2

He kept me waiting for a while, and didn't mind at all. I felt him take hold of my hand, "Keep your eyes closed, Alli; I have a surprise for you." *I love surprises; you know that.* I heard him giggle in my mind and led me to the stairs where he picked me up and did the speed thing. He put me down, covered my head with a hood and padlocked it on. *Let the games begin.*

He guided me for about ten steps; ripped my clothes off really fast and lay me across a padded bar. He buckled a strap on both ankles and fixed them so my legs were spread wide apart. He picked up my right arm, then the left and handcuffed them so they rested on my back.

My head was pulled down and fixed; it couldn't move in any direction and then a gag forced into my mouth and buckled behind my head. He left me for a while so that the anticipation built in my mind until I was at boiling point.

Something warm and liquid touched just above my bum, ran down into my fanny, out over my bump and dripped off. The sensation was amazing and I changed instantly. Both Harvey's hands, covered in rubber played all around my bum, fanny and bump. I was going nuts for him to fuck me. Gagged or not, I made noises which made him play with me endlessly. *This is fucking beautiful.*

His thumb suddenly pushed up my bum and I went to fucking paradise as he massaged it until I came. I could feel my bum squeeze his thumb as my fanny convulsed with the orgasm he prolonged still using his thumb. *God that was good.*

He pulled his thumb out and I felt something thin and long getting pushed up there and then he turned it on. *Your favourite worm; wondered what it felt like, and love it.* It squirmed, wiggled and buzzed at different times. Harvey turned it up making it do all three constantly. It was bloody amazing and distracted me totally as it felt so good.

A heavy weight was hung on my bump ring so it pulled down

hard. *Hmmmmm.* Two more on my nipple rings and extra weights added. He fixed the metal rings around each of my boobs and squeezed them with his oily hands. *They're as hard as rocks now and I love how they feel.*

He undid the handcuffs and poured more oil over my back. He rubbed his gloved hands all over my back and then started on my legs.

I begged him to fuck me after a few minutes of his hands on the insides of my legs, but he carried on until I was absolutely demented, wanting him. He pulled the worm out and pushed something larger up my bum and turned it on. It throbbed; he turned it up and carried on with my legs until I was screaming in his mind. *You've got to fuck me, please?*

He twisted my nipple rings; shocks shot to my fanny and he pushed his cock in hard. All the steel balls in my fanny vibrated with the throbbing up my bum and Harvey moaned and groaned pushing his cock in and out. His hands were all over my back and round my bum. I started shaking as I came and he pushed deeper, coming with me.

He held me tight until we finished shuddering and lay over me just stroking my body until all the feelings calmed down.

I felt him pull his cock out gently and slowly took everything off. He lifted me up from the bar and cuddled me so tenderly.

"You are amazing Alli, I love you," lifted my chin and kissed me as if I was made of paper. Tears filled my eyes. I get overwhelmed when we kiss like that. He kissed both my eyes and played with my fringe, staring into my face.

"It's you that makes everything work for me, always has Harvey. I think you know that." I got hold of his still erect cock, "Come on we have to feed and then you're all mine." I heard him say 'promise' as we hurried to the blood room.

He looked down at the thing in my hand, "You found another one."

I giggled, "I have my sources. I know how you loved it last time. It was a shame you buckled the last one as I had to send to Germany for this, you naughty boy." I flicked the end of his cock with a riding crop and he giggled in anticipation of what was to come. I knelt down and sucked his cock until he was almost coming. I opened the iron maiden for his cock and balls and clamped it on. As the spikes went in, his knees almost buckled.

He took hold of it and moaned with pleasure, "I love this, Alli. I didn't think you'd ever find another one."

"Hands off," I handcuffed his hands behind his back. "I'm slipping upstairs for a moment, so don't be naughty when I'm gone or I'll have to whip you."

Please? I giggled at him and hurried up.

I stood at the door and watched him. His hearing was so acute he knew I was there and continued to push the iron maiden on to the side of the single chair to feel it dig in just a bit more.

I lashed the back of his legs. "You will insist on being naughty."

He giggled and looked at me, "Jesus, Alli, you look incredible."

I had on a black rubber one piece, finishing just under my ears. Black 'killer heel' shoes and a whip. My hair pulled up into a knot on top of my head with the red spike through it. Eye make-up, very heavy and red lipstick, to match the spike.

I climbed on to my white Baby Grand and sat on the top. "Come here!"

He got to about a foot from the piano. "Stop there!" I opened my legs and the rubber parted from my bum to my pelvic bone. I played with my bump with my gloved hands and changed immediately. He watched intently, every movement my hands made and kept going, it felt so good. "Finish me off!"

When he bent his head I dug each heel of my shoes into his back.

Dig them in harder, please? I pushed hard with my heels. *Perfect.*

The first touch of his mouth had me screaming for more. The heat he generated in me with his mouth was incredible. I loved it. I kept raising my fanny higher and the heels dug in even more. *That's fucking heaven for me, Alli.*

He ran his tongue round and around my bump, picked up the ring through it in his teeth and pulled hard. That made me hornier than ever. His mouth went over my fanny and I nearly fainted. *I love that so much.* From there his tongue moved to my bum and when he played with it with the ball in his tongue, heat pulsed through my whole body. I came there and then unable to hold it any longer. The lightning bolt hit my brain. I passed out.

When I woke up Harvey was licking me dry, and the feelings from that were heaven, every time his tongue touched me. *Absolutely delicious*.

I lifted his head with my rubber clad hands, laced my fingers together behind his neck and wrapped my legs around his body.

"Step back!" When he did my body went with him and I lowered my fanny down on to the iron maiden. I let my legs come round to his front, trapping him between my legs. His eyes lit up, he knew what was coming. I took a key from my mouth and undid his handcuffs.

The first thing he did was cuddle me. "Thank you," he whispered in my ear. He moved his cock back and forward quite slowly at first, testing things out. The whole of my fanny from the front of my pelvic bone to my bum was smothered in metal balls and that huge thing was made of iron. Neither of us knew how this would end up. He picked up the pace a little at a time and heat started to build really fast.

He slowed down. "I don't think this was a good idea Alli. We've hardly got going and it would get too hot for you."

"Let's go into the pool. That should keep the heat down."

"We can try." He wrapped his arms around me and did the speed thing. The next second we were under water and swimming up for a lung full of air each to sink to the bottom again.

It was much better and we must have heated the pool by a few degrees, but neither of us got too hot. Harvey loved it and so did I. We came together and lay on the bottom in each other's arms until the feelings stopped and the heat cooled. He lifted me off carefully and we swam to the surface.

"I can't believe we did that, Alli. Are you sure you're okay."

"I'm absolutely fine, no damage done to me. My biggest concern was what your cock would look like. We were at it like rabbits down there."

Harvey started laughing: "All I know was, it felt fucking de lux, to coin one of Hillary's sayings."

"Get out and we'll take a look." Harvey hauled himself straight out of the pool, sat on one of the chairs and waited for me to unlock it.

I giggled when I saw it. "Some of the rivets are worn flat." I touched underneath, found the release bar and pulled. It opened slowly because the spikes were embedded very deep. Harvey prised it off and we both watched the holes close up in seconds.

"Just as well you only fire blanks. That could have damaged your manhood. That was a stupid thing to say. Who in their right mind would put that on if they were human?"

"You did say it came from Germany." Harvey was laughing, "I could think of quite a few that would try it. Anyone into fetish or S&M, even gay men."

"I bet their bloody eyes would water, even putting it on, let alone shagging."

"I can see your point."

"Ha ha, very funny. You better watch out Mr Burgess. I might have to send the worm up there." Harvey's eyes bulged at the thought.

I made tea for me in the special white cup and saucer for the next little event for Harvey. I put the tea down so he could see it where he was standing. Standing, wasn't really the right word. His wrists were fixed to a bar with a ring in the middle. Through the ring was a hook from the frame where our basket chair hung. The frame was no ordinary chair hanger. The chair was only there to disguise why we had it in the kitchen, and was really a hoist.

His ankles were strapped to a metal bar and each end was fixed to the floor with a Bungee strap. He was so strong it was the only way to contain him. Before I hoisted him above the floor I gagged him with a ball.

I picked up the cup and saucer and drank the tea right in front of him. The whole time his eyes followed the black gloves. Between sipping the tea I ran my fingers along the row of balls implanted under his cock, and he shuddered every time he felt my hand covered in rubber.

That is fucking, amazing.

He couldn't see what I was doing down there but his mind pictured it. I watched it with him, in my mind. I put the cup down, held his cock in both hands and rubbed the head of it over the rubber I was wearing, and he moaned like crazy.

Hmmmmm, you're driving me nuts.

I picked up the cup and saucer again and made so much of drinking from the cup, his mind was getting fucked as he watched. I knew he loved it and made the tea last so much longer for him. When the tea was finished I put the cup and saucer where he could still see it and went behind him.

I played with him on the inside of his legs with my hands and he writhed at every touch. I put one hand between his legs and gripped his cock. *That feels so good.* My other thumb found that place above his bum that always sent him crazy.

I wanked him off as I moved my thumb around. The noise coming from him, told me he was enjoying it and I stepped up the pace a lot. The whole frame behind me shook as he thrashed and moaned when he came. I pushed my hand forward to catch as much of his semen as possible and squeezed his balls with my other hand. I ran my tongue from his bum, all the way up his back when I stood up. I'll lick it off the gloves; where he could see me.

His eyes watched every movement and when I'd licked all his semen off I pushed each finger in and out of my mouth a few times in a very suggestive manner. I bent down and licked his cock to make sure I'd missed none and left him, to get his favourite toy of all.

I didn't try to hide it. His eyes sparkled when he saw it. I played with his cock for a while and picked up the toy. He closed his eyes and waited for it. I clamped it on to his cock and let the heavy iron ball, on the thick chain, drop. All the spikes bit in at once and he moaned in ecstasy. *Hmmmmm, just perfect.*

I left him to wash my gloved hands and walked into the sitting room to play my piano for an hour.

He heard me coming and had his eyes on the doorway waiting for me to appear. All I had on were his favourite red 'killer heel' shoes, the rings around my boobs and long, red rubber gloves. I walked over seductively. He watched every move I made and strained to watch me go behind him.

I ran my hands all over his back and up the back of his legs, let them wander around his body to play around his groin. My boobs, like rocks now, rubbed up and down his back.

I played with the base of his cock and he thrashed around on the hoist. The noise he made was incredible as I slipped my fingers between his cock and legs. When he came he went rigid and made the loudest sigh I'd ever heard from him. I held him tight until he stopped bucking and his body relaxed. I kissed his back and walked around to his front.

I slowly took the cage off his cock and carefully pulled the spikes out of his flesh. I pressed a button on the hoist and his feet touched the floor. I undid the Bungee straps and took the straps off his ankles then unbuckled the ball from his mouth and eased it out to kiss him.

"I didn't expect to come like that, Alli. It was unbelievable. Alli, I want to thank you properly. Lower the hoist and bend over in front of me."

I did as he asked and he thanked me alright. It was heaven every time his tongue touched me and got me to the point where my legs had turned to jelly.

"Undo my wrists. I need to hold you up."

He held me with his strong hands, and brought me to screaming point with his mouth all over my fanny. He flipped me and rammed me on to his cock, facing away from him. *I've wanted that for hours*.

He put his arms around my body and did the speed thing up to the big mirror on the landing. I watched his cock disappear inside me as he played with my bump and I rubbed my nipples to send shocks to my fanny.

He put his hands on my waist and lifted me up and down his cock ever-so slowly. I put a finger into both nipple rings and pushed them away from me. He teased me with the head of his cock, just on the lips, before pushing me down hard. I screamed when I came. He held me tight until I stopped shaking and the feelings had gone. He gently lifted me off so I could cuddle him.

"I love you Mr Burgess. That was quite a night."

"Well wifie, you surpassed yourself tonight. Seeing you on your piano covered in black rubber, did my head in before all the games. I have to ask, how did you get that one piece on and off by yourself?"

"You forget; I ordered from Germany. What they had over there was totally different from the things we've found here. There was a hidden zip from my bum right up to my neck and you wouldn't have realized the fanny bit opened until I opened my legs. They seem to have been making the stuff a lot longer than most and it was more refined.

"I put in a big order. I could bring things out over time, but only when you're naughty," I told him with so much innuendo in my voice he pictured other things in his mind.

I slapped his bum hard, "Don't be naughty and spoil the surprises Mr Burgess." He giggled and picked me up, carried me to my bedroom and sat me on my bed.

He took the shoes off and stroked them before putting them on the tall boy where he could see them up there whenever he wanted. He didn't sleep at all and I had felt him play with me in my sleep. I would wake as horny as hell and I had to shag him as soon as I opened my eyes. It was totally his fault.

He knew I was exhausted tonight and cuddled me so I could sleep the few hours I needed each night.

I opened my eyes to the sun on the curtains which filled the bedroom with a warm glow. I turned my head and Harvey's eyes were closed until he heard the fabric of my pillow move and realized I was awake. His eyes smiled inside his long lashes before it got to his mouth. By that time I was giving him his good morning kiss. He wrapped his strong arms around me and rolled me on to his chest so I could face him.

"You let me sleep soundly last night. I didn't feel you playing with me at all." A huge grin filled his face.

"You were knackered for one and two, I kept going over in my head you sitting on your piano in your black rubber. I couldn't get it out of my mind." I started giggling.

"I'll take the riding crop to work and every time you think of it I'll put you over my knee." He couldn't help laughing.

"I think Jo would be the first to hit me or she'd ask for the rest of the day off, to go and shag Hillary." I giggled at him, he was probably right, she loved rubber.

"I'm going for a bath but before I do that I think we should give Olli and Gina some cash. He's looking for a job and they'd need some money to do that. I don't think they have a penny to their name, Harvey."

"It's alright Alli I've thought of that. We'll get ready for work, see how they are and give them some. I think I should tell Ron we have another two Hybrids living in Jenny's cottage. You never know, he might want to recruit them both. We already know Gina reads minds."

"Bloody good idea, Harvey; Gina said she wanted to stay, she told me last night and she thought Olli would if he found a job. Right; we should get cracking."

We both hurried to get ready. I loaded a bag with things like tea, milk, bread and anything else I could think they might need during the day and they could eat with us at night.

Harvey knocked on the cottage door and it opened immediately.

"Hi," Gina had a huge smile on her face, "I heard you coming. Come in, we're in the kitchen."

I closed the door behind me and we followed her. Ollie was drinking water and stopped when we walked in and got hold of Gina.

A smile grew on his face, "I couldn't put into words how lucky we've felt since bumping into you two. I'll find a job here if it kills me. I suppose it was stupid saying that, but I think you know what I mean. We want to stay."

"Sit down Olli and you Gina, we want you to stay. The Home Office and my boss, the Commissioner of Police in this area, look after Alli, Jo and me. We're looked after by them because they know we're Hybrids.

"We already know Gina reads minds and she could probably do more if given the chance. We have no idea yet what you'll be able to do but it could be something they want to use. Do you have any objection to me having a word with him about you two?"

"Fucking hell; that was the last thing I expected you to say, Harvey. I've bummed around since I was sixteen and didn't take any exams at school. Then there's Gina; she doesn't even know who she is."

"None of that matters, Olli. They're not interested in your past. They're losing the war against crime and they need us to tip the balance in their favour. You'd get well looked after, I promise you that."

"What do you think; Gina?" I asked, hoping she liked the idea.

"It sounds good to me. We'd have to go through training somewhere to join the police and I've no idea if I have the brains for that."

"You're not getting it, either of you. I had no training at all. I went in with Harvey one day because he couldn't read someone's mind. The Commissioner heard the tapes after I'd helped him a few times and offered me a job because I work well with Harvey. We're not saying you'd be working with us, you may not but you're good with cars, Olli. They might want you undercover on car ringing for instance. The pay is good, the work really interesting and you'd get to play hard after work."

"It wouldn't harm to see what your Commissioner says. I like the idea," Olli started smiling and had something else on his mind, we waited.

"You were right, Harvey. I'd never had sex like it. It was the best thing that ever happened to me apart from finding Gina." We both laughed at him.

"I don't think I should say anything about that to the Commissioner, he'd have a bloody heart attack." Harvey could hardly keep a straight face.

Olli was howling with laughter and hugged Gina who came out with, "You were swimming late last night."

I looked at Harvey; he burst out laughing and then answered, "We had to go in there to cool something down. I'm not telling you what."

Gina started giggling, "It sounded painful. Are you alright?"

I was sniggering at Harvey's face as his mouth hung open for a moment. There was a glint in his eyes when he asked, "Did you hear us in your mind or actually hear us."

"Both," she admitted.

"So you got the lot in stereo, great."

Gina giggled, "I enjoyed it."

"Not as much as me," Harvey told her. "We don't care. Jo could hear in our minds from twenty miles away. That's what Alli meant by play hard and we do."

"I'm all in favour of that, Harvey, where do we sign?" Olli was really up for it.

Harvey smiled at him, stood up and took a roll of notes out of his pocket. He handed it to Olli who looked at it in shock.

"You shouldn't give us that. I'm sorry I wouldn't take it." Harvey sat down.

"I didn't get to finish what I was telling you last night. I played the stock market for over fifty years and I'm loaded, multi-millionaire loaded so please take it. We both said this morning you should have some money to tide you over until you get a job and we're taking you shopping tonight. We're only passing on the help we were given in the past, I promise you." I could still feel they wouldn't take it.

"Jenny, who owned this house, left me her money when she died because Harvey didn't need it and I have nearly as much as him. She helped Harvey, sixty years ago. Harvey helped me, when we met and we both want to help you, please let us.

"I was the same as you, ask Harvey. I wouldn't accept anything off him at first but he genuinely wanted to help me and his kindness won me over long before we became a couple. I'd never had anyone so kind to me before and I found it hard to come to terms with."

"Okay, you win," Olli said to us. "We'd like to return the favour one day and thank you. What you said about kindness, Alli was just how I felt all my life. I have always found it difficult to accept. Gina was the only one who had ever shown me any until we met you two."

"Thank God that's settled," Harvey said with a smile and handed the roll of notes to Olli.

"Thank you, both of you and we really do appreciate it."

"We know that Olli. I brought a bag of groceries for you during the day and you're eating with us after we take you shopping. You're not paying for anything tonight. Accept it as our treat to you for wanting to stick around. Harvey was right last night; your lives will change for the better, from now on, so embrace it."

"We have to get to work and should see you around six." Olli got up, shook Harvey's hand and gave me a hug.

Gina said, "Thank you," as she hugged us both.

They came out and waved us off to work. "Thank god you persuaded them in the end, Alli. I have a feeling Ron would be thrilled to have another two Hybrids to look after."

"I think you're right, Harvey. You should see him straight away."

"You're coming up there with me, Alli." I smiled at him.

Ron was really interested and told us to leave it with him. He'd get back to us before the day ended.

Jo came in and made sure she closed the door behind her.

"Hello, you pair of buggers. How have they settled in? They're staying I hope."

"They want to Jo," Harvey told her. "We've been up and told Ron about them. He said he'd get back to us by the end of the day. How's Hillary taking it? It was shit for her to hear it like that, but she'd have been mortified if we hadn't told her and it slipped out in conversation."

"That's more or less what she said on the way home. Please don't worry about it. We like them, they're good fun."

"Gina could hear and read minds at a distance. She might as well have been with us when we were shagging last night." Jo was creased up.

"You can laugh, we don't know how far she'd be able to do it in the future. She had no idea how long she'd been turned."

"Sounds interesting. I bet Ron was peeing in his pants, when you told him he had another two. We won't know what Olli would be capable of, for a while I suppose."

"I don't know. I dug inside his head when we were talking to them this morning. He has a very practical and logical brain. If he'd been tested when he was at school, he'd have been in Mensa by now and would have one of the highest scores." Harvey and Jo were stunned for a few moments.

Harvey picked up his phone and told Ron exactly my findings. Ron talked to him at length about both of them and hung up. Harvey sat there and didn't say anything.

"Are you going to tell us or not Harvey?" I hated it when he did that and I couldn't read him.

"Ron was told they wanted them in London and he was pissed off about it. I said they'd refuse to go. He said that would force them to change their minds at the Home Office." Harvey was really hacked off.

"That's okay then. I thought you meant they wouldn't be needed at all. They could get settled in properly and if Olli found a job in an ordinary garage it would force their hand even quicker."

"If he took a job sweeping the streets they'd be pissed right off," Jo threw in.

"See: why didn't I think of that?" Harvey smiled at us both, "I feel better about…"

Harvey didn't get another word out, the door knocked and Jamie came in.

"Sorry, Sir. We've been called out to the houses they're knocking down behind the High Street. They started bulldozing this morning and found three bodies under floorboards."

"Right, come on." Harvey grabbed his jacket and we left the office. "Bring half the team with us Jamie. Call the doctor and ring Socco. Are Uniform already there?"

"Yes, Sir. They were called out first."

"Good, we'll meet you there." We hurried to Harvey's car and Jo sat in the back.

I turned to her. "We were near those houses last night when we picked up Olli and Gina's belongings. People pretended to be cops and made them leave all their stuff saying they're moving all tramps out of town. They were only in there out of the rain."

We pulled up beside the heavy plant at a standstill near the houses. When we got out to see which house had the bodies in, a group of men were shouting and swearing at the Uniform Officers standing in front of a house. The hedge at the front was flattened and the corner wall was caved in at the bottom. The heavy plant with a bucket attached sat across the hedge and the bucket lowered to the floor.

"Could I help you gentlemen?" Harvey asked in a calm voice.

"You can keep your bloody nose out!" a man in a hard hat yelled at Harvey.

"I'll say it again. Could I help you gentlemen?" Harvey waited.

"I've just told you, fuck off!" the same man yelled.

"I'd fuck off, but you'd be with me and locked in a cell if I heard any more of that language from you. There are ladies present." Shock filled the man's face. The two Uniform Officers had smiles on their faces.

"Now, would you kindly answer my question?"

"It's like this Gov'na they're stopping us from getting on. We're under contract to get this whole row knocked down in two days."

"Could you tell me your name, please?" The man looked worried.

"Colin Watts."

"He's lying, Harvey." Harvey didn't look at me but the man glared.

"Cut the bullshit. I want your name now!" Harvey demanded.

"Who's asking," he said cockily.

"Detective Inspector Burgess and I will have you arrested if you try to hold me up any longer." Harvey was furious now and the man knew it.

"Sorry; it's Colin Wicks."

"Right Mr Wicks, you'll stay here until I've taken a look. If there are bodies in there you wouldn't be able to touch this site for at least a week. Do I make myself clear?"

"Yes." Harvey turned to us and the rest of the team behind us.

"We'll go in and take a look. Jamie, stop all work along this row now, please?" Jamie ran to the plant still moving further along the road.

I opened the boot of Harvey's car and pulled out forensic suits to cover our clothes. It took a few minutes to get ready. Harvey picked up a large crowbar from the boot and gave us hard hats. The two Uniform Officers stood back to let us through and we followed the path to the rear of the house, to gain access that way. The front door was locked..

Chapter 3

The back gardens along that row were filled with the district's discarded white goods. Fridges and old washing machines, along with piles of black bags, everywhere.

We saw rats scurry away when they saw us, as we picked our way to the open back door. Everything we stepped on moved, layered with black bags; filled with rotten waste. Finally we got to the back door and stepped inside. I could smell the bodies straight away. Harvey glanced at me; he knew I could smell them.

"You go ahead, Alli. You'd find them quicker than us." I passed him and walked slowly through the filthy kitchen and made sure I didn't step on evidence to be gleaned later.

I turned into what I thought was a small sitting room. There was a window facing the back garden. I stood in the middle and closed my eyes, to concentrate. The smell for me was very strong in here but the floor hadn't been disturbed at all. *How would anyone know they were under there?*

I took a few steps towards the back window and opened my eyes.

"There are two under here, where I'm standing but I sense more and I don't only mean in this house."

"Jesus Alli. Jo could you go back to the road, please? You and Jamie clear all the workers off the site; arrest anyone who won't leave."

"It would be a pleasure. I'll see you later."

Jo left us and Harvey used the crowbar to lift the floorboards. He used it to lever enough wood up to get his hand under, then ripped them up with his hands. It was very quick and we faced two bodies.

"Bloody hell; they look like 'Mummies', Harvey. What the fuck's been going on here. We should find the others." Harvey followed me out of the room and I turned down the hall to the other interior door at the bottom, to the left of the front door. I opened the door and the smell of death hit us both, this time.

"This is worse than a post-mortem, Alli; are you okay?"

"I'm fine. I've had worse than this in the past, Harvey." When I stepped into the room, three bodies were half out of the floor and broken up in places. The bandages that once held everything in were seeping bodily fluids on to the wood.

"I'll get Hillary down here." He pulled out his phone and waited for her to pick up.

"Hillary, are you too busy to join us at a scene?" He listened. "Half an hour would be fine. We're at Chelsea Avenue, behind the High Street. I'll tell Jamie to look out for you. We've got five bodies in one house and Alli knows there are more in other houses. Thanks Hillary; see you soon." He hung up. "Alli, I should break open the front door. Socco will need better access than this. I think you and I should go into all the houses down the row."

"I think that too. Come on Mr Muscles get that door open." Harvey grinned at me and stepped out of the room.

I walked around the bodies half out of the floor and wondered why anyone would try to pull them out like that and heard wood split and groan and a loud bang when the front door hit the wall behind it.

Sunshine streamed into the hall and some of the smell started to clear. We both walked out of the house to silence. Jamie and Jo had done a good job clearing everybody out of the street and were waiting to hear what we had found.

"Five in there. Alli says there are more so we have to do a house to house down the whole row. Hillary is coming soon so keep an eye out for her Jamie. Tell whoever's on the road block to let her through."

"Okay, Sir." He shot off.

"How strong is your stomach Jo; it's fucking gruesome in there. Join us if you want?"

"I'm coming Harvey. I've got to get used to it at some point." He smiled and we walked to the beginning of the street.

He broke open every front door so we didn't have to pick our way to back doors. The first three houses were clear, but the forth was unbelievable and worse than the one with five bodies. Harvey ripped up the whole floor in one room and bodies were wedged on their sides between joists across the room. All bandaged like before. I'll give Jo her due she didn't puke but shock filled her face.

“That’s thirteen so far, anymore in this house?”

“No. I can’t fucking believe it. Let’s carry on.”

“I think we should have a break. I’ll get Jamie to muster up some tea from some region of the globe.”

“Good idea Harvey, I could do with a drink.” We left the house and sat on the curb outside. Harvey pulled his phone out. “Jamie, send someone for tea, we’re gagging. We’ve got thirteen and only done five houses so far.” He listened. “That’s exactly what Alli just said, thanks Jamie.”

“Is that what they pay you for; sitting on your arses.” Hillary was getting out of her car which we hadn’t even noticed.

“Cheeky bugger,” Jo called. “You’ve got enough work here to last ‘til next Christmas. I hope they give you a bonus.” Hillary crossed the road with a grin on her face.

“How many?” She looked at us in turn.

“Thirteen and counting Hillary. There are more,” I told her.

“Fuck; I’ll ring for more help.” She took her phone out and spoke at length, ordering different things and people to arrive pronto. She hung up and stared at the houses.

“They’re all wrapped in bandages Hillary,” Harvey explained. “The ones we’ve found so far didn’t seem to be newly killed. The house behind us has eight; wedged between joists in a downstairs room. The house with the JCB outside has two in the back room and three in the front.

“The three are broken up and parts of them above the floorboards. I don’t know if that happened when they pushed the corner of the house in. I couldn’t see what the JCB did, that could have done that damage to the floorboards. I may be wrong,”

“You’re not wrong about many things Harvey,” Hillary told him.

Jamie came down the street with a carrier bag and a smile on his face.

“Sir; I got you tea and a sandwich each, that’s if you could stomach it.”

I ripped my gloves off. “That’s great Jamie thanks; I’m starving.” I took the bag off him, “We’ll give you the money later Jamie.” He went back to the road block.

I handed out the tea and found a sandwich I wanted and

opened it.

"How could you eat when you've seen all that, Alli?" Jo was surprised.

"If you saw the dead everywhere and wouldn't eat because of it, you'd get bloody thin." Jo started laughing and chose a sandwich.

While we ate, people and equipment arrived for Hillary and she gave out instructions.

All the bodies in the house behind us had to be numbered and photographed methodically. No mistakes could be are made at this stage. It was slow but vital before they were moved. At least they're being demolished. Joists could be cut one at a time to make it easier to extract each body whole.

Harvey rang Andy, who was still at the nick. "Andy, get on to the local council. I want a list of tenants, from the last twenty years. It may be longer but we couldn't say how far until the PMs are done. When you get the names, start tracking everyone, even if they've left the country." He listened. "No; we've hardly started and we've found thirteen. Start a list for anyone you couldn't contact as we may have them here." He hung up.

We looked in two more houses and were about to pass the one with five bodies in when Hillary caught us up.

"They're away and coming back for the next lot in about an hour. I need to look inside to assess their extraction."

"I'll come with you, Hillary. It's fucking horrible in there."

"Thanks, Alli. It's been a while since I saw this many at once. I was called to an air crash just after I qualified. That's ingrained in my memory forever. It shocked me rigid."

We walked through the front door and turned into the room.

"Now I know why you said it was horrible, bloody hell!"

"The smell was putrid when we first opened this door. Harvey broke the front door open. We could hardly breathe in here without tasting it. He's had an insight into my world and he's really worried about me. I've seen and smelled worse than this; they've walked beside me talked their bloody heads off."

"Fucking hell; I don't envy you at all. Let's see the others."

Down the hall, she only glanced at the other two and we left the house. Harvey got hold of me for a cuddle. He'd heard every word of my conversation with Hillary.

“We ought to crack on Harvey; we don’t want to be doing this when it gets dark as it’ll creep Jo out.”

He squeezed me. “Okay, Alli.”

It took us another five hours to go down the row of houses and we found another twelve. Even Hillary was shocked.

We waited until all the bodies had been removed and took the forensic suits off.

“I could do with a swim, I don’t know about you three.” Three smiling faces beamed at me. “Stay the night you two, please. We should have some fun after this shit of a day.”

“As long as I get some sleep we’ll stay. I’ve got a heavy day tomorrow and with this amount of bodies I could call on extra help, but that shouldn’t stop me from doing my fair share.”

“We were taking Olli and Gina shopping tonight,” Harvey reminded me.

“Even though we’d have stopped at the sex shop; I don’t think I could face it.”

“Today must have really got to you, Alli. Let’s go home.”

I knocked on the cottage door and Olli opened it. “Hi, Olli. Could you and Gina come round? I know we were taking you shopping but we’ve had a tough day at work. I really couldn’t face shopping tonight.”

“You’re worrying Alli; don’t.” Gina came to the door, “We know what you’ve had to do, today; I heard it all in my mind.” She turned to Olli, “I’ve got the keys; let’s go.”

“Now I am gobsmacked.” They laughed and followed me indoors.

With all the greetings over and done with, Harvey got the wine out and we sat chatting for a few minutes about how Gina knew everything that went on today.

“Olli has an announcement for you; over to you, Olli.”

“I went to the council offices, today and I’m officially your local road sweeper. We’re not going to London; they can swivel on it until they take us on. I’m not too proud to sweep the streets; a very good idea, Jo.”

“Yippee!!!” I screamed.

“That’ll fucking show them!” Harvey yelled and Jo was in hysterics.

Hillary didn’t know what was going on for a few seconds, but soon caught on after she read Jo's mind.

"I think that's priceless. I know Ron would be thrilled you want to stay here and so are we," Hillary told him with a grin.

"I was very interested when you told Harvey I could've been in Mensa, Alli." Olli was surprised, I could tell.

"You've got one of those brains that could work out weird logical things and you're already hearing us through Gina, aren't you?"

"Yes, I've got a confession."

"Oh fuck; I can see what's coming here." Harvey was almost cringing.

"You're right Harvey, sorry; it got us going, thanks."

"I don't care; it'll make things more interesting knowing we have an audience of sorts. What you heard last night was pretty tame by our standards, I warn you."

"The black rubber one piece on Alli, sitting on her piano sounded fucking excellent to me." I started giggling and Harvey's eyes sparkled.

"Perhaps Alli would like to give us a twirl, later?" Harvey told him knowing I'd love to. I could feel Gina getting excited.

Jo and Hillary were sitting there, open mouthed.

"You're catching flies you two; are you hungry?"

"Just waiting for the show to begin," Jo giggled.

"You'll have to wait Jo, sorry. What time are we eating because I have to go for a swim?"

"I'll order for an hour's time, Alli. We could go for another swim later; if you want?" I just giggled and ran for the pool room; everyone bar Harvey followed.

I dived in and went through the synchronised swimming I could do and now had it much longer than before. Olli and Gina treaded water at the side of the pool, spellbound.

Harvey dived in just as I was finishing and I came up for air with him. Hillary and Jo were shagging in a corner at the far end of the pool and we dived down to the bottom, to do the same. When we came up it was time to get out, the food would be delivered shortly. Harvey hauled himself out really fast and took hold of my hands to pull me out as if gravity had never been invented and we headed for the towels.

"How do you feel now Mrs Burgess?" Harvey had a twinkle

in his eyes.

"Delicious Mr Burgess; fucking de lux." Four lots of laughter rang out in our heads and we both giggled.

The meal over, we had coffee and I slipped away to get changed. They all knew I was coming down and watched me come through the door. I climbed on to my piano and lay along the top, crossed my left leg over the right and placed my black shoe flat on the top with the heel in full view. I rested on my right elbow and held the whip in my left hand. I had my hair on top of my head with the red spike through it and my make-up, the same as last night.

"Anyone for tennis?" Harvey roared with laughter at me but the others just looked. Jo was the first to speak.

"Sorry Hillary, I've got to say this, Alli. You look fucking gorgeous."

"I don't blame you for saying it Jo. She does to me, too."

"We're not getting left out of this?" Gina piped up, "Where could I get something like that? I know Olli would love to wank at the moment." She looked at him with a smile on her lips and he nodded. I started giggling and Harvey was trying so hard not to burst out laughing, failing miserably.

He got up, came over to me and kissed me for ages and knew I was turned on by the audience. I uncrossed my legs and he put his hand between them to play with my bump. I knew they were watching and played up to it. Harvey loved it and he played with me until I was moaning and I had to lift my bum up to his thumb. I lay back; my head and arms hanging over the keyboard. *Please don't stop? I love it.*

I've no intention of stopping Mrs Burgess, I love you.

His thumb never stopped moving on my bump. *That's delicious Mr Burgess.*

For you; anything.

Harvey brought me to climax and I screamed his name in my mind and my love for him escaped my mouth. He held me tight and kissed my neck and ran his hands all over my body until the shuddering stopped. He cuddled me and lifted me up to carry me back to the others and sat down with me on his lap.

"Sorry, chaps; couldn't help it."

"Don't be sorry Alli, we fucking loved it," Gina giggled with a glint in her eyes when Olli cuddled her, after pulling his hand out of her jeans. I looked at Jo and Hillary who were doing the same. Jo had her hand down Hillary's jeans and was still playing with her. She made no attempt to remove it. Hillary had her eyes closed and we could hear what was going on in her mind.

"I'm glad I wasn't flying solo." Jo looked at me and grinned.

No one else spoke until they'd finished and then Olli asked Harvey, a question.

"Harvey; could I see the two things Alli put on your cock last night? I couldn't picture them at all."

"It would make your eyes water, just looking at them. Give me a minute." He sat me on the sofa and went down the cellar. Hillary and Jo looked mystified; they were in for a fucking shock.

Harvey left one in the kitchen and showed him the 'iron maiden', first. When he opened it up Olli gasped and put his hand over his cock.

"Show us?" Jo asked and Harvey glanced at her.

"I hope you're ready for this?" He turned towards them and we could tell by their faces they were horrified.

"You've got to be fucking nuts putting that on Harvey! My eyes are watering and I haven't even got a cock!" Jo yelled. Harvey giggled at her. Hillary was too shocked to speak.

"I don't know what you'll make of the next one then." He went back to the kitchen and changed it for the iron ball and chain; opened up the cock piece and came in to show them.

All the spikes curved down making sure they bite and when it was closed, they almost touched. Harvey held on to the cock piece and let the ball drop; now they could see how heavy it was.

"Believe me or not I love them both. We had to go into the pool because the first one got red hot rubbing between Alli's legs."

"Why's that?" Gina asked innocently. Hillary and Jo were already there and winced.

"I'll show you Gina." I pulled my feet up and spread my legs. They saw the metalwork over my whole fanny. Her hand shot up to her mouth and Olli couldn't believe it.

"We don't feel pain only pleasure."

"I don't feel pain but I wouldn't go that far," Jo admitted.

"If you could feel this Jo, you would. I promise you that," Harvey told her, referring to the ball and chain.

"Bring it on," Olli said to himself. Harvey glanced at him and smiled.

I closed my legs, "Shows over." We heard everyone groan in our heads and smiled at each other. Harvey took the contraptions down to the cellar and we listened to Olli and Gina talking about it in their minds. They would definitely go down the same route as us.

I looked at Hillary; I knew she was itching to ask something.

"Go ahead Hillary; just ask?"

"Years ago I wanted my nipples pierced and bottled it but I'm thinking of having it done again. I just wondered how they go about it."

Jo's eyes took on a sort of glazed look when she pictured how fantastic she thought it was. Hillary looked at her and giggled.

"They put a clamp on and leave it a few minutes and by that time your nipples would be numb. Geordie explained all that to me. He didn't know he was wasting his breath at the time, but I let him prattle on." Hillary laughed at me. "They put a larger needle through than the ring or bolt you want in. The wire of the 'said' thing is pushed inside the end of the needle and when they pull it through the ring or bolt is through your nipple. Then they take the clamp off and either do it up or screw a ball on the end. I couldn't say how long it would smart, I don't know. I presume it could be a few days to a week."

"Well that's made me decide on Saturday; are you coming, Jo?"

"Absolutely Hillary; I may get something done with you." Jo was thinking of a row of balls, implanted over her pelvic bone.

"Good idea Jo; I'd love it." Jo cuddled her and smiled.

Harvey was listening at the door. "It feels good to me so I'm sure you'd like it, too, Jo. It definitely isn't one sided."

"Music to my ears, Harvey. It's a pity they don't work through the night or I'd be down there now." Harvey laughed at her.

"We don't know if we feel pain or not. I've never given it a thought," Gina stated.

"Lie on the floor, Gina. I'll do something on your sternum, paramedics do, if they're not sure someone is pissed. If you feel pain, you would feel this."

Gina lay on the floor and Hillary knelt beside her. She pressed a knuckle into her sternum and Gina didn't move.

"You should have yelled Gina; give me your hand." Hillary rolled her fingers and squeezed them hard. "You don't feel pain or you'd have felt both things."

"Try me Hillary, please?" Ollie jumped up. Hillary smiled, "Swap places."

She did the same to him. "You're like Gina, Olli." A smile broke out on his face immediately.

"Now I have a question for you Harvey as you've been turned the longest."

Harvey waited for her question. "What would happen if you bit me?"

"Jesus Hillary! I've no fucking idea. I don't think it would turn you. Alli fed off humans, remember? Sorry, Alli; I shouldn't have disclosed that."

"That doesn't matter, Harvey. I drank from them but didn't push venom into them. The only venom I used was to heal the bites. Remember when I healed Jo's finger. The venom that got into her blood, from me, must have topped her up, to be like us. Maybe it would work if enough venom got into you, Hillary." *Fuck; I've said too much.* Harvey was gobsmacked.

Everything got very serious from that point on.

"I want you to bite me, Alli?" Hillary was adamant.

"What if something goes wrong, Hillary? I could kill you if I feed off you and I'd never forgive myself!" It came out louder than I wanted. *I'm scared, Harvey.* He put his arm around me and kissed the side of my head.

I didn't mean to shout, Hillary; sorry.

"When I was bitten do you think whoever attacked me gave me a specific dose of it; I don't?" Olli threw in.

"Do it Alli, please?" Hillary begged. I looked at Harvey.

"If you don't give her enough you could top it up, later. She'd be like Jo was in the beginning."

"You're agreeing with it, Harvey?" He nodded.

"You'll die first; you know that, Hillary?" I had to get that across.

She looked at Jo, “You know I want this more than anything else, Jo.”

Jo, cuddled her, “I want it too; you know that.”

“Bite me Alli, please?” There were tears in her eyes.

I couldn’t answer at first. I kept going over in my head everything I’d been told my other ‘self’, used to do. What if I couldn’t control myself?

I looked at Harvey; he’d been following my thoughts. *You wouldn’t hurt her, Alli.*

“Okay; come upstairs. You should be lying on a bed in comfort before I do it, Hillary. You three come too? Harvey, if I start drinking off her, pull me off please or hit me or do something to make me stop? Don’t forget; I still can’t remember doing any of that.” I waited for his answer.

“It’s okay Alli, I’ll keep you right.” I trusted him implicitly.

We ended up in my bedroom and Hillary lay on my bed. Jo held her left hand and I stood on her right.

“Are you ready, Hillary?”

“Give me a minute?” She looked at Jo, “I love you Jo, please remember that.”

Jo kissed her, “I know and I love you too, Hillary; forever.”

Hillary turned her head to me, “Let’s do it please, Alli.” She closed her eyes.

Jo watched as I leant over her and sunk my teeth into the left side of her neck. This was really strange for me. My teeth pierced into her neck so easily. I felt Hillary tense because it hurt her but she made no sound.

Instead of sucking to drink; I reversed it and pushed. The feeling was really weird to me. The pressure to push came from all over my body, instinctively. I held it for a minute and stopped. I gently pulled my teeth out of her neck and looked at the two marks, dribbling blood. I licked them; they healed and disappeared before my and Jo’s eyes. Now we had to wait.

I looked at Harvey who was just behind me, “Can you hear her heartbeat?” He knew I was really worried about it.

“Yes Alli; it’s slowing down slowly. You must have pushed venom into her or that wouldn’t be happening.” I sat on the bed and took hold of her other hand.

Harvey turned to Olli, "I couldn't hear your heart because the rain was coming down in bloody stair rods and the commuters pissed me off and wouldn't move."

An hour had passed and Harvey could hear her heart, but we couldn't feel a pulse at all. The wait was agonising and endless.

"She's getting stronger, Alli; it's speeded up again." We both tried to feel a pulse and couldn't yet. We waited another twenty minutes and I put two fingers on her neck, detecting a tiny movement. I looked into Jo's face and smiled.

Thank you, Alli. I'm sure you know what this means to me.

"You know I do, Jo." There were tears in her eyes and they trickled down her face. She made no attempt to hide them. We knew the depth of feeling they had for each other.

Harvey put his hands on my shoulders and squeezed them gently. We had no need for words or thoughts, it was just a knowing.

Jo tried for a pulse on her wrist and felt it clearly and a smile spread across her face when she looked at me then Harvey.

I felt Hillary's hand grip mine and relaxed again, "She's coming round, her hand moved in mine." I felt my eyes fill and brim over and the tears rolled down my cheeks, dripping on to the rubber I still had on.

She opened her eyes; blinked a few times and looked for Jo who bent over and kissed her. Hillary squeezed my hand tight as she kissed Jo. I knew it was a thank you.

When her hand relaxed I let go. She wrapped both her arms around Jo's shoulders.

We left the room and went downstairs to give them some time on their own. Harvey cuddled and kissed me, as soon as we got to the sitting room.

"Dry your eyes, Alli. You gave her something she'd never have had and they'd always be thankful you had the courage to do it."

I felt a hand on my back, it was Gina's. "Alli, I've made you some tea; come and sit down. Olli and I were really moved watching the kindness you did for her. Don't be upset; you've given them so much."

Harvey kept his arm around me and we sat on the sofa. "Thank you Gina; I'm just pleased it worked and I didn't kill her."

"You were never going to do that, Alli; you haven't got it in you. I know you were worried in case your other 'self' appeared, but she's gone now and you are in control." Gina and Olli looked puzzled. "We'll tell you one day, just not tonight," Harvey told them gently. They both smiled as we drank tea and waited for them to come down.

They walked in laughing and Hillary put her arms out to me. I got up and cuddled her. "Thank you, Alli. I'll never be able to repay you for your kindness." I gently pulled away and looked her in the face.

"Just have a wonderful life with Jo. That's enough for me, Hillary." Jo wrapped her arms around us both and we hugged for a while.

"I expect you could do with a drink, Hillary?" Harvey asked her.

She started laughing and we pulled apart, "Could I! I've never been so bloody happy in my life." She squeezed Jo and they sat with us on the sofa.

Olli got up and got them wine. I was pleased they felt at home here and knew they could do whatever they liked.

"Thanks, Olli. When I heard about you yesterday I cried, well you saw it. I never thought I'd be like you now and I know you must have been in turmoil like I was about aging and leaving the one good thing you've ever had, behind?"

"You're right; I thought of it every day, it bloody haunted me. It probably sounds stupid, but that's exactly how it was for me and I knew it was cutting Gina up. I had no way of changing it. Whoever attacked me deserves a medal as far as I'm concerned."

"It's about time you played your guitar, Harvey?"

He looked at me, "I will; if you play your piano with me, please?"

"How could I resist you Mr Burgess; you start and I'll join in."

"Have you ever listened to Duelling Banjos, Alli?"

"If you've got it on CD, then yes. I've heard all your music."

"It's there; see how you get on," he got up for his guitar and walked me over to my piano.

"I'll play an opening few bars and if you remember it just carry on playing it with me." I glanced at him and nodded.

He started playing and I joined straight in; I just seemed to know it and had a hell of a time. The piano arguing with the guitar through the whole piece. It was so much fun I started clapping when it ended. I'd never played that fast before and all of it just with one hand.

I was so excited I forgot about them until I heard them clapping.

"That was fucking brilliant!" Olli yelled and stood up to clap for both of us. I got up to take a mock bow, nearly fell over my own feet and giggled.

"I'm blaming it on the shoes," and went over to Harvey to kiss him.

"You really enjoyed that; didn't you?" Harvey asked me with a huge smile on his face.

"It's confession time?"

Harvey giggled, "Go on; I'd love to know."

"I loved it and the speed of it was mind blowing. I never thought my hand could play that fast."

"You're ready for some really challenging music now, Alli. We'll go to the music shop and buy some CDs for you to listen to at the weekend. Perhaps we could join these two buggers when they get their bits changed and go to the music shop from there." Jo and Hillary laughed at him.

"We're coming, too." Gina was almost jumping up and down.

"Couldn't be seen with a road sweeper, sorry; have to keep up appearances. What would the neighbours think?" Olli howled with laughter. "I suppose they could walk two paces behind us or in front and we could pretend we didn't know them. Has anyone else, got any suggestions?"

"I think we should let them come, Harvey. They would keep Jed and Geordie busy for a while. I saw it in my crystal ball."

"Your crystal ball told the truth. I'd be able to get an inch of tattooing done, each week on road sweeper's wages. I'd be happy with that."

"I'm sure I could sort that out for you. Pay me back when you start earning decent wages when the bastards take you on, Olli?"

"You don't have to do that, Harvey. You've done enough for us already."

"Gina, would you talk to him, please?"

"I'll try but I make no promises. He's a proud man, Harvey."

"I know that but why not have it now and enjoy it for much longer. I told you this morning; I wouldn't even know it was gone."

"I'll think about it, Harvey; thank you for the offer."

"There's one thing you could take off him," Jo told Olli. "If you want tribal tattoos why don't you let Harvey design one for you? He designed ours and Alli's back and his drawings are amazing."

"There you go Harvey that's something I'd love if you have the time."

"I'll make the time because I love drawing, Olli. All you need to tell me is what styles and shapes you liked and then I'd draw something for you."

Chapter 4

"It's time to feed Harvey and Hillary needs some sleep," I reminded him.

"We'll go home," Olli said to us.

Harvey smiled, "I've got a surprise for you two; you don't have to go home."

"How come; you haven't got room for us here?"

"We have Olli. When I had the swimming pool built I had a shower and bedroom added on to the back, in case we wanted to swim. The surprise was not just staying here, the shower room is black marble and the bedroom is also black. Don't put a light on in either and you'd enjoy it so much more. That's all I'm saying. I'll show you where it all is when we go to the blood room."

Jo looked a bit miffed and Harvey noticed. "Jo; I didn't offer you it before because you both had to be turned to appreciate it. One of you would've been harmed. Once you and Hillary feed together and she's accustomed to the feelings and the change combined, you could use it."

"I understand Harvey. I look forward to it already." She looked at Hillary, "If it's as good as Harvey's made out, I could see us changing things at yours if you wanted to, Hillary."

"I can't see a problem with that, Jo. I have plenty of spare bedrooms and four bathrooms. If it's as good as you're saying, Harvey; I'd get them all done and then you could stay whenever you wanted. I'll get you to come over if it kills me," she giggled at her last words.

"Come on then; let's get them sorted and we can come down for ours, Harvey."

"Could we see what your shower room and bedroom looks like as we're up here?" Jo asked.

"Of course you can, Jo; I'll show you," Harvey took them both in and put on the light.

"Bloody hell; I see what you mean. What's that?" she pointed to the large sunken bath.

"It's a Jacuzzi with really strong jets of water," he giggled, "I used it a lot before Alli came into my life." Hillary and Jo looked at each other and giggled.

"Sounds like it would be perfect for us," Jo told him. He smiled; knowing exactly what she meant. "That'll be on our shopping list."

Harvey took them into his bedroom and turned on the bedside lamp.

"This is the only light in the room. There are no windows in here or the shower room. You get the same experience if you shag during the day or you're up late."

"It's getting better by the bloody minute. Come on Hillary, you're going to love this." She took her to the blood room grabbing two handfuls of blood bags and they ran along the hall, to my bathroom. The door was closed behind them.

We sorted out Gina and Olli and selected what we wanted from the fridge. When we passed my bedroom door they were having a whale of a time. We hurried down to the other shower room and drank it really fast as we'd waited longer than normal.

Harvey took hold of my hand and led me out of the shower after the feelings had hit and we changed into what we really are.

"I have something special for you, down in the cellar. I've been keeping this for a special occasion."

"What special occasion; have I missed something?"

"The first time I saw you and Adey in the cafe."

"Oh my God, Harvey; I never expected you to remember that!"

"You made such an impression on me, Alli; that will be with me forever. You forget; I watched you for a long time before the day I sat with you."

"I didn't notice you at all, Harvey." *I must have had my bloody eyes closed.*

"I always sat behind you, Alli; so you wouldn't notice me. I told you I didn't want to disturb your life if I didn't have to. Let me show you your surprise. Close your eyes, Alli and I'll take you to it." I smiled at him and closed my eyes.

Harvey picked me up and did the speed thing and put me down gently. I felt him let go to leave me standing there, with my eyes closed and wondered what it could be.

A hood was firmly pushed over my head and the padlock

done up so I couldn't see, couldn't hear and wouldn't know what's coming next. *I'm getting horny Mr Burgess.*

That's perfect for me Mrs Burgess.

Harvey placed his hands on my shoulders and walked me a small distance. I felt him pulling the zip down my back and he peeled the rubber suit from my body, raising each leg to pull it off me completely.

He turned me and lifted my left hand buckled a strap on to it and fixed it out to my side. He buckled a belt around my waist and I felt a strap touch the top of my back and the hood.

He pushed me back slightly for me to feel something soft and pliable against my back. He picked up my right hand and buckled that one to fix it at the same height as the other.

He spread my legs and buckled straps around them both, above my knees and other straps on my ankles. My whole body was pulled up and fixed with the strap at my back which raised me up from the floor.

My knees were pulled sideways and fixed. My ankles pulled straight down and tethered. *This already feels fucking gorgeous. Be patient Mrs Burgess. I've hardly started.*

Hmmmmm; I like the sound of that.

A gag was forced into my mouth and buckled behind my head. Then something soft touched the front of my body, coming no higher than my shoulders. His hands were doing something on the top of my left wrist. They travelled up to my shoulders and right up my neck. He did the same to the other arm. I felt him press down on what he'd done already, on both arms.

He fiddled at my ankle and his hand moved up to my thigh and stopped abruptly. Shivers ran up my spine when one of his hands touched me and turned me on. He copied that on the other leg. Then I felt him press right up the inside of my legs; from my thigh, up and over my pelvic bone and down the other side to my other ankle. *This is interesting; my husband. I love to feel your hands on me*. He ignored my thoughts.

A few moments passed and he touched the back of me above my bum and down through my legs, pressing as he went.

His knuckles touching the balls that covered my fanny, which heated them up momentarily. *I like the feel of that.*

The heavy rubber hood was put over the first hood. It covered my shoulders and was padlocked part way down the back. Now I couldn't breathe the same amount of air and would have to be very careful.

Suddenly; whatever was at my back and front touched me everywhere and got tighter and tighter until I couldn't move a muscle. I changed; the anticipation tipped me over the edge and I felt moisture running out of me. Harvey ran his hand all over my fanny and turned me on even more.

I was trapped completely in that thing but I liked the thought of only my fanny being exposed. It was strange; I felt that my fanny was the only part of me alive at that point.

Something pushed me at the front of my body and caused me to bounce back and forward. Then it dwindled until I was rigid again. *I'm encased in rubber. That's good, I love it.*

I must have been upended although I hadn't noticed it. The next sensation was something warm that trickled into my fanny. It heated all the balls up until my fanny was lovely and hot. *Fuck; that feels so good.* Something strange was put over my bump and pushed hard on to the balls around it, pressing them into my skin and then a drawing feeling started to happen. My bump was pulled out under tremendous pressure. *Whatever you're doing feels fantastic to me.* It pulled harder and then stayed at that pressure. *You can do that again, I love it.*

A buzzing thing was moved over my nipple. I felt him press on both sides of it and the thing stayed there. He did the same to the other one. Shocks shot to my fanny. *I love it.*

I managed to keep my breathing steady, so far and still enjoyed everything that was going on.

I felt something go into my fanny and out again very fast and then pushed up my bum. It was wide, soft and kept going up, very high and then my bum pinched a narrow bit and it stayed in. I loved how it felt and squeezed my bum to feel it in there. *Christ, that feels good Harvey; you'd love this.*

Christ knows what he was shoving up my fanny, it was huge and I felt him push hard to get it in. Then he got hold of my fanny lips and pulled them together to cover it over. It actually felt good up there and was warm like my fanny after it heated up with whatever he poured in. He was fiddling around with the balls and when I twitched my fanny it didn't move anymore. *What have you done; wired it up?* I heard him laugh in my head. *You have; you bugger. What's he done that for?*

I didn't feel him for a while and thought he'd left me until I felt him push gloves over my hands and covers on my feet. He pressed around my ankles and then around my wrists. *What the bloody hell, he was doing, I haven't a fucking clue. Whatever grabs you; I suppose.* I heard him giggle in my mind.

I felt a rocking movement across my back and after a few minutes that stopped. The front of the mask was pulled and stayed pulled. I felt enormous pressure across the back of everything; back, legs and arms and my head was pushed forward really hard, which made my chin, encased in the heavy mask, pushed against my chest. Then everything relaxed and something crept over the front of me. *I've got to be under water.*

Clever girl.

I felt Harvey's hands touch all over my back, down my legs and every time he passed my bum he squeeze my cheeks. Whatever was up my fanny started to buzz until all the balls became hotter and made me warm all over. *That feels so good.* The thing up my bum moved around slowly and really turned me on.

The buzz on my nipples was turned up high and stronger shocks, shot to my fanny. The balls gripped on to the huge thing in there. I held my breath. I wanted to enjoy everything without the panic, like the first time I wore that bloody thing.

Now, the thing over my bump kept up a rhythmical pull, which was bloody beautiful.

Leave it all running, Harvey. I love it.

I can feel you love it but I want to fuck you up the bum, too.

Try and get in there with it. You know I'd love it.

A couple of minutes went by.

I wouldn't be able to do it justice, so could I have more air please?

The airway was opened immediately. I filled my lungs full of delicious oxygenated air.

I felt the bum thing being pulled out a little way and Harvey forced his cock in my bum with it. I heard him groan in my mind. *I knew you'd like it and you feel so good to me.*

I can't get enough of you, Alli; you know that. Let's go on the journey?

He began fucking me and I yelled and screamed with him in my mind. Our journey sent us to paradise for a while and when we came together it blew my mind. I passed out.

I opened my eyes and Harvey was looking down into my face. I could still feel him up my bum, pressed against the thing that was still inside my fanny. I still felt the suction on my bump and the only thing not going on was the movement up my bum beside Harvey's cock. Instead of the buzzing over my nipples they were pulled up to something above his new bed. I looked up but couldn't see what they were hooked onto. I didn't care because he knew how I was feeling. Fucking sensational. He pushed his cock in and out very slowly.

"How are you, Mrs Burgess?" He straightened my fringe with his little finger.

"I feel very greedy tonight, Mr Burgess. I hope you don't mind."

"There's no such word in this house Mrs Burgess, you should know that by now. Your choice to have anything you want."

"I'd like to wear the chastity belt and you could hold me over your mouth to do wonderful things to my fanny and bump. Talking of bump; what's that on it now? I'm not saying I don't like it, I do, but I'm intrigued."

"I've rigged a small water pump with a suction cup on the end. I was thinking of putting two over your nipples but I couldn't find anything to split the hose to feed off two tubes." I started giggling.

"Come on, you've got to tell me?" He smiled and waited.

"If you could find what you're looking for, why not get two? You could do my nipples and bump at the same time. See; I told you I was feeling greedy Mr Burgess." He started laughing and couldn't stop.

"Now what's tickled you?"

"Let's go the whole hog and get enough to do four, one for my cock. I think I'd have to invest in a bigger pump; probably the size they use at the fire brigade…one of their huge trucks, maybe."

I couldn't stop laughing and squeezed his cock up my bum, so much, he couldn't help moaning.

I pulled my pelvic floor up really tight and everything down there became rigid with the thing wired up my fanny. He loved it and fucked me hard until he came in gasps and yells and finally groaned through gritted teeth, whilst he pushed his cock as far inside me as it would go. He held me tight until he stopped shuddering and the feelings had died down.

"How are you feeling now Mr Burgess?"

"Mrs Temptress Burgess; that's your name from now on. I think you could say well fucked. I enjoyed that Alli. Your muscles are so strong down there. I'll go and get your chastity belt. Before I do that I ought to get that thing out of your fanny."

"Just undo the wires, stand at the end of the bed and be ready to catch it."

"They give you a handle that screws in. It's so big it wouldn't come out any other way?" I smiled; opened my legs and waited for him to do as I asked.

He grinned and knelt on the bed between my legs to undo the wires. It took a few minutes, "I'll take this off your bump."

I put my hand over his, "Leave it on until you come back; I love it."

"Fair enough; I have to order that bigger pump tomorrow." I couldn't stop the giggles.

"Stand at the end of the bed and be ready." I waited until he had his hands out to catch it and pushed with my muscles. It shot out and Harvey caught it against his chest. It was a slippery little fucker; wrong words, big fucker and he nearly dropped it.

"That was like being hit by a cannon ball, bloody hell. Now you know why I love to fuck you; your muscles are incredible. I better get your chastity belt."

I hardly had time to blink and he was back with the belt, and the shoes I wore with the rubber.

I was hanging by my nipples, and had been since he left me to undo the wires. I didn't think he realized I was raised up when his arm was under me. He lifted my bum and I started swaying.

"Christ Alli; sorry."

I put my hand up, "Don't be; I've loved every second of it, Harvey. Don't put the belt on yet. You'll have to deal with my fanny this way up and you could pull those hoist wires up higher, please. I have another request; hook my bump up there, too."

He wasted no time to grant my request and added a few extras. He pulled me up as high as his head after strapping my wrists and ankles together onto the wires hooked on my nipple rings, pushed a ball into my mouth and buckled it behind my head. Handcuffs were looped through the ball strap and locked either side of my face and then on to my wrist straps. *I want you to watch my every move, Mrs Temptress Burgess.*

The whole of my rear end was visible to me and I was at his disposal. I couldn't, fucking wait.

He looked into my eyes the whole time and knew exactly what was going through my mind. He gripped me in his hands either side of my bum and started.

He blew on to my fanny and my stretched bump pulsed; it felt tremendous and he kept doing it until I screamed in his head. He pushed something up my bum and turned it on to throb. I moaned and thrashed about but everything between his strong hands was rock-solid still.

His mouth covered my fanny; I almost passed out. He kept his eyes on mine and blew warm air inside me and everything twitched for more.

He pushed his tongue inside and I squeezed my muscles. The balls touched his tongue and became hot; instantly. *Fuck me, that's gorgeous.*

He did it again and licked all the balls that cover my fanny area and they all heated up. I was on fire down there and loved it all the more because I could watch. His tongue ball touched my bum and I screamed for him to do it again, in his head. He ran it round and around my bum until I was fucking demented.

The feelings from that were indescribable.

He let go of me with his right hand and touched something beside him. I started to drop until I was at his cock level. He put his hands at the front of my legs and pulled me on to his cock. I watched his cock dive into my fanny, over and over. The shakes started. What I felt and the sight of it brought me to orgasm quicker and I didn't want it yet.

I gripped his cock each time he pulled out. He moaned and rammed it back in for me to do it again. Now I was in charge of what happened next; trussed up as I was and he knew he was putty in my hands and flashed his eyes at me.

I squeezed harder. He pulled harder to get it out but came back for more. I turned up the pressure so he couldn't pull out at all and stood there with his eyes closed, thrilled as his cock was squashed inside me. All the metal balls pressed into his cock and the images that ran through his mind were filled with his love for me.

Play with my bump, Mr Burgess. I want us to come together.

His thumb massaged my bump; my moans kicked in, I relaxed a bit on his cock and he hammered it in until I came with him. He held me tight on to his cock when my fanny contracted with the orgasm. We both went nuts in our heads. When the feelings stopped, he put his hands around my back and picked me up to cuddle me. He unclipped the ball straps and eased it out of my mouth so we could kiss.

As we kissed he held me up with one hand and the other one undid the wires on my nipples and bump. He swapped hands, made sure the wires wouldn't get caught then walked down off the bed. I was still impaled on his cock and it felt lovely when he walked around with me to get the handcuff keys. He sat on the bottom of the bed and opened all the handcuffs to free my arms and legs.

I gave him a cuddled and kissed his lips, "Bloody hell, Harvey; I enjoyed that."

He squeezed me tight. "I'm gobsmacked at the strength you have down there. I couldn't pull my cock out for fear of pulling it off; not that I wanted to, I was enjoying it too much."

I giggled and he felt it again and moaned, "They're definitely getting stronger, it must be like weight training all the shagging we do."

"That thing I was in at first; what was it?" He smiled at me.

"It was heavy rubber with the zips they use on dry suit water skiing equipment. I didn't trust the zips and stuck black gaffer tape over them as we were going in the pool. That was all the pressing you felt. I flicked a switch on an air extractor and it sandwiched you between the two layers. What did it feel like?"

"It held me so tight I don't think you'd get out of it. I couldn't move anything. The fact you put that air restricting hood over my head, didn't make any difference. I couldn't open my lungs much anyway, it holds you so rigid. The only part of me that felt alive from that point on was my fanny until you stuck the things that buzzed over my nipples. It heightened everything you did to me. What the hell did you pour into my fanny?"

He smiled, "Warm honey. I had to put something in there to push that huge ball in. Oil would have seeped out even though I wired you shut."

"I almost got the same sensation off that, as your fist up me. It didn't move around the way your fist did but it was good and I liked it wired shut."

"I could leave the handle on and still wire it in. Could I try it now?"

"Yes please." He lifted me off and sat me beside him. He went over to the tallboy, picked up the handle and screwed it into the huge steel ball and put it beside me on the bed.

"I'll be back in a minute." He rushed out and was back with a jar of honey in his hand. He opened it, scooped a handful out and rubbed it all over the ball.

"Lie back Alli and open your legs." I lay back but rested on my elbows to watch. He put the ball over my fanny and rotated it as he pushed. It slipped in to fill me with the most amazing heat, which spread everywhere as he turned it back and forth. I lay right back and dug my heels into the bed and my body arched up as he screwed me with the ball. He felt my ecstasy and enjoyed the pleasure he gave me. He touched my bump with his other thumb and in seconds the thunderbolt hit. I passed out.

When I woke up I was handcuffed to the four corners of the bed. A gag was in my mouth and a hood on. I was face down over something hard and the huge ball is still in my fanny. I flexed the balls on my fanny lips and felt them wired shut. The suction thing was back on my bump and pulled hard when it throbbed. *I don't know where you are, Harvey. Everything feels really good already.*

My bum was touched; something cold pushed inside and slowly opened. Warm liquid dripped into my bum, the cold thing closed and pulled out. The ball in my fanny turned very slowly and something the shape of a cock, rammed up my bum. *That isn't you, Harvey. It doesn't feel right to be you but I like it all the same.*

It was pulled out and felt wet and was pushed back in easier. Heat started to build when he fucked me with it and then he turned it on. That sent me crazy.

The ball rotated faster and he knew I loved it all and listened to my shrieks of delight in his head. He rubbed the head of his cock over the balls outside my fanny. *I knew it wasn't you; you naughty boy. I'm going nuts for you to fuck me.*

He pulled the dildo out and rammed his cock up my bum. Just the feel of his hot cock when he fucked me was out of this bloody world. *That's just perfect for me.*

The implanted balls on the underside of his cock rubbed the huge ball as it rotated faster and faster. Heat shot from my fanny to my brain. I shook from head to toe as the convulsions hit me over and over. I knew he'd come with me because he'd pushed his cock in so hard and lay across my back and stroked my body until the feelings died down. *God, I love you Mrs Burgess.*

I know and I love you with equal intensity, Mr Burgess.

He gently pulled his cock out and took everything off me until I was naked in his arms.

"I think you should get some sleep now, Alli or you'll be whacked tomorrow and we have a heavy day ahead of us."

"I am tired now but couldn't have asked for more tonight, Harvey; I love you."

"I love to please you and what you did for me was fucking amazing. Turn over. I want to hold my cock between your legs and feel the heat from you when you sleep." I turned away from him and he pushed his cock through my legs. I gripped on to it and as I closed my eyes he put his arm around my body and rested; he never sleeps.

As soon as we opened our eyes we could hear the banter from the others talking about our antics through the night.

"Christ Harvey, I completely forgot they were here."

"You're not the only one. The chat over breakfast should be interesting." I laughed at him, he was right.

He picked me up and took me through to the shower room. He stood me beside the marble bath and headed for the shower.

We walked in with towels on because our clothes were still

upstairs.

"A good night was had by all, listening to you two," Olli couldn't help saying. We must be programmed to tell the truth because he was embarrassed after he said it.

"We forgot you were here. I'm pleased you enjoyed it because we certainly did."

"You must have one hell of a toy box," Jo stated.

"You know how long we've been together, Jo; we've been collecting for most of that time."

"Delivery guys must love you two," she bounced back.

"I'm bloody sure they'd have memorised this address. If only they knew what they were delivering." They giggled at the thought of some of the things they'd seen.

"We'll give you a key Gina and you could let anyone in with deliveries and use the pool any time you like but I warn you; we have a cleaner every morning and we never skinny dip when she's about."

"Understood Harvey and thanks for trusting us."

"We trust you implicitly, Gina. As you love the piano so much, why don't you learn to play it? Harvey bought me a course of lessons and I've never used them. They're yours if you want them." She looked at me then Harvey, who nodded in agreement.

"I'd love to learn, thank you." She came over and gave me a hug.

"How did you get on last night, Hillary. We were too engrossed and didn't hear any of you." Harvey waited.

"I'll say you were. It was bloody fantastic. The feelings from the blood and then the change took me over the top straight away. I know Jo hasn't got to hold back anymore and that's made me so happy for her."

"And you two?" he looked at Gina and Olli.

"I'd never have thought being in such a dense blackout would've made that much difference," Olli answered. "It doubled everything and we had a ball," he giggled. "Ball being the operative word of the night."

We laughed at him, "I want to try it, Olli," Gina told him and his eyes lit up.

"Did you get enough sleep, Hillary?" I asked her.

"I'll be like Jo, I'm pleased to say. I couldn't sleep and feel as strong as an ox. We've got a shitty day ahead of us and I feel I could cope with anything now."

"We're going up to get dressed so we won't be long." We raced upstairs and separated to our different bedrooms. Harvey turned on the speed thing and watched me dressing from the doorway, smartly turned out for work.

"It's alright for you Speedy Gonzales. It takes me ages to get ready."

"I don't mind Alli. The view is always good in here." I giggled at him.

"Perhaps you could show me how to do the speed thing some time. It could come in useful."

"Only if you show me how to do what your other self did. I know you said you couldn't but I think you should try it. We did say ages ago we'd give it a go and to be able to think yourself somewhere else is brilliant."

"Do you honestly think I could do it?"

"Yes Alli. You both used the same body and brain, so it has to be in there somewhere." I sat down and started my make-up. Harvey came over and sat on the floor beside my make-up table, leaned his back against the wall to wait for me.

"When we have the house to ourselves we'll try it. You've interested me again. Christ; it seems like years have passed since you told me she did that."

"The vampire that told me how to do it said you have to have the place you want to end up, in your mind, before you will yourself there. When you're ready we'll stand at the top of the stairs and both think of the kitchen to try it. Yes?"

"Okay; we'll give it a go. I'm nearly finished." I screwed the mascara brush into its holder and stood up. "I'm all yours."

"I know and I'm fucking delighted." He was standing before I moved and held his hand out for me. We walked to the top of the stairs and stopped.

"Think of the kitchen and will yourself there." He let go of my hand, I concentrated hard and the next thing I knew, I was beside Harvey in the kitchen.

We were laughing and yelling. I hugged Harvey and made so much noise, Jo came in to see what was up.

"Have we missed something?" She looked confused.

"You most certainly have." She was still puzzled.

"We stood at the top of the stairs and willed ourselves down here."

"How the fuck did you do that?"

"My other self used to do it and Harvey was told how, by a vampire a long time ago, so we tried it and it worked."

"Do it again; I want to see?"

"I want some tea, Jo."

"I'll make your tea and take it to your piano and when I come back here, try it again. It'll shock the pants of them and me."

"It might not work but we'll try it." She boiled the kettle, made the tea and took it to my piano. When she came back in we concentrated hard. We appeared in the sitting room and picked up the tea. When we turned round their faces were unbelievable and Jo stood grinning at the kitchen door.

"What's wrong?" I asked them as if we'd done nothing unusual.

"You kept that bloody quiet." Hillary was laughing now and a smile brushed the others' lips.

"We've only just tried it but apparently my other self did it a lot and Harvey told me how."

"I think that's fucking genius!" Olli yelled. "Shit, I'll have to go. My first day as a road sweeper and I don't want to be late. They start at the crack of fucking dawn." He bent over and kissed Gina, "No peeking in their toy box when I'm gone." She went with him to the door, to see him off.

"We'll have to get going soon; what time is the first PM Hillary?"

"Nine thirty on the dot. We've a massive amount to get through and I couldn't be sure how many extra staff they'd allow, yet."

"Let me know if they don't send enough. I'll get Ron to prod them from our end. I won't tell him you're like us until you want me to. He'd wonder how it happened."

"We'll leave it for a bit and I could say I was attacked; too obvious so near Olli's. We're leaving now. We have to get changed before we go in."

We hugged them; ate our breakfast and drank tea before we left.

Everyone was working hard on the phones when we arrived. Jamie came over to us, "We've tracked half the names and we have ten untraceable on the list so far, Sir."

"Right, carry on Jamie. Until we have dates of death we don't know if the list you have to track, will grow? I'm praying it won't." He turned to Jo. "Come with us to the Commissioner's office, we're debriefing him about yesterday."

"Okay, Sir." She got to her feet and waited for us to move on. "Jamie have Socco finished on the site, yet?"

"Not to my knowledge, Sir; do you want me to find out?"

"Yes but don't let that crew back on. I want nothing demolished, yet?"

"I won't, Sir." He turned away and headed for the phone.

"Let's go; we'll have to make this brief and tell him we have the PM at nine thirty."

Ron was in a chatty mood and we had to remind him we had a PM, twice. He was pleased we found them all so quickly and wanted to know the findings of the first PM as soon as possible.

Harvey told him Olli was now our local road sweeper and he rubbed his hands together, "That'll show the bastards who's in charge."

We left him in high spirits and Jo came with us to the PM.

They were just putting the first body on a table so Hillary made us tea as we were a bit early.

"I hope your stomach is strong, Jo; this isn't good I warn you?"

"It's got to get easier, surely."

Hillary replied, "If you feel sick just come in here. Put some of this under your nose and put your mask on before you come in." She handed her a small pot.

"Ron's been told of Olli's new job and he was thrilled. How many extra staff have they sent?" Harvey was concerned she got enough help.

"Two and they're not here yet. I'll be pissed off if they don't arrive soon."

"Make sure you don't lose your temper, Hillary. I'll get Ron to sort them out after the first PM."

"Thanks Harvey. They've done the dirty on me before and

nothing like the size of this case."

"Don't worry. Anything that holds you up slows us down considerably. Ron will bash a few ears. He's itching for another fight with them after Alli." Hillary looked at her watch.

"I bet he is; finished your tea? Let's go to work."

Jo wiped some of the white stuff under her nose, put her mask on and followed us into the pathology room.

On the table was a body wrapped in bandages. One of Hillary's colleagues was photographing it from every angle. Hillary waited for him to take a last shot and stepped towards the table on the other side of it from us.

She pulled down the microphone to give a running commentary on everything she had to do.

She spoke at length on the condition of the bandages and gave the measurements of the body. She looked everywhere for an end of a bandage to start taking them off and couldn't find one. I wasn't looking at her but at the person covered in bandages, looking at his body, to her right.

"What do you want?" They all turned towards me.

She can't find the end, can she?

"You're right. Do you know where it is?"

Of course I do but I'm not telling her, a woman.

"Why not?"

I would never go to a woman doctor. I wouldn't discuss things to do with down there, with a woman.

"Tell Harvey; you're safe with him." He walked around the table and stood next to Harvey.

It's up my bottom.

"That's okay; thank you for telling me." Harvey tried not to smile, "It's up his bum, Hillary."

Hillary kept her face straight and turned to one of her attendants. "Could you roll him please?" He came over and rolled the body away from her and she used forceps to pull the bandage out. "Lay him back down and you better hang around, Danny or this could take all day." He stood to one side until asked to do something.

Hillary un-wrapped the body and found most of the original clothing was still on the top half. From the waist down it was naked and his genitals had been removed. I was shocked and after looking at everyone else, so were they.

"Whoever removed the genitals did a clean job, Harvey. A scalpel must have been used making precise cuts. No hacking at all."

"Have you ever seen anything like this before, Hillary?"

"Only in the dissecting room in training. Danny could you remove his clothes and we'll see what's going on inside." More photographs were taken as each piece of clothing came off.

She took a scalpel and cut the 'Y' incision down his body and Danny handed her an electric saw to open his chest. Next; she cut his ribs off with what looked like loppers you'd use in the garden.

Hillary smiled when she heard my thoughts.

From then on the PM took no longer than any other. Hillary estimated his age at sixty-five after taking X-rays of his joints. It left us with nothing to go on apart from his missing genitals and the fact he'd been embalmed about ten years ago.

Two men came into the room as Hillary was finishing.

"You took your time. Had breakfast on the way, did you?" She knew they had after reading their minds. "You better have your work heads on gentlemen as there are another twenty-four and I don't intend doing them all, myself. Have I made myself clear?"

"Abundantly, Miss Stokes."

"You can cut the Miss Stokes, it's Hillary and you know it. I haven't forgotten you two, don't think I have."

"I don't know why they were shitty to you when you first came here, Hillary. They had a quick shag on the way, after breakfast."

They both went white. "If you're not careful, I'll dig around inside your heads and find a few more little gems, you bloody hypocrites."

"Well done, Alli," Harvey was delighted.

Hillary faced them. "I suggest you get to work right now." They left the room.

"Am I pleased you were here, they were bastards to me."

"I know, and they were coming for round two, Hillary. If you have any trouble from them I'll dig a bit deeper. There's plenty where that came from and they've got horrible minds."

"They're going to see a lot of us this week and be crapping in their pants, every time they see you, Alli. I'd dig away and arm Hillary with other little gems, as you call them, for when we're not here."

"I look forward to it. I don't like them at all. When is the next body coming?"

"We'll have tea and give Danny a chance to clean down."

They were in the staff room drinking tea when we walked in.

"Are you taking the piss?" I just came out with it, I was incensed. They smiled and carried on drinking, I couldn't fucking believe it.

"Like to dress in women's clothes when you shag, Blondie? Haven't told Glenda, have you. She doesn't know you're a tyranny." He looked up from his cup horrified.

"And you!" I looked at the dark haired one, "Love it up the bum. Not cocks, cucumbers are your speciality. Had a problem once though, snapped didn't it? They had a fucking laugh at you at the hospital. Made their day that did. Must be monotonous on night shift, until you arrived."

"Who the fuck are you?"

"Your worst nightmare, and I'll be here every day until this job's finished so I expect you to fuck off and get to work!" They got up and left.

I sat down and started laughing. Slowly the other three came out of their coma and shrieked with laughter.

Hillary gave me a hug. "You're priceless, Alli. I thought I was hearing things at first." Jo and Harvey were holding their sides.

"You should hear her in an interview, Hillary," Jo told her between giggles. "They don't stand a chance. Everything she sees is fired at them like a fucking machine gun."

"Jo's right. I actually feel sorry for them sometimes." Harvey giggled and came over to give me a hug.

"It just popped into my head. I was incensed when I saw them drinking tea; bloody cheek."

Chapter 5

The next body had been broken open. Hillary couldn't un-wrap it so she cut through all the bandages, keeping a check she wasn't disturbing anything underneath.

Jo left for a moment to put more stuff under her nose. The smell from this one was really bad. I looked across to the two men, checked if they were working and caught them looking at me a few times. They were wondering how I knew all that. They'd only had a taste of the stuff that flowed from their minds.

Before we came back in here, Harvey rang Ron and asked him to get more help. The wankers they'd sent were rough on Hillary the last time they were here and it had already started again. He told Harvey to leave it with him. He was pissed off because it held us up.

Once all the bandages were off, Hillary looked over the body. She had a puzzled look on her face.

"What's wrong, Hillary?" Harvey asked.

"This is strange, Harvey. I know it's decomposing but I couldn't tell you, until I open up the body, if it was male or female. There are no genitals at all and only a tiny hole to pee from and an anus. I don't see any signs of surgery either." She picked up a scalpel to open the body in the usual way for a PM. The blade cut into mush really and the smell got stronger. Jo left us and I don't blame her. Hillary opened up the abdomen to look for any sign of gender and found none.

"This could be a freak of nature but it doesn't feel right to me," she told Harvey.

She went over to the two other pathologists and looked at their bodies. They were annoyed she was poking her nose in so I went to stand next to her.

"Have you found anything weird regarding the genitals on your bodies?"

Blondie answered her. "You'll get the report when I'm finished and not before." He stared her down.

"Hillary is polite to you both because that's the sort of person she is but I'm not Hillary you piece of fucking shit. Be civil to her or I'm going to the press with all the other crap I dragged out of your heads. Think you'll have jobs at the end of it, I don't and your families will disown the pair of you."

"Who are you, nothing but a jumped up copper?"

"From two weeks time she'll be a Detective Inspector; is that good enough for you! The Commissioner is getting you removed from this case as we speak! I wouldn't be clever about your standing as a Home Office Pathologist in the future!" Harvey yelled at him.

"Oh fuck," Blonde said to himself under his breath.

"Oh fuck, indeed. Now answer Hillary's question, please?" Blondie looked at Harvey who was the other side of the large room and heard him whisper.

"What are you people?"

"As Alli told you, your worst nightmare, so get on with it!" He was bloody worried now and looked at Hillary.

"The testicles had been removed and replaced with pebbles. They're over there on the bench and all the internal parts of the penis, except for the urethra, so he could still pee. It was packed out with wadding to make it look like nothing had taken place. The penis was opened from the underside and the scrotal sack opened at the back. It must have been done long before the person died because healing had taken place and the scars almost undetectable."

"Who the hell in their right mind would want that done?" Hillary was mystified, like the rest of us. She went over to the other pathologist and just looked at him waiting for an answer.

"I'm sorry, Hillary."

"It's too late for sorry. I've had years of shit from you two. What have you found?"

"This man was in his early twenties and had the same done to him as Peter's body."

"What number was on your body?"

"Five."

She asked the same question to Peter. "Seven," he answered.

We could see her thinking. "Make sure you both select your next bodies between one and eight, please?" She walked over to Harvey, and I followed.

"Harvey, I'm betting all the bodies from house four have had the same surgery."

"Christ Hillary, what the hell have we got here?"

"I don't know yet. The quicker we get PMs done the better. We might have more of an idea."

At the end of Hillary's PM we went to the staff room where Jo was.

"I think I'd be better use to you back at the nick, Harvey. Hillary said something that set me thinking. Do you think they may have all been in a mental hospital at some time in their lives? As Hillary said, who in their right mind would put themselves through that?"

"An excellent idea, Jo, run with it. Jamie has a list of untraceable tenants, so work off that list and see what you come up with. Keep us posted if you find anything out?"

She gave Hillary a hug. "I'll see you later Babe," she gathered her belongings and left us.

"Jo's bloody brilliant at coming up with theories. She set us on the right path for the last big case we had," Harvey told Hillary.

"I keep telling her; she thinks she's thick because she hasn't done a degree of any sort. Exams mean bugger all as it's how you use your brain that matters."

"I know how she feels, I was the same, wasn't I, Harvey?"

"Yes you were but don't forget, Jo put up with the same crap as you at school. Now there's the place to fuck your confidence."

"Here, here; let's go to lunch. I think we've earned it and I'm starving. What do you fancy, Chinese or Indian?" Hillary asked us and knew full well what we'd choose, so she didn't wait for an answer. "Indian it is," and giggled.

While we were eating we heard Jo talking to Jamie about what she was there to do. He said he'd give her any help he could. We didn't tune in any longer as they were going to the canteen.

"Jo seems to get on well with Jamie now. She was telling me about some problem they had on your last big case."

"Yes, she wanted to talk to Social Services and Jamie had always done it. He runs everyone on the team brilliantly without me getting heavy handed with them. I suppose he felt her step on his toes and I had a word. He'd never have gleaned all the information she did. The whole office stopped and listened. She nearly ripped the guy to bits on the phone and got everything we needed to take the case forward. I wish we'd taped it for training purposes. You'd have been proud of her, Hillary. She was like a bloody terrier and read him the riot act, threatening to ring the papers."

"She sounds a bit like you, Alli, with those two bastards."

I giggled, "I suppose she does."

We watched another two PMs in the afternoon. The two men only did one each and their findings were as before. Hillary's bet looked promising.

Before we left for the night, Hillary's phone rang. We didn't read her mind but all the way through the conversation a smile got wider on her face. When she hung up she cheered, left the office and walked over to the two men.

"Leave that; I've had word from the Home Office. You're on the train back to London tonight." They were in shock. "Harvey told you what would happen and you chose to think it was an idol threat. I couldn't say I'm sorry to see you go, I'm not a hypocrite. Goodbye!" she turned and came back in, wedged the door open to check that they actually left.

"Ron's organised six pathologists. They're coming tonight and will work in shifts all over the weekend so I haven't got to work. Four are staying on until they're all done. He has his faults like the rest of us but I could kiss him at the moment, but on second thoughts, maybe not."

We laughed at her. "I'll go and make sure they go and don't do anything stupid before they leave, I don't trust either of them." Harvey left us.

"I'm pleased Hillary. You would've worked the weekend just to keep things moving. You can still go to the tattoo parlour with Jo now."

"With all this going on I'd already told her I may have to work. Bless her, she said she'd come in with me. I know she feels sick every time she comes here."

Harvey came back in. "They've gone with their tails between their legs, serves them bloody right. Have you got to stay until keys are exchanged Hillary?"

"No, I'm to leave them at the station with your lot and they're picking them up from there. I feel like I've been given a bloody holiday."

"You'll feel even more like that when you use the black shower and Jacuzzi tonight."

Her eyes lit up. "I completely forgot about that. Thanks, the pair of you."

Harvey pulled his phone out and waited for whoever to pick up. "Jo, wait there as Hillary's coming back with us and you're coming to ours tonight." He listened. "Yes, you're using it, don't worry. See you in a bit." Harvey laughed. "I think you'll find her a bit excited, Hillary. I don't think you'd mind that at all."

"Absolutely not, let's get out of here." She locked up behind us and we headed for our cars.

Hillary gave the guy manning the front desk her keys and we hurried up to our office. Jo was there by herself drinking tea and looking over lists of names.

"Leave that Jo," Harvey called from the door. She looked up with a grin on her face, picked up her jacket and car keys. She looked different. I couldn't put my finger on it. She walked with more confidence. I might be wrong.

We all pulled up at our house. Gina and Olli came out of the cottage to join us. I noticed Jo, put her finger to her lips when she looked at them both and they just smiled at her. I thought nothing anyone could pick up and said nothing. Whatever surprise she has for Hillary, I won't spoil it.

The pool was where everyone headed and Jo was first to dive in before anyone could see her. She still had a grin on her face. Hillary used the steps and swam over to her. They were kissing for a few minutes when Hillary let out a cheer and Jo pulled her to the other end of the pool and shagged her. She looked like a man, going at it. Harvey watched and smiled and then noticed I looked puzzled. He took hold of my hand and ran it over the five balls implanted above his cock. I got in front of him and rubbed my pelvic bone over his, then dived to the bottom.

He followed and shagged me the same as they were. We hadn't done it like that since I had all the extra hardware put in and it brought us both to the brink in minutes.

Harvey got behind me and pushed his cock up my bum and we floated to the surface with me on top. He moved me up and down him as we lay in the water. No one knew what we were doing until I started to come and yelled for him to push harder. He put his arms around me and took us to the bottom to finish down there.

We got out, Harvey ordered the food and I went upstairs to dress in something different. He came up and watched me pour myself into a little rubber outfit he hadn't seen before. He dropped his towel and held his cock as he watched. I made out I wasn't aware he was there and exaggerated every movement I made, until he couldn't help himself. He put his arms around me and ran his hands all over the rubber.

It was the thinnest black rubber that covered everything but left nothing to the imagination. You could see right through it and I nearly had an orgasm when he touched me.

"I haven't finished yet, Harvey." He let go and watched me put on a tiny black leather waistcoat and a short black leather skirt. I took the shoes he loved from the tallboy and slipped my feet into them, combed and twisted my hair and pushed the spike in, checked my make-up and turned to him. "I'm all yours now and I have a present for you. Would you like it now or later?"

"Now please."

"Are you sure; we have guests and we're going to eat."

"Please Alli; I want it now." He knew it was something he'd love.

I turned into my dressing room. "Close your eyes and open your legs a little." He closed his eyes and I slid the thing on to his cock. He'd never had anything like that before and never anything that went inside as well as around it. The metal rod was about half an inch thick with a ball, on the end. He took a moment to get used to it and smiled. I locked the metal band near the base of his cock. It stopped the rod and metal cover from being removed. The ball was deeper than that, which made it impossible to pull out.

"I haven't finished yet, stand still." I encased his balls inside a metal ball and padlocked it. The ball was extremely heavy and I let it drop. It pulled his balls down and Harvey moaned with the weight of it.

"I wouldn't let you go down with your cock sticking out like that. I have something else for you. Turn around a second." He turned and I pushed an anal hook up his bum and pulled the long solid end up between his cheeks, hard. It was attached to chains that I brought round the front, lifted his cock and padlocked the chains across it, very tight.

"How does that feel Mr Burgess?" Harvey put his hand on the thing over his cock and then on the heavy ball between his legs. He lifted it and let it drop a few times. He put his hand on the hook, pulled it up and moaned.

"Could I look now please, Alli?"

I stroked his cock. "Please do. I hope you like it?"

Harvey opened his eyes and looked at everything in the mirror, even the hook up his bum. "Alli, I love it all, it feels really good."

"Now I know you don't mind something inside your cock I found quite a few things you'd like. If you're naughty enough tonight you may get something else. Are you able to walk with that ball between your legs?"

He tried a few steps. "It swings and twists when I move my legs and that adds to the pleasure. I'll put tracky bottoms on."

"Try to sit?" He sat on the stool beside my make-up table.

"That thing up my bum pushes up higher. Very nice indeed, Alli. Thank you and you look good enough to eat tonight." He got up and cuddled me running his hands over the rubber on my arms and at the top of my legs. I picked up his towel and gave it to him.

"Go and put some clothes on, the food will be here soon."

I watched him walk along the hall and his gait wasn't any different.

Harvey paid for the meal and we all dived in to get what we wanted and headed for the sitting room. They all knew what we'd been doing upstairs but no one said a word about it. We ate and talked on other subjects.

"You looked like you were having a good time Hillary, and you Jo."

"I had to pass the tattooist's on the way to work from the lab and just stopped to make an appointment. Geordie asked what I wanted and he had time to do it. I wasn't going to say no, was I?"

"I'm pleased she did, that's for sure," Hillary giggled.

"How's the road sweeping coming along, Olli?" Harvey asked him.

"I got a tip today. An old lady put twenty p, into my pocket. I swept the path beside a bench she'd donated for her husband's passing. I'm starting a tip jar and should be full in about twenty-five years." Harvey laughed at him.

"At least I won't look any older when I go to spend it," and laughed.

"What did you do today, Gina?" I asked because she was quiet tonight.

"I came in here, tinkered around on the piano and went for a swim. I missed Olli and you lot. I know I heard you all and I could talk to Olli in my mind but it wasn't like being there in the flesh."

"What did you do when Olli was at work, before we met you?"

"I went with him."

"She did more than that, she's a bloody good mechanic and as good as me," Olli pushed in.

"Bloody hell. Why didn't you say that before? I think it's brilliant."

"I don't know if I trained as a mechanic. I went with Olli and just knew I could do it. Wherever he got a job I'd go with him and they took me on as well. I loved it, that's why I was at a loose end without him."

"Ron knows now you've taken a job sweeping roads and he had to ring the Home Office on Hillary's behalf today. I bet he made sure he told someone what was decided by you two and I don't think it should be long before you both get the call," Harvey told them.

"Alli, I love what you've got on; would you let me touch it please?" Gina asked.

"Yeh, go ahead." She got up and came across to me. She ran her hand down my leg and the thrill from her touch was evident to everyone. *That felt, fucking gorgeous.*

Harvey put his arms around me since he knew why I was so excited.

"You and Hillary should get one of these body suits. If you'd touched me with the sole of your shoe I'd have felt the same,

Gina. The fine rubber intensifies a touch to such a degree I could come right now, with Harvey's hand on me. I have to be good tonight or it wouldn't be fair on Harvey if I wasn't."

"Alli, do whatever you want. The very fact I couldn't, would heighten everything for me, you know that." They all listened but no one dared ask the question.

"Just ask, I'm not embarrassed. Fuck, you should know that by now."

Olli was first to ask anything, "What has Alli fixed on your cock, Harvey. I know it wasn't like the last things you showed us."

"There's a metal rod inside and the top has a metal cap to cover the head of my cock. A metal band locked tight around the base of it and the ball at the end of the rod, stops it from being removed. I love the feel of it and she has other things I'm looking forward to later." The three women were in shock but Olli asked again.

"Tell us the rest Harvey. I'm really interested. In fact, I'm getting a fucking hard on just thinking about it." Gina giggled at him and put her hand over his jeans where his cock was.

"My balls are encased in a heavy metal ball and a huge hook up my bum with chains on and they're padlocked around my cock so I didn't upset the delivery man." Everyone was in hysterics.

"I want to see it Harvey. I like the idea of the hook," Jo asked.

"You do?" Hillary looked amused.

"Oh yes. Hillary; I do."

"I have another one if you want to try it, Jo." Her eyes lit up.

"I want to see it on Harvey and then I'll try it, Alli." Harvey grinned at me and dropped his tracky bottoms, turned to show her the hook. He got hold of it and pulled it up.

"Yes please, Alli," came out of Jo's mouth. I left them and headed for my dressing room, picked up the hook chains and padlock and appeared before them with everything she wanted. Harvey was showing Olli everything else he was wearing.

"Here Hillary, you should put it on her." She panicked.

"I couldn't until I knew for sure it wouldn't hurt her. You do it Alli?"

Jo looked at me. "I don't give a fuck who puts it on, I just want it."

"Come in the kitchen, Jo." She followed me in and dropped her jeans and boxers.

"See this ball on the bit that goes up your bum Jo, you'd like it when you sit on it but wouldn't hurt you at all. Shove it up your fanny to get it wet and it'll go up easier." She took it off me and pushed it up her fanny then handed it back.

"Stand still Jo." I pushed it up her bum and let her get used to it before I did anything else. "Are you okay with that?"

"More than okay Alli…finish it off." I pushed the metal between the cheeks of her bum and pulled it up to make sure it was tight and took the chains around the front and padlocked them up.

Nice.

"When you bend or sit down you'd feel it pull up tighter because of the chains and when you sit on it, I'm sure you'd love it." She bent over and moaned.

"I never thought my bum would feel that good." She pulled up her jeans and did them up.

When we went back in, Hillary kept her eyes on Jo when she sat down. Jo moaned and screwed around on her bum to really feel it up there.

"I didn't know you could get stuff like that Alli, it feels really good. Have you tried it?" I smiled at her.

"Not yet. I have one that's different to yours. I haven't used it yet and I've not even shown Harvey. The hook has chains that go through a collar for my neck and finish with a ring to hang me up." Jo and Hillary were shocked.

I felt Harvey's arms around me. "That sounds just right for you, Alli. I hope you bought plenty of rope to go with it."

I laughed at him. "As if I'd forget that. I was hoping you'd use it on me tonight as you wouldn't be able to shag me. No, I'm changing that statement. You shouldn't be able to shag me."

Harvey cuddled me. "Oh, you know me so well. Perhaps we'll shock this lot and they could watch."

"You know I'd love it Harvey so you could start as soon as you liked." Harvey laughed at me. I looked at Jo and Hillary, who were sat there wanting to watch but didn't want to say and then I heard Gina giggle.

"We might as well show them all the stuff we have, Harvey.

Gina and Olli are headed down the same route as us anyway. I don't know about you two." I looked at Jo and Hillary. "I think Jo would like to try other things." Her eyes flashed and Hillary laughed.

"Take us on a tour, then," Hillary piped up.

"Upstairs first Hillary because we have a soundproofed room up there." Harvey took hold of my hand and we ran up.

Before Harvey opened the door he waited for them all. "Alli's never seen what was in this room as she always had a hood on and some of the things I haven't tried on her yet. She's in for a little surprise." I could feel the excitement build in the four of them but it wasn't as great as mine.

The door opened and Harvey put a light on. I walked in with him and my eyes were everywhere and he watched the smile grow on my face.

"Fucking Nora. I like this Harvey." It was like a medieval dungeon. Everything was black and that meant he could get as much enjoyment as me in the darkness. There were wooden frames like I'd seen on our stay at the 'try before you buy' place and something that looked like a rack. Cushioned bars with manacles either side on the floor. Everything had either straps or ropes on. There were chains grouped together and hung from the roof. Most had leather straps attached.

Harvey saw me looking up at it and put his arm around me. "That is on a hoist and you'd be face down when you were on it, Alli."

"Use it on me now, please."

"Are you sure you want them watching?"

I turned to look at the others. "I've asked Harvey to put me in that." I pointed above my head. "If you're squeamish we'll see you downstairs later. I'd like you to watch if you want." Smiles filled their faces and they stood back to give us some room.

"Take off your leather gear, but leave the rubber suit on. I knew you'd love this, Alli." I took them off quickly as I was horny already.

Harvey held a metal bar behind me, the full length of my back and head.

"Hold on to that, Alli." I put my hands behind my back and gripped the bar. He forced a ball into my mouth and buckled it across the bar which held it to the back of my head really tight.

He selected a heavy leather strap from the array that hung on the wall, put his hands around my body at my hips and buckled it, with the bar trapped in it. He pulled hard to make sure there was no slack.

"Let go now, Alli." He went over to the wall and pressed a button and the chains above, lowered slowly. He moved me to one side as they neared my head and then lay me face down on the floor. The straps on the end of the chains he buckled around my ankles and wrists and carried on to buckle another one around the metal bar behind my neck. He strapped metal bars down each leg so they wouldn't bend. He spread my legs and buckled a bar between my ankles to hold them wide apart and now my fanny was at his disposal. He opened the zip across my fanny, stuck his finger up my bum and pulled up hard. I moaned. He took his finger out and I felt something cold pushed in there instead. It moved and became wider until Harvey couldn't pull it out. *A bum hook?*

Absolutely.

A thin rubber hood was forced over my head and I couldn't see but I could still hear. It was a bit muffled, but at least I could still breathe okay. My hair was pushed up into the back of it and tape, I presumed, was pressed down over the bottom to keep my hair inside.

I began to lift off the floor and started swaying. Harvey's hand held my leg and one on my back to stop me moving. Nothing happened for a while and then I felt something warm spread across my back and down my legs. Harvey's hands moved all over my body and the rubber suit heightened every touch until I was screaming in his mind for him to fuck me. I changed and thrashed about. *Please fuck me. Please fuck me.*

He lifted me higher and he did the same all over my front. He hung a heavy weight on my bump ring and found my nipple rings under the rubber and hung weights on them, too. Now my boobs a were pulled down he fixed the steel rings on them and squeezed hard. *I love that, thank you.*

Something changed; all my weight hung from my bum. *Christ, that feels good Harvey. You'd love this.*

He touched my stretched bump with his tongue. I loved it so

much I ended up screaming and moaning.

I felt his hand push inside my fanny and balled into a fist. He pushed and rotated it so fast the thunderbolt hit and I passed out.

I heard muffled voices. "She's alright she's had an orgasm that's all."

I'm fine. Carry on Harvey please, that was beautiful.

"Some fucking orgasm."

Was that you Jo? I couldn't hear you clearly.

Yes Alli, we were worried.

Don't be, this has always been normal for us. Sometimes four or five times a night. You'd love, the hook.

Not like that, I wouldn't?

I bet you a hundred quid, you would.

Get on with your orgasm and leave me out of it. I have to say, it was good to watch.

We heard Harvey laughing. *Do you want your garden fence, back?*

Harvey still had his fist up me and moved it slowly. The pressure left my bum and I could feel everywhere I was strapped again. While he moved his fist his other hand ran up and down the inside of my legs until I was demented and shaking all over. *Keep going, please don't stop.*

When I came that time, Harvey pulled his fist out and put his mouth over my fanny. The heat from his mouth sent me reeling and screaming his name over and over in my head. He licked from my bump to my bum and extended the orgasm until I was completely drained.

He held me tight until I stopped shuddering and the feelings calmed down. *I love you Mr Burgess.*

Likewise Mrs Burgess. I'll get you down now, Alli. I can't cuddle you properly up there. A few moments later I felt my stomach and feet touch the floor first and Harvey took everything off. He picked me up to cuddle me and I flung my arms around him to give him a kiss.

I looked for the others.

"They left just before I got you down to give us time together. I think they enjoyed watching you. A lot of groping was going on when I caught sight of them. I was a bit busy at the time." We laughed all the way to the shower. I had to wash all the oil off me.

Harvey helped and his hands felt lovely soaping my back over the rubber. Once I was dry I went back for my leather bits.

"You've been busy in here. I had no idea you'd done so much shopping." I giggled at him. "How are your bits? You haven't crushed it, have you?"

"No, I've been very good this time, Alli and I have a request."

"Go on," I waited for the question I knew was coming.

"Could you change the thing on my cock for another surprise, please?"

"As you've been so nice to me I will but your legs might buckle a bit with that one." Harvey's eyes lit up. I held my hand out and took him to my bedroom.

I took the padlock off and let his cock free from the chains and locked them back up.

"Won't you need that undone for the next thing?"

"I'm not sure how much of the other thing you'd be able to stand. You might have to try it a few times before you use it all."

"What the fuck, is it?" He wasn't worried, he was fascinated. I went into my dressing room and brought it out to show him.

It was a huge screw made of heavy steel and tapered from a point to an inch and a half wide in eight inches with a T bar handle. Harvey took it out of my hand, felt the weight of it and smiled at me.

"Take this off Alli, I have to try it. Don't you worry I'll put it in. I think I could enjoy this," and grinned.

"It's your funeral," and laughed with him. I unlocked the ring holding the rod inside his cock and pulled it out slowly.

"That feels really good when you pull it out, Alli."

"Before you put that in, come and see some of the other things I have for you to insert up your cock."

He followed me into my dressing room and looked at all the steel rods on my dressing table, with different shapes on the end.

"You've been busy Mrs Burgess." He picked one up with a bullet shape on the end and pushed it up his erect cock. He closed his eyes and I put my hand over his to take over. He moaned and groaned when I pushed it in and pulled it out. "I fucking love that, try another one, Alli."

Each one I tried was wider than the last and over a period of time I was pushing things up nearly the width of the screw. I picked it up and screwed it in, right up to the handle.

He got hold of me. "Thank you, Alli. You know exactly what I crave. I want you to chain it up and later you have to whip me, please?"

"Stand back a minute and close your eyes." He did as I asked and waited. I put a wide metal band down the middle of his cock and tried to lock it together.

He opened his eyes. "Let me do it, Alli?" He squeezed it together and gasped. He took hold of his cock and lifted it up. The reason I couldn't do it up was because of all the balls, implanted underneath. When he squeezed it shut the metal stretched over each ball and they were still prominent.

"Made to measure, now."

He started laughing at my quip and picked me up, straddling me over his cock. "Warm it up with your fanny. It's a pity it's got that sort of handle. I couldn't fuck you with it in."

"That's possibly why the handle is like that. I've no doubt you could get something made to suit you. You always say money talks."

"I'd never even thought of that, Alli. That's set me thinking," and he lifted me off. "Chain me up as we have guests we're ignoring." I took the padlock off and pushed his cock to his stomach, put the chains across it catching the handle of the screw inside.

He put his hand on it and pressed. "That's something else, Alli. I love it. You enjoyed your hook, then?"

"I loved it. The end must be different to yours." I looked at him puzzled.

"Yours winds out so you were hanging on a two inch wide, flat piece of metal. You couldn't hang anyone human on one like you used on me. It would do a lot of damage."

"I've made tea, if you're interested!" Jo yelled up.

Harvey giggled beside me as we walked towards the stairs. "I wouldn't be getting the white cup and saucer out with this in. I think I'd explode."

"That sounded fucking interesting, show us?" Jo asked.

Harvey dropped his tracky bottoms and they all gasped.

"You're fuckin nuts, Harvey Burgess! How the hell did you get that up there!"

"It's like a cork screw. Alli used lots of different metal rods with shapes on the end to dilate my cock and screwed it in. I loved it Jo. Would you go without something you love because someone thought you nuts?"

"Putting it like that, Harvey; no. It's like someone asking me to be straight and I couldn't. I'm sorry."

"There's no need to be sorry, Jo. When you lot have gone up, Alli will be whipping the shit out of me with a bull whip for a couple of hours and I'd love it. It's different to the things I do to her but when you boil it down we're only feeling pleasure. I'm just sorry I couldn't fuck her with it in, the handle will do her damage. I'll contact the firm she bought it from and get something made with a different handle so that I can."

"I think it's fascinating, Harvey," Hillary told him. "I couldn't understand humans using stuff like that but if you don't feel pain, why not?" Jo was surprised she'd said that.

"Would you go in for anything like Alli has, Hillary?"

"I don't see why not. I know those buggers giggling over there, would; written across their faces." She laughed at Olli and Gina, who were both masturbating, staring at Harvey's screw.

Gina giggled. "We've been found out Olli, what a shame."

"I think a bottle of wine should be opened to celebrate." Harvey burst out laughing, pulled his tracky bottoms up and headed for the cellar.

Chapter 6

Saturday morning and we were heading for the tattoo parlour. Before we left home, Harvey showed Olli the design he'd drawn for him.

"That's bloody brilliant Harvey, thank you. You should be an artist, you know that?"

"There aren't enough hours in the day now, Olli. Personally, I'd like forty-eight." Olli laughed at him, rolled the drawings and followed us out of the house.

Jed wasn't in as it was Saturday and we'd forgotten he didn't work it. Geordie came out of his piercing studio when we were being told.

"Hi, we haven't seen you for ages; keeping alright?"

"Hi Geordie. We've been fine, you?" Harvey asked. Geordie's face twisted slightly.

"Jed's girlfriend's mother died, two weeks ago. Jed's back but his girlfriend stayed on to sort the house sale and he's really pissed off at the moment."

"We're really sorry to hear that, Geordie. I forgot he didn't work on Saturdays and we've brought some friends in to see him. Jo came to see you last week but her partner wants you to do something for her."

Geordie nodded; smiled to Jo and asked Hillary what she wanted him to do.

"I want my nipples and clit piercing, Geordie. Have you got the time, today?"

"Okay. I'll see when I can fit you in." He looked in his diary. "I've got time in an hour and a half I couldn't do it before, I'm afraid." He waited for her.

Hillary looked at Jo. "We can wait, can't we?"

"I want you to get this done as much as you, Babe. Of course we can." Hillary smiled at Geordie and he wrote her name in the book.

"Does anyone else want anything pierced? I have more free time after I finish Hillary."

"You do, Gina." She shook her head. "Gina, you're having it

done today and you can owe me for the rest of your life, I don't care. Tell Geordie what you want and won't take 'no' for an answer." I stood there with my hand on my hip.

She looked at Olli. "Olli wouldn't accept anything off Harvey so I couldn't, sorry."

I stared at her.

"What the hell are you two doing in here?" Jed stood before us with a grin on his face.

"You're a sight for sore eyes. We heard about your bereavement Jed, we're both sorry."

"Don't be Harvey, she never liked me. Thought I was beneath her daughter; because I'm a tattooist and Abbey only stayed on to sell the house, only child and all that. What have you come in for?"

"Our friends want some work done. Olli, show Jed what you want?"

Olli pulled the drawings flat and showed Jed. "I only want a price, today."

"No he doesn't, I'm paying Jed." Harvey stated and looked at Gina. "Tell Geordie what you want, Gina and Alli's paying for yours. When we get home I'm confiscating your tip jar, Olli." Olli laughed at Harvey.

"I told you, it would take twenty-five years to fill."

"Time's meaningless Olli. You're getting it done today, if you could do it, Jed?" He looked at the drawings.

"I've got the whole weekend free, perfect timing really. I'll get the transfers made, come with me Olli, I have to measure you?" Olli went to the transfer machine and Jed measured him, keyed everything into the machine, laid the first drawing into the top and switched it on.

"It won't take long. Christ; he'd never be able to get all this done at once, like you Harvey. He'd never stand the pain."

"Yes he will Jed, pretend he's me." Harvey nodded to him.

Jed smiled back. "That's good, it's better for me. Did you draw this?"

"Yes, I did it last night. Have you used any of the others, yet?"

"They're going like hot cakes." He heard the machine bleep and went over to change the drawing. When he came back,

"People love them, Harvey. Can I get you all a coffee?"

"I'll make it Jed, you've got enough to do." I left them all to it as I felt a bit left out, being here and getting nothing done.

I felt Harvey cuddle me from behind. "Do you want something else done Alli, I know how you're feeling."

"It just seems weird coming here and getting nothing added, that's all Harvey."

"I'll get some paper from Jed and design something to go on the outside of your thighs to go with the tattoo on your back, if you like?" I turned around and hugged him.

"I'd love it, Harvey but I don't think Jed would have the time."

I looked into his face. "He'll have the time tomorrow, Alli. I'd love to do that for you."

"Thank you, Mr Burgess. Help me carry out these coffees, please?" We grabbed three each and handed them out.

When I gave Geordie his: "Did Harvey like all your extras, last time." His eyes sparkled.

"He loved it and so do I. You'd never believe the difference it makes to some things." He laughed at me and took his coffee into his studio. He wasn't daft, he knew alright.

I joined Jo and Hillary. They were looking through some of the tattoo books. They didn't look very interested in any of them. Harvey pulled a chair opposite me and started drawing the designs for my legs.

"What are you drawing, Harvey?" Hillary asked as she watched him.

"Designs for Alli's thighs," he glanced up to me, "and up to her hips I thought." I smiled. He knew I'd love it.

He'd been drawing for a few minutes when his phone rang. "Fuck; this better be good or someone will fucking cop it."

"Yes!" he was really blunt and they'd know he was hacked off. He listened for a few minutes. "We'll be there in fifteen minutes. Sorry Alli we have to go, you and I are needed. Jo, tell Jed and Geordie we'll be back later."

"Don't you need me?" she asked.

"They need someone who sees the dead, Jo."

"Okay, good luck." I grabbed my bag and followed Harvey out.

"Where are we going Harvey, this isn't a murder, is it?"

"No Alli. There's a girl in the same position as you were as a child. Social Services have asked if you could help. The girl's parents don't believe her. Well…you lived through it, you don't need to guess."

"How do they know about me?"

"Nick knows of the parents and someone from Social Services. It came out in a conversation. If the girl hasn't lied you'd probably see them, too. You don't mind trying, do you?"

"Of course not. If she sees the dead and they're anything like my bloody parents, she would be going through hell."

"We're nearly there, Alli. Nick's meeting us at the house." We drove on to one of the huge housing estates and Harvey made a left and then a right. I could see Nick, leaning on the boot of his car.

We pulled up and joined him. "Sorry to drag you out on a weekend but things kicked off last night. I can't stand back and watch this, anymore. They are distant relatives of mine and I've heard enough about how the girl is mental. She plays with my kids and she's fine. I shouldn't be saying this because I'm a Solicitor but her parents want stringing up."

"It's alright Nick. I feel like killing some of the guests we get," Harvey told him. Nick gave Harvey a look of, 'I totally understand'.

"I'll take you in. The house is a tip and you can say anything you like to them, Alli. I'm past caring about them. It's Josie we care about."

"How old is she, Nick?"

He turned to me. "Only seven." He knocked the door and we waited, He knocked again.

The door opened and a woman with a cigarette hanging in her mouth stared at Nick. "I thought I told you to sod off, last night. Poking your bloody nose in." She slammed the door, only Nick put his foot in to stop it.

"I'm calling the police, right now?" She glared at Nick.

"I am the police!" Harvey raised his voice.

"And I'm Princess bloody Margaret," she answered, loaded with sarcasm.

"I'm Detective Inspector Burgess and this is PC and Psychic,

Alison Burgess." He pulled out his warrant card to show her.

She turned white and backed away from the door. Nick pushed the door wide open and asked us in. The woman backed up the hall to a shit-hole of a kitchen and sat at the table. There were empty Cider bottles, lined up along the kick-boards of the units and the place was filthy.

"Where's Josie!" Nick demanded.

"In her bedroom, where I put her last night! She's driving us fucking mad, talking to fresh air. I'm having her certified!" I could stand it no longer.

"Do you know something, you disgust me! I had parents like you who beat me within an inch of my life for talking to the dead! I see them everywhere and have done, since I was tiny. You're nothing but a fucking alcoholic!"

"Here, you can't talk to me like that!" she spat back at me.

"Got any witnesses, have you? No one here heard anything, did you boys?"

"No," came from them both.

"Go and get your daughter, down here now! I'd like to talk to her, please!"

She hauled her body up from the chair and passed us muttering under her breath.

"I can hear everything you're saying; hold your tongue!" Harvey yelled at her; forcefully. She looked shocked and hurried out of the stinking kitchen.

"This place is worse than the houses they're knocking down."

"I heard how many bodies you found, the human race has a lot to answer for," Nick said to us.

"You wouldn't want to know what they've had done to them, Nick. Hillary's wading through it all. They've had to ship in extra help for her so she could have the weekend off."

"Christ; it's unbelievable." Nick turned to the doorway and his face lit up. He held his arms out and the most beautiful child ran to him.

"Hello, Uncle Nick. Why have you come round this early? Aunty Jess usually picks me up later."

"I've brought someone to see you Josie. This is Alli and Harvey. Alli would like to talk to you for a little while." She turned and smiled at me.

"Yes, I don't mind; she looks nice." I could have cried. *Having to live in this shit-tip, with that mother. God only knows, where the father is.*

"Shall we go to my car and you can sit in the back, with Alli."

"I'd like that Uncle Nick. Is Aunty Jess still picking me up for swimming, tomorrow?" She looked worried. "I can't find my arm bands."

"Don't worry about that Josie, we'll find you some. Let's go to the car." He put her down and she ran ahead of him.

"What a beautiful little girl, Nick."

"Jess and I would like to adopt her, but the witch wouldn't have it, we've tried several times."

"Would you like me to have a word with her, she'd change her mind." Harvey glanced at me and a smile tinged his lips. He knew what I'd do and liked the idea.

"You can try Alli, but don't hold your breath." We followed Josie to Nick's car. *The mother must have stayed upstairs, I'll find her later.*

Harvey put his arm around my shoulder and squeezed me gently. *I totally agree with what you propose, Alli.* I looked at him and smiled.

Josie got in the back, next to the child's seat and waited for me. Nick and Harvey sat in the front and talked quietly so Josie wouldn't feel they were waiting for her to speak.

"How are you getting on at school, Josie?"

She looked coy but said quietly, "Everyone in my class thinks I'm weird. I answer the people who talk to me."

"Let me tell you something Josie, I could see them at your age and had the same trouble at school. If you like I could show you how to make them stop so you can get on with your school work. I found it really annoying when I wanted to hear the teacher. Do you find that?"

"Yes, I think they wait until I want to listen and start screaming at me."

"All you have to do is scream at them, in your head, not out loud. They'd hear you. I used to scream leave me alone and I'll talk to you later when I've finished my work."

"Is that all I have to do?" She looked amazed.

"That's all. Tell me, can you do anything else your cousins

can't do."

"I know what they're going to say before they say it." She looked proud.

"I do that too, anything else?"

"I know when someone is lying. I don't know how I just know."

"You like swimming then, I love it."

"I have to wear armbands. The lifeguard keeps trying to rescue me from the bottom but I love swimming down there."

"How long do you stay down, Josie?"

"Ages that's why they're fed up with me."

"I'll let you into a secret. At school I swam on the bottom faster than anyone who swam on the top."

"Really, they won't let me do that."

"Nick, do you know about her swimming on the bottom of the pool."

He turned around. "Jess has played hell with them at school and the pool. If she doesn't wear armbands, they won't let her in."

"We have a pool at home, Nick. Do your other kids swim properly?"

"Yes Alli, they're all older than Josie."

"Our whole pool is twelve foot deep so you could bring your kids early on a Saturday morning a couple of times a month, if you like. At least Josie could swim how she wants. Harvey and I hold our breath under water for a long time. I was trained in synchronised swimming but they couldn't find anyone who could hold their breath as long as me."

He looked at Harvey. "It's okay with me, Nick. Perhaps Alli could show Josie how to do it. She could've won medals, she's that good."

"Bloody hell, Harvey. I can't thank you both, enough."

"I've told Josie how to tell the dead to leave her alone at school. Her work will improve from now on. She definitely gets harassed by them. She has the same trouble I had at school."

"I knew it, but couldn't get her parents to understand."

"They look and sound just like mine. I couldn't get out of there quick enough. Josie is lucky to have you and your wife looking out for her, believe me." Harvey leaned over to Nick and spoke to him quietly so Josie couldn't hear. *Alli was taken to loads of psychiatrists by her parents.*

Nick looked at me and I nodded, he was horrified. I leaned over the front seat.

"I'll have that word with Josie's mother. You may find she'd be living with you quicker than you thought. Social Services wouldn't know about the family for no reason."

"Please do Alli. We'll be forever in your debt."

"Don't think of it like that. She'll have a good life with you two." I looked at Josie. "When we go back in you can't tell your mother anything we've talked about, Josie."

"I don't tell her anything Alli. She always calls me a liar."

"I'll talk to her before we go, Josie. I'm sure you'd like to see more of Uncle Nick, Aunty Jess and your cousins, wouldn't you?"

"Yes I would. Uncle Nick's asked her loads of times."

We left the car and returned to the house. On the way back, Nick said something to me. "Alli, Josie's father isn't her real dad. You only have to get permission from her mother."

"Even better Nick, this won't take long."

I couldn't see her mother downstairs, caught Nick's eye and pointed upstairs. He nodded and I climbed the staircase to find her.

She was lifting a glass to her mouth when I walked into the front bedroom. The whole house was a tip and didn't smell very healthy to bring up a child. Just like my parent's house.

Her head turned towards me immediately. "Get out! Who said you could come up here?"

"I don't need permission from you. You're just like my mother and I've no doubt you beat the hell out of Josie."

"I'm allowed to hit my own kid." She's so fucking brazen. *I'll knock that out of you.*

"That's where you're completely wrong, lady. Look into my eyes? I have something to tell you." She stared at me. "You're going downstairs to write a letter giving full custody of Josie to Nick and Jess. After you've done that you're packing Josie's things and handing her over to Nick. You will remember nothing of our little chat and never contact Nick and Jess again about your daughter. Have I made myself perfectly clear?"

"Yes." I stood aside and let her go. She went down to the kitchen and asked Nick for some paper and a pen. He looked shocked but pulled a letter from his inside pocket and gave it to her with a pen. She pulled the letter out and turned it over. Nick just stared as she wrote the letter I'd asked her to write.

She signed the bottom and handed it to Nick. He read it as she looked under the sink for a black bag and hurried upstairs. Nick looked at me for an explanation. I just smiled at him.

Her mother came into the kitchen with a full black bag and gave it to Nick. She grabbed Josie's arm and held it out to him. He was completely flummoxed.

"Take her hand and ask no questions, Nick. You have a daughter." He smiled at me, took Josie's hand from her mother's grasp and walked out of the house. We followed them and talked with him at the boot of his car. Josie was already inside in the child's seat, a huge smile on her face.

"I don't know what you did, Alli. I don't want to know. She'll have a good life from now on, I promise you that."

"I already know, Nick. You have a good heart. Don't forget about the swimming? Just let us know when you're coming and if she needs anymore help with the dead people, I'm only a phone call away."

He gave me a hug. "Thank you, Alli." Harvey shook his hand.

I put my head into the car and kissed Josie on the cheek. "If you have any problems at all with the dead people, ask Uncle Nick to ring me?"

"Thank you, Alli; and for the swimming."

"I'm looking forward to it already, Josie; we'll have some great fun. We'll see you soon. I know you'll be happy from now on." She put her arms out for a hug and tears filled my eyes.

Harvey felt it and put his hand on my back. "Let them get off, Alli, so Josie can settle into her new home."

"Bye Josie." She waved her small hand and I closed the door. Nick smiled at us and got in the driver's seat. "Thank you," he mouthed as he closed his door and started the engine. We watched them drive off and Harvey cuddled me until my tears stopped.

"I wish someone was around to do that for you, Alli?"

I smiled at him, "We'd never have met if they did, Harvey." He knew I was telling the truth.

We joined the gang in the tattoo parlour. We'd been almost two hours and Hillary was in Geordies studio with Jo. Gina was making a list of things she wanted doing, as soon as Geordie was free. We looked in on Jed. He was filling in Olli's back tattoo.

"And what have you been up to?" Jed flashed his eyes. "Jo said you were called out."

"It wasn't a murder Jed, more like an errand of mercy. Alli sorted it out and we have four kids coming to swimming, twice a month on a Saturday morning, from now on."

"I know you have a pool bigger than a foot bath, according to Jo, but wouldn't it be crowded."

"We haven't seen you for ages, Jed. We have a fifty foot, indoor pool behind the house," Harvey informed him, with a huge smile.

"It's fucking brilliant, Jed; we swim every day." Olli backed Harvey up.

We laughed at Jed's face, he was staggered.

"Do you swim, Jed?" Harvey asked him.

"I like nothing better, Harvey but I wouldn't go in the public pool if you paid me."

"Nor would we, that's why we got ours built. You're welcome to come back with us for a swim when you've finished here. I warn you; we skinny dip." Jed laughed at Harvey.

"The only two of you I haven't seen every crevice of are Gina and Hillary. I expect they'll be next in the queue to see me." Harvey giggled knowing Jed was right.

"I forgot about that but the next one in the queue is Alli. I've almost finished a design for the outside of her thighs to go with everything else that's on her."

"Nice. Tomorrow afternoon suit you, after I've finished Olli?"

"That would be perfect, Jed. Gina hasn't asked me to draw anything yet." He looked at Olli. "I'm sure she's going to."

"Correct." Olli giggled. "We'd have to see what piercings she's had before you do anything, Harvey. I've an idea she's going nuts with them, she loves, Alli's." Jed grinned at me.

"Geordie told me what you had done last time. I didn't believe him at first."

"You'll see it later, it's fucking excellent for both of us and we've had some bloody good fun with it." I laughed at Jed's face.

"Haven't we just," Harvey added with a twinkle in his eyes,

which didn't go unnoticed by Jed. He grinned at Harvey. He'd guessed exactly what he meant.

Hillary and Jo came in looking happy. Jo went straight over to see Olli's back. "I like it, Olli. Gina's gone in and she wouldn't tell us what she wanted and just kept giggling."

"I think I ought to warn her about the first twenty-four hours, Harvey. It looks like she's going the whole hog."

"I should before he starts." I hurried out to tell her and heard the conversation between Jed and Harvey.

What's wrong for twenty-four hours?

Nothing serious. When Alli got aroused she was so horny it scared the shit out of her and took about an hour of shagging to stop it. If she goes ahead Olli, be ready, that's all I'm saying for now.

Olli must have understood since I heard nothing else on the subject.

I went into the piercing room and asked Geordie to step out for a moment. Once he'd gone I told her how it was for me. She said she'd go ahead anyway so I left and told Geordie she was fine. He didn't understand but I wasn't explaining it to him. I was sure Jed will.

"She's still having it done Olli, just be ready to shag her for an hour." They all started laughing.

Jed looked tired after ten hours of tattooing and Harvey told him to call it a day. He'd done Olli's back and down both his sides. "I'll finish it tomorrow, Olli." He got up and went over to look in the full length mirror just as Gina came in.

She ran over to him. "You look gorgeous Olli, don't worry I haven't had as much done as Alli. I could have a bit more done another time." She ran her hands over the tattoo on his back. "I love it."

He put the small mirror down hugged her and they came back to us. "I love it Jed, you've done an excellent job. I'll get my kit back on." He got dressed when Jed cleared up and we all left for home, and Jed followed in his car.

Jed couldn't believe how brilliant the house was. He loved all the tribal furniture in the sitting room and when Harvey showed him the pool room he whistled.

"You lucky buggers using this, every day." He stared at

everything.

"The depth is twelve foot the length of the pool, you'll see why." No one wasted a second getting in and Jed stripped quickly, dived in and watched me swim along the bottom. He went up for air after half a length.

Harvey swam to the bottom where we shagged and were down so long I could feel Jed getting worried. *Tell him Jo, he's worried.*

We both heard her explaining how long we hold our breath and he stopped worrying. When we came back up he was swimming lengths of the pool. Harvey didn't swim with him, he'd have known something was weird as Harvey swims so fast. No one else shagged in the pool, they do it at the top and must have felt self-conscious. If Jed comes again he should bring his girlfriend and then they wouldn't feel like that. I didn't think Jed would give a shit anyway.

I got out and pulled loads of towels out of the cupboard, wrapped one around me and felt Harvey's arms circle my body.

"Are you okay Mrs Burgess?" He kissed my neck.

"Perfect Mr Burgess, and you?" He kissed my neck again.

"I think you know what I want, Alli." I turned and handed him a towel, which he wrapped around his hips and took him upstairs to my dressing room.

He put his hands above his head, held onto the edge of the arch to my dressing room and closed his eyes.

I took off his towel and rubbed my hands under his cock until he had a hard on. I held his cock in my left hand and picked up the first metal rod. I went through them all until his cock was ready for the screw, picked it up and screwed it in fast. He sighed when the handle touched the tip.

Harvey opened his eyes, "Put some gloves on and play with me, Alli."

"You're kidding me."

He cuddled me and whispered, "I'll come in my head like we did in the shower, when you were tied up, remember." I did and picked up the red rubber gloves. He closed his eyes again and waited for the first touch of them.

He made no sound verbally but went mad in my head. He really enjoyed it and went rigid when he should have come normally, when the powerful thunderbolt hit his brain. He didn't pass out like I did, just cuddled me and told me how much he loved it.

"Take it out, please, Alli. I'll tie you up later on and you could try out your new hook." I flashed an excited look at him and held his cock to unscrew it again. It was harder to get out. He'd refused to come down his cock but he loved the fact it took longer and moaned with every turn.

"The feelings I got from that were incredible, Alli. I'm so pleased you got it. Do they have any other things I might like?"

I giggled at him. "I have a catalogue for you to look at Harvey. I'm sure you'd find something else you'd like to try." He put his arms around me and kissed me.

"Show me later. We ought to go down. They'll be out of the pool and hungry." I dropped my towel and threw some loose clothes since I was being tied up later. Harvey did the speed thing and was dressed before me. He held my hand down to the others in the sitting room.

"Are you staying for something to eat, Jed?"

"I can't thanks Harvey. Abbey will ring at eleven and if I'm not there she'd worry. The swim was great, thanks. Is nine too early for you at the shop?"

"No Jed, that would be great." Jed gave us women a hug and shook the boy's hands and included Jo in that. She loved the fact he considered her more male than female. He could hardly think anything else. She stood before him with as many muscles as Harvey and only a towel around her hips.

He grinned at her. "You're not on steroids are you, Jo?"

"No Jed; just fucking hard work at the gym."

"You look good Jo, see you all tomorrow." When he left Jo was made up and we were extremely chuffed for her. I caught Hillary giving her a hug and what passed between them was lovely to hear.

Harvey ordered the meal. "You've got time for a shag now. We were a bit greedy, sorry." They threw the towels and headed for the pool. Harvey stayed with me and selected the wine from the cellar. I sat at my piano and played the music Harvey bought on the way back from Josie's house. We'd listened to it on the way to Jed's.

I felt him standing behind me, he listened with his eyes closed. When I finished he wrapped his arms around me. "Christ Alli, I didn't think you'd pick that up straight away. It was note perfect."

He kissed the side of my neck. "Even I didn't think I'd remember it, Harvey." I stood up and cuddled him.

"Put him down you don't know where he's been," Jo giggled. "I take that back, I almost forgot your bloody dressing room. It must be fucking good or you'd not request it again that quickly." We laughed at her.

"If you were a guy Jo, you'd want it I promise you."

"I'd never want a cock Harvey. Might fancy it up my bum, though." We both giggled.

After dinner we cleared up and Harvey went down to our toy room to collect the things I wanted. When the others saw everything he brought up they were a bit unsettled. Harvey and I glanced at each other and giggled in our minds.

The hook I'd described to them yesterday was very different. It wasn't only one hook for my bum but a second one for my fanny. That one was shaped like a cock with a difference. It was stainless steel and a vibrator but they couldn't have guessed. There were no wires as it was remote controlled.

"Get changed into your black strapping, Alli." I glanced at him and hurried out of the room. The questions the others had in their minds were funny and we listened with amusement since they had come nowhere near the answer.

It took a couple of minutes to put everything on and I thought myself down onto the lid of my piano. Harvey saw me appear but they didn't. I sat there and waited for them to look.

Jo was the first to notice. "I'd like you in that, Hillary." The rest of them turned with gaping mouths.

I got down and walked over to Harvey who was waiting with handcuffs and the hooks beside him on the floor.

He locked my wrists behind me, just below my waist, to the strap down the centre of my back, using the handcuffs.

He stayed behind me, asked me to open my legs and to bend them a bit. I felt the hooks go in and smiled to myself as they felt so good inside me.

Harvey put a wide collar around my neck and buckled it at the front. He picked up the heavy chains attached to the top of the hooks. He pulled them up hard. I moaned with delight and changed. He buckled the chains behind my neck loosely and made sure they ran through the collar unhindered. The excess he let drop down my back. He forced a ball into my mouth and buckled it up after putting a hood over my head and padlocking that.

I felt him tie the tops of my arms together very tight and loved how that made my boobs stick out further. He put his hand on my back and bent me forward and the hooks pulled up higher. I couldn't stop the moan that escaped my mouth.

I felt rope around each boob that was pulled hard to tie the knots. *Christ, that feels good Mr Burgess.*

He laid me on the floor and felt a strap being buckled just above my right knee. He pushed my legs wide apart and strapped the other leg to the bar holding them rigid. I felt a manacle lock around one ankle and then the other. They were pulled together, locked to each other and pulled behind me. He fed a rope behind my handcuffed wrists and my ankles were pulled back to meet them and tied off.

He rolled me onto my front. Everything tightened when I was lifted off the floor and felt movement for a short while.

Solid floor squashed my boobs and touched the front of my thighs. My head rested inside the hood at the front and I waited for the inevitable pleasure to come. He would hang me from the hoist in the kitchen in a minute.

I was lifted again and the chains through the collar around my neck pulled up tight and the hooks dug in delightfully. *Hmmmmm.*

I swayed for a few minutes, it dwindled and then I was still.

The hooks feel delicious and pull up really high. Thank you, Harvey. I can feel you're all worried, believe me I love it.

I was left for a long time for the anticipation to build. No one thought anything. Classical music was the only thing I picked up.

The first thing I felt was cold air on my fanny and then buzzing started inside me. That made all the balls vibrate. My knees were pushed down hard, I changed again. The metal cock and bum hook pushed up higher. *Fuck me, that's good. Do it again, please.*

My knees were moving and I felt the tension on the collar around my neck change. Harvey's hot tongue played with the balls around the lips of my fanny. The heat from his tongue sent me reeling and I begged for more in his head. He squeezed my boobs and they were rock-hard. My nipple rings were twisted. Shocks shot to my fanny, the balls hit the metal cock in there and gripped onto it. The buzz was turned up sky high and the thunderbolt hit with such force, I passed out.

He must have changed my position when I was out cold. Now my knees were right up at the front of me and my ankles were tethered to the leather straps on the sides of my thighs. The metal cock had gone from my fanny and my arms were bearing my weight on the rope with the hook up my bum.

Harvey's hot mouth covered my fanny and I changed instantly. *Keep going, it's fucking gorgeous.* Suddenly; vibration started in my bum next to the hook, sending sensations right up my spine and pins and needles shot all over my body.

Harvey's mouth stayed on my fanny and my bump ring was pulled down hard. *Do it again, please.* He pulled harder.

Hmmmmm, perfect.

I didn't feel him near me anymore. *Where have you gone?*

My nose caught the scent of my bath oil. That broke the suspense and I knew what was coming next.

Harvey's hands, covered in rubber, touched all over the inside of my legs, smearing the oil as they moved. I changed and thrashed around as he picked up the speed, faster and faster. Now I was fucking demented, for him to fuck me.

He rubbed it all over the balls covering my fanny area and pelvic bone. The next thing was a vibrating dildo that moved over them. That made everything tingle so much I moaned and sighed, it felt so good. It was pushed up my fanny and Harvey's hands started again on my legs and the balls until I screamed in his head. *Please don't stop this, I love it.* He kept going. I tried not to come and held off as long as possible. When the thunderbolt hit; I screamed his name and saw stars for a moment before everything went black.

I opened my eyes and I was in Harvey's arms. He was naked and was sat on the floor of the kitchen with his back to a unit. His cock was inside me and I was still trussed up the same, but only with rope. He knew I loved the feel of it. The hood, ball and all the black strapping had gone and I have always felt safe tied up like that.

"They've gone to the pool to give us some time alone. Did you like that, Alli?"

I smiled at him. "I loved it all and thank you for tying me up."

"You do enough for me, Alli, and I want to give you what you love." He kissed me and I got tremendous feelings in the pit of my stomach. We still kissed as he raised me up and down his cock, slowly and rhythmically. We both changed and Harvey kept up the pace. We both moaned and groaned until we could hold it no longer and both came together. He pulled me on to his chest, his cock pushed up higher until he was completely drained.

He held me like that to let all the feelings calm down and rocked me until I wanted to be untied. He knows I love it so much.

"Oh, sorry?" It was Jo.

"It's okay, Jo, we've finished. Alli likes staying tied up for a while."

"I didn't hear you and thought you'd gone upstairs, I'll leave you to it."

"You don't have to leave if you're putting the kettle on. Harvey could do the speed thing and take this off upstairs, Jo." She smiled and lifted the kettle.

Harvey lifted me off his cock and laid me on my bed. He untied all the ropes and cuddled me when I stood up.

"I love you, Alli." He put his hands either side of my face and kissed me so tenderly, tears filled my eyes. He pulled back and wiped the tear off my cheek. He knew how emotional I got when he kissed me like that.

"Would you like the screw back in, Mr Burgess?"

"I would Mrs Burgess but could you dilate my cock really slowly as its fucking delicious when you do it." *You know I can.*

"Lie down on my bed and close your eyes." As he did that I pulled on a pair of long rubber gloves. I played with his cock with them until he almost came. I left him for a moment and gathered all the steel rods and a couple of extras he hadn't had yet, plus a screw. Not the same as the last one he had.

I straddled his legs and laid all the rods and screw on to his six-pack. Starting with the smaller rods first, I played with them slowly. I moved them from side to side as I pulled them out and pushed them back in. He moaned out loud but told me in my mind how good they felt. It took about two hours to get him ready to accept the new ones.

He gasped as I pushed the first one down his cock. They were covered in bumps and nodules.

"You were holding out on me, you little minx. I love it, Alli." I giggled and changed it for a wider one.

His body moved under me and a smile grew on his lips. "You like?"

All he said was, "Perfect."

I pushed a wider one in and he moaned really loud. I thought I'd gone too far but he put his hand over mine. "Keep going Alli, and don't stop, please. This is ecstasy for me, truly." I played with that one longer and he loved it. Next would be the new screw. It didn't taper much, like the last one. The tip was rounded off and all the screw edges, the full length of it, were covered in nodules.

I pulled the rod with the widest head out slowly.

"Take a deep breath Harvey, your present is next." When he drew in his breath, I screwed it in fast, right up to the handle. His hand went to his cock and he gasped. He felt the width of it and opened his eyes to look.

He was shocked at first but a smile grew on his lips. He looked at the array of things I'd used to get his cock large enough to accept that huge screw and giggled. Some of them were two inches wide and he hadn't noticed how wide they were getting as I'd played the game to distract him.

"How does it feel now, Mr Burgess?"

He got hold of my hands with the gloves on and wrapped them around his cock. "Play with it Alli, I haven't got words to describe how it feels. The nearest is out of this world, thank you." He lay back and I ran my hands up and down his huge cock, he changed and thrashed about as he came in his head. I stopped playing and just held it.

"Do it again, Alli, please."

After he'd come four times he asked me to take it out. He couldn't go down with it in, they wouldn't understand at all. I held his cock and took it out slowly. I was amazed how quickly it shrank back to its normal size.

"Thank you Alli, that was fucking amazing for me and I know

you enjoyed getting me to that size."

I giggled. "You know me so well."

I gathered all the rods and screw, to wash them in the bathroom sink, ready for the next time.

He cuddled me and started laughing.

"What's tickled you?"

"They'd have heard it all. God knows what they're thinking right now, Alli."

I giggled. "We'll find out soon enough, let's go down.

We walked in and they looked at us from the sofas. "We totally get it now, Harvey, you could have left it in. We're sorry we've made you feel uncomfortable." Hillary got up and gave him a hug. "I'm sorry," she said to him quietly.

Chapter 7

"It's okay Hillary, I understand. It must seem bloody weird to you. I'm pleased it won't be a problem now. Alli has a catalogue with other things to choose from and I would be ordering from it."

"Could I be a cheeky bastard and ask to see what you used, Harvey."

Olli would go down that route and Harvey smiled at him. "I'll get it stay there."

He did the speed thing and brought it down with the steel rods I'd used on him. He handed them to me. "Lay them out in the order you used them, Alli, and let Olli see how you got me to that screw size."

Hillary and Jo sat forward on the sofa and watched me lay them out.

"It took two hours to get him to the size he could accept the ones with the nodules on and a lot longer to accept the screw." Olli couldn't take his eyes off it all.

"Hours of absolute fucking bliss, for me," Harvey told them.

"Would you have left it in, if we weren't here?" Jo asked. She was still sorry for making him feel uncomfortable.

"Honestly? Yes I would Jo, until the morning."

Hillary asked the next question and I knew it was coming, she was fascinated.

"Harvey, would you let us watch you have it put back in. My medical training tells me, that's impossible and it obviously isn't." A smile grew on Harvey's face.

"I'm sure if I was human I wouldn't be able to stand even the first screw, Hillary. I had my eyes closed and felt the size of my cock and gasped. I couldn't believe it was that wide. I'll let you watch but stay quiet, please. I want to enjoy it."

He moved the coffee table and took his jeans and boxers off, lay on the floor and closed his eyes. I gathered all the rods and screw, straddled his legs and pushed his T-shirt up to lay them on his stomach. He got hold of the T-shirt, took it off and threw it behind him.

I played with his cock until he was hard and picked up the first rod. I pushed it in slowly and drew it out even slower, ran it up the inside and moved in different directions to get him used to the next size up.

He moaned and thanked me in my head for the next one. They could see how much he loved it. I went through the small ones and started with the wider ones I'd used for the first screw. Harvey moaned, groaned and loved every movement of the rods and my hand on his cock. He spoke to my mind all the way through and when I got to the ones with the nodules on he asked me to stay on each of those longer.

All I wanted was to please him and spun it out longer than last time. The bigger they got the more I moved them from side to side and stretched his cock wider and wider. The two inch one was the last before the screw. I used that the longest time of all and Harvey came in his mind with the anticipation of what was next.

"Take a deep breath, Harvey." He breathed in, I took out the rod and screwed in the huge screw, right up to the handle.

He breathed out and held his cock for a minute and smiled at me. "Thank you, Alli." He held his arms out for a cuddle and I lay on his cock so he could wrap his arms around me. "Christ, that feels good between us." He moved me from side to side, feeling how solid it was and moaned with delight.

Harvey started giggling. "I forgot we have guests." I looked up. Hillary and Jo were kissing, stretched out on the sofa. I looked the other way and Gina was giving Olli a blow job.

"Would you like to be tied up when we feed, Alli? I told you I was keeping this in."

"Yes please. Could you tie me in a ball and cuddle me. No, it's alright. You go in the Jacuzzi if you want. I don't mind, you've done loads for me already tonight." He smiled and it turned into a grin.

"Why don't I tie you in a ball and take you in the Jacuzzi with me. I could hold you on the jets. You haven't been in there yet and I know you'd love it, Alli."

"What are you two plotting?" Jo was sitting up and giggling. "You turned us on and those two buggers over there." She smiled at them trying to get in some weird position to shag.

"It certainly turned me on," Harvey admitted.

"I think you'd make a good article for the Lancet, Harvey." Hillary giggled at him. "They'd never believe it even with photographs. They'd think we'd done a job on it on some computer programme." Harvey started laughing, I sat up and his huge cock stood to attention.

"I think I ought to strap that down before it pokes someone's eye out." They were in hysterics.

"When I stand up Alli, it'll drop being so heavy. We're having the black bathroom upstairs, tonight. Alli requested to be tied up and we're using the Jacuzzi after we feed. Alli's never been in there and should love it."

"We can vouch for that, Alli. Thank you Harvey, for letting us watch. I was bloody fascinated how large Alli got your cock, as you call it." She giggled. "I only learned the real names of everything but that's changed very fast around you lot." Harvey laughed at her.

"They must make those things for humans but I've no idea if they actually use them," he explained.

"I think some would try. You ask any A & E doctor what unusual things they've found up people's bums. You'd be bloody amazed, loo brushes being one of them. We heard all sorts when I was training." I thought that was really funny and couldn't stop laughing.

"What was the weirdest thing you used, Alli?" Hillary asked me. I had to think for a moment.

"It had to be a toss-up between the ball Harvey wired into my fanny or the double ended dildo as well as Harvey's cock up my bum and a large dildo up my fanny, all at the same time. No. The suction thing on my bump or those bloody weird hoods. The chastity belt, I couldn't choose really." Harvey laughed at me.

"I'll tell you exactly what it is, Hillary, a normal shag. Now that's weird for us."

She laughed at us, understanding completely. "What's the chastity belt like?"

"Whoever designed it got it all wrong. It's beautiful and feels good to wear but they're supposed to stop you having sex and it forced you to have it."

"What do you mean?" Harvey asked me to get off him. He

would go up for it, to show Hillary, and put some track-suit bottoms on. He took two seconds to appear back with us, with the belt in his hand and the handset.

He handed it to me. "Put it on Alli, show Hillary what you meant." I stripped off and stood into it. The things for my bum and fanny, slipped in easily and I locked the belt on. The key was put on the coffee table.

Jo's eyes were riveted on it. "Would you like that Hillary, I could still shag you with it on." The metal over the whole of the clit area was cut away and would give good access for Jo to please her.

"I'm sure I would, Jo. What else does it do, Alli?"

"Lie on the floor Alli and we'll show, Hillary." He gave me the handset. I lay face down and felt Harvey's hands under my thighs. He got hold of my hip bones to pull me gently over his face and held me above him.

"Turn on whatever you like, Alli." Once I turned the dials I put the handset to one side. Harvey waited until I was so horny I changed and begged him to begin. He still held off until I was demented and had squeezed my fanny onto the things throbbing inside me. The first touch from him was his tongue ball on my bump and I begged him for more. He held off again. I screamed for him to touch it again, the throbbing up my bum and fanny was driving me nuts as I waited for him. The noise I made had everyone in the room as randy as fuck. I could feel it and that added to the pleasure for me. Harvey licked my bump and held his hot tongue over it. I shuddered and screamed with delight. The thunderbolt hit and I passed out.

I opened my eyes. I was tied into a ball ready to go up to feed. Instead of my arms tied together above my head like before, they were tied behind my back and my arms were tied together at the top very tight. It felt fucking lovely for me.

I looked for Harvey and couldn't see him from where I was in the sitting room and couldn't see anyone else, either. *They must have gone to feed.*

"Are you ready, Alli? I had to show Olli and Gina the rooms behind the pool." He picked me up, cradled me in his arms and kissed me on the walk up the stairs to his shower room.

"I'm looking forward to this, Mr Burgess." He smiled at me

so tenderly I almost cried. *He's done so much for me tonight.*

"I could say the same to you, Mrs Burgess; loved every second of it. Now for the Jacuzzi, Alli and I think that would be the high point of your day, especially as you're tied up." I smiled at him and imagined how it would be.

"A thousand times better than that, you'll see." He propped me up in the corner of the shower and went out for the blood. He gave me three and had four for himself. He quickly opened another three for me, so the feelings would hit hard. I changed and everything heightened. I thought it couldn't get any better than that. Harvey picked me up and gently carried me into the Jacuzzi.

When he turned on the jets they pummelled everything which set all my nerve endings ablaze. He held my fanny over one of the jets and I shuddered, coming so violently in his arms. He held me there being fucked in mind and body.

How he found my bum with his thumb, I was tied up so tight, but find it he did. I screamed with pleasure as he massaged my bum with the jet, still blasted on my bump. The fact I was tied up heightened everything and Harvey was turned on. He'd always enjoyed pleasing me.

Keeping his thumb inside me, he lifted me on to his thighs. The jet between his legs played on my bump, too. I could feel his cock with my tied hands, and squeezed it hard onto the screw. When I came again I held it so tight he went rigid, coming with me in his mind.

He held me close for a few minutes to start again, over and over, until he knew I'd completely had it. He cuddled me for a while and I told him to set me free of the ropes. He lifted me out to take them off.

When all the knots were undone he helped me to my feet and cuddled me, for the strength to come back in my legs.

He looked down into my face. "Alli, that was perfect for me and I know you loved it. We'll have to come in here more often or I'll get another one in the other black bathroom behind the pool. I'm sure they'd get used."

He giggled, thinking about the arguing that went on about whose turn it was to use the black bathroom again.

"I missed all that. I think we should get the cottage rigged up for Olli and Gina." Harvey was thinking about something else and

I didn't catch it because I was talking. "What were you thinking about?"

He smiled at me. "What do you think of joining the cottage to the house?"

"They're here all the time anyway. I think that's a good idea. They could have their own black bathroom in there and there'd be no squabbling. Would it be difficult to do?"

"I don't think so, Alli, they're very close and a door could go in the alcove beyond the fireplace in the hall. The only objection would be if you didn't think we'd have enough privacy."

"We get up to what we want if they're here or not and I shouldn't think we'd shock them after today, do you?" Harvey laughed at me and his cock tried to lift and couldn't because of the weight.

"Is it alright? I gave it a hell of a squeeze when I was changed." He lifted it up with his hand and I couldn't resist putting my hands all around it. "Hmmmmm, that feels really good, Alli. You've done no damage I promise you."

His eyes were closed and I played with it running my fingers underneath, touching the implanted balls until he pulled me forward to squash it between us. He went rigid and groaned. The sinews on his neck stood out as he was coming in his mind. He cuddled me really tight until the feelings died down.

"Thank you, Mrs Burgess. You certainly know how to turn me on. I love you, Alli. Who would have thought we'd be where we are today when you moved in. I certainly didn't?" He looked down at me and smiled.

"I'd have called anyone a liar if they'd told me. Am I pleased I did. I have everything I want in you, Mr Burgess.

"You were so kind to me when I moved in, Harvey. How could I not love you from the beginning? I was too afraid to say anything and you won me over with your empathy, sincerity and above all, trust. I know what flashed through your mind. It wasn't your fault Harvey, or mine. That's been wiped from our lives for good. It didn't happen as far as I'm concerned. Don't think of it again, please."

He took my face in his hands and kissed me until I was melting. He picked me up and took me into his bedroom.

"You need sleep, Alli and I want to cuddle you." He laid me

on the bed, got on behind me and put his arm around my body. He kissed the back of my neck. “I didn’t know you loved me from the time you moved in. I felt the same, Alli.”

I pushed my body closer to him. “I know, Jenny told me when we became a couple.” He squeezed me tight and kissed my neck again.

“Try to sleep. I’ll draw your tattoos in the morning at Jed’s. Goodnight Alli.”

“Thank you, Harvey. Night.”

I opened my eyes and Harvey was looking at me. “Good morning, Alli.”

I kissed him. “Good morning my husband, how are your bits. I hope I can get it out.” Harvey giggled.

“I don’t think that’ll be a problem. If you can’t, I will, Alli. If it wasn’t for the fact it wouldn’t go into my jeans I’d leave it in only I’d look a bit deformed if I tried.” I pictured it and started giggling. Harvey tickled me to stop my mind seeing his huge cock bursting out of his jeans.

“Take it out, wench,” and giggled. I sat up and he rolled on to his back.

I took hold of his cock, tried to turn it and didn’t have the strength. Harvey got hold of the handle with one hand and held his cock with the other. He turned it a couple of times and I took over. He moaned as it turned. The nodules were a great pleasure for him as they moved round and around the inside of his cock. He loved it and wanted to come but he held it off until I got it out and had the biggest ejaculation I’d ever seen, when I took it right out.

I cuddled him until his feelings calmed down and looked at his cock. It was back to its normal size already.

“Christ Alli, I might have come in my head but I must have been storing that up somewhere.”

“It was like a bloody damn bursting, Harvey.” He laughed at me and got up to go for a shower. I pulled the black sheets off the bed for the wash and got new ones from the trunk.

Jo and Hillary went shopping to the sex shop at Darwin’s Heath and were joining us later. Jed was ready for us at his shop.

He had the kettle boiling as we arrived for coffee. He knew we were never late.

“Hi, you lot look happy. Had a good night?” He had a twinkle in his eyes as he was getting to know us.

“Fucking amazing Jed, thanks,” Harvey told him with a huge grin on his face.

“That pool of yours is bloody fantastic.”

“Bring your girlfriend some time and we’d like to meet her. Would she mind us skinny dipping, we don’t swim any other way.”

“She walks around naked at home so that wouldn’t be a problem, Harvey.” I handed out the coffees and we went to his studio. Gina and I sat at the table in his room and watched Olli getting tattooed.

“Right Olli, could you hold an erection. You’d have to if I’m to tattoo your penis properly.” Olli looked flummoxed.

“I’ve never tried, Jed.”

“I’ll tell you what I thought of, Olli.” Harvey tried to help him. “That Alli was doing what Jed is doing and it wasn’t a problem for me.” Olli smiled at Harvey and glanced at Gina. She was giggling and thought she’d make a right hash of the tattoo if she was doing it. We all laughed in her mind.

“Carry on Jed, I’ll be fine.” Jed placed the transfer right down Olli’s chest, abdomen and erect cock, then got started.

Harvey picked up some paper and a pencil from the stack on the table beside us and drew the designs for my thighs. *They look beautiful.*

Harvey smiled at me. “So are you Alli, you’ve no idea how beautiful.”

“I still think you need an Optician.” Harvey giggled at me and continued drawing.

Jed had filled in the design down Olli’s cock and was moving up his abdomen.

“Can I ask you something, Harvey? If I’ve got this wrong, forget I asked.”

“Go on Jed.” Harvey was excited about his question.

“Are you into bondage?” The smile grew wider on Harvey’s face. Jed knew he was on the right track even before Harvey answered.

"I think you know we are." Jed was happy to hear that, we both felt it.

"My brother was a mountaineer and into rigging, using only ropes." We both listened intently now. "He also teaches bondage to couples. Would you be interested?" *Tell him, we're interested, Harvey.*

Okay Jo.

Olli's eyes were riveted on us before we answered. Harvey nodded to him.

"He'd have three couples for classes, Jed. Let him know, please."

"I certainly will; he goes to couples houses. If you're all together he may do a special rate."

"We will be together but he doesn't have to do a special rate Jed, you know why."

Jed nodded to Harvey and said thanks in his head. Harvey answered. "You're welcome." Jed looked surprised. "It's not just Alli, Jed, all of us do it."

"I'll have to watch what I'm thinking around you bloody lot," Jed said with a grin. Harvey laughed at him.

Jed was getting to the top of Olli's chest when Harvey asked Olli what he thought about joining the house to the cottage.

"A fucking brilliant idea, Harvey. Does that mean all the alterations, too?"

We knew exactly what he meant, a black bathroom.

"Absolutely Olli, the whole lot would be done together." Olli put up his thumb and moved his head to one side so Jed could join the tattoos over his shoulder and finish the top of his arm.

"I'll order some lunch, Jed." Harvey pulled his phone out and asked Jo in his mind how long they'd be.

"Hi, that didn't take too long." Jo and Hillary strolled in to Jed's studio giggling. *We were talking to Geordie, booking the next things, Hillary wants doing.* Harvey ordered lunch and listened to all the banter.

You can't think that and not tell us, you buggers. I stared at Jo and she giggled.

Alright; she's going the whole hog.

What! You better have plenty of toys Jo, you're going to fucking need them. Fuck being the operative word, you get my drift.

She nodded to me. *Why do you think we went shopping?*

"When are you getting something else done, Hillary?" I asked out loud.

"In about an hour, Alli." Hillary smiled. "I'll be okay." She came over to me and looked at the drawings for my legs. "These are beautiful Alli, lucky you." *We've got two pairs of hands to sort me out, don't worry.*

"You should ask Harvey to draw something for you Hillary or maybe you can draw, that never crossed my mind."

"I'd like Harvey to do something for me, Alli. His drawings are really beautiful. I want something with a Japanese feel to it, including butterflies." Harvey came over to us and picked up more paper. He sat down and began drawing a picture of a mountain with draping willows at the base and butterflies dancing around bamboo leaves for the frame of the picture. Hillary watched in amazement as he drew in such detail and so fast.

At the bottom of the whole picture he wrote Japanese symbols going down. To be tattooed down her spine if she liked it.

Harvey looked up at Hillary. "You have to imagine it with colour, Hillary. Jed had free rein colouring Alli's, he's brilliant."

"I think the pair of you are brilliant, I love it Harvey. Could I add to this later?"

"Of course Hillary. The main theme on Alli's are the briars. Jed did them free hand, I just followed the theme. Your theme could be the leaves, butterflies and symbols, making it unique to you." Harvey handed her the drawing. "It's yours, Hillary."

"That's bloody amazing, Harvey. I saw how quickly you drew it."

Jed was shocked. "I don't know how he does it either, Hillary, hidden talents." Jed smiled at her. "I wish I had them Hillary. That would have taken me a couple of days. I can enlarge it to fit you exactly, when you want it doing."

Geordie came in. "Harvey, your meal has arrived." He went out to pay and we all headed for the room used to eat in.

We were having different conversations around the huge table, two pushed together. I heard Jed ask Hillary if she worked with us.

"I see a lot of these buggers. I'm their Pathologist, Jed."

"I would have said brilliant Home Office Pathologist." Harvey pushed in to the chat.

"Bloody hell, I'm sitting with royalty here." Jed giggled and Hillary smiled at him.

"I may have to come in on your late nights for my tattoo, even then if I made an appointment with you and I get a rush job from this lot I wouldn't want to have to cancel."

"Are you free next Sunday, Hillary."

"As far as I know at the moment yes, but that could change."

"Get yours done today Hillary, I can wait," I threw in.

"I can't Alli, nice of you to offer. I'm getting pierced and it would take hours. Jed couldn't fit it in before they close."

"I tell you what, if Harvey has somewhere well lit, I could come with you tonight and do it at theirs. I have a mobile kit because I get asked to tattoo disabled people all the time and a lot can't leave their homes."

Hillary looked at Harvey and he smiled at her. "You're welcome to do it at home, Hillary. The kitchen is the brightest place in the house. Would that do, Jed?"

"That would be perfect in there. I have something to cover the floor so there'd be no mess."

"That's organised." I stacked all the plates and Jo helped clear all the cartons. I had a quiet word with her when we took it all to the kitchen. I told her my fanny dribbled all the time, for a whole day and she'd need something to stop that if she was getting tattooed. Jo told me Hillary would use pads anyway, in case anything bled. She wasn't sure if she'd heal as quickly as us. That was a load off my mind.

When it was my turn to be tattooed Harvey looked through the catalogue that came with all the metalwork I'd bought for him. Jed did all the outlines and asked me to take a look. Harvey must have been engrossed. He didn't notice me looking in the mirror. I walked over to him.

"Found something more interesting than me, have you?" Harvey looked up and ran his hand over the outline on my leg.

"I wondered what you'd say if I kept my head in this book." He started laughing and stood up. "Nothing is more interesting than you for half the men on this planet, Alli."

I looked at Jed. "Are you sure his drawings aren't in Braille, he's got a serious vision problem." Harvey giggled at me.

"Have you looked in the mirror lately, Alli?" Jed said to me. I was bloody shocked.

"I kept telling you Alli, heads would turn." I felt myself going red. "Don't be embarrassed Alli, I like it if others find you beautiful. I know you're mine; that's the difference."

"He's right, you only get one true partner and mine will be home in a few days. I didn't tell you, we're going to be parents. Abbey's two months gone."

"That's brilliant Jed. You have to bring her to meet us at the house now, when she gets back; after your reunion bash, of course." Jed grinned at me. "I'll give you my mobile number to ring us. Harvey's is a hot line for work and you'd be bloody deaf if he answered your call."

I wrote my number on some paper and gave it to him.

"Well, do you like it Harvey? Jed's about to start colouring it." He grinned at me knowing the change of subject was just what I wanted.

He twirled me around and pulled his hands up my legs to my hips. *Careful, I'm trying hard not to change.*

Oh, shit.

"It's perfect Jed, get some colour on it. I'm going back to the catalogue."

Jed got back to work and spent the next three hours transforming the lined tattoo on each leg into masterpieces.

He cleaned down each tattoo for the last time and I went over to look in the mirror. Tears pricked my eyes; they were so beautiful. Harvey felt me get emotional and came over to me.

"Alli, they're stunning. I'm not surprised you feel like that." He cuddled me and told me not to cry. I got dressed and thanked Jed.

"The colours are amazing Jed, thank you so much." I gave him a hug.

"We should see where the other buggers are. Hillary must be finished by now," Harvey stated.

"You go and find them. I'll just clear up here and get my kit out," Jed told us. We left him to see where they were.

"Why are you all waiting out here?" I asked no one in particular.

"It's my fault," Olli said. "I didn't want to disturb you and they stayed with me."

"Daft bugger; you've seen it all already."

"Under different circumstances, though. It just seemed wrong here, sorry."

"Don't be sorry, it's nice to know we have a gentleman among us. Thank you for your concern, Olli." Harvey was giggling, in my head. I turned and smiled at him.

Jed came down the hall dragging a large steel workbox. Harvey hurried over and picked it up. "Where do you want it?" Jed couldn't believe his strength.

"Come on Jed, move yourself. The muscles I've got do work but it would bloody hurt if I dropped it on your foot." Jed opened the shop door and held it for Harvey. I had a little chuckle. Harvey had picked it up without thinking and got out of it pretty well. The others don't know how strong he really is. Jo and Hillary knew he was strong but had no idea he could pick our car up if he tried.

Jed came back to see if Geordie had finished for the day.

"Can I pay the bill at home Jed, there's money in the safe. I had no idea how much it would cost." Jed nodded.

"I'll pay for Gina's work now, Geordie." I pulled out a debit card for him.

Harvey carried Jed's workbox into the kitchen and left him to set everything up. "I'll get you some chairs and there's a massage table upstairs, I'll bring it down Jed."

"Thanks Harvey that'll be great."

I put the kettle on. "Anyone for tea?" Five hands shot up.

Hillary asked if she could use my bathroom. "You don't have to ask, Hillary." *Are you alright?*

I'm fine; just checking really, Alli.

As her and Jo left, Harvey came in carrying a huge suitcase. He opened it up and turned it over.

"I didn't know you had that, Harvey." He looked at me with a twinkle in his eyes. "I'm sure we might be using that some other time, please."

There's still a lot you don't know about, Mrs Burgess. I have to have things in reserve, for you.

I glanced at him, handed out the tea and Gina came in. "Play for us, you two." Jed's ears pricked. "What do you play?"

"I play the guitar and Alli the piano." Harvey waited for more questions from Jed. He didn't ask anything else.

"Do that fast thing you played the other night, please." Gina was very persuasive.

"Come on Alli." He grinned at Gina. "She won't leave us alone, until we do." She started clapping and cuddled Olli.

Harvey started it and I jumped in a few bars later. We played "Duelling Banjos" for them and this time I used both hands and was exhilarated when we finished. A round of applause rang out and the loudest came from Jed.

"I've heard people say they play and they're crap. I couldn't say that about you two, it was excellent. How long have you been playing?"

"They've driven us mad for fucking years. Practice, practice, practice." Jo's face was beaming. "Sorry, I had to tell it how it was." *You're a genius, Jo.*

Hillary was right behind her. "I'll second that; we wore earplugs, for ages."

"Well thanks; now you tell us." Harvey laughed at them.

"Come on Jed, let's get this tattoo started." They took him into the kitchen.

Three hours later the tattoo was finished. Hillary came out with a towel over her front to show us.

Harvey went into the kitchen to pay Jed. "There's extra for you and Abbey, get the baby things with it." Jed tried to give it back.

"We can't have kids, Jed. This is the nearest we'd get, a friend having one. Please take it from Alli and me." I walked in. "We insist Jed, please."

We could see tears in his eyes. "I think Abbey will insist you're god parents, after this. Thank you." He gave me a hug and shook Harvey's hand.

When Jed had gone we looked at Hillary's tattoo properly. "Sorry about disappearing like that, Hillary."

"It's alright Alli, you'd make very good god parents, I'm really happy for you both. Now, as for my bits they're healed already, so Jo can shag the arse of me, tonight. She's well equipped I promise you." We laughed at her. Jo looked embarrassed.

"We're going home to feed. I couldn't do what I have to for Hillary, with you not far away."

"We totally understand Jo, don't worry about it. We'll see you tomorrow at work." As soon as Harvey told her that she relaxed and cuddled Hillary. They said goodnight a few minutes later and left.

"I felt sorry for Jo, tonight. She has to go against everything she is, Harvey."

"I know, Alli. It just shows you how much she thinks of Hillary. Hopefully it should only for one night, it could be more. The hoods sorted you out, remember? Let's go up to feed. I can hear those two at it, already."

Chapter 8

Jo was at her desk when we walked through the outer office.

"Do you want to come in for a chat, Jo?" She looked up at me and grinned.

"I'll be in, in a moment I'll just finish this, Alli." Harvey went over to Jamie to ask him something so I ambled into our office and sat at my desk.

I opened my computer and looked for any sites that covered the removal of genitals. The first thing that popped up was on the Eunuch. The Egyptians castrated men who looked after the harem. Next was the practice of Castrato. Boys with exceptionally high singing voices were castrated to keep the voice from breaking. *Poor sods*.

Jo came in and closed the door. "Sorry Alli, I would have lost my train of thought if I'd come straight in."

"How did it go?" I didn't read her mind; I wouldn't be so rude.

"I don't know how to tell you after my speech, last night."

"Jo, just say it, you know I won't be judgemental."

"When we went to the sex shop yesterday I looked for a strap-on, which I'd have hated. We came across one that had no straps. One part went up my fanny and another up my bum to stabilise it. When I saw how much Hillary loved it and I didn't feel odd using it on her we had a fucking good night. Excuse the pun."

"What was she like after you went to feed?"

"Rampant like you said she'd be. I'm pleased we tried it out before we did that. We had a few false starts getting used to it. I know I'd never have sorted it out without that thing."

"I said to Harvey you're going against everything that you are."

"I heard you, Alli. You understand me better than I do sometimes. I'm not sorry we got it and I'd use it as long as she wanted me to. If it's forever then it is. The one saving grace is I could feel I was shagging her. It was inside me and rubbed my clit so we both come together."

I got up and gave her a hug. "I'm glad you got over that little hurdle, she'll be in control of her body quite quickly. It only lasted on me for one night because Harvey used those weird hoods over two days. I had to control it; mind over matter played a huge part. When he put the first one on it felt in my head, I'd been buried and had to be very careful. You wouldn't want to go down that route. I don't think either of you would like it one bit."

"Like what, Alli?" Harvey came strolling in.

"The air restricting hoods."

"I never left her side when she had them on, they're scary shit. Are you alright Jo?" He was really concerned about her after our chat last night.

"I'm fine and it went okay last night. Alli can fill you in on the details. You're going to the lab, aren't you?"

"Yes, just to see what they've found out over the weekend. Have you tracked anything regarding mental hospitals?"

"None of the untraceables on the list have been in one, that's for certain. I've not only checked in this area but nationwide. They still have a few, to trace and we'll see what comes up."

"Jamie told me he only had a few left to do. Alli, we're off to the lab. What are you looking up on your computer?"

"Anything to do with genital removal but I've only just started. I'll get on with it when we get back." I picked up my jacket and bag. "See you later, Jo."

"Hi, Hillary."

She smiled at us. "How are you two, and more to the point have you spoken to Jo?"

"She was pleased it went okay and so are we. I knew she was worried last night."

"I felt really shitty for her but she handled it extremely well. The good thing is I won't want it after things have calmed down. It reminded me too much of being shagged by a man. Sorry Harvey." Pictures of her being raped flashed into my mind.

"I'm so sorry, Hillary. I had no idea you'd been raped." I gave her a hug. Harvey stood there in shock. "You haven't told Jo have you?"

"She'll know now but I couldn't tell her. I knew she hated using that thing, and we had too."

"She'd be made up you wouldn't want it anymore from what she said to me this morning. It won't be burn your bra it'll be burn the cock."

She started laughing at me. "You're like a breath of fresh air Alli, thank you. I'm not sorry I had it done. That part of things felt bloody lovely." She looked at Harvey. "I've never felt threatened by you or Olli. You're the first males I've had any friendship with since then and I value that."

Harvey gave her a hug. "I'm honoured Hillary, thank you."

I put the kettle on and got mugs ready. "Let's have some tea now that's out of the way." Harvey giggled at me.

"Mrs Burgess's cure all." Hillary couldn't help but laugh.

"I noticed. You do drink a lot of it, Alli."

"I couldn't drink wine like you lot. One glass and I would be tipsy, two and I'd be on my back. Ask him, he has to keep count."

Harvey sniggered, "It's true."

"What's a girl got left, tea and he loves me drinking it at certain times." I flashed my eyes at him. He knew what I meant.

"True again, I fucking loved it," his eyes really sparkled.

Hillary sat behind her desk and looked over the reports of the PMs already done. We stopped talking. We didn't want to break her thoughts.

"There's something really weird about all of this. I can't put my finger on it. Eighteen have been done so far and they've all had ops or complete castrations."

"I suppose until they'd all been done we wouldn't have a complete time span for when they were operated on and killed. I haven't asked before Hillary, what did they die from?" Harvey was baffled.

"The most recent date; eight years, so far. That could change I'm afraid. Most of them died when they were embalmed. It replaces the blood with chemicals and we wouldn't know if they were drugged at all, until we have the tox reports back from the lab."

Harvey's phone rang. He stood up and left Hillary's office. When he came back in: "Alli, we have to go and we'll see you later Hillary."

I got up, picked my bag up and hugged Hillary. "See you soon." I held Harvey's hand out of the lab.

On the way to the crime scene he told me what the call was about. "This looks like it's linked to our case now."

"What! Jesus, Harvey, I don't like this."

"Me neither, Alli. I thought this was a cold case."

"What do you mean?" I looked over to him driving fast and dodging traffic.

"A cold case is something not currently happening now or something opened up because more evidence has come to light. The cases opened up again because DNA has flagged up a perpetrator who'd had his or her's taken for another crime entirely."

"Where are we going, then?" He didn't answer. A taxi was blocking the street, double parked. Harvey flicked a switch on the dashboard and a siren blasted out from under the bonnet.

The taxi driver took off at speed looking in his rear-view mirror.

"Look ahead; you fucking idiot!" Harvey yelled at him. The taxi screeched to a halt at a pelican crossing and barely missed a family halfway across the road. Harvey jumped out of the car and hurried to have words with the driver.

"If I wasn't in a hurry to get to a murder scene you'd be getting a visit from Traffic, think yourself bloody lucky mate!" The guy said sorry and Harvey returned to our car. People behind us honked their horns again. Harvey flicked the siren and the horns stopped immediately.

We pulled up outside a ramshackle house that didn't look habitable to me. We got out and walked to the front door.

Before Harvey knocked, "How did you find out about this, Harvey?"

"An anonymous tip-off, Alli." He knocked hard on the door.

The old man who opened it was hardly alive. He looked so infirm let alone, capable of murder.

"Yes, if you're selling anything I don't have money in the house."

"I'm Detective Inspector Burgess. We've been called out to your house. A phone call was received at the Station regarding a body at these premises."

"Is this some practical joke?" He looked astounded. We both felt he knew nothing about it and Harvey spoke to him in a more gentle tone.

"Could we come in and speak to you, Sir?" The old man let his door open wider and showed us into his sitting room.

The smell of a body hit me. Harvey looked at my face, for a moment.

"Could I ask your name please, Sir?" The old man smiled.

"It's Henry Shaw, Sir."

"Mr Shaw, there's no other way to say this, I'm sorry. We've had a tip-off about a body in the shed in your garden." He looked physically shaken.

"I don't understand? I haven't been out there for years."

I stood up and sat beside him. "Mr Shaw, I'm Alli. I work with Harvey as I pick up on emotions, the dead and know when someone is telling the truth. I know you haven't a clue about the body, please don't worry. Do you have any family I could contact for you?" He smiled at me and patted my hand.

"No dear; there's only me left in our family."

"I know the body is in the shed, I can smell it from here. You don't have to watch what's going to happen now and you certainly don't need the press on your back from the local rag. I'm putting you into a hotel while all this is sorted out."

"I can't afford anything like that my dear." *The poor old bugger.*

"I can and won't even notice the bill. Could you pack a few things and I'll get an officer with an unmarked car, take you to a good hotel." He looked shell shocked, "I'll help you pack if you like, Mr Shaw."

"I don't know what to say." I took hold of his hand; he was shaking.

"Please let me help you. I know it's an awful shock but we have to get the ball rolling on this, I'm afraid."

"It's alright dear I understand, you have to get on with things. I'll go and pack a bag." He got up to leave the room.

"I'll carry your bag down, Mr Shaw. I don't want you lifting anything heavy. You'd have to pack enough for at least a week," Harvey told him.

"Okay son; thank you." He left us to wait for him.

He came into the room again. "My suitcase is in the front bedroom Detective Inspector."

Harvey got up and put his hand on his shoulder. "It'll be better for you to be away from this. Sit down and Alli will ring Andy. He'll take you to the Carlton and if you need anything from here ring this number." Harvey gave him a card. "We'll get finished as quickly as possible, that's a promise."

Mr Shaw nodded to him as he left the room. He sat beside me. "What is this world coming to?"

I took my phone out and organised Andy for the mission.

"Mr Shaw, he's young but you wouldn't want anyone else sorting this out. He's a bloody good copper. Sorry, I shouldn't have sworn."

"It's okay with me. I expect worse things are said in your job."

I giggled. "The air is quite blue at times, you're right." He smiled at me just as Harvey arrived with his case.

"We both feel like killing half the people we deal with." Mr Shaw smiled at him.

"I understand that perfectly. You must be good at your job or they'd never have put you in charge."

Harvey grinned at him. "We must look like kids to you, being the age you are."

"Everyone looks like that to me now, I never thought I'd last this long."

"Andy's here Harvey, could you let him in, please."

Harvey got up and Mr Shaw looked at me. "I read minds and could hear him out there. He's singing to something on a CD."

"I can see why they employ you," he laughed. "I bet nothing gets past your little gift."

"Not a lot. They don't stand a chance in an interview room. It all pours into my head as soon as I look at them."

He chuckled, "I'd love to hear that."

Harvey came in with Andy. "She's right. The interviews are brilliant to listen to. Ask Andy on your way to the hotel, he's heard them."

Andy giggled. "Come on Mr Shaw; your carriage awaits. I'll give you a rundown on the way." A glint touched the old man's eyes and he got up.

We helped him into the car and Andy started talking as soon as they left. More to keep his mind off what was going to happen here than anything else. Andy has a very happy attitude to everything. Perfect for that little job and he gets on with the elderly better than anyone else in the team.

Now we got down to business. Harvey pulled his phone and got things moving really fast. People turned up within minutes and got going on securing the scene and keeping the press and onlookers away. *It always amazed me how the press got hold of anything. They must pay a lot, or the public wouldn't bother; would they?*

"The thought of a big payout motivates most, Alli and then their picture in the paper or on TV. The 'fifteen minutes of fame' syndrome. Let's get suited up. Christ knows what we're going to find."

We stood on the road behind the car and pulled on forensic suits, covered our feet with plastic and then pulled on our gloves as we took the path at the side of the house to gain access to the back garden. We could see the shed door half open as we turned the corner at the back of the house. It was roughly twenty feet from us and the smell was very strong to me.

As we walked closer our eyes scanned the ground for anything Socco might want.

Harvey was in front of me and pushed the door to see if it would open any wider or if the body was stopping it in any way. The interior was dark so Harvey pulled a small torch from his pocket and switched it on. When he shone it into the shed I was by his side. We both stared at a mummified body sprawled across the floor. The foot on the right leg was behind the door and stopped it from opening further.

The shed behind the body was full of boxes and they looked like they'd been there for years. The cardboard was filthy, covered in dust and they hadn't been disturbed for a long time.

The body was totally different from the others. The bandages were virtually new but there was dirt in places where whoever had carried it here must have touched mud at some point. Essentially, this was a new body.

"Hillary might want to collect this, herself." Harvey found her direct number and waited for her to answer.

"Hillary you're not going to believe this; we've got a fresh one, here." He listened for a minute. "Okay we'll be waiting. 20 Fisher Close and on the left from your end, see you soon."

We walked back to the front of the house. Jamie was waiting for us with two men from Socco. Harvey looked at them. "I don't think you'll get much. Do your best. It's in the shed at the back." They nodded to Harvey and took the path.

"This is a fresh one Jamie, bandaged the same as the others. I want doors knocked along this street and the one behind. Get Uniform on to it and find out if any CCTV cameras are working around here. They put the bloody things up and half of them aren't working. Target practice for kids, most of them."

"Okay, Sir. Is the house derelict?"

"Unfortunately not. A Mr Shaw lives here. We've put him in the Carlton; our expense in case anyone asks. He's over ninety, Jamie, and the council's temporary accommodation is bloody awful. They'd just say put him in a home. He's a nice old man who's looked after himself so far and he couldn't handle the press, at his age."

"I quite understand, Sir. I'll get things moving." Jamie shot off.

We sat on the curb and waited for Hillary.

"When was the last time it rained, Harvey?" He looked at me strangely.

"About a week ago, why?"

"There was mud on the back of the right leg. It could have got there from whoever looked in the shed but I'm guessing it happened when it was brought here." A smile grew on Harvey's face.

"Quite the little Sherlock today, Alli. I didn't notice that. There may be footprints if it was wet."

"My head's nearer the ground than yours so it's not your fault." I elbowed him and giggled.

"You haven't done that for ages, Alli." He put his arm over my shoulder.

"What are you on about?"

"When you first moved in you did it a few times, elbowing me, remember?"

I giggled, "Yes I do, even in the Morgue. We've been to some thrilling places." Harvey sniggered and we shouldn't be laughing out loud.

I told you I'd take you on the journey. You've had it with frills. Morgue, work, Pathology labs. What more could a girl want, Alli? You get to dress up in the latest fashions. Forensic suits, gowns and the shoe wear is fabulous.

Mr Burgess, you've been so kind.

"I tried to shut you out but found it fascinating." Hillary stood behind us with a smile almost splitting her face.

We both grinned at her. "We get fed up waiting around Hillary and I see you're sporting the latest Pathology Chanel suit or should I say shell?"

"Nearer the truth, Alli. Where's our victim?"

"In the shed at the back. Alli says there's mud on the back of its right leg so it may have been moved here when it was raining."

"I'll take a soil sample just in case we need it. Have Socco finished?"

"We'll take a look Hillary. I can't see them getting much?" Harvey led the way and Socco were packing up their things.

"Did you get much, Keith?" Harvey waited.

"A couple of smudged fingerprints on the handle. I'm not holding out much hope I'm afraid. Whoever put that body in there laid it down without disturbing anything and it's not a small body."

"Thanks Keith, have you looked for footprints?"

"Yes, we saw the mud on the leg and had a good look around. It may have come from wherever it was killed. I'm saying 'it' as we don't know the sex yet, that'll be Hillary's domain." He nodded to her. "Is this linked to last week's?"

"We'll only know that when the bandages come off. Thanks Keith."

They picked up their cases and left us to it. Hillary went to the shed with a torch. "He's right, we might have to take the front off this shed or clear everything out."

"If you get it in a body bag, Hillary, I'll lift it out as long as you get rid of your staff for a couple of minutes."

"Understood Harvey, thanks." Hillary looked relieved. She left us to get some help.

Harvey put his arms around me. "Are you okay, Harvey?"

"I just want a cuddle from my wife, I'm fine. I was thinking we haven't taken Olli and Gina shopping yet. It would take our minds off this shit."

Before I could make any comment, Hillary was back with two men wearing forensic suits. I recognised one, Danny who helped at the first PM in this case. He nodded to us both and went over to the shed with Hillary. In his hand was a body bag. The other guy was carrying a stretcher, laid it on the grass and he left the garden.

"Sorry, I had to ask you to do this Danny. You're the only one who could fit in here. I'll keep a torch on you as you may have to shut the door a bit to roll the body. Just get it in the bag and zip it up, then wait for me by the van, please." Hillary knew he was really puzzled, I could feel it from here. He did as she asked and a couple of minutes later he pulled the door open, enough to get out and left us.

"Do your stuff, Harvey." Before she had the last word out the body bag was on the stretcher and Harvey was beside me again.

"You could be a bloody magician, I didn't see you move," she giggled. "We better wait a minute or they'll smell a rat. I'm going to say you and I got it out Alli. They can believe what they like. They'll know Harvey couldn't get in there."

"Very good Hillary. I'll take the head end and you two can take a handle each. You'll have to pretend you're knackered."

We picked up the stretcher and carried it to the van. Her staff looked in shock.

"Take it from here, lads. I have to sit a minute. There was only room for Alli and me in there. We didn't want you to watch in case we dropped it and I'd never have lived it down."

Danny laughed. "As if?"

"You forget, I know you buggers." They loaded the body and drove away.

"Thank you Harvey. That saved a lot of time and we can't afford to waste any. That body was fresh and I have a horrible feeling you'll find more."

"I've been thinking that since we got here, Hillary. I can't smell them or see them but my gut instinct tells me something is wrong, Harvey. I think you should get Uniform to check all the sheds near here and especially the houses at the back of these. My mind keeps me drawn to them and I don't know why." I sat on the curb and Harvey sat beside me. He pulled his phone out and waited for Jamie to answer.

"Jamie I want all sheds opened at every property in this street. Especially the street behind us. Alli says her mind is drawn to the houses back there." He listened. "Good man, get it done."

"He seems to be on the ball, Harvey." Hillary looked impressed.

"I'd be sorry to see him move on but it's inevitable. Have you thought how you're going to cope with the age thing Hillary, with your workers I mean?"

"I'll have to do the same or pretend I've had twenty-five facelifts." I started laughing. "What's tickled you, Alli?" Hillary waited.

"When Harvey worked out I'd never age since I'm stuck at twenty-two, I could only say I'd never need a facelift." She giggled at me.

"That's good, I hadn't thought of that. Think of the money we'd save, Alli. Believe me, I'd have had at least two and dyed the hair until it fell out. I'd have ended up like Joan Rivers plus a wig." Harvey was giggling beside me.

"What's so funny, Mr Burgess."

He looked at me. "You two, once you get going there's no stopping you. I'm seriously thinking of investing in a garden fence and position it in the sitting room. You can lean on it and talk your heads off."

"Watch it, Mr Burgess. I brought a cane to work. They sent me to sleep him and Jed. I was getting my back done and they never bloody stopped. Worse than women you two are. Cars and motorbikes, that's all I heard for three bloody hours." Hillary was laughing at Harvey who was pretending I was lying. "I'll get you later, Mr Burgess."

"I hope that's a promise. Cool it, Jamie's coming."

He wasn't just coming, he was running. "Sir, you'll have to come and see this."

Harvey got up and ran with Jamie, back to wherever he'd come from.

Don't go yet, Hillary. I have something for you.

We looked at each other for a second and then we got it. Harvey had genitals from a dustbin.

He handed a black bin liner to Hillary and when she opened it she saw what we'd seen in Harvey's mind.

"A dog knocked over a dustbin and was about to run off with it. Jamie had his wits about him and told the dog to sit. Then he said drop and the dog put it down, it was nearly bloody dog meat. He's checking the rest of the bin."

"Which house did it come from, Harvey?" I asked as this wasn't anything to do with the gut feeling I had before.

"It's alright Alli, they haven't stopped looking." He turned to Hillary. "If we find anything else we'll bring it to you unless it's another body. I'd call if we found another. It's a good job you've still got help, you'll bloody need it."

"I'll do the PM on this body when I get back to the lab to make sure we're dealing with the same MO and let you know what I find as soon as possible, Harvey."

"Thanks Hillary, that would be a great help. We might be taking Olli and Gina shopping later, we haven't decided yet. If you want to come over give us a ring, I couldn't see us being out to late."

If you're going near Darwin's Heath, I think we'd like to come with you.

Okay Jo, we'll let you know if we're going.

Harvey started to grin. "Nothing slips past her." Hillary giggled.

I heard that, Harvey Burgess.

"We should get back to the job in hand so we'll see you later, Hillary." She gave us a hug and drove off.

"Alli, the street behind Mr Shaw's house is Milton Crescent. I think we should walk the whole length of it. You might be able to hone in on something to do with this case. It could feel totally different to you, once you're in the street."

"I think it's a good idea. Maybe that's why I couldn't be specific about anything. Which end do we start at?"

"We'll use the cut to get into the street and start at number one, that way we won't get confused trying to work backwards."

I linked Harvey's arm and we used the cut, ending up in Milton Crescent. We walked to our right and paced half the crescent to number one. I stopped myself from picking anything up until we were there, to keep a clear head.

Harvey pulled his phone out and waited for Jamie to answer.

"Jamie, I want a road block on both ends of Milton Crescent. Alli's walking the centre of the road to pick up anything from either side." He listened for a moment, "Okay Jamie." Harvey closed his phone and looked at me. "He wants a couple of minutes, Alli."

We heard sirens on the main road that joined the two ends of the crescent. A squad car stopped behind us and blocked the entire road. Harvey's phone rang. "Yes," he listened. "Thanks Jamie. We can go Alli and take as much time as you want."

"I could pick them up better if my eyes are closed, Harvey. Hold my hand and guide me please. If I give you a squeeze, stop."

He took hold of my hand and we began the slow walk up the centre of the street.

We hadn't been walking long when I heard a car engine at speed. I opened my eyes and Harvey told me to leave the road. He stood his ground and the car screeched to a halt inches away from him. The driver was white with shock. Harvey opened the driver's door. "Get out now, please."

"But."

Harvey's voice got a lot louder. "No buts! Get out now, please!"

The driver got out and was visibly shaking. "I'm conducting a murder enquiry in this street. I'd like your keys." The lad handed them over.

"Walk to the end of the crescent to the road block and when I've finished you'll get your keys back. What's your name?"

"Jason Hicks. I was only visiting my girlfriend."

"Do you know the speed limit on this road, Jason?"

"Thirty, I think." Harvey could see he was scared.

"It's twenty and has been for the last two years. What would you have done if a child ran into the road? I'm really visible in this forensic suit, a child isn't. You would have killed them, Jason. You were hitting forty at least. Families with young kids live on this street and that's the reason for the speed limit. You're lucky I've more pressing things to attend to. Kill the speed before you end up killing someone else or yourself."

"I'm sorry, I'll be more careful."

"Right. Go to the road block, please." He turned and walked towards the beginning of the crescent.

Harvey put his hand out to me. "Come on Alli, we could have done without that." I joined him at the back of the lad's car and closed my eyes when I touched his hand. We continued down the crescent and I started hearing an argument. I squeezed Harvey's hand and we stopped walking.

"Do you hear that Harvey or is it only in my head?"

"I only hear it in your mind, Alli. Where are they? Open your eyes, you might see them anywhere."

I opened my eyes, looked over to my left and scanned the houses for any sight of the two ghosts I could hear. They were arguing about the operations they'd had. One bragged he'd had the most extreme one done therefore he was more superior to the other one. Harvey listened with me and knew this was linked to our murders. I moved on a little further and looked between the houses. After we passed three I saw them, both leaning on a fence as if they'd done it for years; gossiping .

"I can see them Harvey. I'll push it into your mind, ready?"

He squeezed my hand. "Thanks, Alli. I see them." Both men were covered in bandages from head to foot, they obviously didn't see them on each other and talked normally.

"I bet this is where they used to live, Harvey."

"I'll jot down the house number and we'll come back to it." Harvey made a note of it and we carried on.

My mind was pulled towards a certain house. I tugged on Harvey's hand and he told me where the curb was and a gate to navigate and steps on paths, until I stopped and opened my eyes. I stared at a weird shape, covered in grass at the bottom of the garden we were in.

"What are you doing in my garden and why are you staring at that old shelter?" We turned to the voice. The woman was probably in her late forties.

"I'm Detective Inspector Burgess, Ma'am. We have the whole road blocked off as we've found a body in Fisher Close and we're searching for more."

"Why have you come in my garden? I live on my own." She looked really shaky. I walked over to her.

"What's your name, please?"

She took a few seconds to answer. "Pam Clarke, why?"

"I'm Alli, and Harvey over there is my husband. I work with

him. Have you always lived by yourself, Pam?"

"No, I was married. He just left one day without saying a word. I didn't have a clue our marriage wasn't working. They say love is blind, don't they."

"How long ago was that?" I could see she was counting in her head.

"Twenty-six years, now. We'd only been married a year." I could see tears fill her eyes, she still loved him.

Harvey came over to us. "Could we talk to you indoors, Mrs Clarke?"

"Yes, follow me." She turned to the back door and took us in to her kitchen, "Please sit down." We pulled chairs at the kitchen table, opposite her.

"Pam, do you know Mr Shaw?" a smile flashed in her eyes.

"Yes, he's a lovely old man. I used to talk to him over the back fence years ago but the hedge has grown so thick we can't see each other through it. I do a bit of shopping for him, have done for years. Is he alright? It's not him, you found."

"No Pam, he's fine but the body was in his shed. Harvey and I have put him in the Carlton until this is sorted out. We're paying so don't worry about that. He doesn't need the stress of reporters hounding him."

"Please don't take this the wrong way. You're very caring for the police." I smiled at her.

"We aren't your ordinary police, Mrs Clarke. I run the murder squad but we're millionaires, both of us and if we can help someone like Mr Shaw we do it gladly. Alli works with me because she senses things, sees the dead and reads minds. She has since she was a kid." Pam looked at me and I nodded. She had her hands on the table; I took hold of one of them.

"Pam, I was drawn to your garden when we walked the street. I could sense something in that shelter of yours." The tears came again, in floods this time. I got up and sat in the empty chair beside her and put my arm around her shoulder.

"I know you still love him Pam, I felt it. I don't know if he's in there. I sense more than one. Do you have any family you could go to?"

"My sister lives in Australia and the only family I have."

"Pack enough clothes for a week. You're joining Mr Shaw in

the Carlton. We'll probably fill the place, by the end of this."

"I have some money put by," she said through her tears.

"Keep it Pam, this is on us. You wouldn't want to be here when they open it up, go and pack. Andy will take you, he took Mr Shaw."

"Thank you." She got up and left us at the table.

How many do you think, Alli?

It's stuffed, with them. Her husband is one of them Harvey, so we're going back twenty-six years.

When Andy's taken Mrs Clarke that will be his first job, contacting the council for more names. Harvey pulled his phone to Andy for Mrs Clarke's trip to the hotel.

"Jamie we're at 43; bring the lot. There's an Anderson shelter in the garden full of bodies." He rang Hillary and waited for her to pick up. "Hi, it's me again. We're just about to open an Anderson shelter, Alli says it's full. 43 Milton Crescent, yes," he listened. "We'll see you soon." He rang Ron next and gave him a rundown on what we'd found so far. Ron told him that Hillary would keep the help she had until this was over.

"She'll be pleased you said that Ron. She's coping now but we don't know how many more we'll find here. I think you should get more pathologists on standby. Okay, thanks Ron."

He rang Andy on his mobile. "Have you dropped Mrs Clarke yet, Andy?" A few moments passed. "When you get back to the nick ring the council again. The years have clocked up to twenty-six now." He listened. "I want the tenant list for Milton Crescent as well, going back thirty years. Well done, Andy."

"Andy booked Mrs Clarke in and took her along to see Mr Shaw."

"How did he know, they knew each other?"

"She must have told him on the way. At least the same thing has happened to them both and they won't feel so cut off from everything. Come on Alli; let's have a look at this shelter."

On the walk to the back garden, I had to ask him a question, "What's an Anderson Shelter, Harvey?"

"I forget you're not as old as me, sorry. They were used in the last war. Families had them in their gardens in case of air raids. I shouldn't think there are many left in the country, now."

"That wouldn't have stopped a bomb, Harvey."

"I know that and I should think everyone who had to use one knew it, too. The stiff upper lip was well used at that time. I'm just pleased Jenny and Charlie had their country shop when the war was on. I was at the quarry and none dropped near us."

Harvey looked at the front of the shelter. "There's supposed to be a door here, and its bricked up." Harvey pulled his phone out.

"Jamie, go to the tool hire place, get a Kango gun with a wide chisel bit and a small generator. Tell them it's for me and you won't need to pay anything. Make sure you have the right fuel, petrol or two stroke; whatever it takes."

"I've never seen you use any tools, Harvey." He smiled at me.

"You forget, I did all of the work on the house before I met you. I have an account there. I could break through with my bare hands but I think I'd cause a bit of a panic." I giggled trying to picture it.

"Socco are here, Harvey." He turned to face the two men coming towards us.

"Bit of a hold up Keith, sorry. Jamie's bringing tools for me to break it open. A crowbar won't do it."

"We'll go to the cafe on the main road for tea. I bet your gagging for one."

"You could say that Keith, thanks. We haven't bloody stopped. One sugar for me and two for Alli, please." They left when Jamie was carrying a generator across the garden towards us.

"I'll get the gun, Sir, I won't be a minute." Harvey moved the generator nearer the shelter and got it going with one pull of the cord.

"Quite the little handyman."

Harvey glanced at me with a glint in his eyes. "I show you how handy later, Mrs Burgess." I giggled.

"I wonder how long we'll have to wait for our lessons." Harvey laughed in my head. *Not too long, I hope*.

Jamie came running across the grass, carrying a huge drill with a chisel on the end. Harvey took it off him and plugged it in. I stood back when he started drilling between the bricks. It wasn't long before some were falling at his feet. He kicked them to one side and carried on. The smell began escaping from the shelter. Jamie started coughing and was almost sick. I held my breath. *I'm doing the same, Alli.*

Harvey carried on until all the bricks were out and we could see the door. He moved the bricks to one side with his foot, turned the generator off and opened the door. "Let's get out of here."

We stayed by the road until the tea came. "Jamie, I got you one."

"Thanks Keith I bloody need it. That was bad." He was still white.

"It's a bit rough Keith. I opened the door to let the smell out but didn't look inside. I wouldn't start just yet, give it chance to clear."

Hillary's car pulled up and she got out to join us. "It's bad isn't it?"

She gave us all a pot of the stuff she gave to Jo. "Use it, I am." She opened her pot and put some under her nose. "I'm taking a look, anyone coming."

"I will, Hillary." She smiled and put her arm out for me to link it.

"Aren't you going to use it, Alli?"

I giggled. "I'll hold my breath Hillary, we both did when Harvey opened it." Hillary looked at the pile of bricks.

"Bloody hell, I didn't realize it was bricked up." We approached the door and Hillary pulled a torch from a pocket and shone it inside. What we saw was a wall of bandaged heads.

"Fucking hell!" I felt Harvey getting closer and we turned around. "I've never seen anything like this Harvey?" Hillary was shocked.

She stepped back from the door so he could see. He was speechless for a minute. "I'll get Socco to ship them to a temporary morgue. How many do you think, Hillary. Bear in mind there are two steps down into it."

"Anything between twenty and thirty. How could one person have done it all?"

"Maybe it wasn't just one Hillary, we could have over fifty bodies."

Out on the street, Harvey gave the car keys to Jamie. "He's Jason Hicks, you'll find him at the road block at number one, Jamie. His car is the Golf blocking the road. Drive it down there and remind him of the speed limit on this road, when you hand them to him, please. We need the road clear for this lot to be moved."

"Okay, Sir. I'll have a word with him."

Chapter 9

A sports hall was requisitioned for a temporary morgue. The security was stepped up to keep everybody out.

Television crews and the press were at the gate and everyone had to wade through them to get any bodies out for PMs.

The afternoon we opened the shelter Harvey and I went back to the path lab with Hillary to watch the PM on the fresh body from the shed. She hadn't been able to get started when she went back before as the tables were all being used by the other pathologists. I'll give them their due, they work their socks off for her and never complain at all.

This body didn't smell half as bad as the rest and Hillary started the PM after all the photographs had been taken. She did the usual commentary as she measured the body and talked about the state of the bandaging, etc., etc.

"Hillary, can I say something."

"Yes Alli, it's okay."

"You're about to take the bandages off and I've noticed something you might like to look at."

Hillary came around the table beside me. "Show me, Alli."

I pointed to the wrist. "There are dents around the wrist as if wide strapping was over the top of the bandages at some point and the same at the ankle. Maybe the shadow that's cast on this side made it more prominent for me to see it."

Hillary looked carefully. "You're right, Alli, well done for spotting it. The only reason for applying straps means this person was still alive when they were bandaged."

"What the hell's going on Hillary, I'm bloody baffled?" Harvey looked at her.

"I'll get on with it Harvey and we may have more answers as this is a fresh body."

He put his arm over my shoulder. "Well done, Alli. I didn't see it either."

Hillary started taking the bandages off the left arm first. She stopped near the elbow. "John, could you take a shot of this please?" John came over with a high tech camera and took a photograph of the inside of the elbow.

"There's blood on the bandage and a large needle hole in the vein at the elbow. I think this body was embalmed with the bandages on. This is bloody strange to me." She carried on and found a tiny needle mark further up the arm but no blood on the bandage. John took another shot with a short ruler beside it, for scale.

She un-wrapped the other arm and found the same sized hole at the elbow, which meant she was right.

Danny helped her un-wrap the legs and she did the head. It was definitely male and he wasn't more than twenty, I'd say. His head was shaved and had a designer stubble beard. He was a good looking guy and shouldn't be lying on this table.

You're fucking right, there. Hillary and Harvey's head shot round to look at me. I turned towards the young man at my left.

"My name is Alli. I can see you. Could you tell me your name, please?"

Jay. I've come to see what the fuck he was doing to me.

"Was it just one person who killed you?"

You're having a fucking laugh, aren't you? He didn't just kill me.

"My name is Harvey. I can hear you through Alli. Give me a minute. Alli, would you push his vision to me. I'd like to see who I'm talking to, please."

I closed my eyes and sent him the sight of Jay, to his head.

"That's better, Jay. I can see you now. I run the murder squad and we've got almost fifty bodies, bandaged like you. Twenty have had post-mortems and they've had things removed or been operated on. Do you know the person who did this to you?"

I had a hood over my head, the whole time.

"What do you think he's done to you, Jay?"

He must have injected me with something because it's all a bit hazy but it didn't stop the pain. He cut me at my balls and dick. I think he's cut them off.

"Can you cut the bandages of him Hillary, please?"

"I shouldn't but I'm going to. Jay, I can hear you, too, and I'm sorry I have to show you this."

I can feel you're all gutted, just do it please.

I took hold of his hand as she cut them off. I felt him tense as she got near his abdomen. When she pulled back the thin gauze where his cock should be he yelled out in agony.

What the fuck has he done; turned me into a woman! His voice broke and he sobbed next to me. I cuddled him and a few minutes later he stopped crying.

How come you can see and feel me?

"Jay, I've been visited by dead people all my life and I'm used to it. It's only recently I've been able to feel them. The first was a little boy named Jimmy. I held his hand over his dead body and we had quite a chat. We caught his killers quickly but this case is different. We have a huge number of bodies and no leads. Is there anything you can think of that might help us in any way, it doesn't matter how small. Jimmy gave us things like a nickname and we found the man. You may not think it's important but everything helps."

Hillary, when you've finished the post-mortem could you take that thing out of me, please?

"I will I promise you, Jay."

Thank you. I heard a cat quite a lot. He had me strapped down for days and did bits at a time. I wish he'd just got it over and done with. I couldn't fucking believe he hummed tunes all the time he was changing me. To me; it was like a kid making a model or something. He sounded happy and jolly and talked to that fucking cat, endlessly as if he wasn't cutting me up at all. He must be fucking mental.

"Did he call the cat with a name, Jay?"

I thought he was calling it Puss, at first, but he was saying Puds. Funny name for a cat.

"What is your surname Jay? We'll have to inform your family."

It's Henderson. I lived with my sister and her boyfriend at 14 Milton Crescent. Her name is Natalie, she's away on holiday I think. I've lost count of days.

"Don't worry about that we'll find her. I want to thank you for all your help as everything you told us will be useful."

Thank you all three of you. I'm pleased I came now, I nearly didn't, bye.

"Bye, Jay." I turned to Harvey and cried on his shoulder and he cuddled me.

"You did really well Alli. He gave us a hell of a lot to go on."

"I hope we catch the bastard that did that to him. I'd like to ring his fucking neck." I looked up over Harvey's shoulder and all the pathologists were watching us and started clapping. Hillary turned around, she was shocked.

The nearest one to Hillary walked over to her. "I'm making a cup of tea after that. You three look like you need one and we have to get over the shock." Hillary laughed at him.

We sat around Hillary's office and talked about everything they'd seen and heard.

"I've never seen one psychic let alone three. It was bloody fantastic to listen to. How long have you been psychic, Hillary."

"All my life Derek, it's bloody useful working with these two."

"I was fascinated what you told Jay about Jimmy, Alli. You're in the right bloody job for your talents."

"You don't know the half of it, Derek. Alli reads minds and knows when someone's telling lies. She digs about in people's heads for anything, we need to know."

"You want to hang on to her."

"I am; we're married." Harvey grinned at me and they laughed at him.

All the pathologists had a good look at Jay's body before they returned to their own. Hillary got on with Jay's PM and at the end she took the small amount of flesh and lips of the vagina out and sewed him up.

Thank you, Hillary.

My pleasure, Jay.

"I'll do a DNA test on the genitals retrieved from the bin, also on the woman's bits and put them on ice. You'll come across a body, somewhere without one or whoever is doing this has a place he can get them from. A hospital maybe?"

"Bloody good idea Hillary, we'll look into that. Alli do you still want to go shopping tonight?"

"No Harvey, I just want to go home, sorry."

"It's okay, it's taken a lot out of you doing all that. You look tired Alli. We'll have a quiet night, watch a film maybe, eh."

"I'd like that; I'll try and have a kip in the car on the way home so I have enough energy to have a swim. I need to wash all those ghosts off me."

"I forget you see more than we ever need to know about, let's go now. We're off, Hillary. Tell Jo we're sorry about the shopping and we'll go another night."

"You get Alli home and we'll ring later, bye."

Harvey waved to the other men and carried me to the car.

I couldn't remember the journey. I woke as Harvey opened my door to carry me indoors. Gina and Olli were already in the sitting room with a cup of tea for us both.

"You've had a fucking horrible day. I can't believe what you've had to do." Gina was very concerned about them staying. I could feel it.

"Stay here, I'm fine. I had a sleep coming home. All I want is a swim and something to eat. Harvey's putting a film on and we could all watch it. If I fall asleep just leave me, I'll wake up for the credits as usual."

"It's true, she finds out who's been in the film and doesn't actually see any of it." They both giggled at Harvey.

I drank the tea and felt a bit better. "I'm going for a swim now, are you coming?" They got up and followed me. I got undressed and dived in to swim on the bottom and Harvey swam on the top, keeping an eye on me. He knew how knackered I was.

I didn't stay in long as I got tired, quite quickly. When I got out they all did. "You can stay in longer."

Harvey insisted on staying with me. "Olli, you and Gina stay in. I'll call when the food arrives." He picked up a huge towel and wrapped it around me, handing me another for my hair.

"Come on, Alli. Get on the sofa and have another kip and I'll wake you for something to eat." I didn't argue and was asleep in seconds.

I opened my eyes and couldn't see anything; my eyelashes touched something over my eyes. What the hell's going on? I tried to move my arms and they were strapped down and my legs wouldn't lift.

A searing pain stabbed me between my legs and I tried to scream but the thing in my mouth stopped it coming out and the pain; Christ it's not stopping? All the time he hums those bloody songs. What's he pulling out? It's fucking killing me!

"Alli, wake up; you're having a nightmare!" Harvey cradled me in his arms until I was properly awake. I glanced at his face, he looked really worried.

"I'm sorry, I've worried you."

He smiled at me. "Alli, you were dreaming the story Jay told you. He must have been in agony, we heard what you were dreaming."

Gina and Olli were stood beside us. "I don't envy you, Alli; having all that in your head." Gina knelt down and took hold of my hand. "You see it all don't you, when someone is telling you something."

"And you do Gina, you don't fool me."

"The difference is I don't remember anything further back than six months but you've had thousands of visions, equally as bad as that and they're still in your head. If ever you want to unload some of them I'm here, that's all I'm trying to tell you Alli."

I sat up and gave her a hug. "Thank you, Gina." Harvey put his arms around us both and said thank you to her. He knows how loaded my mind was, he'd been in there enough times.

The doorbell rang and when Harvey went to get the meal Olli left us for the kitchen. Harvey said, on his way past us with the food, "Stay where you are, we'll get your meals." We heard them chatting and giggling, playing mum as they plated up the meals and smiled to each other.

They came in with a plate each on trays so we could eat off our laps instead of the coffee table. Harvey knew I was still knackered and pushed it near us so our wine was in reach. *He thinks of everything.*

I try to.

"Well done boys, this is great."

Gina looked at me and said in a posh voice. "It's nice having live in waiters, isn't it? We'll have to get them proper uniforms but they forgot the cloth over their arms. The tip's going to be small because of that little flaw, sorry boys. It's impossible to get the right staff these days." We laughed at her and started eating.

Harvey had just put a film on when his phone rang. "Yes!" he listened. "She's very tired Jo but she's had something to eat. I expect we'll have an early night, that'll be a first." He looked at me and smiled when he was listening. "Bloody good idea, now we know why they've all been killed. We'll see you tomorrow, night Jo."

"She's changed tack, hasn't she?"

Harvey grinned at me. "As soon as she heard how Jay had been changed she started looking for any of the residents who might have worked or are still working in any of the hospitals around here."

"I wish we were helping you on this," Gina said out of the blue.

"That's a fucking good idea Gina." Harvey's face had lit up and I started smiling. I know where he was going on this.

"What is?" She looked flummoxed.

"Come into work with us tomorrow, Gina." Her face became serious.

"I couldn't do that Harvey, I'm not allowed." She looked at Olli and he just smiled at her. "Do you think I should, Olli?"

"It's one way to get you in by the back door. Prove your worth and they're hardly going to tell you to fuck off, Gina. I think it's a brilliant idea."

"What about you?"

Olli grinned at her. "I have other plans. I'm getting my round changed to one that's near the hospital. You never know what I might find out. I could turn out to be quite a good spy." Harvey howled with laughter and I started giggling.

"I'd love to see those bastards' faces at the Home Office if we crack this case wide open using you two." Harvey couldn't wait.

"So would I," Olli told him. "It's got quite a ring to it, Olli 007." We fell about laughing.

Olli left for work at the usual time and I took Gina upstairs to sort some clothes for her.

"Wear your jeans and Doc Martins but choose any of these tops and jackets, Gina. I don't mind what you wear. I promise we'll take you shopping soon? My clothes are going down slowly. Harvey gets a kick out of ripping them off me at times, I can't think why." Gina giggled and looked through the clothes.

Harvey was waiting for us with toast and tea and a huge grin was plastered across his face. He didn't have to say anything. We both knew why it was there.

"I'm curious, Harvey. How are you going to explain why I'm with you two?"

"I have a sneaking suspicion I won't have to Gina. You're going to do it for me." I smiled at him, he was right.

"Now I know you're mad." Gina ate her toast and drank her tea. She had no idea how good her brain was. I looked at Harvey and he winked. He knew it had clicked with me, too.

Jo had her phone to her ear when we walked in. She saw we had Gina with us and put up her thumb. We got a few odd looks from some of the team. It didn't last very long and they knuckled down and got on with their work.

We took her into our office and Harvey gave her his desk and computer. He opened it up and left her and pulled another chair from the wall and sat at mine.

He had calls to make and I got on with looking at the site I was on before.

After a short time I heard typing from Harvey's computer and Gina was hammering away at the keys almost as fast as I type.

Harvey was also looking and glanced at me. Neither of us talked in our heads. We might have broken her train of thought and she'd tell us when she was ready. Harvey made another call and a Trans Gender site popped up for me to look at.

I was fascinated how they do it these days. Totally different to the first sex change, done in South Africa to somebody called April. The skin on the man's cock was used to make the vagina.

The poor sods had to go through two years of electrolysis to get rid of every hair follicle before the main operation. Whoever was learning how to master the technique on our poor victims had no fucking idea how it was done. Perhaps he hadn't got the Internet or watch TV. Maybe he was fucking mental as Jay said. Barbaric I bloody call it.

My phone rang. I knew who that would be as there was only one person with the number apart from our little click.

"Hi Jed." Harvey's eyes lit up. "We're fine, you?" I looked out of the window as I listened. "I'll put Harvey on and he'll say if that time is okay. Bye, see you soon."

I handed it to Harvey. I need to visit the ladies room.

On the way I stopped at Jo's desk. She was just finishing a call.

"How's it going, Jo?"

She grinned at me. "I'm glad Gina's here at last, have the powers that be changed their minds?"

"Absolutely not. Harvey says she would shock the lot of us by the end of the day. All I know is she offered to take some of the shit from my head last night and when I cuddled her as a thank you, something happened between us and I could see how good her brain was. Harvey picked up on it straight away and she sees everything she's told, like me."

"I could hear her mind racing but it was going so fast I only pick up a bit."

"For someone who couldn't remember longer than six months ago she's bloody good on a computer and typed almost as fast as me."

"Do you know what she was actually doing?" Jo was puzzled.

"Harvey gave her his computer and just left her."

"How interesting is that," she giggled. "I'd love to see their faces if she's that good."

"Olli's changing his road sweeping round to one near the main hospital; and he called himself Olli 007." Jo laughed and a few heads raised, saw it was us and carried on working. They're used to us nattering but wouldn't get pissed off. Jo was like a terrier when she worked and they all had the occasional little chat. The job was so intense there had to be some let up or we'd all go nuts.

"I was going for a pee, I think I should go."

"Keep me posted." She was back to work when I turned my head. "I will."

Gina looked up when I returned to our office. "Alli, could you help me with something please?" I walked over and looked at the screen on her computer. What I saw surprised me. Harvey looked at my face but didn't comment.

"Sure Gina, what can I do for you?"

"I logged onto that internet chat room and pretended to be a guy that needed gender reassignment. Someone answered and has asked me to tell him more about me. What the fuck would I say to him?"

Harvey came over and looked at the screen. The man she was talking to was in shadow. His features were really hard to make out. "You play it really slow Gina and you give him nothing that is real. He may just be gay and looking for sex but you may have someone who is really fucking weird. What have you told him so far?"

"Just that I feel like I'm in the wrong body, and have seen loads of psychiatrists who say the same about me. Only general stuff and nothing specific."

"Good, keep it like that and wait for him to push it further. Is that site just for gender reassignment or is it a general site?"

"Gender reassignment only. I've trawled through all the ones used through the medical profession but this one stuck out like a sore thumb to me. There's something not quite kosher about it. I think the picture on the screen isn't who answered me.

"The way he phrased things made me think he was older than this guy." She pointed at the face.

That pricked our ears instantly. Gina looked at us. "Am I doing alright?"

Harvey started laughing. "I think that's fucking excellent but be very careful."

"Gina, what were you typing before? You were going hell for leather for about three hours."

"Oh that. I sent in a dissertation for an Open University Degree on Psychology. Why, have I done something wrong?" Harvey was speechless and me.

"Did I hear that right?" Jo came through the door with a huge grin on her face. "I obviously did by the look of you two." We just giggled.

"Gina, that's fucking priceless and you've done nothing wrong. I look forward to your results." Harvey was really chuffed with her.

She giggled. "I'll get on with it then. Oh, 007 is sweeping near the hospital as we speak."

"I think that calls for a celebration. I'm buying lunch in the canteen."

"Can you afford it Harvey? We'll go Dutch if you like."

He grinned at me. "Pick up your bag wench, let's go." I giggled and he got hold of my hand.

We sat away from most of the team and Andy was the nearest to us. Once we'd eaten he turned and spoke to Harvey.

"I called in at the Carlton last night on the way home. They've settled in okay, Sir."

"Thanks for doing that Andy. Have the press found them yet?"

"I asked the receptionist to call me if they get any bother. She left a note for the night staff and I've heard nothing yet, Sir."

"Good; let's hope it stays that way Andy. Are the council playing ball?"

"Not at first, Sir. I took a leaf out of Jo's book and blasted them. I soon got a response." Jo pushed her fist in the air.

"Keep it up, Andy," Harvey said, giggling.

"Will do, Sir." He got up and left us to talk.

"He's gay, did you know," popped out of Gina's mouth. She was so shocked her hand covered it. "I've spoken out of turn, sorry."

"Well join the club," came out of Jo's, in an American drawl. We fell about laughing, remembering Harvey's last words to him.

I caught Jamie smiling at us. He knew Harvey had a lot on his shoulders and liked to see us let off steam, even if it was only in the canteen.

"Andy doesn't know you're gay Jo." She was shocked.

"Is he blind? Perhaps he wasn't in the pub that night and that proves Jamie doesn't blab."

"We already know he doesn't Jo, he's very discrete. Oh, what did Jed have to say for himself, Harvey?"

"Tomorrow night, seven o'clock. We have to go shopping tonight. We need masses of rope. I'll ring John and ask him to hold a load back for us to pick up later."

"Music to my bloody ears." Jo giggled, she was itching to go shopping. "I'll ring Hillary when we go back to work. Are we going straight from here? That's no good. We couldn't leave Olli behind."

"I wonder how 007's getting on," Gina said with a grin.

I've got my eyes peeled. Shopping sounds great and I'm glad you've taken your exams. We heard him giggling.

"He doesn't miss much."

"Nothing," Gina answered.

The afternoon seemed to fly by and during that time Harvey went up to see Ron. We heard him tell Ron he couldn't be on call tomorrow night, and of course, he had to tell him why. I was shocked when I heard Ron giggling when Harvey explained he was into bondage and might be a little tied up as we're all booked in for lessons. Because it was impossible for us to lie, unless to save someone's feelings or to keep what we are a secret, it just flowed out of Harvey's mouth.

When he came back down he closed the door and dropped to the floor in a fit of laughter. He had to hold it in until he got back here. We sat at our desks in hysterics.

"I should think he's heard it all now; what was his face like?"

"It wasn't straight, that's for sure," Harvey said with difficulty through the laughter and got up.

There was a knock at the door and Harvey turned to open it.

Hillary was laughing at him. "I nearly crashed the car I was laughing so much," she said as she walked in.

"How come you got away so early, Hillary?"

"Derek heard me talking to Jo on the phone and must have had a word with the others. They told me to go and have some fun. Little did I know it would start before I got here. Jo's making us tea. I bet Ron's had twenty-five cups since you left his office. I'm surprised he didn't have a bloody heart attack." She started giggling and couldn't stop.

"I think he must be de-sensitised by now. We've always thought our place was bugged and probably have cameras in there, too."

"They've had a few fucking laughs if they have, Alli," she dabbed at the tears in her eyes.

"Harvey reckons there'd be a lot of wanking at the other end if they have."

"Nothing but filth talked about in here." Jo carried in a tray of cups and it shook as she giggled.

"Put it here Jo." Gina made a space on the desk.

Jo put it down. "Did you hear about this one?"

Jo asked Hillary and pushed her thumb back to Gina.

"No, what?"

"Gina only took a degree exam for the Open University on Psychology this morning in three hours flat." Hillary just stared.

"Three and a half Jo," Gina told her and giggled.

"What's half an hour between friends, tea?" Jo could hardly lift the cups.

"I think I need a stiff drink after hearing that. Well done Gina. What made you even consider doing it? I think that's fascinating." Hillary went over to her desk and pulled up a chair.

"Well I thought if I had to get inside the head of whoever's doing this, I'd have to actually know about it. I looked at the University site and thought of enrolling for a course. When I looked at the exam itself I knew all the answers and typed a full dissertation and emailed it to them. I didn't know I could type, let alone fifteen thousand words."

"Fucking hell, Gina." Harvey was astounded like the rest of us.

We drank the tea and knuckled down to work again, Gina talking to the weird guy on line and I trawled through anything I could find, regarding sex changes. The rest of the afternoon went by in moments.

Two hours later we were just about to leave when Ron came into the office for a chat.

"I won't keep you too long. Alli, you're right about the bugs. They're not in your house anymore, but they are in here." We stood there with open mouths.

"You're all worried, don't be. I haven't come down here to bullock, you just listen." He turned to Gina. "I heard everything that was said about your exam today. I phoned the Open University and had a Psychology Professor look at the submission you made Gina and he told me you'd get at least a 2.1 degree or higher. I've also been on to the Home Office and they've finally agreed to me looking after you and Olli." Ron's face burst into a smile and we all laughed and hugged. It was crazy.

When the hilarity died down a bit Ron had a quiet word with Hillary.

"I know what's happened to you Hillary and I don't blame you one bit. You have a stable relationship with Jo and I'm very pleased for you both."

"We weren't sure how you'd take it Ron."

"With all the shit you've put up with over the years and then found you want to be with someone forever, I'd have asked Alli myself if I was in your shoes."

"You really don't think it was wrong."

"Hillary if May and I were young again and knew how you lot live your lives to the full, I'd have asked the question. Don't ever think I'd be judgmental about anything." Hillary gave him a hug and kissed his cheek.

"Thank you Ron. Today has been a bloody good day."

"You're all going shopping and I've held you up; have a good night. Harvey, bring Olli and Gina to work with you tomorrow, please?"

"I will Ron. Come on you lot, we have rope to buy." I gave Ron a hug and said thank you to him.

"Get off Alli, I'll see you tomorrow."

I glanced back at him. He was a very happy man today.

Hillary left her car in the car park and travelled back to ours in Jo's. Harvey was driving and hadn't said much about today. The problem was, he had so many questions to ask and couldn't decide what to start with. Maybe no words were necessary as we were all so fucking happy. I looked at Gina in the back seat. She had a smile on her face and was staring out of the window as she talked to Olli in her head. He was waiting for us outside the house and jumped in when we pulled up.

We took them clothes shopping; plus some for me and picked up the rope from John who had a twinkle in his eyes when he gave Harvey the huge sack full. Harvey ordered the food before we left Darwin's Heath and it was delivered not long after we got home.

The wine flowed before it arrived as we were so excited with the outcome of today. I forgot about only having one and acted the fool because I was pissed, much to everyone's enjoyment. I tried walking on my special shoes I'd just bought at John's. Black Patent Leather with two inch platforms which made the heels seven inches high. I'd still have broken my ankle if I was human but everyone had a good laugh and I didn't give a shit as it mended in seconds and I didn't feel a thing.

Olli and Gina were ecstatic about their new jobs and stole the show for the evening.

He handed Gina a carrier bag and told her to put it on. Olli cleared the space between the two sofas and pulled another bag from behind the sofa we were sitting on.

"I nipped back in my lunch break as this was delivered, today," Olli announced with a grin on his face. "Gina has always wished I had two dicks and she will get her wish tonight. Alli, Gina said she'd need help with my surprise. Could you give her a hand, please?" I giggled at him and headed for the stairs.

"Gina, Olli said you need me?" she was struggling with the ties down her back.

"I should've been a bloody contortionist." I smiled at the pickle she was in.

"Leave it Gina, I'll do it. How tight do you want this, it's a hell of a wasp waist."

"Pull it right in, the tighter the better." When she turned towards me I was surprised by the piercings she'd had on her nipples. She had bolts through and the inside of each bolt had a chain attached to the other nipple; heavy chain and thick bolts with rings instead of balls on the outside. In fact, the hole through her nipple was an eyelet, like the lads have through their ears nowadays.

Gina saw me looking and giggled. "I had to go the whole hog on my tits."

"I didn't notice those piercings when you were swimming, Gina."

"I've got smaller bolts to put in for daytime wear as it was a bit difficult to hide them under clothes. Remember, I didn't have this in this morning."

"Turn around you naughty girl and hold onto the bedpost. I'm going to pull pretty hard to get this laced up tight."

Every time I had another lace to pull I asked her to breathe in before I pulled. Her waist was getting really narrow and then the corset fanned out over her hips. I tied the laces with double bows and now they wouldn't come undone when they played.

"Anything else I could help you with, Gina?"

"Could you help me get my hair up like you have yours but I want this tiny hat put over the knot please? Sort of have it off centre a bit. Do you get what I mean Alli?"

I picked up my comb. "Leave it to me Gina, I know what you

want." It took me a few minutes and slipped a band over her hair before I fixed the hat on top.

She looked in the mirror "That's perfect Alli. I just fancied looking like a bordello whore tonight." I laughed at her.

She turned to me with a huge grin on her face. "I'll finish it from here and thanks for the help, Alli. Don't let on. Olli didn't know what was in the bag."

I went back down. Harvey was watching Olli build a weird contraption on the floor between the sofas. When he saw me coming he giggled with sparkling eyes. He was more than turned on with the anticipation of the event to come. Jo and Hillary were equally intrigued with the building of what looked like an artist's easel. It was fixed to a large metal plate on the floor. I sat beside Harvey and he handed me a mug of tea.

"Thanks for making this. What on earth is that for?"

"All will be revealed Alli, you have to be patient," Olli told me.

Harvey's eyes darted to the doorway as he'd heard Gina come down. Four other pairs of eyes waited with him for her entrance.

The first thing we saw was a black ostrich feather fan move down the edge of the door. It came into the room and Gina's legs with white stockings and high heeled white leather ankle boots, showed beneath the fan.

She moved into the middle of the floor and the fan was never still as she shook it constantly and started lowering it to reveal her head and neck.

Her eyes had the longest false lashes I'd ever seen and she fluttered them, to give more effect. There were feathers tucked into the brim of the tiny hat and a white velvet choker around her neck. She suddenly closed the fan to reveal everything she was wearing.

She was stunning to look at and the corset was covered in tiny beads to match the white silk. I hadn't taken much notice when I was upstairs with her. The antics with her tits threw me a bit.

Olli's mouth was open as he watched her walk towards him. She took his clothes off slowly and kept eye contact with him the whole time.

To me, the rolls had completely reversed and Gina was in control. Harvey squeezed me gently. I glanced at him and detected the tiniest of nods.

Hillary and Jo's eyes had never left her; enthralled, not only by her beauty but what she was doing to Olli.

When he was stripped naked she took hold of his cock and knelt in front of him. She put her mouth over it and Olli closed his eyes and moaned every time she drew her mouth up. When he was almost coming she stood up and turned away from him.

She stood with her back to the frame, lifted each foot and stood on a crossbar ten inches off the floor. She sat on something and put both feet to the floor again, with a deep sigh.

"Come here, Olli." He moved closer to her. "Lock handcuffs through the nipple rings and on to my wrists, then fix them above my head, please."

He was a bit shocked. "There's plenty of slack on the chain between my nipples, don't worry." He undid the handcuffs where he'd attached them, for his idea for her and complied with her request. The chain between her nipples ran easily through the eyelets and pulled her boobs up a bit higher.

He was so close to her he couldn't wait, spread her legs and pushed his cock inside her. They both changed together.

When he pushed her up she moaned and when he pulled out she moaned again. She was fucked up her bum by a dildo on the frame and loved every time Olli pushed his cock in since she knew what was coming next. The volume of noise that came from them got louder by the minute until they both screamed.

His hands around her tiny waist pushed her down when he pulled out so she got more of the dildo inside. She screamed for him to do it again every time he pushed her down.

As they got near their orgasm he held her down on the dildo, bent his knees and pushed his cock in hard. She screamed with joy and was delighted with her fantasy shag.

Apart from the noise coming out of their mouths their minds turned us all on. We couldn't escape it, not that we wanted to. We soaked it up and played with our partners on both sofas.

Everyone changed when they tipped over the edge and my clothes were ripped of me in seconds when they climaxed together. Harvey picked me up and did the speed thing to the mirror on the landing. He pushed me backwards on to the mirror, stripped before I could take a breath and shagged me with my hands held above my head. *This is beautiful, please don't stop, I'm begging you.*

Harvey, spurred on by my pleading pushed in harder. The implanted balls over the base of his cock ground against my bump and give us more pleasure. We both yelled and groaned when the shaking started at the beginning of our orgasm.

Harvey knew I was coming and pushed much harder and we both shook violently when we came seconds apart. He pushed his body against mine, and had me pinned to the mirror. He let go of my hands and ran his up and down my body until we finished shuddering. I cuddled him then lifted his face to kiss him.

I loved it Harvey, the same as I love you. That was better than any porno movie, not that I've ever seen one. I think you know what I mean.

I certainly do, I've watched a few. He giggled. *When I worked in vice.*

Yeh, right, that's a porky if ever I heard one. He laughed out loud.

"I bet you've got a few stashed around this house."

"Who me?" His body moved against me trying to suppress a laugh.

"I'm taking that as a yes, Mr Burgess. Don't dig the hole any deeper."

"I give in. They don't hold a candle to what we've just seen."

"I would never have thought watching someone else shag would get me that switched on. Did you hear what effect she looked for when I helped her get dressed?"

"Olli was giving a speech on how to make that contraption. I missed most of you talking."

"A bordello whore." Harvey giggled.

"I think she looked beautiful except for the eyelashes, they were tripping her up. I didn't notice the dildo and she knew exactly what he intended to do to her."

"You could imagine it going through his brain when he was sweeping and she'd heard it all. He was sunk as soon as he saw her as I am with you Alli." I kissed him again and that set us off on another journey of our own which lasted about an hour in the plunge pool.

"We ought to go back down Harvey. I'll put my dressing

gown on. I want a proper swim later."

He hauled himself straight out of the water and lifted me out with no effort. "I'll grab mine on the way down, Alli."

We held hands when we left the marble pool room and heard Hillary and Jo in our upstairs play room. As we passed the open door we caught sight of Hillary shagging Jo up the bum. Jo was strapped over one of the bars and loved every minute of it.

Hillary sensed we were there, smiled and carried on.

We giggled to ourselves, collected our dressing gowns and heard the crack of a whip from downstairs.

"They're still at it the buggers."

Harvey looked at me. "I bet I know who's in charge of the whip."

"It doesn't take a brain to work that out, Olli's just like you, Mr Burgess. Could we watch do you think?"

"I'm sure they'd love an audience. Gina's just like you, Mrs Burgess."

I pointed to my chest. "Moi?" He just giggled.

The crack of the whip got louder as we got nearer. She was giving him a hell of a thrashing.

When we walked in I was actually shocked. Olli was on the frame, facing it and his wrists were handcuffed to the top as hers had been. What shocked me was what she was lashing with the whip. His cock and balls were through a solid piece of wood, only when I looked again I realized it was two pieces locked together, like stocks. Olli made no sound and had a permanent smile on his face, which broadened every time the whip made contact. It was obvious he loved it and Gina, with her back to us, turned and giggled. She kept it up for ages before she tired and played with a dildo to change her so she could carry on.

I told you she was like you.

I elbowed him, he picked me up and did the speed thing up to my dressing room.

"Why are we here, Mr Burgess, you want to be screwed?"

"No, I have a little job I'd like you to do for me."

"What sort of little job?"

"You know when I was tattooed, Jed shaved my hair off where he was tattooing me but it left quite a bit outside that. I'd like you to shave off what's left Alli. I've booked a really early appointment with Jed to have my balls tattooed black."

"I like the sound of that Harvey. Where he shaved you before hasn't grown back so it would look and feel lovely for us both and you wouldn't get any hair caught on your toys anymore."

"I don't shave so I haven't got any shaving cream. What could we use?"

"It's alright. I'll use one of my make-up brushes and make a lather with some soap. Have you any razors?"

"No, but I know where there are some. Jenny kept all sorts of Charlie's things to remind her of him. They're in her loft. I'll think myself up there. I won't be long."

He was back before I blinked. "I need a torch. She said she had boxes she'd never unpacked and I landed on a huge pile in the dark." I laughed at him and he disappeared again.

After couple of minutes he appeared with a packet of razors. "The box was marked Charlie's so that made it easy."

"I bet she'd laugh at us now."

Harvey gave me the packet. "I'm pleased these are safety razors. I'd have cut the buggers off with a cut throat."

Harvey put his hand on his cock and said, "Ouch," and laughed at me. "You could have held them back in place and they'd have healed very nicely thank you."

I giggled at him as it sounded ridiculous. "We should do this on my bathroom floor. I'm bound to make a mess, I can wipe it up in there Mr Burgess and it's a good job you won't feel it if I nick you." Harvey didn't give a hoot and followed me into my bathroom.

I found a bar of soap in the marble cupboard under the sink and ran some hot water into the basin. I selected a brush that would be perfect for the job and made lots of foam. I turned around to tell him to undress and he was already stripped and waiting on the floor with a smile on his face.

"You're enjoying this, I can tell, Mr Burgess," and burst out laughing. "Hold that thought." I thought myself down to the kitchen and still heard the whip when I picked up a bowl to put the foam in and appeared in my bathroom with it in my hand.

"That didn't take long." I scooped the foam up into my hands and filled the bowl, picked up the brush and packet of razors to kneel beside Harvey.

He was in hysterics. "What's so funny? Remember I have the razors Mr Burgess." He could hardly tell me for laughing.

"You ran your hands through your hair when you thought of a bowl so it's a good job they're still at it or you'd have scared the living shit out of them; look."

I went over to the mirror and looked. "So I did and I'll leave it there. We'll have twenty questions later. I bet none of them get it right. Now let's get to the job in hand." I picked up the brush and loaded it with foam. "Turn over and kneel up because I'm starting at the back."

He was there in a second and I painted the foam below his tattoo. I know it tickled him but he didn't move. It was easier than I thought it would be and finished his bum in no time.

"I think you should be on your back when I shave your balls. I don't want to attack the back of them through your legs."

"Nor do I Alli." He got on his back and pulled his balls with his hand so they were stable for me to shave them and finished with no problem at all.

"It looks a bit weird on your legs. Do you want me to shave it all off?"

"Please Alli. You're right it does look weird. I thought it would grow back. I've seen other guys with tattoos are under a load of hair."

I got up and made another batch of foam, filled the bowl again and shaved his legs. When I ran my hand over them they felt really smooth and he got a hard on.

"Stop it, Mr Burgess! I'll have to smack you as I may not have finished."

Harvey giggled at me. "Just one more place please, Alli. Above my back tattoo up to my hair line and over part of my shoulders needs shaving, too. I'll let you do something naughty to me when you've finished." My eyes flashed and he knew I was hooked, what girl wouldn't be. He sat up and stayed very still while I dealt with the last little job. I soaked a towel in hot water, squeezed the excess water out and cleaned him down everywhere I'd shaved him.

He got hold of me for a cuddle and he was as smooth as a baby's bum. I ran my hands all over him and he loved it. "I wish I'd asked you to do it ages ago. It feels good to me, too. Thank you Alli; do what you like to me now."

Chapter 10

We arrived at Jed's for six o'clock and he was waiting with coffee already made for us.

"Good morning. I've never had such brilliant time keepers."

"We hate people wasting our time and we wouldn't do it to others Jed. Good morning and thanks for the coffee. Alli shaved me last night so that's a little job you don't have to tackle."

Jed winked at me. "I wish all blokes came prepared like that, they're a bit touchy around that area. You wouldn't believe the tears when I've shaved some people and that's before the tattoo's bloody started. It'll be a doddle for you."

"We have to be in work by eight Jed?"

"It won't take long Harvey since you won't feel it. I have to take my time on the bellyachers. I bought today's paper for you to read and it'll be finished in no time. Let's get on with it."

Jed was right. He was finished in under an hour so we chatted to him and had another coffee before we left.

"I think they look lovely and mysterious now." Harvey was giggling beside me in the car.

"What mystery have you cooked up for them Mrs Burgess." I giggled and looked out of the window; he knew I had something in mind but I'd buried it so deep, he wouldn't find out until it was about to happen. I looked at him and grinned.

We pulled into the car park at work. Jo, Olli and Gina had waited for us to arrive, in Jo's car. We saw no one last night after I shaved Harvey because we were a little busy.

They got out of Jo's car and she couldn't contain herself. "What's the big secret Harvey, leaving a note for us?" Jo's face was splitting.

"Just had a little job done at Jed's, no big deal."

"I'll have to black ball you if you do it again." He could hardly speak for laughing and Jo sniggered beside him.

As we walked into work I had to ask. "I'm surprised you can walk, Olli." Gina giggled.

"A good thrashing never hurt anyone, Alli. That's what I was taught. Why change a habit of a lifetime." I didn't hear him laugh but his shoulders were shuddering uncontrollably.

Harvey spoke to them before we went inside. "We're serious in here apart from odd times and we never talk about what we are except to the Commissioner. You'll be coming up to see him with us and he'll tell you what's what. He's a good laugh but takes this job seriously as we do. Gina met him informally yesterday. He looks after us really well because he knows we get results. Jo works in the team's office but I think Gina will stay in with us. I've no idea of his plans for you Olli but you'll find out soon enough. Are you ready?"

"For anything he wants to throw at me. I'm so pleased to be here, you've no idea."

"I feel the same as you Olli. I love this job, always will." Harvey clapped him on the back and we went up to our office.

Another desk was already installed for Gina when we opened the door.

"I was right about you Gina so let's see what fate has in store for you Olli."

Harvey knocked on Ron's door and opened it straight away. "Come in, come in." Ron looked at us, "Where's Jo?"

"She didn't think she was needed Ron," Harvey told him.

"I'm sure she's listening. Come up Jo. Grab a seat; tea?"

The door knocked and in she came wearing a cheeky grin. "I didn't know we were having a tea party, Ron; I'd have come up with them." He grinned at her, and always liked her humour.

Once he handed out tea and had settled down he became serious, stirred his tea and gathered his thoughts.

"Gina and Olli, I'm so pleased they finally came to their senses. The very fact you get on with these three already made it criminal if they'd split you up. Gina; as you've guessed, will stay with Harvey and Alli. They have already shown me how connected they are.

"I want to use you in a different way, Olli. You're not scared to get your hands dirty, you've proved that already and the name Gina called you yesterday tickled me when she said it, but 007 is probably quite apt for the roll I want you to play." Olli was smiling at Ron.

"It's not going to be glamorous by any means but the pay is

good and you'd be feeding information to this lot." He grinned at us. "Harvey will tell you where he wants you to work. Do you drive, Olli?" He nodded to him. "You'll get a new car as I'm sure Harvey will have you moving around quite a bit, solving this horrendous case."

"Thank you and I can't think of anything I'd rather be doing, Sir," Olli spouted. Ron smiled at him.

"You call me that in front of the rest of the team. In private, my name is Ron to you both. The others already know that Olli. I look on you all as my family. I look after the whole team but you five are special and I'm adding Hillary into the mix." He smiled at Jo. "She'll get no more shit from anyone again and I'll make damn sure of it, Jo." *Tell him thanks, Jo.*

"Hillary says thanks, Ron." He smiled at Jo.

"Christ, I wish I could do that; you're welcome Hillary."

"Gina, Olli; you'll be on Inspector pay for the first year and then you'll be promoted Inspectors from then on. Thank you for wanting to stay here to work with me and your friends. Together, we'll sort the bloody mess that mars this life, for people who want to lead a decent life."

"I'll drink to that." I raised my cup, "Together."

They all followed my toast and finished their tea.

"Thank you, Ron. Come on you lot, we have work to do." Harvey cracked the whip, not that he needed to, we wanted to get on. We said bye to Ron and hurried back to work.

Once in the office, Gina got on her computer straight away while Harvey had a word with Olli.

"I'll be ordering you a new BMW but I think you should also have a banger so you're not noticed. I'd like you to get a job at the main hospital. I think a porter could just about go anywhere in a hospital, without looking out of place. As you'd be new you could say you were lost, if anyone sees you where you shouldn't be."

"The car is brilliant, thanks Harvey and I'd make a good porter and could get lost quite a bit."

"You'd have to be careful; hospitals have cameras all over the shop. This morning I'll sort you both mobile phones and order the cars. What sort of banger would you prefer?" Harvey grinned at him.

Olli pretended to weigh up his options. "Hmm, an old Volvo.

They're more reliable and I may need to shift in a hurry."

"That's fine Olli, I think it's a good job you're a mechanic. I'll get a plan of the hospital this morning for you to look at and Ron would have already made sure you're taken on. He has friends in high places, Olli. He can hear what goes on down here."

"Bloody hell, you move bloody quick in here. I already love this."

"That'll be music to Ron's ears, believe me.

"Now; have a look at the site Gina's on. It's a chat room on a gender reassignment site. She's sure the guy on the screen isn't the one she's talking to. Did she mention it to you?"

"No, she wouldn't divulge anything to me Harvey, it wasn't her place to. We might be a couple but we both knew what you do here, stays here. I didn't ask her anything about it. We wanted nothing to jeopardise us being taken on."

"You're going to make a fucking good spy Olli, good to have you aboard." Harvey grinned at him, "Go and see how she's doing." Olli picked up a vacant chair and took it over to Gina's desk.

"How are you getting on, Alli? I've hardly had a word with you today, sorry." He put his arm over my shoulder and kissed the side of my head.

"Hello Mr Burgess. You've had your hands full don't worry. I've been looking for crimes that involve illegal operations. Lots of things have come up on organ theft, mainly on illegals. I expect Immigration have a lot to do with those cases. Abortions don't happen much these days but I've found one site that offers to do small ops on genitals. It also mentions Gender Dysphoria."

"What sort of ops Alli, does it say?"

"Some women have huge fanny lips and want them reduced and for guys it's penis enlargement, mainly. Gender Dysphoria means someone in the wrong body."

"Is it possible to pull up more information from them, Alli?"

"I'll try, hang on a minute." I followed the instructions on which tab to open.

Harvey's phone rang. "Hi Ron."

While Harvey listened to Ron I pulled up the bumf on the site and started reading. The more I read, the hairs on the back of my neck prickled. I had a gut feeling that this didn't smell right and alarm bells rang in my head. I got up and went over to Gina's desk.

"Gina, could you write down the web address for your site, please."

She looked up at me. "You think the site you're on is linked to this, don't you?" I nodded. She wrote the address and followed me back to my computer.

"It's different Gina, shit!"

"What's up, Alli?" Harvey was off the phone.

"I think the site Gina is on, is this site, too. The problem is, the address is different."

"That doesn't mean you're wrong, Alli. You could have loads of web addresses at the same place. Different Servers; different computers, the numbers are endless. Tommy from upstairs is our computer geek. I'll get him down here now."

He got on his phone and waited for someone to pick up. "Tommy it's Harvey, would you come down please if you're not busy." He listened for seconds. "Great, that's fine."

"Fifteen minutes girls, we'll have tea while we wait."

"I'll make it with Gina to show her where everything is out there."

"Olli, you come, too. I better tell the team who you are and what you'll be doing." Olli got up and followed us.

We went into their office and Harvey asked them to stop work. I left Gina with them and made the tea myself.

"You've probably been wondering who these two reprobates are. This is Gina and her partner Olli. Gina is working with Alli but Olli will be out in the field, undercover. He'll be a porter in the main hospital and I'll explain why.

"The last PM Alli and I attended was different from the rest, up 'til now. Part of a woman's vagina was sewn into the body of a twenty year old male after his genitals were removed. What we're looking for is someone practicing gender reassignment.

"Alli spoke to him when Hillary was doing his PM. His name is Jay Henderson from 14 Milton Crescent. He came to his PM to see what the sick bastard did to him. He was strapped to a bed and operated on while he was awake and felt everything. The man we're looking for has done over fifty so far and there may be more, we don't know yet.

"Jay told Alli this man has a cat called Puds and sings when he cuts away at his victims. He didn't do a quick job either, he took days. Once he'd finished he bandaged the victims and embalmed them when they were alive. We don't know as yet, if they were drugged. The tox report hasn't come back yet. So you see what we're up against now.

"The partial vagina came from a body we haven't found or from a medical institution, hence having Olli working there. Gina has talents like Alli's, she doesn't see the dead, yet but will keep in contact with Olli, in her mind when he's at the hospital."

"That's seven miles from here?" Jamie said to himself.

"You could probably treble that Jamie and it wouldn't be enough. Gina came in here yesterday and I gave her my computer and left her to see what would happen. Alli said she didn't know how clever she was.

"She had an accident and can't remember anything further back than six months. Gina knew she'd have to know something on Psychology to get inside the head of a weirdo and in three and a half hours she typed a fifteen thousand word dissertation on Psychology and sent it in to the Open University by email.

"The Commissioner contacted them and asked a professor to check her submission. He said she'd get at least a 2.1 or higher degree. She has an extraordinary brain and we're going to make use of it. I hope you'll all make them feel welcome. Thank you."

Before Harvey moved, they all stood up and clapped. He was ecstatic with the team's reaction.

Olli's and Gina smiled at them and said thank you.

"Mind your backs." I was holding a tray of cups. "Jo I need you for a minute." She got up, opened the door for me and came in. The other three followed and holding up the rear was a lanky, mop-haired guy, I'd never seen before.

"Hi Harvey. What's the problem with your computer?"

"Hi, Tommy it's not a technical problem. We have two computers logged on to different sites with different addresses. Alli and Gina think they're coming from the same place. Could you trace them for us?"

Tommy's eyes lit up. "At last; something interesting to work on. It'll take a bit of time but I'll trace them, Harvey. I'll copy the sites up to my computer and get started straight away." His fingers were already twitching to get on the computers.

"We'll drink our tea so do what you have to, Tommy." He went to my computer, typed for a couple of minutes and then to Gina's.

"I'll make this a priority Harvey," and almost ran out of the office.

"Olli, your new car was delivered to the cottage and the keys will be delivered here. We're picking up the Volvo on the way home because you start work as a porter tomorrow morning at seven. Twelve hour shifts I'm afraid, Olli."

"Harvey, I don't care how long the shifts are. I wouldn't be getting tired like the rest of the staff and that's when people make mistakes. I've been thinking Harvey, have you thought of Funeral Directors. They use embalming fluid all the time and could get their hands on body parts as no one would know if something was missing, once clothes were on."

"Fucking good idea Olli. I'll get Jamie to compile a list."

Harvey went into the big office, had a word with Jamie and came back in.

"That's sorted. Once they have a list he'll put Andy and Craig on it, to get all employees names from every one of them."

The door knocked and Jamie came flying in. "Sir; we've got two bodies in the alley, down the side of the cinema. Uniform, just rang."

"Right. Alli and Olli, come with me. I'm leaving you here Gina. Keep up the dialogue with that bastard and remember what I told you yesterday. If you need anything, ask Jo."

"Okay, Harvey." We left the office on the run.

"Jamie, Andy could finish the list. You know what you're doing with it Andy?"

"Yes, Sir."

"Jamie, bring three people with you; call the doctor and inform Socco."

We hurried to Harvey's car and Olli sat in the back.

Harvey pulled out of the car park. "Do you think this would be linked to your case?" Olli was really excited.

"Probably not, Olli. This sort of thing happens on a daily basis. It's been too quiet over the last few days." We met a log jam in town and Harvey put the siren on until we got past it all.

He stopped the car and we jumped out. I handed Olli some gloves and gave him some instructions.

"Don't touch anything Olli and keep your eyes peeled so you don't step on anything that could be evidence." We hurried towards the two Uniform Officers.

"What have we got?" Harvey asked as we looked across at the bodies.

"We haven't touched anything but it looks like one was shot, although we're not sure about the other one, Sir."

"Thanks." We walked over to the bodies and Olli stayed back and watched us.

One was definitely shot in the head. Harvey took a pen out and used it to move clothing on the chest of the other victim.

"This looks like a knife has gone through his T-shirt, Alli. Do you sense anything?"

I closed my eyes and heard a huge argument with more men than I'd like to count. Boots breaking bones and a loud thud, over and over.

"These two have had a hell of a beating, boots and a baseball bat. Lots of voices egging them on and bones breaking Harvey."

The two Uniform Officers weren't surprised by my statement as they'd been on some of the cases with us before.

"Well done, Alli. We'll wait for the doctor and Socco. Let's have a look round."

He called Olli over. "We're taking a look down the alley and I think you should come with us Olli."

As we walked down, the walls on either side had blood smears on both sides of the alley. There were bins at the bottom; huge commercial bins and the sides were covered in blood.

"There's a hand print here, Harvey." Olli showed him.

"Let's go back; Socco, will get what we want from this."

The doctor had arrived and Socco. "Get your photographs first Keith, then the doctor could move them. Hello Brian, we'll have to stop meeting like this, people will talk." Brian laughed at him.

"If you don't have a sense of humour on this job you'd put a gun to your head. What do think happened here that you want me to move them?"

"Alli said they were beaten with boots and a baseball bat and they've also got broken bones, Brian." He looked at me.

"Hello Alli. I bet you could tell me which bones."

I giggled. "Ribs, pelvis, leg, arms and spine, Brian, how's that?"

He smiled at me. "I bet you cut down on the workload Alli."

"She's saved us a bloody fortune, so far in man hours alone, Brian."

The photographs were finished and Brian bent down to the bodies. He turned over the guy who was shot in the head as he was face down over the legs of the other body. He pulled his jacket back from his chest and pulled his T-shirt up. The bruises were extensive but would have stopped forming, not long after he was shot. He looked at the other one and bared his chest. The whole of it was black with bruises.

"This one bled to death; a knife wound there, Harvey." He pointed to an inch long dark red slit, almost over his heart. "I'll get them shifted to the lab. Hillary will love you with all she's dealing with at the moment."

"She has six other Home Office Pathologists, Brian. They work bloody hard for her."

"I'm pleased to hear it. She was usually left to struggle."

"Things have changed Brian. We're getting everything we need now."

"About bloody time, I've no doubt I'll see you soon. I'll fax you the paperwork Harvey, bye."

I talked to Harvey on the way back to the nick. "I'm sure it's drugs Harvey."

"You'd be right, Alli. Tox will find some on them I'm sure." He drove back much slower than our journey there.

Jo heard us and was ready with a list for Harvey to look at, as soon as we got into work.

"Harvey, these people have worked at the hospital at some point, cleaners mostly women. Two men worked there some time ago and are now unemployed. One of them lives opposite Mrs Clarke." Harvey stopped dead.

"What's his name, Jo?"

"Gerard Withers and before you ask, I've no idea how old any of them are. The only details Jamie could get were names and addresses of employees and no personal details."

"Jo, ring the hospital and see if they have a personnel office. Someone will have other details on everyone they employ. When you've found the right person, give them hell!" He smiled at her. "You know exactly what I mean."

"Eye, eye, captain; sorry, Sir." A few of the others looked up and grinned at her. It was a good job Harvey had his back to the team, he was grinning. Jo sat down and picked up her phone.

We went into our office and Gina was still at her computer. She waved us over and finished typing before she spoke to us.

"This guy is bloody persistent. I told him I was scared and would have to think it over. He's emailed me a dozen times in the last half-hour. Look at your computer Alli. Loads of emails came through for you after you left and I didn't know what you'd said to them so I had to leave it for you."

Harvey followed me over and the same email message was in the inbox; eight in total. I sat down and opened the first one.

"They must have a way of linking whoever looks at their site straight back to you; is that possible? They're asking for all my details." I clicked down the list and they were all the same. *Persistent isn't fucking strong enough.*

Harvey glanced at me. "I'll ask Tommy. He'll know, Alli." Harvey pulled his phone. "Tommy. Sorry it can wait, I can hear you're in the canteen." I listened to Harvey's mind.

Harvey, come up. I don't mind answering a few questions over lunch.

"We'll be up in a few minutes, Tommy." He hung up. "Let's have a spot of lunch, talk to Tommy and we can crack on after."

We trouped up to the canteen, picked what we wanted to eat and Harvey picked a table near Tommy.

He looked up as we sat down. "Hi, Harvey. I haven't finished tracing the sites yet but what do you want to know."

"Alli has a question for you. I'm sorry I didn't introduce you when you came down earlier. Alli is my wife, Tommy and Gina is Olli's partner."

"Pleased to meet you all. I've heard about your gifts, Alli. I don't think there's anyone here who hasn't. What do you want to know?"

"Hello Tommy. I logged on to the site you're tracing to look at the bumf about it and they emailed me constantly, when we were out of the office. Can they automatically link back to you if you've not emailed them at all?"

"No Alli. Whoever's running the site must have some really sophisticated equipment and know exactly what they're doing or they have someone helping them with brilliant technical knowledge."

"The time span for the bodies goes back twenty-six years, Tommy," Harvey explained to him.

"I'd say he has others helping him or he's loaded with money to burn; he'd pay heavily for that sort of information. Mind you some of the kids these days have hacked into government sites and they've been teenagers.

"In the states, kids have hacked into the Pentagon. They've had them in court for it. Our computers are really difficult to hack into. I won't say impossible as we have highly sophisticated security to side step. It would be bloody difficult. It makes it even more important I trace them as quickly as possible."

"We won't keep you Tommy, thanks." Harvey turned from him and we finished eating. Tommy left the canteen soon after and as we got up to leave, Jamie came in to have a word with Harvey.

We left them talking and headed for our office. I sat next to Gina to see what had happened on her site and Olli looked at the plan of the hospital he'd be working at.

"Gina, what have you called yourself to this weirdo?"

"He just knows me as David, Alli. I didn't give him a surname."

"Has he told you about the operation you'd have to have if you wanted one?" She looked baffled.

"I think you should ask him what it entails. You couldn't be expected to make a decision like that when you don't even know what's going to happen. I think he would expect you to ask those sorts of questions."

"So do I," Harvey said as he came in. "Have a shot at it Gina. If he's not forthcoming then you'd have to prod a bit. Ask his name. He might be so up his own backside to actually give you his real name." Gina smiled and opened up a dialogue with him again.

"I'll stay with you Gina, don't worry."

Hello, it's David again. I've been thinking about the operation and I'm scared. Could you tell me a bit more about it please?

Hello David. I'm so pleased you got back to me. I know it's a scary thing to go through but think how much better you'd feel after it was all over.

What's your name? It feels weird talking to you and not call you anything.

It's Anthony, David. Do you live with your parents or are you living alone? I need to know this, David.

I live on my own Anthony, is that a problem?

It's perfect David, don't worry about that. I only need to know as I'd have to provide a nurse for a few days after you get home. It's all part of the service.

How much would it all cost Anthony?

I keep the costs down to a minimum David so we could come to some arrangement about the money.

I thought it would cost thousands?

Normally it does but I do special rates for special people and I consider us friends.

"Harvey; look at this." He came to Gina's computer and read it over my shoulder.

"He's grooming you, Gina. A proper site wouldn't talk to you like that. I still can't tell if he's gay or he's our man. Ask him to describe the operation to you?"

I feel we're friends, too. Could you tell me how you do the operation, I've no idea how it's done?

I put you to sleep and take away your penis and testicles and then insert a vagina, to make you into the person you should have been; when you were born.

"Tell him you'll think about it and contact him very soon, Gina."

Anthony, this is a lot for me to think about. The operation sounds straight forward but I need a little time; I'll get back to you soon.

"He's our man, well done Gina. Now we wait for Tommy to trace those sites." Gina left her computer and went to see what Olli was doing.

"Harvey do you know if Jo's found out about Gerard Withers yet?"

"She's on the phone to them now Alli. I'll ring Andy and see how he's getting on." He pulled his phone, sat at my computer to talk to Andy and had to wait for him to pick up.

"Andy, how many have you done?" He listened a few moments. "Come back and we could get started on the names you have now. You can get the rest tomorrow so bring the list in here and get some lunch." Harvey stared at the computer screen in front of him.

"Alli, since Gina came off her computer, you've had loads of messages from the same site. I'm sure they're linked now. That bugger's switching from one computer to another." I looked at the screen and watched the emails load, one after the other into the inbox.

"Do you want me to start a dialogue with him, Harvey?"

He twisted his mouth. "I'm not sure Alli. Give it an hour and maybe open one then. We wouldn't want him to cotton on, that we knew what he was up to. We don't know what sort of equipment he has."

Tommy opened the door, saw Harvey and came straight over to him.

"Harvey that bugger must have money. He has servers that are linked and bounced from one server to another, before he gets to you. I've tracked seven so far and I know there are more. The next one down the line is from the states."

"Shit, Tommy. Do you think there's any point tracing any further?"

"To be honest Harvey, no. I've looked at the dialogue to Gina's computer and he's definitely British. If he was American I'd know. The phrasing and words they use would stick out a mile; my wife's American."

"We're back to square one. Could you keep an eye on the sites? Alli's talking to him in about an hour. You never know he might slip up, Tommy."

"I was going to suggest that Harvey. I don't think we're done here yet."

"Thanks for all your effort, Tommy."

"I've enjoyed doing it. It's more interesting than the normal run of the mill stuff I'm asked to do. If I pick anything else up I'll let you know straight away. I'll get back to it." He turned and left the office.

"Why doesn't he call you Sir, Harvey? Is he a higher rank than you?"

Harvey smiled at me. "He's not actually in the Force, Alli. He just works for us. Quite a lot of civilians work for us. It would be hard to find computer geeks joining up. They have a different mindset to normal humans. Their brains are wired totally obscurely. Most of them couldn't do a normal job."

"You learn something new every day." Jo came hurrying through the door and pushed it closed behind her. Her face was full of excitement.

"What is it, Jo?" Harvey and I waited for her to explain.

"That Gerard Withers who lives opposite Mrs Clarke, is in his fifties. He has a nephew living with him, a Jason Hicks."

"Fucking hell, Jo. No wonder he was bricking it yesterday."

"Get this. Withers worked in the hospital Morgue. I've looked him up on the electoral register. Hicks is registered as a student. I got on to the local colleges and University. He's doing a degree in IT." Harvey's eyes sparkled.

"Was Withers sacked or did he just leave the job at the

hospital?"

She started grinning at Harvey. "He left because he was caught messing with one of the bodies. They gave him the option to leave or be hauled up to answer questions in an enquiry."

"Sounds like our man Jo, well done." Harvey strode out of the office to talk to Jamie. When he came back in, "Alli, start a dialogue with that bastard. We're raiding the place and I want you to keep him talking."

"Okay, Harvey. It'll be a bloody pleasure."

"Olli, Gina; you're coming on the raid and Jo will tell you what to do. We're waiting for the warrant from Ron and we'll go as soon as we have it. Jamie's got Uniform ready and some of the team. I hope Andy and Craig get back here in time."

"Alli, I'll send thoughts back to you, to keep you in the loop."

"I didn't know you could do that, Gina." Harvey was surprised.

"I wouldn't know how far away she'd be able to hear you but she'd be able to hear me from about forty miles." She giggled at Harvey. "Our brains got linked the other night when Alli had the nightmare."

"I felt something happen then Gina, I wasn't sure what it was. I only realised about your brain capacity, not anything else."

"I've started seeing the dead, the same as you, Alli. I don't know how you coped when you were young. Some of them are bloody awful to look at."

"Tell me about it, Gina. I'm so sorry you've got that from me."

"I just push it into a place in my head and bury it. I haven't got as much shit to store as you have."

The door knocked and Andy came in with papers in his hand. "Sir. Here are the lists of employees from the Funeral Directors." Harvey took the paperwork from him.

"Thanks Andy. Has Jamie filled you in on the raid?"

"Not yet, Sir. We ate a sandwich on the way and I'll catch up with him now." He left the office and Harvey heard him talk to Jamie.

Harvey gave me my seat at my computer and I logged on to the last email that was sent.

Dear Sir,

You emailed me about the service you provide to people who want gender re—assignment.

Could you give me more details on how to proceed as I'm feeling very wrong in my body and don't know where to turn for help.

I cannot afford the horrendous fees that are charged and don't know if I could wait the years, to get it done on the NHS.

Please get back to me as you seem my only hope.

Yours sincerely,

Lewis.

I pressed the send button and sat back in my chair. Harvey looked at the email I sent after I opened the "sent items" tab.

"What do you think, Harvey?"

"Perfect Alli. That should wet his appetite." I clicked on the inbox and a new email was already there.

Dear Lewis,

Please go on to the site and click on to the dialogue tab. I would like to talk to you personally. It's much less formal than email.

I look forward to talking to you about your predicament.

Yours faithfully,

Anthony.

"That's proof they're linked. He used the same bloody name. Has Jay's sister come back from her holiday yet, Harvey?"

"I sent someone round this morning and she wasn't back. I would be interested to see if Jay used either of those sites. If he did, we have him for murder right now."

Jamie came in with a smile on his face. "Sir, the Commissioner handed me the warrant as he left the building. He said something about an Optician's appointment."

"Jamie, let's go. Alli, start talking to him and keep him at the computer. It would be good to catch him in the act." He gave me a kiss and left the office with everyone who was going. Only a few of the girls were left, still trying to contact people on the list for Milton Crescent.

I pulled the site up again and logged on to the dialogue box.

Hello Anthony,

Thank you for getting back to me so quickly. I'm at my wits end. I hope you can help me as I can't think of another way out of this body I'm in.

Hello Lewis, of course I can help you, that's what I'm here for. You sound like you've had enough. I'd like to arrange a meeting as soon as possible.

Anthony, I'd like to know a bit more about the operation. You can appreciate I'm worried. I've never had an operation before and I know I need it to be done but I'd like you to talk me through it if you would.

Alli, we're just pulling up to the house. Uniform

have broken the door in and Harvey has stormed in with the other lads in the team. Jo and I are following. Shit. The house is empty with just a few clothes left upstairs. Harvey is pissed off.

I'll keep up the dialogue with the man, see you soon.

Lewis, I do understand so please don't worry. I've done hundreds of these ops. I put you to sleep and remove your penis and testicles and sew in a vagina. Everyone I've done up until now have gone without a hitch. You'd get the best of care I promise you that. Wouldn't you meet me somewhere as this chat with you would be so much easier, face to face?

You haven't told me how much it will cost Anthony. I need to know that. I have some savings put by for the operation.

Lewis, don't worry about that now. We could come to an arrangement. My costs are cut to a minimum and I could take instalments if you wish to do it that way. Please let me meet you somewhere. You could bring a friend if you wish.

Someone's just knocked my door; I'll get back to you Anthony, I'm very interested.

I sat staring at the computer and decided to get some tea. On the way to the kitchen, Harvey and the rest of the team came in with sombre faces.

"Gina let me know how it went; you don't have to tell me.

The good news is he wants to meet whoever I'm supposed to be. Maybe you could catch him if I set it up. Tea everyone?" Their faces relaxed and some of them smiled and everyone put their hand up for tea.

"I'll help you Alli as I need to know where you make it." Gina grinned.

"Let's not have tea, we're opening a bottle of Champagne to welcome you and Olli to the team," Jamie told Gina.

One of the girls that stayed here stood up with a large bottle and the girl sitting next to her produced a tray full of empty flutes to be filled.

"Get that bottle open Jamie, we're all dying of thirst!" the girl with the glasses yelled. Harvey put his arm over my shoulder and gave me a squeeze. He was thrilled they were taking the trouble to welcome them properly.

It took a few minutes and the glasses were filled and handed out.

Jamie raised his glass. "Welcome Gina and Olli. As you can see we're a weird bunch but just ask if you need to know anything. You might be working away from here Olli but you could drop in for a cuppa anytime."

"I'll be glad of that when I'm freezing my balls off somewhere Jamie and thank you for the welcome, we both appreciate it." Olli got hold of Gina and kissed her. The jeering started and they both put up their middle fingers. The laughing nearly lifted the roof. They stopped kissing and drank the Champagne with the rest of the team.

Once the glasses were empty they slowly returned to their desks and got on with their work. The girl who produced the glasses brought them into the kitchen to wash them up. I was in there making tea.

"Didn't you get a drink Alli, I'm Debbie."

"I did Debbie, thanks. I gave most of mine to Harvey. I couldn't drink in the day and only have one glass of wine when we eat at night as it's never liked me much. I drink tea most of the time at home."

"I should knock it on the head but it's forced at you when you go out. No one listens when you say no."

"They should, half of them won't have livers in ten years

time."

"I worry about that. Perhaps I could suggest they donate some of the drink money to charity. It would probably go down like a lead balloon but I shall give it a go. I wouldn't want to be ill, later on in my life because I hit the bottle now."

I stirred my tea. "I think that's a bloody good idea, Debbie. I've seen the bags under the lad's eyes after a binge drinking session. Not a lot gets past me Debbie."

"I know I think it's brilliant. I'm pleased we had this chat, Alli. I'll bend a few ears the next time we're out." I grinned at her and left her drying the glasses.

Harvey watched me carry my tea in and his face was happy. I sat beside him. "Have you read it all, Harvey?"

"I was listening to your little talk with Debbie. If she gets the ball rolling we ought to put money into the fund and they could decide which charity to donate it to. It might help them get away from the binge drinking mentality that's swept the country. We all like a drink but you're right Alli, some of them will end up on a transplant list somewhere, it's a bloody shame. Go out and tell her what we'll do and it might spur her on to do it." I smiled and left him at my desk.

"Debbie." She was surprised to see me next to her. "Harvey and I will put money into the fund if you get it going. You will all be able to decide which charity to donate the money to. We're very concerned about your health and this may be a way to get the lads, more than you girls, to think what they're doing to their bodies." She smiled so wide I was chuffed.

"Thanks Alli. Tell Sir, I'm pleased to do it. Half of them look like bloody zombies, the next day. I'll get everyone in the building involved. Watch this space." I giggled and left her to get on.

I sat next to Harvey and picked up my tea. He was on the phone so I looked at the inbox on my computer. I pulled it over and opened the email that was waiting.

Dear Lewis,
I've been thinking. I'm due a holiday soon and would like

to see to your problem before I go. Is there no way you could hurry your decision as I have a slot free at the end of next week.

It's first come, first served, I'm afraid and you may have to wait until I get back.

Yours faithfully,

Anthony.

"He's a pushy bastard." I jumped when Harvey spoke and he cuddled me. "Sorry Alli, I didn't mean to do that. It went alright with Debbie, then?"

"She's really up for it Harvey, did you hear it all?"

"Not the last bit. Ron phoned to see how it went. He's as pissed off as we are."

"I bet he is. Debbie's getting the whole station involved. Her parting words were, watch this space."

"Good. We can't dish out the punishment if we're as bad as they are. Christ; I'd hate to deal with the drunks in town on a weekend."

"What are we going to do about this bugger?" I pointed to the computer.

"Nothing yet, Alli. I want you and Gina on the gay sites. See if you could spot him on there. He must have another source he gets victims from. Jay didn't look the sort to want a sex change."

"You're right Harvey, he didn't." I shut my email down and got on to Google. Gina was already on a chat line and trawling down pages of different messages. Her brain was reading it so quickly, I could hear it but it was just a dirge to me. Harvey looked at me because he could hear it, too.

"Bloody hell. I've never heard anyone read that fast."

Gina looked at us and giggled. "I'll shut it off so you can't hear it, sorry," and got straight back to it. We looked at each other and laughed.

"Where the hell did she get that brain from?"

"Some mad scientist I think."

Chapter 11

An ear piercing scream hit my brain from Gina's mind. My hands flew up to my head, trying to stop it. Harvey grabbed me and looked at Gina. She was doubled up on the floor with her hands above her head, fending off something invisible. Olli was by her side first and we rushed there to help him.

She started babbling and pushing Olli away. He couldn't understand it and tried to cuddle her again. He looked at us worried to death.

I closed my eyes and concentrated hard, to see what she was so frightened of.

Men in white coats, dragging her into a room. A deranged looking man; teeth bared and moving towards her.

I knelt beside her and took no notice of her pushing me away. I had to hold her. "Gina stop! They're not there now. It's Alli, they've gone, they've gone. You're safe with Olli. You're okay now. They've gone for good." She flung her arms around me clinging on so tight.

I looked at Olli. "You cuddle her Olli, come on." He knelt down and she let him cuddle her.

"I'm sorry Olli. I didn't realise who you were." He rocked her and let her cry.

"I think I triggered that, Harvey. Remember my last sentence to you? That's how she was bitten. Some fucking laboratory project; the bastards!"

"You mean they're making Hybrids on purpose!" He was livid.

Ron came through the door with Jo, who went straight over to Gina.

"Is she alright? I heard you calming her down, Alli. What happened?" Ron's face was full of worry.

"I mentioned to Harvey about mad scientists and Gina got a flashback of why she's a Hybrid. I concentrated and saw it all in her head. She was held down by doctors and bitten. They knew what a brilliant mind she had even then and used her for an experiment."

"The fucking bastards; will they stop at nothing!" flowed out of Ron's mouth really loud.

"You know who did this; don't you Ron?" He wasn't surprised I asked.

"I've an idea, Alli. That's why they wanted them in London, to get her back. It'll be over my dead body now; make no mistake. I'm going to kick up a stink over this."

"I don't think you should Ron," Harvey said to him gently. "Let them think we don't know anything. You may be opening a can of worms. Gina and Olli want to lead a calm life here. If they find out we know they may come and take her; they'd have nothing to lose."

"You're right Harvey. We'd be slapping them in the face and they wouldn't even know it." He went over to Gina and Olli who were standing up now.

"It must have been a hell of a shock for you to remember like that, Gina. Are you okay, now?"

She smiled at him and giggled. "I'm fine now, Ron. I'm bloody glad I'm with this lot. We've all been through it one way or another." She cuddled Olli. Ron patted her arm and came back to us.

"I'm pleased they live next door to you; keep an eye on her."

"They've lived in with us since the second night Ron. I'm having the two properties joined together soon. They've got plenty of support as Jo and Hillary are with us most nights, too."

"Sticking together, that's good Harvey. Pack up and go home you've all worked hard today. A few minutes early won't hurt. Have a good night."

He left the office and Gina came over to me.

She held her arms out for a cuddle. "I must have hurt your bloody head, screaming like that. I'm sorry Alli."

"Don't be sorry. I'm just pleased I could see what happened to you and talk you down from it. You heard what Ron said, Gina." She nodded. "He's saying nothing to them in case they snatch you back. They'll rue the day they did that to you."

"If they hadn't, I'd never have met Olli or you lot. I call it fate because my life is brilliant now and I wouldn't swap it for anything."

"She gets more like you every day, Alli," Harvey said with a grin and picked me up. "Mrs Alli Temptress Fate Burgess is always saying it to me."

Jamie came in. "The Commissioner has told us to go home, Sir. Is that right?" He grinned at me in Harvey's arms.

"Absolutely correct Jamie. You can all bugger off home and we'll see you tomorrow." Jamie started laughing and left the office. A cheer rang out to the sound of chairs scraping across the floor, then silence.

"I had a phone call from Jed today. He's bringing Abbey to the bondage class for us to meet her. Let's go home. I want a swim to wash today off me before some fun tonight." He put me down so I could grab my jacket and bag and held my hand out of the building.

"Jo, are you coming straight to ours?"

"Yes Alli. Hillary's knocking off at six so I'll have a swim with you lot. See you there."

On the way to our car Harvey chatted. "We'll have to buy swimming cosies. Josie and her cousins are coming for swimming this Saturday at nine o'clock."

"Whoopee!!! Have you told Nick we're covered in tattoos?"

"So is he, Alli. I was surprised when he told me and apparently Jess has some, too. The kids won't give a damn. I bet half the people in the public pool have them."

"When did you see him?"

"When we came back from the raid. What a fucking waste of time that was."

"Jason must have told him to move the day we saw him. I wish I could remember his car registration."

"You've given me an idea saying that. I asked Jamie if any CCTV cameras were working. We'll look tomorrow and I'm hoping we might have caught it on a camera somewhere. I feel a bit better, now." He pressed the key fob and we jumped in.

I turned to Gina and Olli. "We've got the kids swimming on Saturday morning. If you want to swim then you'd have to have cosies I'm afraid. We'll get some in town tomorrow dinner time, Gina."

"You two will buy Speedo's if I'm not with you," Harvey told us and Olli agreed with him.

"I wouldn't be seen dead in them." We burst out laughing. "Or alive." He said loudly over our noise. "These women haven't a clue, Harvey."

"I know it's serious. I'd be scared of popping out the top."

"I'm not bragging but I'd feel the same. I suppose when they were worn a lot the pools were cold. When your balls and dick shrivelled to the size of peanuts it didn't matter. You'd never expose yourself in a month of fucking Sundays."

Harvey chuckled beside me. "I remember it well Olli. When I was a kid we didn't have pools. The teacher broke the ice on the river for us to swim. I didn't find my cock for days and had to pee sitting down."

Olli was in stitches in the back. "Very painful if I remember rightly."

"I'd already been bitten by then. I always wondered why so many of the kids cried. I didn't feel the cold and they must have been in bloody agony."

"This is all very interesting the size of your cocks in or out of cold water. What do you swim in then, clever buggers?" Harvey gave me a sideways glance and giggled.

He pulled into a garage forecourt. Olli got out with him and they disappeared through a door beside a huge window showing the new cars they had for sale.

"I can't see them getting something like those, Alli." Gina had her head jammed between the seats.

"I think it'll be a part exchange, Gina, nothing flash. Your good car is at home and you'll love that. Jo loves hers."

"I still can't believe all this has happened for us, Alli."

I turned to her. "You and me both, Gina. We have to tell you how we met and what happened before we got married."

"I saw what flashed into Harvey's mind the other night. Those fuckers have a lot to answer for."

"I think Harvey's words, before we left work will come true, Gina. Since I cuddled you after having my nightmare about Jay, our brains are more linked every day."

"I've already noticed, Alli. You got as turned on as me, last night." I giggled.

"I know, I loved it."

Harvey got in beside me and gave me a knowing smile.

"Gina, I expect you'd like to go home with Olli, he won't be a minute."

"It's not going to backfire all the way home, is it?"

Harvey laughed at her. "When I said banger I meant not a new car, not something fit for a scrapyard. It's an S 60."

"I haven't a clue what one of those is. Is that him, coming now."

"That's it. You like white, don't you? By the time it's covered in muck off the roads it'll be perfect cover for Olli."

"Looks very snazzy Harvey, thanks." She opened the back door, got out and pretended to hitch-hike.

Olli pulled up beside her. "You look good enough to eat, get in." Gina giggled at us and ran around the bonnet. "See you at home after I've shagged my passenger, only kidding." We all heard the "Ah" from inside the car. "Looks like I have to make a pit stop, see you soon." His window went up, they pulled off the forecourt and we followed.

"They seem happy enough with that. He'll probably shag the arse of her in a lay-by. Are you telling me what you swim in, I haven't forgotten."

He parked the car as we were home. "Shorts Alli, just shorts." I looked through the windscreen and Jo was killing herself laughing.

We got out. "A very interesting conversation. I can't imagine either of your dicks shrivelling to the size of peanuts but what do I know."

"We'll try them with a bucket of ice, later Jo. Are you taking bets."

I giggled at Harvey and all he said was, "You'll need a pair of tweezers to find it."

"I've gone right off, that idea. You're safe Harvey Burgess."

Harvey came up behind me in the sitting room and wrapped his arms around my body. "You're annoyed with me, Alli, sorry."

I turned and kissed him. "How could I stay annoyed with you for more than two minutes, I love you." He kissed me so tenderly, tears filled my eyes. He wiped them from my cheeks when they spilled over, and then gently kissed my eyes.

"That bugger Jo's beaten us to the pool. I want to ravish you Alli, I've wanted to all day." I held my hand out and we hurried to the pool room. Harvey had stripped and dived in long before me. He'd have to show me the speed thing. I dived in and met him on the bottom. We shagged twice before coming up for air.

"Christ, you were down there for about forty minutes." Jo was shocked. "I was getting bloody worried. I'll get out because Hillary's arriving in a minute." She hauled herself out so easily that it reminded me of Harvey.

"Jo's getting stronger. I expect you've noticed, Harvey."

"I've been watching her over the last couple of weeks. I think I'll have a word with her or she could do something without thinking like I did with Jed's toolbox. I just forgot."

"I think you should go and do it now, Harvey." He swam to the side and hauled himself out quickly grabbed a towel to catch up with her. I listened to their chat as I floated in the pool.

Jo, Alli and I have noticed how strong you are now and we're worried you'll demonstrate it without thinking. Remember when I picked up Jed's toolbox? I forgot but got out of it so it didn't stick in his mind. It may not be that easy in some circumstances.

I thought I was imagining it Harvey and I've been worrying about it. I think I'll stop going to the gym.

It might not be as simple as that, Jo. You may be like me.

What do you mean?

I could lift my car if I put my mind to it Jo.

Fucking hell. Have I caused this to happen by going to the gym.

No. It would have happened anyway. I'm very careful around Alli when she's not changed.

I picked Hillary up the other night with no effort and she's noticed but said nothing.

Tell her everything I've said to you. If you're both informed you'll be fine. Just remember, if you try this bondage thing tonight you won't have to pull on ropes too hard. You'll soon get used to it and ask me if you want to know anything Jo.

"I didn't know about you being that strong and thought I was a freak of nature. I know we saw you pick up Alli that night but I didn't know you could pick a bloody car up.

I could years ago and may be a bit rusty now. I worked in a quarry for years and could break huge blocks of stone with one blow of a sledgehammer. You know when I described the piles beneath the plunge pool, I didn't hire any large plant to push them into the ground, so you can see why I'm careful.

That's fucking scary Harvey. I hope I don't get like that.

The good thing is Alli is as strong as me when she changes and I definitely don't have to worry when we play hard.

That's good news to me. I'd never want to hurt Hillary.

"He's never hurt me, in fact, I've probably been more violent to him." Jo turned to me and laughed.

"She gets very dangerous when she's wearing black, as I recall." Harvey was holding his sides trying not to laugh.

"We couldn't concentrate on our shag for you buggers." Gina was dragging Olli, zipping up his fly with a huge grin on his face.

"A very interesting conversation. Yes I heard it. It's okay Jo and I know you've been worried." Hillary went straight to her for a kiss. "Harvey's right, you'll get used to it and I haven't noticed any difference between us when we're changed."

"That's a relief Hillary. Have you had a good day?"

"Not bad. I've been looking forward to tonight. What's yours been like?"

"We thought we had the bastard and raided his house. The place was stripped when we got there. We'll tell you the rest later as we've only got an hour until our class starts."

"I've got lots of snack things for everyone before the class. Have a quick swim and I'll make tea. We could eat something before they get here and we'll order a curry later. Does that suit everyone?" I didn't get an answer; they just headed for the pool.

Harvey helped me get everything prepared for them getting out. I filled the kettle and got mugs ready. Harvey put his arms around me and kissed the back of my neck.

"That feels nice my husband."

He put his mouth to my ear. "So do you Mrs Burgess."

You greedy buggers, you've just been at it like fucking rabbits.

Oh, so we have Jo. Sorry, we forgot. Harvey answered her thoughts and we both heard her giggle in our minds.

I switched the kettle on. "I'm going up to put something on. T-shirt and leggings I think."

"We can't exactly meet people in towels. I'll come up with you Alli."

I thought myself into my dressing room and Harvey to his. He watched me from the door as usual.

"You'll have to show me how to do that speed thing. I've asked you a few times. Don't you want to show me?"

"Things have just got in the way when you've asked, that's all. Can you remember me looking through my whole life in a couple of minutes when you asked if I'd ever been hurt?"

"Yes. I watched it with you but I don't see the relevance."

"When I do it I push my mind ahead of what I'm doing and keep pushing. My body races to catch up. You're about to put your leggings on and your mind follows what your body is doing. Your mind should be pushed to the next thing and you'd do the speed with your body to catch your mind. It'll never catch it if you keep pushing until you want to stop. Does that make sense?"

"Yes it does. I'm trying it." I picked up the leggings and pushed with my mind and they were on. "Bloody hell I did it." I jumped on Harvey and planted a huge kiss on his lips.

"Thank you. I want to do it back to the kitchen." I dropped to the floor, left him standing and was next to the kettle before I blinked. Jo's mouth hung open beside me.

"Fuck me. Is that what he was explaining to you?" Before I had time to answer her she saw Harvey stop right behind me.

A smile grew on her face. "I'm trying that myself later on. I'll get those buggers out of the pool." She put her head out of the door and yelled for them to get out or there'd be no food left. That got them moving.

The doorbell rang at seven on the dot. Harvey got up and held his hand out so we could both greet our guests. Jed's smiling face was the first I saw and then his girlfriend, Abbey, who was stunning and just like a model. Jed introduced us and she gave us both a hug.

They stood back for his brother who was the spit of Jed. I glanced at Jed and he grinned. "You kept that quiet, you bugger."

He just laughed and said, "This is Lucas my twin brother."

"He's always doing that. Bugger is a good word for him Alli. I'm pleased to meet you." He gave me a hug. He put his hand out to Harvey. "So you're the artist he's told me about, Harvey. I expect I'll see some of your work later."

Harvey shook his hand. "There's no doubt about that, Lucas. Alli likes an audience. Go on through, Jed, the rest of the reprobates are waiting."

Harvey helped Lucas bring two huge holdalls in and by the time we got in the sitting room, Jed had introduced Abbey to everyone and our lot just stared at Lucas.

"I bet you two had fun with the women when you were younger," fell out of Olli's mouth.

"They tried it with me Olli," Abbey explained. "Lucas forgets Jed has hidden extras and he's lucky he's bloody alive." Everyone giggled and she just grinned at Jed. *I'll tie you up and whip the arse of you.*

I burst out laughing; I couldn't hold it in. Jed must have realixed she'd thought something she'd do to him by my laughter.

"Watch it Abbey, this fucking lot read minds." She looked at us.

"You're going to tie him up and whip the arse of him."

She laughed at me. "Alli, that's amazing. I could have a field day, when we have a row if I could do it."

"It's impossible to have a row in this house, Abbey. Are you all having a drink before we get started?"

"I'll get the wine Alli." Harvey went to the cellar.

"Tea or coffee; Abbey? I don't drink much so you won't feel left out."

"This mind reading cuts down on time," and she giggled. "Coffee please, I don't mind making it." I left them for the kitchen and she tagged along.

"Bloody hell. Jed tried to describe this kitchen. Men are useless looking at things with only half their brain in gear and then get it all wrong, it's beautiful."

I put the kettle on and watched her as she looked at everything. When she got to the pool room doors, which were open, she wandered in there and just stared.

I gave her the coffee and stood beside her. "I must admit, I didn't believe him when he told me how big this pool was. I bet you use it a lot."

"Sometimes twice a day, Abbey. It's good to come home from work and wind down in the pool. Until we got this we used a plunge pool upstairs but we couldn't swim properly in there. We still use it but it depends how we're feeling. You could have a swim if you want."

"Thanks, I'll have one before we go home, Alli. I suppose we should go back in. Lucas goes through safety precautions with all the couples he teaches." *I hope, you heard that Harvey.*

I did Alli. I'd have to work out how much I could tell them. Bugger it, I might tell them exactly what we are.

What!

When we stepped into the sitting room Harvey's eyes never left mine. When I sat next to him and looked at the others' faces I know they'd agreed with him.

Lucas was just about to speak when Harvey got up and stood at the end of the two sofas, facing everyone.

"Before we get started on this evening's class we all feel we need to explain a few things to you.

"Jed, we've known you for a while now and class you as a good friend. I hope at the end of my speech you'd let us continue to call you a friend. You know we're not the same as you and we want to come clean as we hate lying.

"We work for the police for one reason only, to tip the balance in their favour against crime because they're losing the battle. What I'm about to tell you is top secret and will probably scare you and I'm sorry for that.

"I hope Jed you've seen in us, enough to know we wouldn't harm you as we really value your friendship." Harvey hesitated before he went on, looking at the three humans amongst us.

"We were all bitten by a vampire at some point in our lives and weren't turned into full vampires." Their eyes widened at that last statement. "You've already seen we don't feel pain and heal very fast. We eat and drink the same as you but we need to drink blood, which I buy from a private blood bank and the last thing, we're never going to age or die. If you want to leave we wouldn't stop you, we just wanted it out in the open."

Jed got up and threw himself at Harvey for a hug. "You fucking idiot, why didn't you tell me before."

Harvey laughed at him. "They'd string me up for telling you only I know it wouldn't work."

"I almost knew the day you picked up my toolbox." He turned to Lucas. "You needn't waste time on any safety things, they don't bloody need it." Lucas was giggling along with our crew. He turned back to us. "Abbey has something to ask you."

She got to her feet, picked my hand up and took me to Harvey. "We'd love it if you were god parents to our nipper when it's born and thank you for the money for the baby things. For what it's worth I couldn't give a shit what you are as I like you all."

I gave her a hug and pulled back to speak to her. "Thank you for trusting us. It means a lot as you're the only humans we've ever told."

"It'll go no further than these four walls I can promise you that. The trust goes both ways Alli."

Harvey got hold of me to face Jed and Abbey. "We'd be honoured to be your nipper's god parents and thank you for asking us."

We stood nattering for a few minutes and I could feel the impatience in everyone.

Harvey picked up on it. "Go ahead Lucas as the floor is now yours." He grinned at Harvey.

"From what's been said in here tonight I can see the easy stuff will bore the pants off you. Have you all tried some bondage?" Everyone nodded.

"I'll help you out, Lucas. We get into some heavy shit but those two buggers," Jo pointed to us, "top the fucking lot." Lucas's eyes nearly popped and Jed was laughing; he'd guessed what we get up to.

"Perhaps we should take you upstairs. We have a soundproof room up there." Harvey was enjoying it, now he wasn't worried about being found out.

We all trooped up there and when Harvey opened the door and put the light on they couldn't believe what it was like and how much equipment we had.

"I bet you have some fun in here." Jed's eyes were everywhere. "Why is everything black?"

"I'll tell you later Jed as this lot will get pissed off if I hold up proceedings any longer." Harvey turned to Lucas. "You can see what we play with Lucas so could you show us stuff on a par with this."

"Advanced bondage I think. I've only got one couple nearly

ready for that stage." He rubbed his hands together. "I'm going to enjoy this. Have you got a hoist anywhere? Don't worry if you haven't as I've got one in the van I could bring in."

"A few Lucas. One above the plunge pool and one on the landing. One behind the pool downstairs and one in the kitchen as we use the whole fucking house when we get going. There's one above your head but there's not enough room in here to watch." Lucas looked up.

"Who the hell gets hung on that anal hook?"

"Me and I love it Lucas. It doesn't matter what's done to us, we only feel pleasure. The others haven't tried it yet but if they knew what it felt like they would."

"Could you move the kitchen hoist into the sitting room Harvey or is it fixed?"

"I'll move it and by the time you get downstairs it'll be in there." He left us to close up the room and walk down.

Harvey had moved the sofas and the hoist was right in front of them so everyone could see properly. "I need a volunteer." I stood up as I knew the others were dubious. They were relieved, I could feel it. *Enjoy it Alli, strip if you want to.* I looked at Harvey and smiled. *Thank you.*

I took my clothes off and waited for Lucas to begin.

"Could you bear your weight on your rings, Alli? I'll support your weight with rope until the last minute."

"Yes Lucas that wouldn't be a problem but I have to tell you this. I'd get aroused if you do anything with the rings and we change our physical appearance quite drastically. Don't be scared and just carry on. I'll try to control it but it may be difficult."

"Don't control it Alli. I want you to enjoy it and if Harvey wants to shag you at the end we wouldn't mind in the least. Come up here Harvey you can help." I caught the grin on Harvey's face.

"I'll show you how to make a corset with metal supports. We'll arch Alli's back backwards and suspend her from that, until the last minute." I glanced at Harvey and his eyes were sparkling.

"I'm horny just hearing that," I confessed.

Harvey kissed my head. "Go for it Alli and don't hold back. I'll enjoy this, as much as you."

Lucas opened one of the holdalls and pulled out loads of white silky rope and three metal bars that were arched. The bars were flat, about one inch wide and twenty inches long.

"I'll only need two of these bars as you seem to be quite supple Alli but I ought to test you out first. Harvey, could you pick Alli up as I need to see if she can arch her back as much as these bars."

"Sure; Jo give me a hand please." Jo got up. "Put your forearms together and link your hands. I want to rest Alli across them so she can relax her body."

"Jo wouldn't be able to hold Alli up like that!" Lucas pointed out and we could hear the worry in his voice.

"Just watch Lucas. Jo's stronger than she looks." Harvey's voice was calm and I could feel Lucas relax and wait.

Harvey put his right hand under my bum and his left at the back of my shoulders. "Lay back on my hands Alli." I did as he asked and saw Lucas's face when Harvey picked me up so easily. He was staggered.

He lay my back across Jo's arms. "Relax your body Alli." He kept a hand on me either side of where I was rested. I let my arms drop over my head and slowly my back bent backwards.

I didn't feel Jo's arms move at all. "Is that enough for you, Lucas?" Harvey asked.

He picked up a bar and held it against my body. "Perfect. You can lift her down now." Harvey put his hands under me and lifted me off Jo's arms.

"Thanks Jo." Harvey laid me on the floor and let my back straighten out naturally.

Lucas opened a large hank of rope and found the middle. "I'll start at the middle of your back Alli by trapping two bars to your body. I'll be using two ropes and work away from your waist in both directions. Please tell me if you feel uncomfortable at any time and I'll adjust things."

"I'll be okay so don't worry and I'd tell you if I wasn't."

"Could you hold the two bars against Alli's back either side of her spine please, Harvey." He took the bars from Lucas. I felt the cold metal touch my back and his warm hands encircle my waist holding them in place.

I can feel you getting aroused Alli. Change if you want to.

I'm holding off as long as possible. If I black out, tell them not to worry. Harvey gently squeezed my waist for a "yes".

Lucas tied a knot in the centre of the rope making a separate loop to hang me on. He stood in front of me, put one hand holding the rope around to my back and took it right round with the other.

Then he fed the long ends through the loop under the knot at the front and pulled it tight.

"Does that feel okay, Alli?"

"Lucas please don't keep asking me, just do it. I'm fucking enjoying this and you've no idea how much." I heard Harvey laugh in my mind.

"That's told me." He giggled and stepped up the pace.

In no time at all he was using two ropes and Harvey held one when he used the other. He swapped them each time he knotted another circle of rope around me until my back was arching, always keeping the knots in a straight line down the front of my body.

"Harvey, could you support her now. Alli wouldn't be able to stand if her back arched anymore."

"Hang me up now Lucas. There's a button on the back of the hoist to lower the hook." He looked worried and glanced at Harvey.

"She'll be fine and we've done worse than this Lucas. Alli loves being tied up."

Jo added: "We've bloody witnessed it." Harvey smiled at her.

Lucas went behind the hoist and brought the hook down to a height he could work on me. Harvey lifted me by the rope and hooked me on. I relaxed my body and my mind began working overtime. Our lot could all hear what was running through my thoughts.

"Lucas, Alli's getting really switched on and we can all hear her mind. Don't be surprised if a few of those buggers change. They're getting as randy as fuck now." Harvey grinned at them and turned back to Lucas who was laughing.

"It happens in all the classes Harvey, you've just got an added element. I nearly said you're only human."

Harvey started laughing, turned to me and whispered in my ear. "Fill your boots Alli, I love you."

Lucas continued adding bands of rope, until my whole torso was covered leaving my boobs bare and stopped just above the piercings on my pelvic bone. *This is so beautiful*. He started again on my neck right up to my ears. *Hold me Harvey, I want to feel your hands*. He held my shoulders and I felt Lucas on my legs next and trembled with the touch of the rope as he covered each one of them.

I fucking love this Harvey. Lucas bent them back under me and kept them spread wide apart. *Perfect.* Harvey switched ends with Lucas.

My arms were used to trap my head and the circles of rope went from my forehead down to my wrists. He raised the hoist and my body was arched so much he was able to bind my hands to both feet.

I don't know if I can hang on without changing. Fuck it I can't. I changed and everything heightened to such a degree I made more noise from my mouth than ever before. Bound like this was heaven for me.

Put your mouth over my fanny, Harvey.

"Sorry Lucas, Alli wants me to do this." Harvey held my thighs and held his mouth over my fanny. My mind exploded, I blacked out.

Harvey had my head in his hands when I opened my eyes. "Fucking hell. That was excellent."

I looked over to the sofas, I was upside down so took a second to focus. They were changed and groping. I looked at Harvey. "Do you feel left out?"

He giggled at me. "Lucas and I are going for a cup of tea. The rest of the buggers are at it like rabbits. Only kidding, I know you're enjoying this. Your rings are next, are you ready?"

"Play with my bump to make me change before the rings and then you can do what you want with me." His eyes flashed, left my sight and I closed my eyes. His tongue touched my bump for a second and then his thumb drove me nuts. I changed.

"Hang her from her rings Lucas, she's ready." The tension left my back as the rings pulled up hard. Harvey pushed his thumb into my fanny when the shocks hit and then up my bum. I heard shrieks of pleasure and didn't realise it was me. The voice went on and on and begged for more. Harvey put his tongue up my fanny, the balls fired off one another and sent pins and needles through me so fast the thunderbolt hit and I passed out.

I woke up in Harvey's arms and Lucas was taking the ropes

off me as fast as he could. "Don't hurry it Lucas. I really love the feel of it."

"I could hear how much you enjoyed it and when you changed it made it better for you. I think you're all very lucky." He sat in front of us and slowly took the ropes of my arms.

"Doesn't it make you horny as well? Sorry, I shouldn't have asked that."

"I don't mind Alli. When I was younger I had an accident messing about on bikes. I can't get an erection and I actually like guys not women. It means I couldn't disgrace myself doing these classes. I don't think clients would like it if I got a stiffy tying up their wives."

"That would be funny if it wasn't so tragic, Lucas," Harvey said to him. "Is there nothing they could do?"

"Apparently nerves were severed and they didn't do micro surgery then. It happened a long time ago so I'm used to it now. Jed was always safe getting me to pass myself off as him for a joke. We did have a lot of fun winding Abbey up. That was, before she knew about me being gay and the problem."

"We had a gay lad in my class at school. Tell me to shut up if I'm talking out of turn. He told me one day some guys only want to be shagged and nothing else."

"I see where you're going Alli. I'd want to be doing the shagging unfortunately."

As we were talking the ropes were coming off until I'm naked.

"Can I look at your back tattoo, Alli?" I turned to face Harvey. "Is this one of your drawings, Harvey?"

"Jed did the briars between Alli's legs and she wanted it extending, up her back. I kept the theme as I think it's brilliant and added the picture."

"You're too fucking modest, Harvey." Jed was stood over us grinning. "You two turned the rest of us on like a bloody switch."

"Didn't it worry you when they changed, they look totally different."

"Do we look worried, we wouldn't be here if we were. Abbey wants to know if we could go in the pool."

"You don't have to ask Jed, go ahead and we'll be there in a minute." Jed left us. "I think you should get some strength in your legs, Alli." Before the last word was out of his mouth he was supporting me, standing up.

"Sorry Lucas. We feel so comfortable around you we forgot."

Lucas got to his feet and scratched his head. "I wish I could bloody do it?"

He began to pack his gear and when I could stand alone Harvey gave him a hand.

"Do you eat curry, Lucas?"

"I love it Harvey. Thanks for helping with this. Do you have any rope of your own, yet?"

Harvey pulled the heavy sack from behind the sofa. "We have all this."

Lucas looked inside the canvas sack. "That's plenty for three couples so you probably wouldn't need me to show you anymore."

"Yes we will Lucas, every week. We enjoy your company apart from the bondage," Harvey told him. "You're welcome here anytime you want to come; and that goes for Jed and Abbey. Just ring before you come in case we're called out for work."

"What do you actually do in the Police Force?"

"I run the murder squad. Alli sees the dead and reads minds. Jo works in the team's office and is good at tracking down things. Gina has just joined us and has almost the same gifts Alli has and Olli is going undercover for us. Hillary, Jo's partner, is our pathologist."

"Bloody hell. I wouldn't fancy coming up against you lot!"

"Only one person there knows what we are and he's the Commissioner. If ever you see us out on a job just act normal and don't mention anything else. This really is top secret, Lucas."

"I'll tell Jed and Abbey on the way home. No one will find out from us."

"I think we've earned that swim, I'll order the meal and give us an hour in there. Go ahead, Alli; I won't be a minute."

I did the speed thing past Lucas and was in the middle of the pool before he got through the door. I dived to the bottom and swam length after length until I felt Harvey's arms around my body. *Come here Mrs Burgess. I've wanted to do this all night.*

Chapter 12

We sat around the sitting room with a plate of curry each, the wine was flowing and the banter hilarious at times. We cleared all the things away and settled down to some serious talking.

"Jed told us you're a mountaineer Lucas. What have you climbed?" Harvey asked.

"Not any more Harvey. I lost the top of two toes climbing Everest the last time. I was lucky to get away with my life. Frostbite is bloody terrible and you don't realise how bad it is until it's too late. I was concentrating so hard, making sure other parts of me weren't getting into problems I forgot about my feet. I had a good team with me, thank God. I was air lifted out of base camp straight to hospital."

"Christ; how many times have you climbed it?"

"Four, on two different routes. They join near the summit and a lot of lives are lost at that point. I've lost quite a few friends over the years. Jed nearly shit himself every time I went and I think that was the last straw with him." He looked at Jed.

"He's right, I hated him going. God knows what he looked like when he got to hospital. He was a right bloody mess when he got home weeks later."

"To be honest I think I'd bottle it if I tried it again. I didn't set out to climb it that many times. I got asked if I'd take people up and got sucked in to two of them.

The guy who asked me to take him up on my last climb did something really stupid and broke his back. His body is still up there. You have to be bloody hard-nosed. You'd die trying to rescue someone you know wouldn't make it. That side of it was hard to stomach for me."

"I think that's incredibly brave Lucas and I'm sure I speak for all of us, we're pleased you're not going again. Have you got enough clients to teach?"

"I could always take a few more, why?"

"We went to a place out past Darwin's Heath where you could try out stuff before you buy it. Most of the frames in our toy room came from there. Next time we're passing I could take a card in for you. I saw plenty of different ads on a notice board when I was booking us in, none of them bondage."

"Thanks Harvey. Jed's got me most of my clients, then word of mouth. I'll get some cards printed."

"Jamie at work told me about the place we tried and he might be interested so I'll ask him tomorrow. Before you go home leave your phone number and he'll contact you direct, if that's okay."

Our lot were fascinated listening to all that and when they stopped talking it went very quiet for a few minutes.

"This is no fucking good. Get the bloody music started you two, you're not getting out of it that easy." Jo's face was beaming. "I'll get some more wine."

"Good idea Jo," Jed piped up. "They're fucking brilliant Brov. I tattooed Hillary's back here, last Sunday night and heard the pair of them play Duelling Banjos."

"We're all going on strike tomorrow if you don't play that again," Gina informed Harvey. "I'll beg if I have to."

Harvey grinned at her then looked at me. "Looks like we're outnumbered Alli. Come on as I'd hate to see Gina on her hands and knees. I don't suppose you'll mind Olli."

"The view would be quite good from here." Gina; elbowed him. "Watch it. I've got a new whip for you."

Olli looked up to the heavens putting his hands together in prayer. "Thank you God." Laughter erupted.

Jo came in with two bottles of wine. "She wore the last bastard out on his bits last night."

Gina giggled and Olli said, "Fucking de Lux."

They fell about laughing.

I saw a wince flash across Jed's face and Lucas looked stunned. "Jesus, you meant what you said earlier Jo."

"Oh, yes. If ever we were tortured for information they'd die trying because we'd love every minute of it."

"Christ. I wish I was like you lot. I'd get some pleasure at least."

No one said anything out loud. The questions and answers that passed between our minds overrode everything else for a few minutes. Lucas, Jed and Abbey wouldn't have known. We got up to play for them when it was going on.

It would mend him, Harvey.

I know Jo and he could kill a human if he shagged them.

At least he could have a fucking wank, Harvey.

Jo's right Harvey. It must fuck his brain up when he fancies a shag. None of us can truly understand what he goes through. At least give him the bloody option.

I don't know Hillary but this is a critical fucking step. Let me think about it when we play some music.

All I'm saying is, don't waste the moment Harvey.

I won't Hillary. I feel really sorry for him.

We played for them over the next hour and ended up with Harvey playing slide guitar.

"Bloody hell. I could listen to you all night," Lucas stated.

"How long have you been playing?" Jed asked. "I know now, Jo was covering up for you last Sunday after what's been disclosed here tonight."

Harvey smiled at him. "Good guess Jed. I've been playing for about twenty months now and Alli a year."

"I'm bloody gobsmacked I don't mind admitting."

"I've tinkered around with a guitar for years," Lucas told us, "Have I turned green with envy?"

"Not yet," Harvey answered. "You might in a minute Lucas. I'm going to tell you something and when you go home think about it really hard because there'll be no going back if you change your mind after it's done."

Lucas glanced at Jed who was grinning. He'd guessed Harvey's next words and the emotion he felt for us ran riot in his mind for a few seconds. Tears filled his eyes. *Thank you Harvey.* Harvey nodded to him.

"You can't leave me waiting, please tell me Harvey."

"What I'm going to propose to you Lucas will have repercussions, it's not all good. I'm twenty-four and have been that age for over a hundred years now. I can see you're shocked but I told you earlier we never age." Harvey thought for a minute before he spoke again, deliberating over the next words.

"I've only ever told Alli this next bit." He hesitated. *Go on Harvey.*

"I had no idea what I was at twenty-two and the first girl I made love to died in my arms. I'm really strong the same as Jo but our strength when we get aroused is phenomenal and only someone who has been turned could match you when making love for us males."

"I don't understand why you're telling me this Harvey. You heard what I said earlier." Lucas looked totally disheartened.

"I'm not trying to torture you Lucas, just listen please. We have venom running through our veins, that's why we have to drink blood. The venom repairs anything it comes in contact with and your body would be repaired. The downside of Alli turning you means you'd die for a short while but what I mean by that is I'd be able to hear your heartbeat very slowly but a doctor would pronounce you dead. It's undetectable by humans. Hillary and Olli have both been turned recently. Olli was attacked but Hillary requested it, making sure she was with Jo forever." Lucas looked at both of them and they nodded back to him.

"I couldn't say if you'd ever find a partner and forever is a bloody long time to go without."

"You were prepared to do that for me, Harvey."

"I know Alli but the circumstances are totally different. You were living here and been through something, really fucking traumatic. I'd have looked after you, into infinity; you know that." He turned back to Lucas who had a smile for us hovering on his lips.

"You'd have to drop all your friends. If you got aroused or angry at anything you'd change in front of them. We have to be very careful at work, especially if women and kids have been murdered. I can't deal with some of the bastards we get in and I've had a long time to practice self-control. I've had to walk out of interviews or I'd have killed someone. We'd cause a riot if we changed in public so you see, it has a heap of fucking drawbacks."

"I'll have to talk this over with Jed and Abbey before I make any decisions Harvey, this is serious fucking shit." Jed spoke next.

"You should go for it Lucas and you know why I'm saying it. I've hated myself for causing you to be like that ever since. You didn't tell Alli and Harvey how it happened. You've always defended me and I love you for that but it cuts me to the quick at the same time.

"If you don't find a partner you could still have a bloody

wank." He turned to Harvey. "There must be others like you Harvey, out there somewhere if Olli was attacked and turned recently."

"There are, Jed, but we don't know any others personally."

"Was Alli your next partner after the first girl?" Jed asked Harvey gently.

"Yes, Jed. I waited a hundred years for Alli and I'd do it again if she was waiting for me. I was lonely most of the time but Jenny who lived next door helped me, when I was looking for work.

"Her husband died sixty years ago and I stayed on to help her. She put up the money for me to try my hand on the stock market and I made millions for us both. She'd been bitten but aged normally and she didn't need blood like me and she died a few months ago at the age of eighty-two. I met Alli in a cafe up the road and knew she read minds as I'd watched her for months with her boyfriend Adey. That same afternoon Adey was killed during a raid on an off licence. The off road vehicle backed over him in the getaway.

"I knocked on Alli's door to tell her he'd been killed and to find out where his next of kin lived. I saw the tiny room she lived in. I wanted to help her out of there and we got on okay so I asked her to move in. All I wanted was a friend and Jenny didn't want me alone when she died.

"Alli moved in a bit reluctantly as I recall." Harvey turned and grinned at me. "She was here a few weeks before I found out what happened to her, when she was bitten and just wanted to look after her forever.

"When we finally got together as a couple she made my fucking existence worthwhile and I proposed on one knee in the high street three days later. The rest is history."

"And not a dry eye in the fucking house." Jo wiped her hand across her eyes. "That's a love story if ever I heard one." Tears were streaming down Hillary and Gina's faces.

Jo stood up. "How many for tea?" Everyone's hand shot up.

Harvey cuddled me and kissed my head. *Okay, Mrs Burgess. Perfect, Mr Burgess.*

"Harvey, do you mind if I have a word with Abbey and Jed in private somewhere, please?" Lucas asked.

“Go in the pool room. You can sit and talk as long as you like. Grab your tea off Jo on the way through.” They left us and a minute later Jo brought our tea in.

“He’s going to ask you to turn him, Alli,” Gina disclosed. “Tonight.”

“If he does I think he should stay with us until he gets to grips with everything.”

“Who’s going to show him how to feed, Alli.” Harvey wondered.

“I think Jo and I should show him,” Hillary answered. “In your shower room with the light on. It’s the biggest shower, Jo won’t care and I can be quite matter of fact. If he wants a wank we won’t be watching as we’ll be occupied.”

Harvey laughed at her. “That’s actually perfect, Hillary. I think we’d better explain things before he’s turned.”

“Play your guitar Harvey please, until they come back.”

“For you Mrs Burgess anything.” He picked up his guitar from the stand and played some classical music I’d not heard before.

About half an hour later they came back in and sat down again. Harvey stopped playing and Jed was the first to speak.

“Abbey and I want Lucas to go through with your suggestion Harvey. We won’t feel we’ve lost him, it’s quite the reverse, we’ll be gaining a family. I personally have become very fond of all of you as I’ve known you the longest. The trust in us you’ve displayed today has touched me deeply. If you can mend my brother I’d owe you forever.” He put his head down and I saw a tear drop from his cheek. Abbey put her arms around him and Lucas squeezed his shoulder.

“Don’t get upset Jed. Alli I’d like you to turn me please? I’d rather wait as long as Harvey did for you than stay as I am. We’ve talked long and hard about all the consequences and you seem able to deal with them. I’m sure with a bit of guidance from all of you I’ll be fine.”

“Come here Lucas?” I asked him. He took the two strides between the sofas and I got up and cuddled him. “I’d be pleased to do it for you. Harvey has to tell you a few things before I do it. Is that okay?”

"Thank you Alli. You know what this means for me and Jed. I'd take heed of anything Harvey has to say to me. You sit down and I'll sit here on the floor."

"Once you've been turned Lucas you'd have to feed on blood and I know you understand that. What you don't know is how randy you'd be when the feelings from the blood in your body, hits you. I wouldn't feed with Alli before she let me make love to her. I wouldn't have been able to hold back and I didn't want to frighten her. The desire to fuck is that strong. You'd need someone to show you the ropes the first time you feed and for obvious reasons because you're gay, Olli and I don't think it should be us."

Lucas started laughing. "I quite understand; don't worry, I'll do it on my own."

"You don't have to Lucas," Hillary pointed out. "Jo and I will show you and you can wank as much as you want, we'd be too occupied to notice."

Lucas giggled. "That'll be perfect Hillary, thank you."

"There's one other thing we've forgotten to tell you Lucas. You may not be able to sleep ever again. I don't and Alli only needs a couple of hours. Hillary and Jo don't and we've never asked Olli and Gina."

"I'm the same as Alli and Olli just cuddles me until I've had enough, Harvey."

"I never get tired but Alli gets weary when she's been talking to the dead a lot. She has them bombarding her all day long and Gina's starting to get that, too.

"You may have special gifts when you're turned. Jo is as strong as me and can hear our thoughts for twenty miles or so. Hillary is psychic and reads minds. Olli has a brain that works out weird logical things. Gina has the sharpest brain of us all; God knows what she'll be able to do in the future. Alli is brilliant in an interview and the poor sods don't know what's hit them. She pulls things from their minds and fires it straight back. I don't have to say much at all but that's enough of all that. You'll get to know us better after you've been turned. Do you still want to go ahead Lucas?"

"More than ever Harvey. Would you do it tonight please Alli?"

"Of course I will. The initial bite will hurt you. I felt Hillary tense when I bit her."

"Only for a few seconds Alli, it went numb after that."

"That'll be when the venom started to work. I'm pleased it didn't hurt for long. Lucas you will be out of it for about two hours. Are you staying Jed?"

"Until I see he's fine and then we'll go home, Alli."

"Come upstairs then, we'll do it in my bedroom."

I asked Lucas to lie down on the bed. "I'm going to bite the left side of your neck so you'd have to turn your head towards me Lucas."

Jed held his left hand. "I'll see you later, Brov."

I could feel how emotional Jed was. "He'll be fine Jed. I can feel how much you love him. Are you ready Lucas?"

"Do it Alli please?" He turned his head and closed his eyes. I bent over him and sunk my teeth into his neck; pushed the venom for a minute and when I took my mouth away Jed could see the puncture wounds.

"I'll heal them Jed, just watch." I licked the two holes and they healed in seconds. "Now we wait. Harvey can hear his heart and will tell us how he's doing." I felt Harvey's hands on my shoulders as I sat on the bed beside Lucas, holding his hand.

"It's working. His heart is starting to slow down Alli," he squeezed my shoulders gently. I kept two fingers on the pulse at his wrist and we waited. After an hour I couldn't feel it. Harvey felt me get concerned.

"I can still hear his heart. It's beating very slowly, don't worry."

Another twenty minutes went by. "I can hear it speeding up a bit," Harvey told us. Jed looked at me and smiled.

The minutes seemed to take forever to pass and suddenly I could feel the pulse on his wrist. "It won't be long now Jed; I can feel his pulse again." I counted down the seconds in my head for something to take my mind off the wait.

Fifteen minutes later Lucas gripped both our hands and relaxed. His eyes opened and grinned at us. "I'm still here." He let go of my hand and flung his arms around his brother.

"Take your time and come down when you're ready," Harvey told them. I couldn't say anything, I was crying. "We'll go down

Alli." He picked me up and did the speed thing down the stairs.

The first one on their feet when we walked into the sitting room was Abbey. "Is he okay? Why are you crying, did something go wrong."

"He's fine Abbey, don't worry. They'll be down soon. Alli cried when she turned Hillary," Harvey explained to her.

Hillary got up and cuddled Abbey. "Don't worry. Jed has tormented himself over the accident for a lot of years. They need time together to unload the baggage. They'll come through that door smiling, like I did."

Gina came in with a tray of mugs and handed them out.

"Here you are Alli. He'll never forget you for this. Come and sit down Abbey. Hillary was right, they need to sort things out. Have you picked any baby names yet?"

"It's a bit early yet, we thought. We don't want to know what sex it is, like everyone else does these days, we want a surprise. We'd have six weeks to register the birth, so we might wait until it's born and choose a name then."

"I know Alli and Harvey will be god parents but we'll all be interested in your baby. I nearly said I'd take up knitting, who am I trying to kid." Giggles went around the room.

The door opened and the two boys came through mucking about together, like kids. They straighten up as if they'd been caught doing something wrong and Lucas walked over to us.

"Harvey, you don't mind if I give your wife a cuddle, do you?"

"Not in the least, fill your boots Lucas." He held his arms out wide and I got up for a hug.

"Thank you Alli. I can feel everything again thanks to you. I'll never forget what you've done for me."

"You don't need to thank me Lucas. I was pleased to do it for you. It must have been terrible hanging over you both since childhood." Lucas looked shocked.

"Alli can see exactly what happened when someone explains anything to her, Lucas. Do you fancy this tea or do you want a real drink?"

"I think a real drink would go down quite nicely as I feel so fucking happy."

"Not for us Harvey thanks, we ought to get going. I've got a full day booked from eleven tomorrow. See us out and then you can relax in peace."

The hugs and handshakes started in earnest until only Harvey, Jed, Abbey and I said goodbye on the doorstep.

Jed gave me a longer hug than usual. "Thank you Alli, we'll see you soon."

Harvey closed the door. "He's going to cry buckets when he gets home."

I put my arms around Harvey. "Neither of them will forget what you've done for them Alli. I think they'd be like the brothers you never had from now on. I'm very proud of you."

"You promised to have a drink with Lucas. He's waiting for you to go back in Harvey."

"Come on then Mrs Burgess, I know you want the subject changed."

I giggled. "You know me like the back of your hand."

We all decided that after we'd been up to feed, we would stay downstairs with Lucas for the whole night. Jo and Hillary would go home and Olli and Gina could have Harvey's bedroom, out of earshot.

It was going to be strange for Lucas to have feelings again in his cock and he could use the shower room behind the pool if he needed to have a wank or if he got tired there was a bedroom he could use.

Hillary and Jo took Lucas to feed with them, when we fed in the pool shower room. An hour later they came downstairs as if nothing had happened. We said goodbye to them and settled down for the night. Olli and Gina said goodnight and went upstairs.

Once everyone had gone Lucas talked for ages to Harvey. I had my head on Harvey's lap and drifted in and out of sleep.

The next thing I knew, Harvey was stroking my face and asking if I wanted tea as it was morning.

I looked up at him. "Good morning my husband." Harvey lifted me up so we could have our morning kiss.

"You had about three hours sleep Alli. That was good for you. Lucas has gone for a swim."

"How's he been?"

"He won't sleep, that's for sure and he's been fine. Any misgivings he had about not being able to control himself at first were unfounded. We talked all night. He's been all over the world, climbing. I explained in more detail about how we have to live and he's happy with everything. Sit up Alli and I'll make us some tea. Do you fancy a swim before breakfast?"

"Good idea. It'll wash the cobwebs out of my head." I followed Harvey into the kitchen and looked into the pool room.

"Lucas is swimming as fast as you Harvey, look."

Harvey came to the door and watched with me. "He still wouldn't be able to catch you Alli." He went back in and brought out three mugs of tea. We sat in the chairs and watched him plough through the water. He caught sight of us and swam to the edge near our chairs.

"Good morning Alli. I hope we didn't disturb you too much, yapping all night?"

"Good morning to you Lucas. Are you getting out, I'll get you a towel."

"I've got one down there, I won't be a minute." He swam to the other end hauled himself out and wrapped a towel around his waist.

A few moments later he sat down beside us. "Bloody hell. I enjoyed that. I've not been in a decent pool for years."

"Harvey said you were fine last night. I know you were panicking. In your shoes, I'd have been too."

"I was panicking Alli. I thought I'd be trying to shag knot holes in wood."

Harvey started giggling and that set me off. "How did it go in the shower when you went to feed with the girls?"

Lucas laughed. "Can they hear you from where they live?"

"Not this far away, why?" Harvey could hardly wait for the answer.

"Jo didn't have her back to me once. She looks like a lad from the back and I bet she thought I'd forget and shag her." We were in stitches.

"That's made my fucking day Lucas," Harvey was holding his sides.

"Hillary was really kind. She talked me through everything. When we waited for the feelings to hit, Jo cuddled her but she held my hand until I felt okay with everything, I didn't expect that. I'm not saying Jo isn't kind, she was worried about her ring. I can't blame her really. In her position I think I'd have been the same. In fact I think they were brave to do it."

"It was Hillary who suggested they go in with you Lucas. She's put up with some shit from men she's worked with. She's a Home Office Pathologist and fucking good at her job. She lived with a Hybrid years ago. It's different with females but even Jo held back a lot before Hillary was turned."

"They make a good couple, I like them both."

"What are you buggers up to?" Gina came in smiling as usual. "Olli fell out of bed laughing about Jo. Personally I found the knot holes funnier, more tea anyone?" Lucas sniggered.

"We're going for a swim thanks, Gina. What about you Lucas?"

"I'm going back in the pool. I'm making the most of it while I'm here."

I dived in to the bottom and swam down there for ages. I could hear Lucas ask how long I hold my breath. Harvey explained we both stay down for about forty minutes sometimes. I didn't catch the next bit as I was turning at the other end. I did notice they were trying to catch me up and failed. Harvey was right again. I came up for air and carried on. After a few more lengths I floated to the top, got out and did the speed thing up to my dressing room to get ready for work.

I got dressed fast but decided not to put my make-up on at speed, my face would've been a bloody mess.

Harvey came in ready for work. "I told Lucas he could stay here when we went to work but he's going home and back tonight. He's putting his clients off for a couple of days until he's sure he won't hurt anyone pulling ropes too tight."

"I can understand him being cautious Harvey, it could ruin his business. Have you paid him?"

"Yes, Alli. He wasn't going to take it but I told him you'd be pissed off if he didn't."

"You got that right Harvey, I would've been. I expect he'll drop in to see Jed, sometime today. That's me finished, let's go down for breakfast. Did Olli get off to work okay? I've got no idea what the time is."

"It's still early Alli, he left just before I came up. We haven't got to leave for another forty minutes."

As soon as we got into work Harvey got Jamie to gather any CCTV film from the area of the killings to look for Jason's car. Gina logged on to the gay site and started reading fast again, still keeping in contact with Olli.

"He's been on a tour of the hospital with another porter. He'll let us know if he sees anything weird going on. I suppose it'll take him a couple of days to find anything out, he could get lucky." She continued with the website.

Ron came in to see if Gina was okay but didn't stay long.

"We've got a PM this morning Alli, at ten."

"More of the mummies?"

"No. The two bodies next to the cinema. Something different for a change. Derek is doing one and Hillary the other. It'll cut down on time for us."

"Who are we taking with us?"

"I'm not sure if Jo has finished what she's doing; I'll see nearer the time. Andy and Craig have gone to get the last of the employee names from the Funeral Directors."

"Have you thought of taking Gina as both bodies are getting done together?" I knew she'd gone back to the emails from the doctor.

"That may be quite useful Alli." He turned to Gina and didn't have to ask.

"I'll come. It'll get me away from this bastard for a while, he's getting to fucking pushy. Have you thought of setting up a meeting with him and follow him back to where he's based?"

"That would be my last resort Gina. If something goes wrong the consequences are dire for whoever has to meet him."

"I can see that Harvey. I know he lived near the bodies you've found but you found no evidence he was doing it at the house where he lived. He must have somewhere quite large to have the equipment, such as beds for him to work in and help to wrap the bodies. From what I've seen in Alli's mind the bandages have been put on really neatly and to lift a body like that the helper must be very strong. You don't think a Hybrid is helping him; do you?"

"That thought never crossed my mind Gina, you could be bloody right. Christ this is getting fucking serious. If a Hybrid is involved we've no idea what gifts it's got and with that strength some of my team could get really fucking injured. Jo and I would have to go in first as we're the strongest."

Jo came in. "I heard all that Harvey. The other guy who worked at the hospital has disappeared off the map. I can't trace him anywhere and he worked there at the same time as the other one."

"Did you do the self-defence class in basic training, Jo?"

"Yes. It sounds like I'm going to need it. At least I'm stronger than I was then and can't die. I don't care what we have to do. Gina's theory sounds very plausible to me. I think you should tell Ron."

"He's upstairs, he's already heard it Jo. We've got one advantage if it is a Hybrid. We're mob handed not only in strength but the mind reading between us all and Gina seems to be able to predict something's going to happen just before it does."

"What the hell would we do if a Hybrid was involved?" I had to ask. "We couldn't send it to prison."

"I'm sure the Home Office has a way of dealing with them. Personally I think they'd be drugged permanently, in a hospital somewhere Alli."

"I've just remembered something, Harvey."

"What Gina?"

"The lights flickered permanently and I couldn't understand why at the time. I think they must contain them with electricity because I heard a lot of screaming."

"Fucking hell Gina. We've got no equipment like that. If we have to get the Home Office involved you can't be anywhere near us or they'd snatch you back."

"You're forgetting something Harvey. Alli's brain is linked to mine and she sees and feels everything I do so I could be a hundred miles away and still help."

"Give me five minutes. I have to think this through, carefully." He sat with his eyes closed and his brain worked out different scenarios at top speed.

Ron came in but didn't interrupt him. He nodded to us and sat beside Harvey's desk and just waited for him to finish.

When Harvey opened his eyes Ron spoke to him.

"I'm really impressed with you four. Gina's right on how they're contained. I had no idea they were making Hybrids themselves. I was only told they caught Hybrids that weren't towing the line and had to keep them somewhere.

"We will have to involve them if it's a Hybrid helping him. That doesn't sit well with me, you know that. The very fact your brains are linked will give us an edge though, over the Home Office and the Hybrid. They won't be expecting that at all." Ron looked puzzled over something.

"Spit it out Ron, what's worrying you?" I asked him.

"I didn't understand what you said about being strong, that's all."

"That's the one thing no one has known about all along Ron," Harvey told him. "I have super human strength and Jo is the same. I've known about mine for a hundred years but it's come on with Jo over the last few weeks. I could pick my car up Ron and that's before I change." Ron started smiling.

"I think that's fucking brilliant, you've made my bloody day. I don't feel we're on the back foot anymore."

"We know of another Hybrid with the same strength as us. Alli turned him last night Ron and he has skills in mountaineering. He's been up Everest four times." Ron glanced at me. He was shocked I'd turned someone else.

"There's a reason I did it Ron, just hear me out please?"

"Go on Alli."

"The guy who did the bondage class is the twin brother of our friend the tattooist. When they were kids his twin brother caused him to have an accident and he lost all sensation to his genitals. They didn't do micro surgery then and couldn't repair him. He's not even felt anything having a pee.

"Jed who caused the accident is a good guy and has been devastated ever since seeing his brother unable to have a sex life, never having a relationship or kids. Lucas is gay but still deserves to have the life he wants.

"Jed has noticed things weren't right with us, never feeling pain and healing so fast. He's guessed a lot over the year we've known him and last night the story about what happened to Lucas came out. Jed broke down at that point.

“You know we talk in our minds. All five of us bombarded Harvey to give him the choice. Harvey thought really hard as Jed is a friend and he could see how much he loved his brother. It’s been a millstone around both their necks. They’d keep the secret, we’ve read their minds.

“Harvey told them every aspect on how we live and all about us. They talked together on their own for a long time to make a decision.

“Lucas told us he’d rather wait a hundred years to find a partner, like Harvey did than stay as he was. He asked me to turn him last night.

“If we’ve done something so terrible Ron we’ll all resign right now, it’s your choice.”

“After hearing that Alli I think you did the right thing. I can’t imagine what they’ve been going through. We all take that side of life as a right and to have it taken away like that must have been devastating for them both. I think we might use him but I couldn’t put him on the payroll as they’d find out we’ve got him. I’m not sure how to go about this Harvey.”

“Ron, I didn’t touch my pay for the first three years. I only used it then to have the pool room built behind the house. Give him my pay, you know I don’t need it. Jenny left all her money to Alli and combined we’re worth a bloody mint. The interest alone is a small fortune a year and we hardly dent that and the capital just gets larger.” Harvey looked at the clock, “We’re leaving in five minutes; a PM.”

“Thank you Harvey; it won’t be indefinitely. Once this case is over, I’ll take him on permanently because they’ll know about him then.”

“I’ll tell him all about the job tonight and I feel sure he’d want it. I’ll let you know tomorrow Ron. I’m afraid we have to go. Gina’s coming with us as she’s not been to a PM yet and she needs to get off the computer for a couple of hours.” Harvey glanced at us. *We’re ready to go if you stop bloody talking.*

He grinned and picked up his jacket from the chair.

Chapter 13

We left Ron in a hurry. He knows we don't like being late for Hillary. Harvey asked Jo to keep digging. "I'm not sorry I'm not going with you at all, Harvey. I'm much more use to you here."

"That's what I thought Jo. Do your best and we'll see you later."

Hillary was just about to start when we got there. Two pathologists were busy on the other side of the lab and nodded to us.

"Sorry we're late Hillary. I can't blame it on the traffic as it was my gob that held us up."

Hillary laughed at him. "Is everything okay at home?"

"More than okay." *I have a job for him if he wants it.*

That sounds good. Morning you two.

Hi, Hillary. We had a discussion and Ron came down. It got a bit involved so we'll tell you later.

"Gina, is this your first PM?"

"It is Hillary. Hi, I'll be okay."

"If you feel sick you can leave if you want, everyone's a bit queasy at first."

"I'm sure I'll be fine but thanks Hillary."

Before Hillary had time to speak after pulling the microphone down, Derek came in to start on the other body.

"Derek before you get going this is Gina, another psychic."

"Hello Gina. I think you're all bloody fascinating."

Gina giggled at him. "Hello Derek. What you do here is to me, too."

"I didn't know you thought that, Gina." Hillary was astounded.

"I didn't say anything in case you thought I was being a big head."

"I think I've heard that before." Harvey turned to me. "Does that sound familiar, Alli?"

"That was me when I saw what was in Mick's head."

Derek looked puzzled. "Alli saw a tumour and he's had it

removed now Derek," Harvey enlightened him.

"Bloody hell! That takes the biscuit for me."

"Well you better watch this space. Gina can do far more than me. She's an unknown quantity at the moment, Derek."

Gina laughed at me. "You've forgotten something quite vital Alli. Anything I can do now or in the future you'd get as well."

I grinned at her. "I forgot that Gina."

"I think we've held them up enough we'll shut up and let you get on."

"It's okay Harvey. Gina, if you feel you have something to say or show either of us just go ahead. These bodies are linked in the same crime so it might be to me or Derek. Alli and Harvey already know that."

"Okay Hillary, thanks."

They both got on with the post-mortems over the next hour and lots of photographs were taken to make a picture, along with all the samples of the last moments of these two lives lost forever.

Gina walked over to Derek's body and watched him through it all. The whole ribcage was open and it didn't bother her one bit.

"Derek; I think his Large Colon is full of Heroin." Derek stared at her for a moment and then seemed to come back to life.

"Thank you. I'll take a look now. This will smell awful Gina."

"I see as many ghosts as Alli now. Believe me, they're not very bloody fragrant. Could I still watch?"

He smiled at her. "As long as you like."

Gina turned and giggled at us, she's enjoying this.

Derek cut into the Large Colon and the smell was vile from over here and Gina nearly had her nose it as she watched.

Hillary looked at her and smiled. "She'd make a bloody good pathologist."

"You're not having her Hillary, sorry," Harvey said with a giggle.

"I know that Harvey but she ought to come to every PM with you."

One of Derek's assistants took a large stainless steel tray to the table. Derek put his hands into the Colon and lifted out a pile of small round objects and put them into the tray. He went back for more and searched around after that in case he'd missed any.

He washed his gloves off and replaced them with new ones.

He took one out of the tray with large forceps and washed it in a bowl of liquid his assistant provided. He placed it on another bench and cut it open with a new scalpel, changed the scalpel and lifted some of the contents out with the blade, dropping it into a glass test tube which he placed it into a stand. He opened a small dropper bottle and dripped a couple of drops into the test tube and shook the sample for a moment. It turned pink.

"It's definitely Heroin, Gina, well done. I wish I had your bloody head."

"You wouldn't want all the other crap that goes with it Derek."

"Possibly not Gina, I forgot about that. We'll open all the others later on and weigh it. At least that's some that won't hit the streets. I'm finished here and thank you for your help, Gina. I look forward to your next visit."

"Me, too, I've had a ball." Derek smiled as she came back to us.

Hillary grinned at her "Your first fan I think Gina. There's definitely something medical going on in your head from somewhere. You know your way around a body, that's for sure."

Hillary looked at Harvey. "What develops in Gina's mind on the medical side will be invaluable to both of us Harvey. You may be bloody glad of it. She's had some medical training from somebody. I can tell, just by the way she's been here today. I'm sorry I'm talking about you like that, Gina."

"It's alright Hillary, I actually want to come. I've enjoyed it and I'm sure I'd soak it up like a bloody sponge. I've been talking to Olli, Harvey, he's doing fine. He's friendly with one of the security guards who bends the rules a bit. He said he'd tell you tonight."

"Thanks Gina." *Turn your microphone off, Hillary.* She glanced at Harvey, checked she's the only one working now and put her hand up to flick the switch.

"You were being praised this morning by Lucas. He was very touched by the kindness you showed him, last night."

"It was a lot for someone to take in. At least I knew all about it beforehand. I know Jo was a bit concerned as she looks like a lad from behind. I didn't want him to feel alone, so I held his hand until he was okay. It was very generous of him, to say that Harvey."

"I talked to him all night while Alli slept beside me. He didn't have the urges he thought he'd have. He was bloody chuffed about that. He went home this morning and be back with us tonight. He'll feed by himself tonight, now he knows the ropes and I'll tell him about the Jacuzzi. He can have some fun in there."

"He'd like that. We better crack on I'm afraid." She switched the microphone back on and finished the PM over the next twenty minutes.

We found Jo in the canteen with the rest of the team. When she saw us she made her excuses to sit with us. They all knew we knock about together at weekends so wouldn't question it.

"How did the PMs go? I couldn't keep track. I was on the phone for about an hour, just on one of the calls."

"Gina was a star today. She told Derek about a massive amount of drugs, in the body's Colon. I'm surprised he didn't see that on an X-ray, Harvey."

"Derek's body was the one that was shot, Alli. His liver was ruptured which caused all the bruising. He only had a broken Clavicle and the Tibia near the bottom of his right leg. I don't think he X-rayed his whole body. He used the state of his knee joint and teeth to help determine his age. He took fingerprints and you may have him on your files, Harvey," Gina answered sounding very professional and then giggled.

Harvey was amused. "We'll know soon enough. They'll fax them through this afternoon. What are we eating ladies. Have you eaten, Jo?"

"I had the fish and chips. I'll give you a hand, I want more tea. I've talked so much today I've got no bloody spit left."

Take our keys. You need more blood Jo. Do it now.

She looked shocked, took the keys and hurried out. I helped Harvey carry the meals back and we ate in almost silence, worried for Jo. I got more tea and we'd nearly finished it when Jo came back in.

I had three Harvey. Will I need that much extra every day?

No. Whatever you're having now, add two more. Maybe the strength is sapping you a bit, it has come on fast. Don't worry. I have four a day and sometimes I have more. A dry mouth is a sure sign you need more.

I've only been having two or three.

That was fine before you developed the strength. Alli needs six or she starts feeling hungry during the late afternoon. We're all different Jo.

"I'll get some tea, do you all want another one?"

"Alli and I do. I'm getting the tea bug from her." Gina smiled at me.

"I'll have another Jo, thanks." Jo went up to the counter.

"You're getting more like bloody twins every day. It's a good job you don't look and sound the same. Olli and I would get in a right bloody mix up."

"Be safe in the knowledge we wouldn't let that happen Harvey. Even if we looked like two peas in a bloody pod." We both laughed at her.

Harvey had a word with Jamie about the cameras before we left the canteen. He hasn't found film of the car anywhere. Harvey told him to issue Uniform and Traffic with the description of the car and Jason, in case they see either on their travels. All we could do was wait and hope they find it.

It was a good job Harvey has a photographic memory and knew the make and model, the colour and must have stared at Jason through the windscreen. He remembered a small chip from a stone almost in the middle of Jason's face.

We'd been in our office for two minutes, when Jo came in. "Harvey, could I go to the hospital and speak to the personnel woman, face to face. She's being bloody evasive on the phone. I think she knows more than she's letting on."

"Take someone with you Jo. Is Andy back yet?"

"No Harvey, nor Craig. I thought they'd be finished by now. Hang on, they're in the office. They must have had lunch out. I'll take Andy, Harvey."

She rushed out. *Andy, you're coming back out with me, sorry.*

That's okay. Craig, the lists are all yours.

You jammy bugger, Andy.

"They all get on really well. I've not heard one of them moan yet," Gina said to either of us.

“They’re a bloody good team Gina, young but easy to mould,” Harvey told her before he answered his phone.

“Hi Jed, everything okay?” He listened for a minute. “Of course you can, we’ll see you later, bye.” Harvey came over to my desk and put his arms around me for a cuddle.

“Lucas has been in to see him, he’s so fucking happy. They’re coming at seven so that’ll give me time to have a word with Lucas before they arrive, Alli.”

I gave him a kiss. “I’m so pleased we did that last night. If we hadn’t I’d have felt fucking awful today.”

The door knocked and Debbie came in. “Sorry to disturb you. Sir.” She was a bit dubious about coming in, we both felt it.

“Come in Debbie it’s alright, he’s not going to bite you,” I said, smiling.

“I’ve had a good think about an incentive for them to give up the drink, Sir. If they put the price of a pint or shot in the kitty they get a raffle ticket and at a time you decide, one ticket is drawn and one person gets a hundred quid. The rest goes to charity. I know it sounds a lot but you have to lead this lot like a donkey with a carrot. No good, Sir?”

“It’s good Debbie, well done. I think whoever wins it should decide the charity. We’ll bring money in tomorrow to set the kitty away and get the raffle tickets and a few posters made. Whoever collects the money in the pub should give it to the landlord to be locked in his safe. I don’t want any of you getting robbed on the way home, that wouldn’t look good would it.”

Harvey grinned at her and she relaxed, “No Sir. We’d look a right load of plonkers. I’ll get my friend to work out the poster, she’s good at that sort of thing. I’ll get back to work. Thank you, Sir.”

“Well done, Debbie.” She left the office. “She’s true to her word, Alli.”

“Harvey, come here a minute please.” We both looked to Gina and hurried over to her.

“I’m back on the gay sites. Look at the picture of this man. It’s the same bloody one, isn’t it?”

Harvey turned her computer slightly so we could both see. “Absolutely Gina. I’ll get Tommy down here now.”

Harvey rang him and he came straight down.

"What have you got Harvey?" He glanced at the screen. "Christ, it's him. I might have a better chance of tracing this. Can I sit there Gina, please?"

She got up and Tommy sent the site up to his computer, after a few minutes of typing. "Thousands log onto these sites and they're easy to hack. They're not sophisticated like the other two were. I'll get back. This won't take long at all." He didn't wait for anyone to say anything and almost ran out.

"He's like a dog with a bloody rabbit. I'll make some tea." Gina opened the door and almost bumped into Jamie hurrying in.

"Sorry, Gina." She giggled and scooted past him. "Sir. Jay Henderson's sister is here to report him as a missing person. The front desk have just phoned me."

"Jamie, I don't want to explain to her in an interview room. Check the rape suite is empty and we'll talk to her in there. I'll send Alli down to get her, if it's free."

"Okay, Sir. I won't be a minute." He hurried out.

"I didn't know you had a rape suite here."

"That's the first thing I asked for when I got promoted. Vice used to interview the women in a shitty room. The women were scared enough without feeling like a bloody criminal."

"You're my hero Harvey Burgess." Jamie came back in.

"It's empty, Sir."

"Organise some tea Jamie and get one of the women to bring it in please."

As Jamie left. Harvey got up. "Come with me, Alli. Bring her up to this floor; I'll be waiting to take you to the rape suite."

"Hello, I'm Alli. I believe you've come to report your brother missing."

"Yes that's right, I've been on holiday. None of his friends have seen him since just after I left."

"I'll take you upstairs, it's more comfortable up there." She got up and followed me through the door at the front desk.

Harvey was waiting for us on the next floor and opened the door beside him. We went into a very plush room with sofas and beautiful curtains, pictures on the wall and nothing intimidating.

"Sit down please Miss Henderson," Harvey spoke gently to her.

"I'm Detective Inspector Burgess. You can call me Harvey and this is my wife Alli, she works with me. Could you tell us when you last saw your brother?"

Debbie knocked and brought a tray of tea in. "Thank you, Debbie."

"Three weeks ago on the day I went on holiday. I'm Natalie." I stood up and sat next to her.

"Natalie, we've been waiting for you to come home." She stared at me and tears filled her eyes. I put my arm around her shoulder. "I'm so sorry Natalie, I'm afraid Jay died not long after you left."

She didn't just cry she wailed for him. It was heart wrenching to hear it. I cuddled her until her tears dried up and she looked at me for answers.

Harvey told her everything. He was so kind to her.

"I bet someone on that bloody computer has done this to him!" she yelled.

"Tell us what you mean Natalie. Everything you tell us would help to catch who did this." She was wringing her hands in her lap, I put my hand over hers, they were trembling.

"He was gay and sat at his computer every night on the chat lines. I kept telling him no good would come of it. The place to find a boyfriend is in real life not in bloody cyberspace. Sorry for swearing but I'm really angry with him now."

"You can swear all you like Natalie and we understand why you're angry. Jay was not the only victim, we have over fifty bodies." She stared at Harvey.

"Do you want his computer it might help you?"

"That would've been my next question to you. Thank you Natalie. Would you mind if Alli and I had a look in his bedroom? There might be some clues in his personal things."

"No. Go ahead, you look whenever you want."

"Have you driven here, Natalie?"

"No. My boyfriend uses the car in the week. He's a rep in Manchester. That's his area."

"I'll have a Family Liaison Officer stay with you until he comes home unless you have any other relatives who could be with you."

"I've only got my boyfriend."

Harvey took out his phone to speak to Jamie. "Jamie, could you organise Chrissie, to stay with Natalie Henderson until her boyfriend returns. He works away." Harvey shut his phone.

"We'll take you home with us now Natalie, have a look in his room and stay with you until Chrissie arrives."

"Thank you. You've been very kind. Could I see him please?"

"Of course you can see him but have your boyfriend with you Natalie, you'll need his support. Can you get hold of him by phone?"

"Yes, he's got a mobile." I took mine from my bag and handed it to her.

"Ring him Natalie, we'll give you some privacy if you want."

"Please stay."

"I'll get some hot tea, Alli." Harvey picked up the tray of full cups and left us.

"Natalie; before you ring I have something to tell you. I see the dead everywhere. Don't be scared, Jay is standing near the window." Her eyes darted away from me and she looked for him. Tears ran down her cheeks and her hands started to shake.

"He's come to speak to you, Natalie," I said gently.

She stared at me. "Is this some sort of joke!" Harvey came back in, he'd heard me in his head.

"Natalie, Alli wouldn't joke about it. That's why she works with me. Jay has already talked to her at his post-mortem and so did I. We are both psychics."

"Talk to him Natalie and I'll tell you what he says. He can hear you and don't be scared, please." She was in shock and couldn't speak.

I've been a fucking idiot Nat. I'm so sorry.

"He says he's been a fucking idiot Nat and he's so sorry." She stared at me.

"That's what he called me." She looked towards the window, "I kept telling you how dangerous it was, you wouldn't listen. If you weren't already dead, I'd kill you right now!"

I know you would, that's why I waited until you went on holiday. You tried to get me to go with you. I wish I'd listened to you Nat and Gavin."

"He knows you would that's why he waited until you went. You tried to get him to go with you; he wishes he'd listened to you, Nat and Gavin."

"What am I supposed to do now Jay?"

Gavin loves you Nat, marry him. I'll be at your wedding. I believe we'll meet again after talking to Alli and Harvey.

"Gavin loves you Nat, marry him. Jay will be at your wedding and believes you'll meet him again after talking to us."

"I wouldn't marry him. I didn't want you to feel alone."

I know Nat. Marry him now, please?"

"He knows Nat, please marry him now."

"I will Jay, thank you for coming to speak to me."

I'll always be watching over you Nat. Have a happy life with Gavin. Bye.

"He'll always be watching over you Nat, Have a happy life with Gavin. Bye."

"Bye Jay. I love you." She burst into tears and I rocked her in a cuddle, tears streaming down my face, too.

Harvey didn't disturb us and went out for the tea. By the time he came back in we were both wiping our faces.

"Here Natalie, you probably need this." She looked up at Harvey, smiled at him and took the tea.

"Thank you, Harvey, and you Alli. I'll never forget you for this."

After Natalie rang Gavin we took her home. Chrissie was waiting in her car and got out to greet her. She was so kind and relaxed with her, Natalie responded and talked with her when we looked through Jay's personal things.

Harvey closed his lap top and detached all the wiring, "Can you see a diary anywhere, Alli?"

"I'll look through these drawers Harvey." I opened them one at a time and searched for something he may have made notes in. The bottom drawer held what we were looking for.

"Here it is Harvey." Under piles of clean paper was a burgundy hard backed book. I handed it to Harvey. He flicked through it quickly; it was filled with phone numbers, names and messages.

"This would keep the team busy for weeks, bloody hell. We'll take this and the lap top, Alli, we're finished here."

Downstairs we showed Natalie what we were taking and left her with Chrissie. Gavin was due back in a couple of hours and

Chrissie would keep in touch with them until all this was over.

"He's been very active on the gay scene. Beats me why he had to resort to the internet."

I glanced at Harvey. "I suppose it sucks them all in eventually. It's too easy to get on the sites and must be thrilling. You know the whole blind date thing." Harvey took hold of my hand.

"I think you're right. I hadn't thought of it like that, Alli. I bet all his friends are the same. When they hear about Jay it should change their minds, I hope. When I think of all that's changed since I met Jenny it worries me what's ahead of us in the next sixty years."

"We wouldn't be able to control it, we'd have to just ride it out Harvey. I'm bloody glad I'm a Hybrid and have you."

He kept his eyes on the road and squeezed my hand. "Likewise, Alli."

Before we left town Harvey parked outside a department store.

"Come on Alli, we need swimming gear. This won't have to take long."

We hurried inside, split up and headed for the "separates" departments. I picked up two black bathing costumes. Gina was about my size and I met Harvey at the tills.

"Did you find what you want Harvey."

"I got three pairs. Lucas will probably be there early on Saturday morning and I don't know if he has any?"

"I've just thought, I forgot Jo and Hillary. What would I get for Jo?"

"Leave it, Alli, we'll explain to them don't worry."

Harvey paid and we rushed to the car. We're heading for the nick.

"Jo contacted me when you were consoling Natalie. She asked if they could bring in the Personnel woman, she's connected to Withers. Her cousin was married to the other hospital worker who's missing. Ricky Banks."

Christ, Jo's like a bloodhound."

We'll be at the nick in ten minutes, Alli.

Thanks Jo. I'll get the kettle on.

Thanks, we're gasping.

"Alli, give this book to Jamie and tell him to get the team on it. I'm going up to see Tommy to give him this." He had Jay's computer in his hand. "He hasn't got much time left today, unfortunately. He knocks off a bit earlier than us."

"Okay, see you soon."

I saw Jamie talking to Craig and waited for him to finish. He turned from him. "What can I do for you, Alli?"

"This is a book we found in Jay's bedroom. It's packed with contact numbers, names and messages. You know what to do with it I'm sure."

"Yes Alli. Listen up everyone. Debbie, would you make a copy of every double page in this book and hand them out. One of the phone numbers could be our killer. Be careful with the calls as Jay was gay and we wouldn't want to upset anyone, but track the lot down." Debbie came over for the book.

"Hi Alli, thanks Jamie." She headed for the copier and started her task.

I put the kettle on and went in to see Gina.

"You've had a rough day Alli, are you alright?" I sat beside her and glanced at the screen.

Before I could speak Harvey burst into the room. "That picture on the gay site Gina, it was registered to Jason Hicks."

"He's a fucking idiot then, using his real name. Do you want me to start talking to him?"

"We haven't much time today, to get into anything heavy."

"I could start it and say my parents have come home from work and speak to him tomorrow. It would wet his appetite."

"Sounds good Gina, go ahead." Harvey turned to me. "Alli, Lisa is making us some tea; would you be okay to interview that Personnel Officer with me."

"I'll be fine Harvey don't worry." The door opened and Lisa came in with a tray.

"Where do you want it, Sir?" Harvey made room on my desk. "I cut some of the birthday cake and saved it for you. There's some for Jo and Andy when they get back, Sir."

"Whose birthday, Lisa?"

"Mine, Sir. My mum made it to bring in."

"Thank you. When Jo gets back could you ask her to come straight in please?"

"Will do, Sir." She hurried out.

"That was thoughtful of her." I put a slice on one of the saucers and took it to Gina.

Jo came in. "Hi, Andy's got her in room two Harvey. She's furious we brought her in. I forgot to say this morning. I rang the University. Hicks hasn't been in since you saw him in Milton Crescent."

"Well done, Jo. Grab some tea and cake, you're coming in to the interview with us. Stand at the back and if you get a hunch about anything let us know."

"She's fucking difficult to read. I think she's psychic," Jo casually said to us.

"This is what you do then, Jo. If you think anything to either of us, push with your mind when you're thinking it, the same as you bury stuff from Hillary. It'll go deeper and we'll still pick it up, she won't." Jo grinned at me. I've realized how she hides things.

"I'll get my tea, whose birthday?"

"Lisa's."

She was only gone a couple of minutes and came back in with a lump of cake and tea. She sat on the empty chair next to Gina and watched her.

We learned nothing new from the interview but Harvey gave her a bollocking for messing us around and told her we'd be keeping an eye on her from now on. She left the nick with her tail between her legs, promising to play ball in future. She doesn't like Banks and was scared to be linked to him.

We pulled up at home and parked behind Lucas's van. He got out with a grin on his face as we scrambled out of our cars.

"Have you been waiting long, Lucas?" Harvey asked as he locked ours.

"Only five minutes or so. What sort of a day have you had?"

"Not great, let's go in. I have to talk to you about something that might interest you." A glint flashed in his eyes and Harvey couldn't wait to tell him. Gina, Jo and I headed for the pool and left them to talk.

I swam for nearly an hour and decided to get out just as Hillary arrived. I gave her a hug and she joined Jo in the pool. Olli wouldn't be back for another hour yet but Gina was quite content talking to him in her mind as she swam.

I was making tea when Gina came in from the pool. "Make one for me Alli please. What sort of costumes did you get for us?"

"Just plain black Gina, nothing flash. I didn't know what to get for Jo."

I'll cut some jeans off Alli and Hillary's got one. We may not even be here on Saturday morning, don't worry about it.

Okay Jo, thanks.

"Have you made one for me Sis?" Lucas nudged me and I started laughing.

"What have I said?" Harvey was giggling behind him.

"I think Harvey must be psychic. He said you'd be like a brother now." He turned to Harvey.

"I think that's amazing I'd never have guessed."

"Three witty buggers in one house. I'm moving out."

"Watch it Mr Burgess. I'll get the cane out and flog you."

"For dessert please Mrs Burgess. Bring on the dinner." I giggled and handed them a mug of tea each.

"What's been decided and don't keep me in suspense. You've buried it and I can't read either of you. I won't flog you," I pretended to be indignant.

"Christ, that won't do Alli." Harvey's face was so serious. I put my hand on my hip and he knew I was dying to know. I looked at Lucas, his face was dead pan.

"You're in cahoots you buggers." The sniggering started.

"Sorry Alli, we're only having a bit of fun. Lucas is in!"

"Whoopee!!!" Tea slopped out of my mug. "Oh shit." I got a cloth and wiped it up

"I haven't got a brother. I like the idea Lucas. Welcome to the family." I hugged him.

"Put him down you don't know where he's been." Jed came into the kitchen with Abbey in tow.

Olli was behind him smiling at Gina. Out of his mouth came, "I found these two buggers on the doorstep. Do you know them, at all?" Jed elbowed him and giggled.

Abbey stood in front of Jed. "Alli, we've brought you some flowers as a thank you."

I gave her a hug. "You didn't have to do that but they're

beautiful. Thank you so much. I'll put them in water." I laid them on the draining board and let the heads hang over the sink so they wouldn't get crushed.

I hugged Jed next. "Alli, thank you isn't adequate for the way I feel after you mended my other half. He's on top of the world and I don't mean Everest."

"I hope he never goes up there again. You don't know the latest, tell him Lucas." Jed stared at him.

"I'm working with this lot Jed. I can't really fucking believe it."

Jed gave him a hug. "How did that happen?"

Lucas looked at Harvey. "You tell him."

"I mentioned to Ron, our Commissioner we knew of another Hybrid who was as strong as us. Lucas was surprised when I told him. We watched him swim as fast as I can and we swam together this morning trying to catch Alli. That was a waste of time." Harvey grinned at me. "Ron was surprised Alli had turned someone else. She explained everything to him and gave him an ultimatum."

"What was that Harvey?" He then looked at me.

"Alli told him if he thought we'd done something so terrible we'd all resign right now. It was up to him."

"Bloody hell, that was a bit dodgy wasn't it."

"Not really Jed. I read his mind before I said it. He's got a soft spot for something as emotional as that. He told Hillary last week, if he was young again with his late wife he'd have asked me to turn them both."

"That's exactly what he told me Alli." Hillary came through the pool room door. "Hello Jed, Abbey." She hugged them both. "Jo will be out in a minute."

I arranged the flowers and carried them into the front room. Harvey was there with a small table to the side of my piano.

"Thanks Harvey, he looks pleased about the job."

"It's right up his street. He was always been a bit of an adventurer. He knew I would offer him the job, and has picked things up from us all day. That's why he had a grin on his face when we pulled up."

"I like the sound of that." Harvey's phone rang in his pocket. His face dropped.

"Fucking typical. Yes!" he blasted into it. "Sorry Ron. We're just having a get together." He listened for a moment. "He loved the idea and couldn't wait to get started." He listened again, "Perfect. We'll bring him in tomorrow, sorry, what was that." Moments passed as he listened. "We will thanks Ron, see you in the morning.

"He's chuffed to bits Alli." Harvey's eyes sparkled and picked me up. "Christ, I'm surprised he's not bloody deaf after me answering the phone like that."

I giggled at him. "He probably holds the phone twenty feet from his head. He knows what we're like." Harvey kissed me long and hard. I didn't want it to stop. *Christ, I missed this last night Alli.*

Me, too, Mr Burgess but I don't regret what we did instead.

Me neither Alli.

We pulled apart and rested our heads together, lost for a while as our minds mingled. "You should take Lucas down to the cellar. Let him choose something he'd like from our special toy box Harvey." He chuckled.

"We'd have to check if he feels pain before I do that. We wouldn't want him in bloody agony. He won't thank me at all if we let him play with anything that hurt him."

"They're all in the pool and I'd like to give your mysterious bits something special Harvey."

The spark in Harvey's eyes ignited and flashed longer than usual.

"Hmmmmm, that sounds like fun Mrs Burgess."

"Close my piano lid, strip and lie across the top. Keep your eyes closed, I won't be a moment."

I did the speed thing and put on the fine black rubber one piece, along with a 'Red Basque' and shoes he loves. Thought myself to the cellar next and collected a few things and was back beside my piano moments after I left.

"I want your bum on the edge and your bits facing me."

This sounds interesting Mrs Burgess. I'm getting horny just wondering what you're about to do.

You're going to love this Mr Burgess.

Harvey's bum moved towards me.

"Just right. They look good enough to eat now." Harvey

thought of me eating him in the nicest possible way.

"Don't let your imagination run away with you this is something totally different Mr Burgess. Just be patient, please."

I locked manacles on to his ankles and left them. I took his special handcuffs, he couldn't break out of, and locked them on his wrists pulling his arms above his head to dangle over the back edge of the piano. I let him feel what I was wearing for a few moments to get him right in the mood.

The other end of the bungee I fixed into another manacle around the bottom of the piano leg, next to the closed curtains, and pulled it tight.

"Lift your head Harvey, please." He knew what's coming; a smile touched his lips. I slipped the hood over his head and locked the padlock.

His right leg manacle I fixed to another bungee and locked that to the leg at the opposite end of the keyboard.

His left leg was pulled sideways a little for the Bungee to be locked into a manacle on the single leg under the narrow end of my piano.

I left him a few minutes to put the rubber gloves on he loves. When I put my hands on his thighs, ripples ran up his body and down his legs away from my hands. I watched his chest rise and fall faster now as the thrill built for him. His mind was going nuts at that point as he waited for the main event.

I lubricated my right middle finger and played around his bum with it. I held his black balls tight in my left hand. A gasp escaped his mouth when I pushed it inside a little, playing around his ring.

Further Mrs Burgess, further. I obliged him for a second with more of my finger. *Much more please.*

I kept my palm facing the ceiling and rubbed against the base of his cock inside behind his balls. I'd never heard him moan and sigh so loud as I gently played with his prostrate. The male 'G spot'.

I sent him to heaven and know he had stopped himself from coming. I played away from it for a while until he begged for me to carry on.

When I touched it again, the thunderbolt hit his brain and he blacked out for a few seconds. My mouth covered his cock.

He came to, in no time.

That was bloody mind blowing. Do it again, please.

I left him for a second, and thought myself down to the cellar for another delight for him.

Hold on Mr Burgess I have another little extra for you to enjoy; breathe in darling.

His chest rose as he took a deep breath and held it. I slid a ring down his cock and the cage, split for the moment, and ready to encase his balls was so perfect for him. He could see it in my mind. *Lock it tight.*

I held each half in both hands and pushed them together. The clicks of two locks engaging could be heard by me.

The volume of noise that pushed out of his mind turned everyone on and they fucked like crazy in the pool.

Lucas rushed for the shower. *Oh fuck. Sorry for doing that to you Lucas. I couldn't help the moment.*

Don't worry about it, fill your boots. Harvey giggled in our heads.

Carry on Mrs Burgess, you know that was perfect for me.

The cage over his balls had dozens of spikes on the inside.

Mr Burgess, they look mysterious now. He laughed at me. *Play with me again. I had no idea I'd get switched on as high as a fucking skyscraper.*

I started and took longer this time until he begged me to push him over the edge again but I held off a little bit longer. My own mind had me on the journey with him and my fanny was wet, and wanted him and he knew.

Mrs Burgess, finish it please. I know you want me to fuck you as much as I want to?

How could I resist that plea? I sent him over the top and my mouth covered his cock when he came. I ran my hands all over him when he came round.

Unlock me Mrs Burgess, I want to ravish you now. I did the speed thing; freed his wrists and ankles, then took off the hood and waited between his legs for him to sit up.

He held my head between his hands and kissed me so tenderly. "Thank you Alli, that was just beautiful and I didn't know you had this?" He put his hand over the cage, rolled it around with his eyes closed and moaned.

"I'm leaving it on when I make love to you Alli, come with me."

He walked us upstairs to his bathroom. "Take your Basque and shoes off please." I undid the Basque and was slipping out of my shoes when I heard the jets in the Jacuzzi start up. Harvey's hands circled my waist, he picked me up and stepped down into the water.

When he took me under, the rubber suit enhanced the feelings so much, I came instantly. Harvey held me tight and covered me with kisses. He turned me over facing away from him and pushed his cock up my bum, opened his legs and let the jets play on my fanny and bump. His hands never stopped moving over the rubber that turned us both on.

His tongue ball played up and down the back of my neck until I was delirious and screamed for him to fuck me. His hands circled my waist again and he lifted me above his face. His tongue touched my bump, the thunderbolt hit my brain and I passed out.

When I opened my eyes Harvey was grinning.

"What's tickled you, Mr Burgess?"

"We've got guests, Mrs Burgess and we ought to go down I think?"

I giggled. "I'm fine with that and you can carry on later."

"Music to my ears, Mrs Burgess." He lifted me out of the water and reached for some towels.

When we walked into the sitting room a cheer rang out from everyone and we giggled at them.

"Couldn't help it, I'm afraid. I had to give him his present."

"Well, we all fucking enjoyed it and just followed them." Jed grinned at our lot. "What the hell was it that got them so randy?"

"My mind set them off Jed. My present sent me fucking crazy for a while."

Silence descended for only a moment.

"Show us Harvey. I know you still have it on," Jo said with a grin.

"We have guests Jo. I couldn't really."

Jo looked at Jed and a glint flashed in his eyes. "You're not getting out of it that way Harvey, we don't give a shit."

"Well you asked." Harvey dropped his tracksuit bottoms and

Jed gasped. Lucas laughed at Jed.

"I told you, your eyes are watering Jed." Harvey burst out laughing.

Abbey was giggling and nudged Jed. "Could I get you one of those?"

"Over my dead body Abbey." Harvey pulled them back up and giggled at Jed.

"You don't know the fucking half of it," Jo told him. "That's fuck all."

"Hillary, could you check if Lucas feels pain. He gets to go to our toy box tonight, if he doesn't." Lucas smiled at Harvey.

"Lie on the floor Lucas," Hillary asked. He was there before we saw him move.

"How the fuck did you do that Lucas!" Jed was astounded.

"Fringe benefits," Lucas told him.

A huge smile broke out on Harvey's face, then mine and Jo's.

"It comes in bloody handy at times Jed. Harvey's moved bodies for me before I've blinked," Hillary said as she knelt beside Lucas. "I'm going to push a knuckle into your sternum. If you don't feel this you'd be able to play with any of Harvey's toys."

"That sounds good to me Hillary, cross your bloody fingers you lot."

She really pushed hard and Lucas never moved. "You're fine Lucas, fill your boots." Hillary laughed at him.

"Thanks Hillary, you've made my bloody day."

"Have you lot eaten?" He looked at a sea of blank faces.

"We've been shagging. We couldn't think of everything and it was your fault, remember," Jo said with a giggle.

"I suppose it was." He grinned at Jo. "It was Fucking de Lux."

He ordered and sat with me on his lap. The banter carried on.

"Doesn't that hurt at all, it looks like torture Harvey. I know you don't feel pain. I just can't seem to get my head around it." Jed was really mystified.

Harvey smiled at him. "Unless you're like us I don't think you'd ever understand it Jed. Jo's right, some of the things I've got are a lot worse than this."

"They weren't up in your toy room," Jed stated.

"A few things are in Alli's dressing room but most of it is in the cellar. We lock everything away as we have a daily cleaner so we're very careful. We'll show you and Lucas if you want while we wait to eat."

"Go on then Harvey. I'm fucking interested now." Jed stood up with us.

Harvey held his hand out for me, "Your bedroom first Alli."

They followed us upstairs and into my bedroom. I sat on my bed and Harvey showed them the screws and rods.

Jed just stared but Lucas's mind was going nuts with delight.

"It took Alli hours to get me to the size I could accept the big screw. Not because of any pain, it's physically impossible to get something that size in without using all those on me first. Believe me, I really loved it."

"So would I," slipped out of Lucas's mouth. "Sorry, I shouldn't have said that."

Harvey patted his shoulder. "It's alright Lucas, we say what we think and can't lie except for protecting what we are or not hurting anyone's feelings. Let's go to the cellar."

Harvey used the combination to unlock the special room down there and switched on the lights.

"Fucking hell," Jed whispered as he walked in behind Harvey. He turned to Lucas to see what he thought. His smile nearly split his face. We could feel the thrill coming off him in waves. Even though Lucas wasn't human anymore, they were twins and their minds were still linked.

"I'm happy for you Lucas, I mean that." Jed was really sincere.

"I know Jed I can read your mind the same as them now and feel your emotions like never before. This is a different world for me now but the bond we have will always be the same, don't ever think it wouldn't."

He hugged Jed. "I know Lucas I still feel it." They broke apart.

"Are you going to show me what some of these things do then?" Jed asked Harvey.

He picked up the iron maiden and opened it. "That makes my eyes water thinking about it." Harvey giggled, put it back on the bench and opened a few other things. Jed noticed the cage with the ball on a chain.

"I don't want to know what that is, my balls are starting to shrivel." He looked along the walls, covered in rows of hoods, chains, heavy belts, bars with manacles on each end, bars with leather buckles, different frames, all the dildos we use, anal hooks, butt plugs and an array of things to cover Harvey's cock and stopped in front of some new stuff we'd just bought.

"What's all this?"

"We haven't tried any of that yet Jed, we're waiting for our heads to be in the moment for those. Its electro stimulation, I think Alli will love it. It gives you the feeling of being fucked without even moving and she'd be strapped into that when I use it on her." Harvey pointed to the strange looking chair/bed that restricted you from moving. Straps were everywhere on the arm and leg supports. In front, between the leg supports were steel rods to clamp the different items on the wall, onto.

"There are a few things I could use on Harvey, too. I don't get all the fun."

"Alli," Jed giggled. "I can honestly say you lucky buggers, the human race haven't bloody lived."

"When I was first with Harvey and up until recently this place was bugged. What they bloody thought we've no idea and didn't care. It wouldn't stop us having a good time. Now you know why Ron said that to Hillary. He must have listened to all the tapes."

"I hear a car door Alli, we'll have to go up, the food is here." Harvey pulled a couple of bottles of wine when we passed it and I got all the plates and things out when Harvey paid for dinner.

I opened the dining room door, lit the candles down the table and laid out all the cutlery. I put glasses out next and Harvey came in to see if I needed a hand.

"I think we'll eat in here as there are loads of us. Could you put all the cartons on the side table with serving spoons please, Harvey." He smiled and just did it, opened the wine and brought that in, too. I put out cruets and napkins for everyone.

"Call them in Alli, it looks lovely." I poked my head into the sitting room.

"We're eating in the dining room tonight, it's ready."

Chapter 14

“Gina said you had some news Olli?” Harvey asked, when we relaxed after dinner.

“I certainly do, Harvey and I know why I was attacked and bitten.” Harvey sat up and waited for more. “I was in the cafe in the hospital and one of the security guards was in front of me in the queue. When he turned to leave he said, ‘Hello Ricky, where the bloody hell have you been, we were worried’.”

“What did you say Olli?”

“Who the hell is Ricky? My name’s Olli and I’ve only lived here a couple of months. He said that’s genius you’re the spit of him. I said, they say everyone’s got a double somewhere. He was really chatty after that and told me I should come to his office if I wanted to sneak a break at any time. I took him up on it, later on this morning and he never shut up. He told me about loads of scams going on with drugs and some of the Funeral Directors.”

“Fuck, Olli! You’ve dropped into a gold mine. Did he give you any details on the Funeral Directors?”

“I didn’t push it too much until I spoke to you as it was my first day. I’ll be able to milk him for information, he wouldn’t know how to be discrete.”

“Find out what you can but be casual about it Olli. I’d rather we waited a bit longer than he twigs why you’re asking too many questions.”

“Right Harvey. He also has cameras that cover the entire hospital and he can switch them anywhere. He looked at the morgue a lot, I think it fascinates him. I might run with him on that. He’s such a blabbermouth he wouldn’t be able to help himself.”

“Perfect Olli. I’ll tell Ron tomorrow when we take Lucas up to see him. We could have two Hybrids to deal with. Whoever bit you Olli, thinking it was him, would be a bit confused he wasn’t a Hybrid; that’s if he’s still around. I don’t like that much but at least we know what we’re dealing with.”

Harvey gave me a cuddle. “Come on Alli, play for me please.

I may give you a go in the hot seat tonight. I'm in the mood now."

I did the speed thing to my piano stool. Harvey laughed. "Could you lift the lid please as you've christened the top now?" He came over, kissed me, lifted the lid and picked up the manacles and hood.

"Christ, is that where she played with you." Jo was giggling

Harvey laughed, "We've both christened it now, the height is just perfect."

I played for about an hour, moving from one piece of music to another without stopping. Harvey stood behind me through it all, and kissed my neck when I finished.

"I'll make some coffee, get comfortable on the sofa, Alli. That was beautiful, thank you."

Anything for you; you know that.

I stood up and the clapping began. I pretended to curtsey and nearly fell off my shoes. "Whoops. I forgot I had feet."

"You could play in a concert Alli, do you know that," Hillary said with a smile.

"This is enough, for me Hillary. I just like playing for us." I looked up and smiled at Harvey, he was carrying a huge tray filled with cups, coffee, cream and sugar.

I moved some magazines to make room for him on the coffee table. "Thanks Alli."

"I'll pour it Harvey, you sit with Alli," Gina volunteered.

After Jed and Abbey said goodnight and left, Hillary went home with Jo. We told Gina and Olli to use the shower and bedroom behind the pool. Lucas was using the Jacuzzi and my bedroom afterwards. Harvey would be in the cellar for a while with me and we'd use his bedroom, later. We took Lucas down and let him choose what he wanted.

He armed himself with a few things and left us with a smile on his face. *Thank you.*

Fill your boots Lucas, have fun.

I'm sure I will.

We went to feed in my shower and hurried down to the cellar again.

Harvey took hold of my hand and helped me to sit on the weird chair. He let me watch everything he was attaching to me.

He strapped my wrists and ankles on to the supports and then my thighs and upper arms. He picked up a tiny bottle of oil from the floor and everything he put on me had some oil smeared on it. He clipped electrodes to my nipple rings and inserted something up my bum. A steel object was pushed into my fanny and clamped on to one of the rods coming up from the floor.

A small arm on the steel object was lined up to touch my bump and Harvey clipped another electrode to the ring through it, too. The anticipation of what was to come built in my mind at such a rate, I was going crazy before anything had happened.

He buckled a strap around my waist and I couldn't lift my body at all and, last but not least, a hood was pushed over my head. I changed and needed him so bad.

I don't know where he was now and the minutes ticked by. I screamed for him to start. I was so horny and my mind was about to explode.

My nipples felt a steady throb and shocks ran to my fanny making sure I clamped down on to the steel object and begged him for more.

Turn it all on, please. Pulsing ran in to my fanny as if I was being fucked and between each pulse, buzzing touched my bump. I babbled like someone crazy and felt Harvey was turned on with me. He changed things a little.

I don't want you to come too quickly, Mrs Burgess. I see you love this and I want to give you as much pleasure as you gave me tonight.

Perfect, Mr Burgess, carry on.

The inside of my right leg felt fluttering and the feeling got stronger as it got near my fanny. A heavy pulse pushed up my fanny, sparking off all the balls. It started again on my left leg, this time.

Harvey did this over and over and turned up the strength on my nipple rings. Shocks fired unending to my fanny. If someone told me this wasn't Harvey shagging me, I'd have called them a liar as it felt so real. Whoever made that contraption knew his way around a body, that's for sure.

Please don't stop this Mr Burgess. Push me so I pass out and start again.

Anything you ask for, Mrs Burgess, my pleasure.

Harvey took me over the top, again and again until he knew

I'd come three times.

I woke up in his bed and he was stroking my face when I opened my eyes. "That was amazing Harvey, your turn tomorrow."

"I'm already having my turn and if you sit on me you'd have more," I giggled and straddled him. When I sat on his cock the shocks he had running up it ran up me, too. I closed my eyes and soaked it up.

"You like, Mrs Burgess?"

"And some, Mr Burgess." Harvey giggled and I bobbed up and down. "Oh, that was nice."

We played for hours, changing position a few times. We loved it all and finally settled down for me to sleep around four in the morning.

"Goodnight my precious wife, have a lovely sleep. You've earned it with knobs on, tonight." I giggled and kissed him.

Lucas was swimming when we got downstairs and Olli was just about to dive in when we walked into the pool room.

"I'm only going in for ten minutes."

"It's early, Olli. We'll call when it's time to get out." He did a mock salute and dived in. When Lucas turned at this end Olli joined him swimming down the pool. At first he couldn't keep up but as the lengths clocked up he kept pace with him. I looked at Harvey who'd been watching constantly, satisfaction filling his face. He glanced at me, and knew I thought the same.

"I thought he was late for work. What's he doing in there?" Gina looked pissed off.

"He hasn't got to leave for another twenty minutes Gina. The clock in that bedroom is an hour fast. I didn't change it when the clocks changed. Watch him Gina. Do you notice what he's doing?"

"Of course I know what he's doing. I've been telling him for two weeks he was getting stronger, he wouldn't have it."

"A bit of healthy rivalry has made him show us Gina."

She grinned as she watched. "Good. Perhaps I won't have to nag him anymore. I've noticed more when we haven't been changed."

"It's a perfect time for you to get it Gina. I'll call him out now." Harvey spoke in their heads when they swam towards us.

They sat with us in towels, drinking tea. Olli went up to get ready for work, with Gina.

"Olli's speed is another thing to tell Ron today, Harvey," Lucas stated.

"Jo knew she was getting stronger and didn't say anything. I think if they don't have it immediately, like you then they feel embarrassed about it. What happened with me doesn't count. Me and Alli were bitten around the age of four. Jo was bitten in childhood but she wasn't given enough venom to turn her fully. Alli healed her finger which topped her up. She drank blood and never slept but didn't show any other, characteristics. Alli pushed words into her mind one day, before that which kick-started the telepathy thing. She's been stuck at twenty-three for the last ten years. We're all different Lucas, like the human race."

Lucas came to work with us. A few of the team looked up as we walked through their office. They were all tracking down people from Jay's diary and knew how important that was. I stopped at Debbie's desk.

"Here's two hundred to put in the kitty, Debbie." She looked up and beamed at me.

"Thanks Alli, to you and Sir. There's already a couple of hundred in the safe at the pub; guilt works wonders when it's applied properly." I laughed at her and headed for our office.

Gina and I got on our computers as soon as we could. Harvey talked with Lucas at his desk. The door knocked and Andy came in.

"Morning, Sir. The Carlton rang this morning. They're getting hounded by reporters." He honed in on Lucas and stared for a moment.

"Fuck. Sorry Andy. Get the phone book out and put them into a good hotel, way out of town. When you go to move them take a couple of squad cars with you. Is Jamie in, I didn't see him?"

"Not yet, Sir. He's had toothache all night, and said he wouldn't be long. He's got an emergency appointment, first thing. The Commissioner rang, he's picking up new glasses and won't be in until ten."

"Right Andy. Have any of the team checking the Funeral Director's employees come up with anything yet?"

"A few of them have got form, petty theft mainly. I'm keeping an eye on it, Sir."

"Your first priority, moving them from the Carlton. ASAP Andy."

"Okay, Sir; I'm on it." He left in a hurry.

"Looks like we're on hold Lucas, until Ron gets here. I've got phone calls to make, take a look at the sites Gina and Alli are on."

Lucas pulled up a chair next to Gina and watched her for a few minutes.

"Do you mind if I say something Gina?"

"No, go ahead." She turned to look at him.

"This is a gay site Gina. Don't take this the wrong way but gay lads are more upfront and talk about sex a lot. This guy may get the wrong idea if you're not talking to him in that vein."

"Bloody hell, Lucas. I had no idea. Take a look at all my questions and answers please. If I've cocked this up he's going to twig what we're doing."

"Let me sit there for a minute Gina." They swapped seats. "I'll take a look don't worry." He scanned everything at an amazing speed. Even Gina couldn't keep up with him.

"Fucking hell, Lucas. I thought I read fast!" He laughed and carried on.

"What you've done so far is okay but spice it up, you want him drooling for you. Get him really interested, he'll make mistakes and say too much."

"Okay. I'll pretend I'm talking to Olli, we talk dirty quite a lot." Gina giggled, Lucas got up and came over to me.

"Who are you talking to Sis?"

"A supposed doctor on a gender reassignment site. This guy's described the exact op he performed on Jay Henderson."

"So this is who you're looking for."

"The very same. He keeps asking to meet me and offering to do the op before he goes on holiday, saying it was first come, first served and I'd have a very long wait if I didn't have it done now. He's a pushy bastard; I've told him I'm thinking about it.

"Tommy's trying to track the site but this guy's got someone helping him. He's bounced seven servers, so far and the next one's in the states."

"He must have money or knows a good hacker. I spent a lot

of time in my bedroom after I left school, before I got into climbing. Most of it on the gay chat lines, wishful thinking on my part, but I enjoyed winding them up. Some of it was spent looking at people's bank accounts and credit ratings. I couldn't claim to be a hacker but I learned a few tricks from mates I knew. Could I have a go?"

I looked at Harvey and he'd finished a call. *Come here please, love.*

He got up and came over to my desk.

"Did you catch any of our talk Harvey?" He looked puzzled.

"Harvey could I try tracing this site for Alli. I've been telling her about time spent in my bedroom amusing myself, hacking people's bank accounts."

"Go ahead but Tommy can't do it."

I gave my seat to Lucas and watched him. He sat down and started typing so fast, he really knew his way around a computer. Harvey's face lit up and smiled at me.

Lucas spent the first half-hour getting to where Tommy stopped the other day and then carried on. The symbols and letters that launched on the screen were all gobbledegook to us but Lucas was in his element.

Every time he got over an obstacle, his face was beaming and typed another address with a strange looking mixture of letters, numbers and symbols.

Rows and rows of numbers started feeding from the bottom of the screen flowing up to the top.

Another server's name popped up. He typed another address and nothing happened.

"Shit. This is an anagram of the address, give me a minute." He typed the address in a hundred combinations until he was given access.

"That was worrying, I thought I wasn't going to get that." He got straight back to it.

The door opened and Ron came in, Harvey went over and told him what Lucas was doing. Ron came over and stood beside Lucas, just watching. A smile touched the corners of his mouth. He was gobsmacked at the speed he worked and how much he knew about the internet.

Suddenly a UK server's address popped up on the screen.

"This is the server for your site Sis. If I go into it to get the address you want and you're not ready to act, they'll get a tip off and move." I looked at Ron and Lucas followed my gaze.

"Hello Lucas, I'm Ron your Commissioner. I'm bloody impressed." Lucas grinned at him.

He put his hand out to Ron. "I'm pleased to meet you Commissioner."

Ron shook his hand. "I think we should take this to my office. I want you all up there Harvey."

"Okay Ron; come on girls, grab Jo."

Gina went for Jo and we were just about to go upstairs when Andy came in and walked up to Harvey, to tell him which hotel he'd put them in. I noticed the smile he gave Lucas and the light that flashed in Lucas's eyes.

You can't go there Lucas, he's human.

I know Sis, no harm in looking. At least I can put a face to my fantasy.

How did you know he's gay?

You have to ask yourself, how did he know I am. It's called 'Gaydar'.

Harvey had missed it completely and was surprised by our thoughts. He smiled at me as we walked up the stairs.

Gina and Jo followed us up. *That was interesting,* giggling at Lucas.

Ron made tea for us and sat behind his desk.

"How near are we, Harvey?"

"Not near enough, yet. If a Hybrid is involved, none of the team could help with this Ron. It's too dangerous. Olli is in with one of the security guards, at the hospital. This guy looks at the cameras in the morgue a lot and Olli will pretend he's interested, too. Apparently some of the Funeral Director's workers, who collect bodies are on some sort of scam. He'll find out what, very soon. Have you spoken to anyone at the Home Office, yet?"

"I don't want them involved until the last minute. If I contact them now, they'll swamp this place and take over."

"We don't fucking want that, Ron. Olli is getting really strong and we'll have four of us, to go in first." Ron looked at Jo.

"Are you alright with that Jo?"

"I was going to say, I might be a woman but that's fucking

questionable." She laughed at herself. "I'm as strong as any of these buggers Ron, don't worry about me." Ron grinned at her.

He turned to Lucas. "I'm pleased you've got stuck in straight away Lucas. Has Harvey told you everything about the job?"

"Yes, Sir."

Ron smiled at him. "You call me Ron, unless any of the team are near. I think of all of you all as family and look after you accordingly. You'll be on Inspector pay for the first year and then you'll be promoted to Inspector properly. By that time the team will have changed so you wouldn't look like you've never aged."

"Thank you Ron. I'm going to love this job."

"I like the sound of that Lucas. Harvey will give you jobs to do, as he's good at leading everything. Now Alli, have you forgotten something this week?" I must have looked blank. Ron smiled and pulled his drawer open. He took out a small box and handed it to me.

I glanced at Harvey. "Open it Alli." Inside were four silver buttons, that's what I thought.

"Congratulations Alli. You are now a full Inspector. You'll have to be measured for a uniform but don't look so worried, you'd probably never have to wear it."

He didn't shake my hand, he hugged me. "Well done Alli. You've made a real difference since you've been here. I'm very proud of you."

"Thank you Ron. You know I've enjoyed every minute of it. I still don't want to be called Ma'am, Ron."

He let me go. "Alli it is." The others clapped, I glared at them but they didn't stop, the buggers.

On the way down the stairs, "Harvey, Olli needs to speak to you. He asked if you could meet him on his break." Gina looked very concerned.

"Find out what time and where, Gina. We can leave as soon as he likes."

By the time we got to the bottom. "Half an hour, the cafe near the hospital gates. He'll be in the alley, down the side of it, Harvey."

"Thanks Gina. I'm leaving you here to continue on the site you're on. Jo's staying, in case you need help with anything. Alli, Lucas, come with me."

We grabbed things from the office, jackets, my bag and hurried out to Harvey's car.

"They're not buttons Alli. They're called, 'Order of the Bath Stars' to go on the epaulettes on your uniform. They're known as 'pips' and the same insignia as a lieutenant in the British Army."

"Bloody hell!" Harvey laughed at me.

It took about twenty minutes to get to the car park near the cafe, another five to find a parking slot. The overspill from the hospital car park, filled it every day because of prices charged for parking in the hospital grounds. It wasn't enough, a member of your family might be dying or need daily treatment that lasts for months, you're penalised for that as well.

We raced across the car park. No one would think it strange as visitors seeking deadlines for visiting hours or patients for treatment, having been held up looking for somewhere to park.

We turned down the alley next to the cafe. Olli was waiting for us, sitting on a stack of pallets.

"Hi Olli. What's so urgent?"

"Hi Harvey, Alli, Lucas. That bloody security guard takes backhanders from the Funeral Directors, Haddon and Wyatt, Lonsdale road, to keep his mouth shut. He lets them take certain parts of bodies, even if they're not picking them up."

"Fuck Olli. Did he just tell you this?"

"I told you he was a blabbermouth, he couldn't help it. As soon as I showed an interest in the morgue, like him, he just came out with it. He also said there's a job going there. He'd have gone for it but he earned more from them where he is so it wouldn't be any good for him."

Harvey looked at me. "You wouldn't know the name Alli. Remember the creep who came to the house, when we were organising Adey's funeral."

"I do Harvey. Since it all came out how I was feeding I think I must have fed off him. I couldn't be seen by them or you Harvey, until the last minute."

"I know Alli. I think this is a job for you Lucas. You're the right height for a pall bearer."

"Sounds perfect Harvey. Is the job on the boards at the Jobcentre Olli; or do you have to be told about it?"

"I really don't know about that, Lucas. You could always

look, if it's not on the board, ask one of the workers to phone them. Say you've got wind of a job there and you've worked in that industry before. They'll phone them, it's better than just turning up."

"He's right Lucas, it could have been mentioned in gossip. You know how people talk and they'd only be suspicious of their workers, letting it out of the bag."

"Drop me off in town. I'll go in and start the ball rolling."

"I'll get back. I'm supposed to be meeting gobshite in the coffee bar just inside the entrance of the hospital."

"Thanks Olli. This might be the break we're looking for. See you later at home." We left him in the alley and headed for the car.

Before Harvey started the engine, "Lucas, if you get a job there and a Hybrid is working with them, you'd have to have a bloody good story or you'd be in big trouble."

Lucas; thought for a minute. "Harvey, I'll stick to the fact I'm a mountaineer. I can talk about it without thinking and as regards why I'm a Hybrid, that's easy. All I have to say is I had serious frostbite and one of the attendants in the hospital I was flown to bit me. I'd have lost limbs if he hadn't. I could also say, I'm shocked I'm like this now and thought I was the only one."

"That's perfect Lucas. Are you able to send us any conversation you have with any of the staff there. I mean open your mind so we could hear it all."

"Yes. That's not a problem Harvey, I'll send it to Sis. I know you type really fast Sis, quicker than Gina and you could get it all down."

"You're right about that Lucas, she's brilliant. It's up to you Alli, would you get pissed off, typing hour after hour."

"I don't mind at all, I know it's got to be done. If I need a pit stop or have to eat, Gina could take over, she types nearly as fast as me, we can let Lucas know. We'd have to think much deeper so another Hybrid wouldn't pick it up. We'll practice it tonight Lucas."

"As it's Friday Lucas, we could drop you at the Jobcentre and wait outside. Make an appointment for Monday morning, for an interview. You'll have all weekend to practice it with Alli and Gina? When you come out we'll get you a second hand car so you don't look conspicuous."

"Sounds good to me, Harvey." Harvey started the car and drove us into town.

Lucas came out with a smile on his face and jumped in the back.

"That's sorted. They rang through and there is a job. I have to be there at ten on Monday and if I'm what they're looking for, they'll start me straight away."

"Good. What sort of car do you want Lucas," Harvey waited for an answer, so he knew which garage to go to.

"Something like Olli's, they're more reliable Harvey." He started the car and we ended up where Olli's car came from. I went in with them this time.

They walked along the rows of cars, I tagged along not knowing anything about them at all. Lucas opened one of the doors and sat behind the wheel. The keys were inside and he started the engine.

A sales rep shot over to us, thinking he had a sale and commission in his pocket.

"You've made an excellent choice, Sir. You'll have no trouble with this she's a beauty."

"That's a lie and you know it! The head gasket is about to blow and you want it out of here." The bloke's head shot around to me.

"What are you talking about?" He was really condescending.

"You probably think I know nothing about cars and you'd be right. What I do is read minds and that flashed into yours as soon as you saw him in it."

Lucas got out and slammed the door. "Cut the bullshit and show us something decent please, Sir!" The bloke turned bright red and took us to a row the other side of the lot. Harvey put his arm over my shoulder and giggled in my mind. I looked up to his face and smiled.

Lucas picked an S 60 the same as Olli, but a year older. I liked the colour, red being one of our favourites.

We went into the office. "Get it ready on the forecourt for five tonight. I'll get the insurance sorted and pay in cash; is there a discount?" The bloke went in to another office and talked to someone else. He came out and offered five hundred off.

"That's fine, have it ready please. We'll see you later." Harvey was blunt with him but I don't blame him at all.

Our next stop was a bank; I stayed in the car with Lucas. Harvey was only a few minutes and got in to drive us back to work.

Back at the nick we went up to see Ron. Harvey told him he'd bought Lucas a car he could use until was on the books here and gets a new one. Lucas was surprised. "I'll tell you when we go down Lucas, we're keeping your name out of the equation with the Home Office."

"Fair enough." Harvey explained to Ron everything Olli had found out and about Lucas's new job prospect with the Funeral Directors. He was pleased how things had progressed and we left him in high spirits.

I sat on the computer with Gina while Harvey talked things over with Lucas.

"Lucas, Ron doesn't want your name on the payroll until all this is over. If the Home Office know too early we have a Hybrid to catch they'll come here and take over the whole thing and possibly take Olli and Gina back with them. As it is, she'd have to stay right away from us when the shit hits the fan. They made Gina a Hybrid in an experiment and want her back."

"Fucking hell; the devious bastards!"

"Ron's livid about it, the same as us. He's paying you with my pay as I don't need it. Once this is over you'll be on the books and they wouldn't have any say in the matter. He wants to keep you a secret from them.

"They don't know how strong we are either or about the mind talking. Gina and Alli's minds, are linked, she could be a long distance from here and still help us. She also knows something is going to happen a short while before it does, we'd get a bit of warning. She told us you would ask Alli to turn you, half an hour before you asked.

"Alli's brain is as good as Gina's. She sat in an interview with me once. She pushed the guy's thoughts to me, read his mind and sent me messages she'd pulled from his brain. All through that she wrote the whole lot down in shorthand. Our thoughts and what was said, the whole lot. When the Home Office took her on it was because her brain power shocked them rigid.

"The pair of them will be unstoppable, when Gina's brain really kicks in and Alli will get it all as well."

"Jesus Harvey. I had no idea. They're both so 'happy go lucky, you'd never think it."

"The Home Office have no idea how good they are now and we don't want them to find out. I'd kill the lot of them if they tried to take Alli from me."

"You wouldn't be on your own Harvey, I'd help you."

Harvey slapped him on the shoulder. "Thank you, Lucas," and stood up. "Come on, let's get some lunch ladies, you look starving to me." We both looked up and giggled.

"Come and see our fabulous canteen Lucas, the food is memorable." Harvey laughed at me and before we left the office, "I'm not sure I should tell anyone you're working here. Lucas. I'll just say you're here on a time and motion quest if anyone asks.

"People talk and we don't want it getting back to the Home Office. I'm not saying anyone here would say anything deliberately but you never know, tongues wag in pubs."

"Understood Harvey, I'm right with you." Lucas followed us up to the canteen.

When we sat down with our food he sat with his back to everyone. I noticed Andy looking over.

I sat here on purpose Alli. I don't want to lead him on. It wouldn't be fair, to him. I'm not going to be here much so he'll forget me pretty quickly. Gay lads are like that. Some of them fuck anything that moves. Giggles went around the table, between eating. Lucas had shot up in Harvey's estimation, I could feel it.

"Are you going to be swimming with us and the kids tomorrow, Jo?" Lucas asked her.

"I think so Lucas." She looked at Harvey. "Tell me if you mind me wearing a T-tea shirt and cut-off jeans, Harvey?"

"Why would I mind that, Jo?"

She grinned at him. "Some pools won't let you in unless you're in regulation costumes and I wouldn't be seen dead in one." Harvey burst out laughing and we all joined in. Heads turned to see why we were laughing and soon lost interest.

Harvey tried to answer her but couldn't for a minute.

"Have you any idea how daft that was Jo?"

She giggled at him. "Yes. Now you come to mention it. I've

not had to pay once." That set us off again.

I got up to get the tea. "Do you all want some?" They all put their hands up.

"If Andy's gone I'll give you a hand Sis." I looked over and he was sitting by himself with a book. "Jo you help me." *He's still there Lucas.*

By the time we left the canteen Andy had gone.

If it wasn't for the obvious, they'd be good together. It was a bloody shame.

I agree Alli, it is a shame but it couldn't happen and I'm relieved Lucas is conscious of that fact. Harvey squeezed my hand as we went down to the office. Lucas was talking to Gina when we went through the outer office and didn't look at Andy.

Lucas followed me over to my computer. "Sis; do you mind if I try to hack that Funeral Director's computer? We could see what they were up to or find out more about them." I looked at Harvey, he was on the phone but put up his thumb.

"Go ahead Lucas fill your boots." He sat down and logged on. When he started I couldn't keep up with his typing at all.

"Where did you learn to type like that?"

He grinned, "Misspent youth, Sis. I used to cruise the gay sites like the rest of them until I grew up. Nearly dying on Everest, made me change how I lived. None of them use protection and can shag four of five different guys a day. You've no idea what it's like. Aids, hasn't changed them a bit. The clinics are at a loss as they don't even know who they're shagging. If I'd had the use of my dick I probably wouldn't have lived that long. Believe me, I'd have been doing the same when I was younger." While Lucas was talking he was still typing like mad.

"How old are you Lucas?"

"Twenty-nine Sis. I was just twenty-two when I first climbed Everest and twenty-eight on my last climb. I never really had enough time between climbs to recuperate, properly. They reckon at least, three years. I was stupid getting dragged into it that often, it was my fault. Still, I've seen a lot of the world but I've wanted to settle down for a while now. This job will be the making of me, it's right up my street."

"I'm really pleased you like it Lucas, you'll be a great asset to our little band of worriers."

"That's a good word for us Alli." Harvey sat on the desk just as something Lucas was trying to get into gave him access.

"Yes," came out of his mouth and he pushed his fist into the air. Harvey slid of the desk and stood beside him.

"This is their bank account Harvey. Fuck, they've got plenty of money behind them. I'll get their account up at Company's House; they're a limited company and it isn't in their business name. Why are they hiding it I wonder?"

Harvey leaned on the desk. I dragged a chair over. "Sit Harvey, I'll go and get some tea."

"Thanks Alli; this is interesting."

Lucas smiled at him. "This will give us the Board's names in the company; your killer might be amongst them."

"Won't they know we've looked at this Lucas?"

"This is public record Harvey. Anyone can look at this. Here we go, its coming up now."

Company's House

Company Name:- Haddon and Wyatt Ltd.

Chairman:- William Gittings

Board of Directors:-

Dr. Anthony Lewis
James Dixon
Gwen Mears
Sarah Bonner
Dr. Gerard Withers
Richard Banks
Michael Morrison
Brian Trewyn

Secretary:- Jason Hicks
Treasurer:- Mary Gittings

Harvey was sat with his mouth open when I went back in to join them.

"What's wrong, Harvey? You look like you've seen a ghost."

I took one look at the screen. "You ought to get down here Ron, you have to see this." Lucas had no idea why Harvey was acting that way.

"Sorry Alli." Harvey could speak again. "I'm in shock Lucas, four of these names are people we're looking for."

Ron came in and hurried over to the desk. "What have you found out?"

"Lucas has looked in Company's House and the four people we're looking for are on the board of Directors at Haddon and Wyatt, Funeral Directors."

"What made you look there Lucas?" Ron was baffled.

"I hacked into their bank account. They're a Limited Company, Registered with Company's House and they don't have the title on their business. It made me curious Ron."

"I'm fucking glad you're on board Lucas. Harvey, which four names?"

"Dr. Anthony Lewis is the guy on the two gender re-assignment sites. Dr. Gerard Withers is the guy whose house we raided and worked at the hospital in the morgue with Richard Banks and Jason Hicks is the nephew of Withers. I had him in the palm of my bloody hands when we walked Milton Crescent."

"Hindsight is wonderful Harvey, it's happened, to us all. Don't beat yourself up over it. This is good news Lucas. Could you get addresses off this site?"

"I'll try." He hunted around on the site and couldn't find a way to addresses. "I could ring them and ask Ron."

"Give me the phone number and I want the number for the GMC. I'll ring them both. It might need a bit of weight behind the calls." Harvey got him the number for the GMC and Lucas handed him the one for Company's House. "Could you print off that list of Directors, Lucas."

"I'll do it." I took over the mouse and clicked the box. "I'll go out and wait for it to be printed. It won't be a minute." *Thanks Sis.*

Andy's head shot up when I walked into their office. I went to the printer and waited for the list beside Jo.

She turned to speak to me. "Sounds interesting in there."

"Very. Finish making the tea I started and come in." I picked up the sheet of paper and left her.

I handed it to Ron. "I'll be back when I know something, this shouldn't take long." Ron left us just as Jo came in with the tea.

"You buggers are having all the fun in here." She handed out the tea and sat on the edge of Harvey's desk to drink hers. Gina came over and sat beside her.

"I bet they've never been doctors at all, fucking nutters I'd call them."

"Gina you're a gem." Jo jumped to her feet. "I traced all the victims at mental hospitals but not those two buggers, I'll be back." She left with her tea. Harvey had a smile on his face.

"What's tickled you, Mr Burgess?"

"I was thinking back to your first day here. I told you we had the same office because we fire off each other and we're still doing it. There may be more of us but it's still happening."

I sat on his lap. "Yes. I remember that day and I feel the same about the job as I did then."

Jo came flying through the door. "You'll never guess where those two resided." She waited but no one spoke. "Rampton."

"Fucking hell, Jo." Harvey was shocked.

"I'm thick, what's Rampton?"

Harvey cuddled me. "You're not thick Alli. Rampton is a mental hospital for the criminally insane. We can find out why they were sent there and when they were released."

Ron came in, "You beat me to it, Jo." He smiled at her. "They were released in nineteen eighty-two. What they were sentenced for was operating on young rent boys. You've definitely got the right pair of bastards. Which one do you think is the Hybrid?"

"I think its Anthony Lewis, Ron. I can't tell you why, I just have that awful feeling. When we're turned whatever we excel in comes out even more. Whatever he excelled in, being bloody insane has come out in him even worse. He's arrogant enough to tell us his real name on the sites and he sounds a twisted fucker when you're talking to him. He gives me the creeps," Gina shuddered.

"Do you think we could get a photo of him from anywhere? Gina you must have seen him when he attacked, Olli. You even jumped on him."

Gina stared at me. "You're right, Alli."

"You wouldn't think he'd be so arrogant he'd put his page on

Facebook or Twitter, do you?" We all stared at Jo.

Lucas started typing and logged into Facebook. He typed Dr. Anthony Lewis in the box and pressed the mouse.

Up popped a page on the famous Dr. Anthony Lewis, a gender reassignment specialist. Giving contact details, phone numbers and the all-important photograph.

I took hold of Gina's hand and went to the computer with her. When she looked she started shaking. "It's him. I've been talking to the bastard." She cried in my arms.

"Harvey have you got a street map? It's giving an address here." Harvey pulled one out of his drawer and went to Lucas spreading it out on the empty space on the desk.

"Twenty-eight, Stanley Drive, Darwin's Heath."

"Jesus; we've been right near the bastard, so many times."

"Harvey, we have to plan this properly," Ron told him. "I'll have the house watched and see where he goes apart from the Funeral Directors. If he's doing it in there I'll eat my hat. He must have another place he takes them to do the operations. We'll know more by Monday, I'll make damn sure of it. Relax this weekend, we're going to be bloody busy next week."

"How old does he look?"

Ron looked at the screen. "He looks nearly my age. He couldn't have been bitten twenty odd years ago and look like that now. He wasn't a Hybrid when he was in Rampton."

"The nearest date of the bodies Hillary has, apart from Jay Henderson are eight years ago. I'm wondering if he's been bitten in those eight years. I'm thinking quite recently and it's gone to his head. That's why he's started doing more operations."

"You could be right Harvey. Would he be as strong as any of you?"

"What are you thinking of Ron?"

"If he's the only one and not strong, we wouldn't have to involve the Home Office. I'd just have to ring and tell them to collect him."

"I hope it's that easy. If he is strong three of us could hold him until they arrived. Shit. I have to organise some Insurance for Lucas's car."

"Stick it on our Insurance, Harvey. It could be any one of you using it for undercover."

“Thanks Ron.” Harvey opened his phone and pressed in the numbers, he waited. When they picked up he gave them all the relevant details of the car. “That’s done, we’re picking it up just after five.” Ron looked at his watch.

“I think today has been a success, go to the interview on Monday, Lucas. It’ll be good having someone on the inside for a change and we’ll hear it all back here. Alli I mean. I wish I could do what you lot can, its bloody amazing. You might as well get off. I’ll organise Uniform in plain clothes to watch the address over the weekend and we’ll have a meeting first thing Monday morning. Come in with them Lucas and you can hear what has happened, before you go for your job. Have a good weekend.”

“Bye Ron.” We looked at each other and laughed, gathered our belongings and headed for the door.

“Jamie, you can all get off home, you’ve all worked bloody hard this week.” A cheer rang out behind us as we hurried to get out of there.

Harvey and Lucas left Gina with me, chatting, when they went to pay for the car.

“Are you okay now, Gina?” She smiled. “Keep thinking of it this way. Olli, would give him a medal, maybe with a black eye or two.”

She giggled. “I’m stupid for crying like that, Alli.”

“No you weren’t, that day was a bloody shock for you and seeing his face must have brought it back, with a bang. I think I’ll get Lucas to look them all up on Facebook, at home. What’s the betting they’re all on it, the arrogant bastards?”

Harvey got in. “Good idea, Alli. Lucas blagged another two hundred off the price of the car. I wouldn’t have had the cheek. They saw all the money and were dribbling, then he dropped the bombshell. We weren’t having it if it wasn’t reduced further. He stacked the money and pretended to put it in his pocket. The bloke from the back came out, belted the guy who lied, around the ear and accepted the price.”

I laughed at him nearly all the way home, going over the vision of Harvey’s explanation. Gina could see it, too, and we heard her giggle as she told Olli all about it.

Chapter 15

I flopped down on the sofa as soon as we got home. Harvey was surprised and sat beside me.

"What's the matter, Alli?"

I stroked his face. "I'm really tired and I can't understand why. I haven't spoken to any ghosts today, they've been there but I've ignored them."

"I think you should have more blood, Alli. You get like this when you're hungry." Harvey picked me up and took me to the blood room. When he opened the door I started salivating, seeing it in the fridge. He grabbed two bags and took me into his shower. No time to undress, we stood under the water fully clothed and I bit into the bags to get it as fast as possible. The feelings didn't hit so Harvey got me two more and that did the trick. I changed and we made love in the shower under the water streaming down.

We went down in our dressing gowns. They were surprised as we usually go straight to the pool.

"Alli was really hungry when we got home. She's had to have four extra bags."

"Are you alright now?" Lucas asked me.

"I'm fine now, I can't explain why I was so hungry."

"It could be that you'd need more from now on, you're getting everything Gina gets with what you already pick up, Alli. Gina you should have more than you do or you'll get hungry in the day. Your brains are burning it up much quicker now. Don't forget, Jo had to come home for more the other day because she's so strong. How many do you have Lucas?"

"Three, Harvey."

"I think five would be better for you. You're not only strong your brain seems to work at ninety miles an hour. I think we'll show you all how to think yourselves to another destination and how to do the speed thing this weekend. We may all need it next week. Alli and I already do it and it could get you out of a problem. I've been meaning to ask you Lucas, where do you live?"

"Between here and Jed's. I've got a bedsit in a crummy house. I took the first thing I could find when I came home from hospital and spent the first three weeks at Jed's."

"The house the other side of the cottage next door is up for sale. I've talked to the estate agent with an offer. I think they'd take it as the price keeps dropping.

"I've got a builder coming tomorrow afternoon. I'll get a price for knocking them all into one. Would you like to move in with us, Lucas?"

A smile grew on Lucas's face. "Yes I would Harvey. I feel really at home here, thank you."

"No need to thank me Lucas, we feel you're family to us now," Harvey handed Lucas his phone. "Ring Jed and Abbey. See if they want to come over Lucas. I think we all deserve a bit of a party tonight after the day we've had." Lucas rang Jed and I went to answer the door. Hillary and Jo were just pulling up.

"Ready for bed, Alli?" Hillary asked as she gave me a hug.

"No. I needed more blood when we got home, I'm alright now. We're having a party. I expect you heard Jo?"

She gave me a hug. "Yes Alli, are you sure you're okay?"

I giggled. "Yes Jo, don't worry."

Olli arrived home. Jed and Abbey ten minutes later. After all the greetings were over we went into the pool. The meal was due to be delivered so we got out earlier.

I collected all the plates and glasses and had the dining room laid out with cutlery, napkins and cruets. I was lighting the candles when Harvey brought the wine in.

"This looks lovely Alli. It's much easier eating in here with everyone. Are you feeling okay now?"

I gave him a cuddle. "I'm fine, really. That's a good idea buying the next house in the row and I'm pleased Lucas wants to stay with us."

"I feel like he's a brother to me now, too. He'd back me in anything."

"I heard what you said to each other Harvey. I understand exactly what you mean." Harvey kissed me and would have gone on longer but for the doorbell ringing.

"Perfect bloody timing." He giggled and hurried to the door. I stood at the pool room door.

"The food's here everyone." I opened the kitchen drawer and took out half a dozen serving spoons. When I turned to take them into the dining room Harvey was grinning at me.

"What's tickled you Mr Burgess?" I took the bags from him to open in the dining room.

He answered as we laid out, the food. "They've sent extras because we order so much. Apparently they've started a competition at the curry house. Looks like we'll win every month."

I giggled. "We must have kept that place open, all through the recession. Christ, if we ever moved they'd die of shock."

"We'll never move from here Alli. We might buy the whole street before we've finished."

"That looks good, what's this about moving?" Jed asked.

"The only one moving is Lucas. He's moving in with us." Jed's face lit up.

"We're buying the next house down the street and having the three knocked into one Jed. The builder's coming tomorrow to look at the job."

"That's good news to me Harvey. He needs to be around you lot. I was saying to Abbey yesterday, once the money comes through from the sale of her mum's house we should move nearer you. We'd have to shift anyway as we've only got one bedroom and with the nipper coming it's pushing us into it."

"I'll keep my eyes open for you Jed. Are you renting or do you own your place?"

"We rent Harvey. The house money will mean we're on the property ladder at last."

"If you're going to talk I should move, they're coming in Harvey." He picked up a bottle and went around the table filling glasses.

"Why the party tonight?" Jed asked no one in particular.

"Your brother found information on the computer that gave us a breakthrough on the case we're on. Did you know how good he is on the computer Jed."

"I know he could use one, nothing else," he glanced at Lucas.

"He types faster than me and I type a hundred and twenty words a minute."

Lucas choked on his wine; Harvey was sitting beside him and

clapped him on the back. “Steady on Lucas,” and laughed at him.

“Are you serious, Alli?” Lucas asked, tears in his eyes.

“Deadly Lucas. I wouldn’t joke about it.” Harvey grinned at me.

“I don’t believe I’m that fast Alli, sorry.”

“I’ve seen her do it Lucas and she was reading off shorthand notes as she typed. She could set a tape machine to play, type the questions off the tape and read the answers off a pad. They were listed as Q &A right down the page.

“If Alli says you type faster than her, I’m sure she’s right. I watched you decipher that anagram a hundred times to get into that server today. She’s not bullshitting you.”

“This calls for a contest I think,” Jed blurted out. I giggled thinking he was joking.

“Yeh, let’s have a contest,” Jo called and clapped her hands and the others joined in, doing a slow hand clap. Harvey was giggling opposite.

I put my hands up to stop them. “All right Lucas, are you in.” He nodded. “We’ll finish our meal and have coffee. The computer comes out after we’ve had a civilised meal, everyone in agreement.”

They cheered; that was a yes if ever there was one.

Lucas laughed across the table. “I’ll never beat you Alli.”

I smiled back. “We’ll see.”

Everyone helped clearing the dinner things away and waited in the sitting room. Harvey got my computer out and opened it in a word document.

“Lucas, can you read a book and type without looking at the keys or do you want to type anything that comes into your head?”

“To make it fair we should both do the same thing from a book Alli.”

“In that case someone choose a book and toss a coin to see who goes first.”

I looked at the faces and no one stepped forward. “Come on, you wanted this to happen Jo. You do it please.”

She grinned “Where are the books in this house as I haven’t seen one. Too much shagging goes on here to have time for books.” It was true, every bloody word and we burst out laughing.

Lucas put his hand up with a grin on his face.

Harvey straightened himself out to ask, "Yes Lucas."

"I have books in my van, tons of fucking books," he giggled. "I don't need them now thanks to you Sis. Jo, come and choose one." He pulled keys from his pocket and she followed him out.

They came back in giggling and Jo laid them out on the floor, face down.

"Choose one Alli." I pointed to the red cover on the centre book and she handed it to me, fished in her pocket and tossed a coin. "Lucas, heads or tails? Whoever wins chooses first or second."

"Tails!" Lucas yelled.

Jo lifted her hand over the coin and showed it to me. "Lucas; you win."

"I'll go first, Sis."

I swept my hand to the computer. "We need a chair from the dining room."

Harvey went for it and as he put it down he asked, "How long are you typing?"

"I think three minutes each and someone would have to turn the pages."

"I'll do it, Alli." Hillary volunteered.

"Thanks Hillary. Switch that lamp on, would you, please?"

She switched it on and Lucas sat down. "I'll open it anywhere Alli, okay."

"That's fine. Harvey, could you keep time please as you've got a second hand on your watch." He waited for the second hand to reach the top.

"Go!" Lucas typed so fast and I could see the shock on everyone's face. "Turn!" came out of his mouth. Hillary was waiting and didn't hold him up. "Turn!" he said again. I could feel Harvey getting really excited. I looked at Jed and his mouth was open. "Turn!"

He typed for a few more seconds. "Stop!" Harvey yelled. Lucas was almost panting and grinned at me.

"I'll open a new document for you Alli. We'll print them off later and count the words." Harvey got it ready for me. Hillary turned the pages back to where Lucas began. I sat down and waited.

"Go!" I typed for all I was worth. *God, they've gone quiet. I can hardly hear anyone breathe.* "Turn!" *You can hear a bloody pin drop in here, were we like that with Lucas, I don't know.* "Turn!" *These minutes seem bloody long for me. Is Harvey watching the bloody time properly?* "Turn!" *Well, he finished about here so why isn't Harvey calling it. Come on it must...* "Stop!" I lifted my hands off the keys and breathed. I stood up and everyone was staring.

"What's wrong?"

Harvey cuddled me. "You've no idea what you just did, do you?"

"No, what?"

"All through the typing you talked to yourself, we all heard it."

"I bet I've made a load of mistakes, then. You know the rule, Harvey. Dock ten words for every mistake."

"I know," he said and grinned. "I'll print them off and one of you can check them." Harvey sat down and turned on his printer.

"I want tea, anyone else?"

Gina came over to me. "I'll give you a hand, Alli. We'll make one for everyone, they'll drink it." We left them to it.

When we were carrying the tea in there was silence. "Christ, it's like someone died in here." We handed out the tea and still no one spoke. Hillary and Abbey were standing at my piano with the typed sheets in front of them on the lid.

I looked at Lucas and he looked as confused as I felt. I gave Harvey his tea, he smiled and could hear every word but I couldn't read him. He'd buried that bloody deep. He giggled in my mind.

Gina sat on Olli's lap talking to him in her head so they didn't make any noise. I just wanted to hear some. Harvey gave me a little squeeze.

I suppose I have to learn to be patient, that's not going to be easy for me.

Finally they turned to us all, Hillary read out the results.

"Lucas, you typed at two hundred and thirty words a minute, no mistakes. Alli, you typed at two hundred and eighty words a minute, no mistakes."

I couldn't breathe or speak. Lucas came over and put his arms around me.

"Congratulations, Sis. I told you you'd win and you held a conversation with yourself all the way through." The clapping started and I turned red.

Harvey was laughing beside us. "That's a bit better than a hundred and twenty words a minute, Mrs Burgess. I bet your typing teacher would love you now."

"She'd have a bloody heart attack, Harvey." Jed's face appeared over Lucas's shoulder.

"You've both shocked the hell out of me." He put his arm around his brother's neck. "I didn't know you were so fucking brainy, kidder."

Lucas roared with laughter. "I think being turned helped quite a lot Jed, it's fucking shocked me." Lucas turned to me. "You type faster than me Sis, but you won, too."

"What do you mean, Lucas?" He grinned.

"I do type faster than a hundred and twenty words a minute." I smiled at him.

"Let's get down to serious drinking and some music please?" Jo asked.

"Get more wine Jo," Harvey asked and picked up his guitar.

We sat in the basket chairs eating toast, drinking tea and chatting for the last few minutes before the kids arrive. It seemed weird having to wear cossies for swimming and Jo, in her cut-offs and T-shirt but we're all here and looking forward to some fun with the kids. We decided the boys had to use the bathroom behind the pool for changing and girls, mine upstairs.

The bell rang and Harvey hurried to answer it. I cleared all the breakfast dishes away.

Nick came into the pool room first, with Josie. She ran to me for a hug.

"Hi, Alli. This pool is lovely."

I picked her up. "I've been looking forward to today Josie. Hello Nick, how are you?"

"I'm fine Alli, Josie's never stopped asking when she could come here. Jess is with the boys; they're chatting to Harvey about his guitar. We're not stopping with the kids. We never get time to shop without them, what with Christmas coming soon."

"I forgot about Christmas Nick. It's different if you've got kids." Jess came in with the three boys, bigger than I thought they'd be. She gave me a hug.

"Thank you for this Alli and for Josie. I don't know what you did but she's been really happy now she's with us, permanently."

"That's all I need to hear, Jess." I looked at the boys. "Let's have your names then, I'm not a mind reader." They all smiled.

"I'm Gavin."

"I'm Nick."

"I'm Luke."

"I'm Alli and you've met Harvey. This is Lucas, Jo, Hillary, Olli and Gina. They swim here every day with us after work. Your dad knows Hillary and Jo already, the other three have just joined us." I turned to our lot. "Nick is a duty Solicitor and we see him quite often at the nick."

Jess handed me a bag. "They've already got their swimming things on, this is their underwear for when they get out, Alli."

"Thanks Jess. Go and have some free time, we're going to have some fun. The last one in is a sissy." The boys were down to their trunks so fast and in the pool, almost before we could blink. Lucas and Olli followed close behind.

Josie was struggling. "I only said that Josie, so we don't get crushed by them." I helped her get her dress off and walked her to the pool edge. "I'll be last in, no Harvey will he's talking to your dad, sorry Uncle Nick."

"It's okay Alli, I call them mum and dad now."

She dived in to the bottom. I called, "See you later," before I joined her. Jo dived to the bottom and swam to the top, to play with the boys. Hillary joined them with a football. We'd done one length when Harvey caught up with us. The football match went on above us and we came up for air when Josie did.

We had so much fun with the kids; three hours went by in a flash.

"Get something to eat when you're changed boys, it's all laid out in the kitchen. Just help yourselves, I'm taking Josie to get changed upstairs."

Harvey took them to the back bathroom and left them to it. He must have thought himself up to his bedroom because he was knocking on my bathroom door, not long after we got there.

"Are you decent ladies?"

Josie giggled and yelled, "Give us chance Uncle Harvey."

I could hear him giggle in my head. "I'll see you downstairs, don't be long, I'll make sure your brothers don't eat everything."

"Okay."

I helped her get her dress back on. "I've had a lovely time today, Alli."

"I'm glad you did. Tell me, why did you call Harvey, Uncle?"

"Because he's so big, he's huge."

I laughed at her. "Tie your shoe laces and I'll put a dress on. I'll only be in there," pointing to my dressing room. I was dressed by the time she'd tied them. I brushed my hair into a ponytail, twisted it up and put the spike through it. Josie's was next.

"I like your hair like that, Alli. Mine's not long enough, yet."

"Thanks. Get your cossie, we'll put it in this bag. Are you ready?"

She took hold of my hand. "I'm ready, thank you."

Nick and Jess had arrived by the time we got downstairs. Josie ran to Jess.

"We've had a lovely time, mum."

Jess kissed her, "I hope they haven't been too boisterous, for you Alli?"

"They've had so much fun and so have we. We'd forgotten what it was like to play. Come and have a coffee with us while they eat. I was always starving after swimming. Go and help yourself Josie."

I put the kettle on and Harvey took them into the pool room, our lot were lounging around. I carried the coffee on a tray and saw the boys sitting on the floor with Olli, leaning against the back wall of the house with plates still full. Laughing and carrying on like they'd been coming here for years.

"They've made themselves at home," Jess said to Nick.

"We've had fun today Jess," Jo told her. "It's not something we've done in the pool. We just swim, normally and I'm amazed how long Josie stays down at the bottom."

"She's never been allowed to do that at the local pool. The lifeguard is a stickler. We've no idea how long she holds her breath."

"It's got to be ten minutes, Nick. Alli's going to show her some synchronise swimming when we aren't in the pool. We won't be here every time they come but we've really enjoyed today."

Once they'd gone home we sat indoors and talked for a while. Jo and Hillary went shopping and I played my piano. When I looked around Harvey and Olli had gone back in the pool with Gina. Lucas was sitting on the sofa, his head was back and his eyes closed and I knew he wasn't sleeping.

"What's up, Lucas?" I sat beside him, he opened his eyes and stared at the ceiling.

"I've had a weird feeling for the last hour, Sis and I don't know why. It's like something awful has happened. Christ, I wish I knew what it was."

I took hold of his hand and closed my eyes, trying to feel what he was feeling. I got a gut wrenching in the pit of my stomach.

"Alli, I feel it, too." Gina was in front of us wrapped in a towel.

"What the hell is it Gina, I can't see it?" Harvey and Olli came in, worried.

"Lucas, how long ago did you say?"

"An hour ago Gina; what have you seen?"

"We were talking just before everyone left and Andy's face flashed into my head. I thought nothing of it. I daydream sometimes and just thought it was something to do with work." Harvey picked up his phone from the desk and keyed in a number.

"Jamie, I know it's Saturday, sorry. Have you got Andy's phone number? Gina and Alli have had a terrible feeling about him. I just want to check he's alright. I shouldn't disclose this to you Jamie if he hasn't, but I'm worried. He's gay Jamie, now you see how important this is?" He listened and looked for a pen. I gave him one with a pad. He wrote the number down. "Thanks Jamie, if you don't mind. I'll ring him from here. Ring me back."

Harvey keyed in Andy's number using my phone. "Jamie is going to his flat, he lives near him." Harvey waited and waited for him to answer and he'd never be without his mobile.

It seemed to take forever for Jamie to ring. Gina and Olli left us to get dressed. Lucas sat with his head in his hands beside me. Despair hit me in waves from his body. I put my arm over his shoulder while we waited. Olli and Gina came back in the room, just as Harvey's phone rang. I jumped out of my skin, so loud in the silence.

Harvey listened; worry filled his face as the seconds passed.

Alli, I'm coming back.

Thanks Jo.

Harvey hung up. "Jamie said his car is at the flat and he didn't answer the door. He could hear me ringing, hammered on his landlady's door and demanded she let him in. She opened Andy's flat and he wasn't there but his computer was on, on one of the gay chat rooms. I hope that sick bastard, hasn't got him?" Lucas looked up at Harvey, with tears in his eyes.

"Sorry Lucas, I shouldn't have said that." Harvey opened his phone again to ring Ron and explained everything to him. He told us to sit tight; he'd be over after he caught up with the guys who were watching the Doctor's address.

I got up to let Jo in. "We've got to wait here for Ron, he's checking up with the surveillance guys."

Harvey's phone rang again. "Yes Jamie." He listened. "Thanks for doing that. I'll let you know if we need you." Harvey closed his phone. "Jamie's been to his friend's house and she hasn't seen him since Thursday."

Gina made tea, more to be doing something as the wait was horrible for all of us. Harvey nipped up to get dressed. I heard a car pull up and opened the door for Ron.

"Come in Ron we're in the sitting room." His face was sombre and he knew how we were feeling. Harvey followed us in.

"Those stupid bastards watched him go to an abandoned mental hospital, and didn't think to tell me. Wait until Monday, they'll wish they were never born. It's out past Darwin's Heath, about two miles further along the same road, that bastard from Vice lived."

"Right. You stay here, Ron. He may not be the only Hybrid and we couldn't take the chance, taking you. I'll just get something from the cellar, Alli."

Harvey was carrying a huge holdall and flung it into the boot before we set off. Olli had Gina and Jo with him and Lucas was with us.

"What's in the bag Harvey?"

He grinned. "I can't escape from it he fucking won't." I

smiled at him knowing exactly what he'd brought.

It took nearly an hour to get there. The traffic was heavy with Christmas shoppers.

We found the old hospital. "This is bloody spooky, I'm not surprised it's shut down." We pulled up and Olli parked behind us outside the gates.

We got out and talked between the cars. "I'll go and look around first, I'll be back before you know it." He was gone as the last word came out of his mouth.

Lucas stared at the spot he'd been standing on. "Alli can do it, too, Lucas," Jo told him and he looked at me, in shock. Harvey returned to the same spot seconds later.

"His car is parked behind the main building so I've let down all the tyres. I can hear singing in one of the rooms to the left of the main entrance. Jay said he sang when he was cutting him. I think we should just go in and get him, before too much damage is done.

"Run to the building and push ahead with your minds. When you want to stop, stop pushing. It's as easy as that. Let's go." Harvey, Gina and I left them standing but not for long. Jo caught us up, then the boys.

Harvey ran straight through the front wall, bricks dropping behind him. He grabbed the maniac Doctor, trapping his arms so he couldn't fight. He tried to get away but couldn't get out of Harvey's strong arms.

"Who are you! You can't barge into my clinic! What are you doing, let me go. I'll have to call the police. Don't you know who you're dealing with here, I'll get you thrown out."

Harvey ignored the lunatic and turned on the pressure.

On the table was a hooded body without his genitals. I took the hood off and Andy seemed lifeless.

I looked at Harvey. "Alli, I can hear his heart beating, he's only drugged. Look for his bits and put the hood over this bastard's head."

I hurried over with the hood just as Gina found them, under the table. She wrapped them in a piece of sheeting that was on the floor. I suppose it was used to cover Andy up. The hood was on the thing Harvey was holding but it didn't shut him up.

"I'm in the middle of a delicate operation!"

Harvey glared at the thing in his arms. "Shut up, you fucking nutter!" Harvey was wasting his breath. He couldn't hear with the hood on. The arm Harvey clenched around his throat, stopped him speaking.

Olli and Lucas took the strapping off Andy's wrists and ankles. Lucas was horrified and lunged at the Doctor.

Jo grabbed his arms. "Don't Lucas, he's not fucking worth it."

"He's going to wish he was dead by the time the Home Office has done with him!" Harvey yelled at Lucas.

"Go back to the cars, drive mine here and bring the holdall from the boot." Lucas left us and was back in a couple of minutes.

He carried the bag in. "Get the wide Bungee strapping out Lucas, then the manacles and handcuffs. Put them on him first." Olli held his legs so Lucas could fix the manacles on tight. They handcuffed him next.

"You fucking bastards, you'll die for this!" He yelled abuse at them but no one was listening.

Once they were on, Harvey let him go and he fell over.

Harvey used the wide Bungee strapping around his body, from his shoulders to his ankles.

He picked him up, carried him outside and flung him in the boot of his car, slamming the lid.

Lucas and Olli held Andy between them. "Lay him on the back seat. Lucas, sit near his feet and keep an eye on him. We're taking him home, not to hospital." Lucas was shocked. "Do you want him to end up worse than you were, Lucas. It's not just his nerves that are knackered. They won't reattach it. He'll have skin grafts and a fucking tube, to pee from."

"I'm not thinking straight, sorry." Harvey started the car and drove home as fast as possible, siren and lights flashing, all the way back to town.

Ron must have been watching for us. The front door opened just after we stopped. I rushed into the house, up to the linen cupboard for something to put over Andy.

I covered him and Harvey carried him up to my bedroom. Gina followed with his bits. Ron asked what we proposed.

"He's cut his genitals off Ron. What the fuck, do you think we're going to do. A hospital would throw them away so you try telling him he's got to live like that." Harvey was furious.

"I'm not saying don't Harvey, Christ you've got to, I know that. Who the hell's going to explain it to him, he's going to be really scared. He knows nothing about how you have to live."

"I will Ron," Lucas told him. "I know exactly what it's like if Alli doesn't turn him."

Ron put his hand on Lucas's shoulder. "Okay son, thank you."

Harvey took his genitals from the sheeting and laid them where they'd been cut from, "Bite him Alli. Lucas, come and hold his hand." Harvey draped a towel over Andy, up to his chest. I turned his head towards me and Lucas sat on a chair beside him and held his hand.

I bit into his neck, pushed for a minute and took my mouth away. I licked the puncture wounds, they healed and I sat on the bed to hold his other hand. Now the wait started.

"Can you hear his heart Harvey?"

He put his hands on my shoulders. "Yes Alli, it's starting to slow down."

Nearly two hours later Andy gripped my hand, I looked at Lucas.

"I felt it, too, Alli." Andy's head straightened up and he opened his eyes wondering what the hell was going on.

"Andy you're in my bedroom." He looked from me to Lucas. Harvey was beside me and Ron, at the bottom of the bed.

He panicked. "I was being cut to ribbons!" He put his hand down to his bits and felt all around. "Was it a fucking dream! He showed them to me and dropped them on the floor." Tears were streaming down his face.

Lucas gripped his hand tight. "It wasn't a dream Andy, he did cut them off. I'm going to explain everything to you, just listen and try to stay calm. I'm going to start with what happened to me first and the rest will make more sense to you." Lucas was so gentle with him.

"We'll let you talk. Harvey will put some clothes outside the door. Come down when you're ready."

"Thanks, Sis."

Harvey phoned Jamie and told him Gina and Olli met Andy in town. He was Christmas shopping and went by taxi as he'd had too much to drink the night before. Jamie was relieved. He told Harvey, he already knew Andy was gay and not to worry about disclosing it to him.

"I'll probably move Jamie on soon, Harvey. Andy will take over his job running the team. Jamie deserves to be promoted he's run the team really well." Harvey nodded in agreement.

"Wasn't that bastard there?" Ron asked.

Harvey laughed. "I forgot about him Ron. He's in the boot of my car and he can't get out. I suggest you ring the Home Office to collect him." Harvey turned to Gina and Olli. "You two should make yourselves scarce. Go out, you'll hear what's going on, Gina." Harvey gave them some money.

"Thanks Harvey. I think we'll go into town and see a film or something," Olli told us. They went next door to change into something decent and left fifteen minutes later.

Ron phoned the Home Office and asked them to come for the Hybrid.

"They were bloody surprised, more that we'd actually contained one, than anything else. How have you done it, Harvey?"

Harvey giggled at Ron. "Let's just say if we hadn't got up to certain things, living our lives to the full we wouldn't have been able to, Ron." Ron twigged what Harvey meant and laughed out loud.

"That's bloody priceless Harvey. Let me know if you're out of pocket and I'll organise some money."

Harvey laughed at him. "I don't think you'd be able to describe them on any expenses sheet, Ron. I'm just pleased we got to Andy before he was killed."

The door to the hall opened and Lucas and Andy came in smiling.

"Are you alright Andy, about everything?" Harvey asked him.

"Yes, Sir. I'd rather be like this than without a dick or dead." He glanced at the Commissioner.

Ron explained to him about why he was here and the fact he looked after us. He also told him he'd be on higher wages but would stay out in the office with the team, like Jo until people were moved on.

"Would you like to live here with us, Andy?" Harvey asked him.

He looked at Lucas before he answered. "Yes I would, Sir. Thank you."

"You call me Harvey from now on unless any of the team are near."

"And you call me Ron, the Commissioner in front of the team Andy. You'll have a good life living here. Your job is safe for the rest of your life and that's forever. Someone like me will look after you when I retire but I'll keep in touch with you all until I go to meet May." He looked at Lucas. "I think you should go in the pool when the Home Office arrives, Lucas. I still don't want them to know about you, yet. We still have to catch the other three."

"We'll both go in there, that way you could say Andy was attacked away from here. The less they know, the easier it'll be, on everyone."

"You're right Lucas. We don't want them getting wind of anything that happens here."

"Do you want tea Ron or are you having a drink, with them?"

"I'll have a drink I think, Alli. Whisky if you've got it. Just a small one please It wouldn't do to get done for drink-driving." I giggled and opened the drinks cupboard.

"What do you drink Andy. We drink red wine, mainly but I have a few cans of beer?" Harvey asked.

"I drink anything Harvey. Wine will be fine with me." I followed Harvey out to the kitchen and piled a plate with some of the food, left from the buffet this morning.

Harvey glanced at me. "He'll be hungry Harvey, god knows when he last ate anything."

"Bloody hell. I didn't think of that, Alli." He poured the wine. "I'm pleased he wants to stay here. I think Lucas has found a partner."

"I do, too, Harvey. They're perfect for each other. When I think about what that bastard did to him, I could cry."

A couple of hours later an armoured truck pulled up outside, double parking. Harvey went out with his car keys and Ron went with him. Jo and I watched from the window.

Two huge men got out and opened the back of the truck. When Harvey opened the boot we could see them laughing, before they hauled him out. They threw him into the truck and locked the back doors. One of them opened a small door on the back for a minute and closed it. They spoke to Ron for a few minutes and left without coming in. Ron came back in with Harvey.

"That was easier than I expected. I won't stay any longer and thank you for rescuing Andy so fast. The quicker we get those sites shut down the better."

He hugged Jo and me and shook Harvey's hand. He walked in to the hall and turned, before opening the front door. "I won't disturb them saying goodbye. I knew Andy was gay, they'll make a good couple." He left after that last statement.

"Fucking hell. He's more with it than I thought."

Harvey cuddled me and laughed. "That kind of shocked me, too."

Jo came into the hall. "I thought I was bloody hearing things. I'm going now. Hillary's had to do all the shopping by herself and I don't want to take the piss. When are you putting up your Christmas tree, ours is up."

"We haven't even thought of Christmas."

"You've only got ten days."

"We'll have to get some serious shopping done, Alli. I've never had to organise this before. We went to Jenny's last year, Jo. I'm going to enjoy this, thanks for reminding us."

"Are we going to see you later?"

"I don't know Alli. I think we're wrapping presents tonight. We might pop over tomorrow, we'll let you know."

Jo hurried for her car; it was raining pretty hard.

"I suppose we haven't got in the Christmas mood because we don't feel the cold. I think I'm going mad this year. Hold on to your hat Mr Burgess." Harvey picked me up and kissed me for ages.

"I love you Alli. You can go as mad as you like." He sat down on the sofa with me on his lap. "I'll have to find you something special for your present Mrs Burgess. Something you won't be expecting at all."

"Likewise Mr Burgess. My mind will be working overtime,

over the next few days."

“I've already got my Christmas present,” Lucas stated as he came in with mugs of tea, both he and Andy with towels around their waists.

“You're getting it together then?” I asked. They both grinned. “That was a daft question; I'm full of those.”

“Lucas told me he'd have wanted us together but couldn't because he was a Hybrid.”

“We knew that Andy, it's bloody dangerous for male Hybrids mixing intimately with humans.” Harvey looked at Lucas. “Have you explained about feeding Lucas?

Lucas laughed. “Yes, I've explained everything. We've already had a shag in the shower, behind the pool; no lights on. We're going to be fine.” Andy elbowed him but was grinning.

“I can see that Lucas, you'll fucking enjoy feeding then, Andy. Don't ever feel embarrassed here. We say what we think and get up to allsorts in this house. We work hard and play hard. Have you checked if Andy feels pain, Lucas?”

“He doesn't, thank god.”

“That was the first thing he checked Harvey, don't worry about that. He could hardly fucking wait to find that out.” We sat there giggling at them. Lucas grabbed Andy and kissed him to shut him up.

My phone rang. I got up to answer it as it was charging on the desk.

“Hi Jed.” I listened to him. “Its fine, come round. Lucas has something to tell you.” They broke apart as I listened again. “That would be lovely thank you. See you soon, bye.”

“They'll be here at seven, they're bringing dinner. I wonder if Gina and Olli will be back by then?” *We will Alli; we'll make sure we are.*

“Was that Gina I heard in my head?” Andy was astounded.

Lucas stared at him. “I didn't hear her.”

“Yes it was Andy, they're in town somewhere.”

“This gets more interesting by the minute.” Andy's face lit up. I glanced at Harvey. He had a satisfied look on his face.

“You may be able to do other things Andy, you'll find out over the next few days.” Harvey's thrilled he was picking things up, this quickly.

"Lucas, have you tried playing the guitar since you've been turned?"

"No Harvey. I've only spent the first day away from here and I didn't touch mine at my bedsit."

"Have a go on mine."

"I'm no good after hearing you Harvey. I'll show myself up."

"I think you'd surprise yourself Lucas, being turned will have made a huge difference."

"It's your funeral." He giggled at his own words and got up, switched the amp on and picked up Harvey's guitar. He sat beside Andy, thought for a moment and started to play some Spanish music. A smile grew on his face as he played.

Harvey was chuffed for him and when Lucas finished he was the first to clap. "I told you Lucas, play it whenever you like."

"I can't believe it. I've tried playing that for months and it always sounded crap. I kept stopping, trying to remember which strings to pluck next. I've gobsmacked myself. Andy hasn't heard you play yet Harvey, go on."

He brought the guitar over. "Could you pass the bottle neck, it's on the top of the amp Lucas." He got it and handed it to Harvey. I got off his lap and sat beside him with my eyes closed to soak it up.

Harvey played blues, blue grass and rock then ended with my favourite. I opened my eyes and Lucas was lifting my piano lid. "Come on Sis, Duelling Banjos please." I walked to my piano and as I passed him I whispered. "You bugger."

He giggled. "Absolutely, always have been." I could hear Harvey and Andy laughing behind me.

Harvey started and I jumped in with the piano. I actually love playing this. When it finished I got up and did a bow.

"Play something else please, Alli," Harvey asked. *Anything for you Mr Burgess.* I played for about half an hour and stopped when Gina and Olli arrived home.

"I was listening to you playing on the way home Alli. I pushed it into Olli's head. I know I shouldn't have done that, you're not supposed to use headphones when you're driving."

"Don't worry Gina, it's like anyone listening to the radio in the car. You could still hear an ambulance or horns going. Headphones cut everything out," Harvey explained.

As she passed Lucas and Andy she giggled. “You heard us, didn’t you Gina,” Lucas said with a grin.

“Sorry boys, my mind’s like fucking radar. We had to stop for a shag on the way home. Olli’s as straight as a bloody ruler but it got him going.” We were in hysterics looking at the boy’s faces.

“You’ll get used to it Andy, there are no secrets here I’m afraid. What we get up to has had Lucas running for the shower, to have a wank.”

“Can’t deny it Sis, I almost didn’t make it. I meant to ask you, what you were doing to Harvey on your piano?” Andy’s eyes bulged and he grinned at me.

“It’s something both of you would like I’m sure.”

“If Alli had told me what she was going to do I wouldn’t have believed it could feel that good. I’m glad she didn’t tell me and got on with it.”

“Now you’ve got me fucking interested, are you going to tell us Sis?”

“I massaged his prostrate.” Lucas looked horrified. “Don’t knock it until you’ve tried it Lucas. Use plenty of lubrication and be gentle. It sent him to bloody heaven, it’s the male G-spot.” Harvey nodded to him.

“Really, I had an Uncle with prostate cancer and he said it fucking killed him, having the examination.”

“You’re forgetting something Lucas. We don’t feel pain only pleasure. Believe me or not it blew my mind until I passed out and wanted more. Alli’s other present just added to the sensations. I went to heaven, alright.” Harvey looked at me and smiled. A few minutes later the doorbell rang.

Chapter 16

Jed and Abbey were huddled, trying to keep dry. The rain was falling like bloody stair rods.

"Christ, you're soaked come in." They ducked under the drip and got inside quickly. "Haven't you got a brolly?"

"At home Alli, it wasn't raining when we left. The dinner's in the boot."

"We'll get it Jed. Go in, Gina will get you towels." *Harvey, give me a hand please.*

As he came into the hall he held the door for Jed and Abbey. "We'll say hello in a minute, get dried off." Jed handed him the keys.

I picked up a huge brolly from the corner. It took a few minutes to carry it all in. We were glad to shut the vile weather out.

They were stood inside the pool room with towels, drying their hair.

"Come upstairs I've got a hair dryer in my dressing room."

"I'll be alright Abbey. You go up, your hair takes ages to dry, without a dryer."

She smiled at Jed. "He knows I'd look like 'Chrystal Tips' in the bloody cartoon if I don't blow dry it. A frizz bomb has nothing on my bloody hair."

Jed giggled. "I was trying not to tell them that Abbey."

She ran a finger down his cheek. "Such a gentleman, point me to the dryer Alli."

She finished straightening her hair. "I don't suppose you noticed Alli, when I go in the pool my hair is piled on top of my head and I never put my head under water. It's a practiced art. I hope our kid doesn't end up with hair like mine."

I laughed at her. "I'm sure it won't."

Down in the kitchen she put the casserole in the oven to re-heat and filled pans with loads of veg she'd already prepared.

"You've been busy Abbey, this will make a nice change. Thank you."

"This is a thank you for all the meals we've had here and for what you did for Lucas. He's a changed man and I don't mean being turned. We've never seen him so happy. What's he got to tell us."

"I'm leaving that for him to tell you Abbey."

She giggled. "Spoil sport."

Lucas came into the kitchen from the pool room, dressed again and Andy followed. Abbey caught on straight away, she gave Lucas a hug then looked him in the face. "Introduce your partner Lucas. Jed, get in here?"

Jed came in and grinned at Lucas but said nothing, just waited.

"I fancied the pants of Andy, he works with this lot but I couldn't go near him because of the obvious. This afternoon we had to rescue him from the Hybrid whose been cutting up at least fifty bodies. Chopping their dicks and balls off, to be precise. Andy was on the table and he'd already lost his, they were on the floor. Harvey brought him home and Alli turned him to heal him again.

"Andy, this is my twin brother Jed and his partner Abbey." Abbey put her arms around Andy as Jed hugged Lucas.

"I'm fucking made up for you Brov." He put his hand out to Andy and hugged him. "Welcome to our family Andy. This is the best Christmas present I'll ever have." His voice broke as he finished speaking and there were tears in Jed's eyes when he pulled away. Abbey cuddled him.

Lucas put his hands on Jed's shoulders. "Don't get upset Jed, I'm really happy with Andy. The past never happened as far as I'm concerned I've forgotten it, so should you now." Jed hugged him again.

"Does anyone want anymore, we're not taking it home with us." The boys dived into the casserole again.

"Thank you for cooking Abbey, you're a good cook and you brought stacks."

"I thought Jo and Hillary would be here Alli. Have they got a prior engagement?"

I smiled at her. "They're wrapping presents apparently."

No we're not. We're outside and it's pissing down.

Okay Jo, I'll let you in. "I'm just letting them in, they're outside."

I got up to leave the table and Harvey got up with me. "Jo's brought something for me Alli, I'll come with you."

What are you up to, Mr Burgess?

Nothing Mrs Burgess, what makes you think that? I gave him a sideways glance and he just grinned.

When I opened the door Hillary was there with a huge bowl in her hands. "I've brought trifle for pudding Alli. God knows what they're up to, I give up. Let's leave them to it, I want to meet Andy. He sounds perfect for Lucas." She walked through the house as she talked, I just followed. We ended up in the dining room where Lucas introduced her to Andy.

She hugged them both. "Where have they been hiding you, I haven't bumped into you, at the nick Andy."

He giggled. "I've seen you Hillary, killing yourself laughing last week."

"I remember that day. Harvey told Ron he couldn't be on call because we're having bondage lessons. I heard it all driving over and nearly crashed the bloody car, I was laughing so much."

"What! Fucking hell. Sorry Hillary, I didn't realise he knows so much about you all."

Hillary smiled. "He knows everything Andy. That doesn't stop us having a good time. If he was younger and his wife was still alive he'd have asked Alli to turn them both. He told me that, that afternoon, before we went to buy all the rope."

Andy pushed Lucas on the arm. "You didn't tell me it's this much fun here Lucas."

He grinned at Andy. "I didn't want to spoil the surprise."

I brought in a pile of glass dishes. "Who's having trifle?" No one put their hand's up, they just stared behind me. I looked round.

"Would you like to come with me, Alli, please."

Harvey held out his arm for me to link it. "What's all this Mr Burgess?"

"You'll find out if you come with me." I linked his arm and he walked me through the kitchen to the sitting room.

A huge Christmas tree was at the far end of the sofa, before the door.

I looked at Harvey. "Thank you, we'll have to go shopping for decorations."

"Wait, you haven't seen everything Alli." He took me into the hall and another tree was at the far end of the fireplace.

"We haven't finished Alli." He turned me into the sitting room again and straight through the kitchen to the pool room. To my right where Olli and the boys were sitting this morning was the biggest tree I've ever seen. I flung my arms around his neck. "Thank you. They're going to look beautiful when they're trimmed up."

"There's a van full of decorations outside. Pick what you want and I'll pay the man on Monday."

Tears welled up. "Thank you Harvey."

"Don't cry Alli, have some fun the rest of the weekend. Gina will help I'm sure and if you want any help with lights and things there are plenty of men around."

Gina tapped me on the shoulder. "We've got the whole day tomorrow to get this house looking beautiful. Come and have some trifle."

We joined everyone around the table. Jo smiled at me. "He roped you in then, Jo."

"Who else. I drove the van here and the trees were on a trailer behind it. Harvey organised it at work on Friday. Hillary picked up the van full of decorations this morning when we had to rescue Andy. I had to hurry back to get the trees."

"You get better at lying every day Jo."

She laughed out loud. "I have to pretend I'm talking to someone else or I can't, say it." Giggles went around the table.

Lucas turned to Andy who couldn't understand what Jo meant. "It's impossible to tell a lie unless it's to hide what we are or save someone else's feelings. That's why everyone is so up front with everything here, we've no bloody option."

Andy started laughing. "Christ, that's priceless."

Everyone helped to clear the dining room and we all seemed to end up in the sitting room. Lucas stopped by Harvey's guitar. "How did that get here?" I couldn't see what he was talking about, until he picked it up.

"That was me again," Jo piped up. "Sorry Lucas. I heard you playing this afternoon and knocked on Jed's door. He has your bedsit key and gave me your guitar. Hit me with it if you like but you play beautifully. Oh, fuck, you won't hear me say that word again, I'm more butch than Andy."

Harvey was in stitches and Lucas tried to keep a straight face to be annoyed at Jo but failed. He grinned at her instead "You bugger Jo."

"Oh." She pretended to think with her finger to her lip. "I thought that was you; sorry." We fell apart. Lucas got her around the throat and pretended to throttle her. She put her hands either side of her head, spread out. "I'm still alive, try again." She had us in stitches.

When all the hilarity had died down I was sitting between Harvey and Andy. "I didn't know Jo was that funny Alli, she's so quiet at work."

"Not when she comes into our office she isn't. She gets to the door to go back out to you lot and her face straightens before she opens it. She should've been on the bloody stage."

"I'm going to feel a bit weird going back to work." Harvey sat forward.

"Don't worry about anything Andy. Jamie was told Olli and Gina met you Christmas shopping. You went by taxi because you'd had too much to drink the night before. Ron told us after you'd been turned, Jamie will get promoted soon and be moved on. You'll get his job to run the team. Jo will be out there with you and if you get seen talking a lot, no one will think anything of it as you're both gay.

"I've only told Jamie."

Harvey smiled at him. "Jamie hasn't told anyone except me today because of what happened.

"I have acute hearing and I've heard the women talking. They've known for a while you're gay and they like you Andy. You're not rude or bolshie with them and they feel safe with you. They'll work their bloody socks off for you when you take over Jamie's job."

"Lucas explained about me changing if I get angry. I'm worried about that. We deal with some heavy shit at times."

"It's hard for us all at those times Andy. I still have problems. I won't pretend I don't. Before I met Alli, I tried to extend the time between feeding as I had no one to enjoy it with. I nearly came a cropper, a couple of times. I found if I feed daily then I can deal with things much better. Alli used to have problems before she got a proper feeding pattern. We've all been through it Andy. You can ask any of us, anything. I'm pleased you're with Lucas, he has his head screwed on and wouldn't let you down."

"I know he won't Harvey. When I first saw him at work I couldn't believe he walked into my life. The day he wouldn't look at me was a bad day for me. I drank too much and got on the chat lines… you know the rest."

"Do you remember anything about the meeting, or the person you met?"

"Yes Harvey."

"We won't go into it now. I'd like you to write it all down if you could. You can do it in our office and no one else will see it Andy. We're going to catch those other bastards red handed."

"Right you buggers, that's enough shop talk," Jo giggled in front of us. "I know you've bought new equipment of the electrical variety Harvey Burgess. We'd like to see it in action. It must be fucking good, the noise you were both making."

Andy couldn't believe his ears. "Don't worry Andy you haven't lived yet. Wait 'til you've been here a few days you'll get the picture." Lucas was creased up beside Andy. "She's not lying."

"Before you get into all that I'm afraid we have to go," Jed told us all. "I've got a full day booked tomorrow. Everyone and his bloody cousin wants a tattoo for Christmas. It's too fucking cold to show them off but I won't tell them. Some of the jobs are good money." We all got up to see them out.

"Thank you again for doing dinner. Oh, your dishes; Abbey, I'll get them."

"Leave them Alli, we'll collect them in the week. We've had a brilliant night; we always do when we come here." I hugged her and then Jed. They did the rounds and waved goodbye from the car as they drove off.

When we walked back into the sitting room the chair was up from the cellar and Harvey was coming through the kitchen door with all the other bits which go with it. The looks that passed between everyone were fucking priceless. Harvey had a grin on his face. He was up to something. I knew when he glanced at me. He didn't think anything Jo would pick up. This should be very interesting.

They all sat down and said nothing, just watched.

"Right Jo. You want to see it in action, strip and sit in the chair!"

Her face dropped. "I didn't mean me I thought you'd demonstrate it."

"We don't fancy a fuck at the moment Jo." Harvey was fighting to keep a straight face. Lucas looked at me and grinned. He knew Harvey was winding her up.

"I'll have a go," Hillary told Harvey.

"Then me please!" Gina yelled.

"Christ, we've got a fucking queue going on here, anyone else." Olli put his hand up. Harvey cracked then with howls of laughter.

"Jesus Alli, we're at the end of this fucking queue. We'll never see this chair again, at this rate." I sat there giggling unable to speak. Lucas and Andy were laughing their heads off.

"The only way round it is to buy each couple a chair for Christmas, I'm buying." The room seemed to freeze frame, only Harvey smiled at me. *Good idea Alli.*

We'll bloody have to, if we want ours back.

Harvey chuckled and the rest of them came back to life.

"They cost too much Alli, we couldn't let you do that." Hillary was shocked.

"Hillary, I'll let you into a little secret. Three of these chairs cost one day's interest on my money. They're already ordered, I haven't even told Harvey. The day we tried it out I knew you'd all love it." I looked at Lucas. "Even you two buggers will love it. In fact I have something new for Harvey to try." His eyes lit up.

"Strip and sit in the chair!"

Harvey was stripped and in the chair and nobody saw him move. Andy's eyes nearly popped out of his head. I buckled the straps around his wrists and ankles.

I left them for a split second and returned with the little bottle of olive oil and coated the inside of a metal ball going over Harvey's balls.

"Why have you used that oil Alli?" Jo asked.

"It makes a better contact with whatever it touches. It's olive oil and is better than any water based lubricant. It doesn't lose its viscosity. Everything you attach should have some on."

The ball I locked around Harvey's balls and fixed the electrodes to the casing. I clipped tiny crocodile clamps to the bolts through his nipples after smearing oil on them.

"Lift your bum Harvey." He rose up and I slipped something long and thin up his bum. "Close your eyes and take a deep breath." I fed another long electrode down into his cock and fixed another wire to it at the tip.

Harvey let out his breath, "Feels good Alli." I opened the box with the control panel in and lifted it out. It was covered in dials to manipulate how much power to give. I screwed all the wires into the back and started to turn dials a little at a time.

I forgot about our audience completely and gave Harvey the pleasure he deserves, he does enough for me. He changed at the first sensation on the casing on his balls and the noise coming from his mouth wasn't a patch on how his mind was going mental for more.

I set the pulses and throbs at different rates and he loved it. Now I started the thing down his cock, only a bit at first.

"Turn it up, please," escaped from his mouth. I turned it up and he had orgasm after orgasm in his mind. I set the nipple clips away and the thing up his bum. That changed things again for him.

I changed the setting on the thing down his cock.

"Fucking beautiful," came out loud and clear. I turned it up a bit more and his mind went over the top when the thunderbolt hit. I turned everything off and he came round really fast.

"Again Alli please." Who am I to say no? I took him over the top again, twice and then he opened his eyes. I unbuckled his wrists and ankles then took everything off him for a cuddle.

He sat up and held me tight. "Thank you Alli. You certainly know what I want." It was then we both remembered we had guests and giggled. Harvey looked around at the faces watching us.

"Well what's the verdict?"

"I think we'll all be waiting for Father Christmas this bloody year," Jo said with a giggle. Harvey laughed at her.

"Are you staying the night Jo?"

She looked at Hillary. "You haven't enough room we'll go home."

"Yes we have. We're going in the pool after we feed and Alli can sleep on the sofa with me. Lucas do you want anything from the cellar?"

"Not tonight. Andy's feeding for the first time and we'll make our own entertainment." He looked at Andy, "You're going to love it. Andy."

"We'll use Alli's bathroom and bedroom as we wouldn't have been here," Hillary told Harvey.

"You boys use the rooms behind the pool, after we've been in to feed. Olli and Gina, my bedroom and shower are yours. Now that's sorted I'm getting a drink, anyone else?" Everyone's hand shot up apart from mine. "That was a bloody silly question in this house," and laughed.

Harvey went down the cellar for wine. "Remind me to order more wine before Christmas Alli. We don't want to be drinking the shit on the bottom shelf."

"Wouldn't they be open tomorrow, you could ring them then. They might have their delivery schedule sorted already for Christmas."

"I'll get it here by taxi if I have to Alli. We're not drinking the rubbish they sell around here. That's one thing I'm picky about." I giggled at him.

"What's tickled you now Mrs Burgess?"

"The last time you used the word picky was at the sex shop about your gender remember?"

Harvey cuddled me. "I love you Alli."

"It's confession time."

Harvey giggled "Go on Mrs Burgess."

"Not as much as I love you, Mr Burgess."

"We'll call it a draw or this could go on all night."

"You're right. They'd be dying of thirst in there. I'll give you a hand. I'll make my tea in a minute."

"Do it now Alli, I'll sort them out." I put the kettle on and poured the wine, Harvey ferried it in to the sitting room. He came out laughing.

"What's happening in there?"

"Olli's in the hot seat and Gina's giving his bits hell. He's laughing at her and after what she did with the whip I don't suppose the voltage is strong enough for him."

"They'll have to rig theirs to the national grid." Harvey doubled up laughing.

"Our electric bill is set to rise quite a bit then."

"We'll have to go on Economy 7, it'll be used more at night."

I heard that, you buggers.

Sorry Gina we couldn't help it.

When we went back in the room Gina looked at us and giggled as she turned the dial right up. "Fucking gorgeous," slipped from Olli's mouth.

We sat next to Lucas and Andy, they were watching and giggling at Gina's antics. "I bet you never thought we lived like this Andy."

"Not in a million fucking years would I have thought it. You walk around that office like butter wouldn't melt." Harvey was giggling beside me. "I'm not shocked don't think that. I think it's brilliant and I'm so fucking pleased Lucas and I are together and I get to enjoy all this. I can't thank you two enough for letting me stay here with him."

"Both Harvey and I knew you liked him from the first time you saw each other and were so sad you couldn't be together. You must have gone through hell before we rescued you. None of us could imagine what that was like for you."

"I'd go through it all again if Lucas was there at the end of it."

Lucas got hold of him and held him tight. "I love you Andy, don't ever forget that. You never have to feel that pain ever again."

We were chuffed to bits for them. Jo and Hillary looked across and smiled, they felt it too.

Olli got off the chair. "When we get our chair we'll be fighting about who goes on it. We'll have to draw up a rota Gina, it's only fair."

"I don't mind being in control of this little box." Olli laughed at her.

"You might Gina when you've tried the women's bits," I told her.

"Where are they then?" She looked around on the floor.

"I'll get them for you, I won't be a moment, boys." I vanished to the cellar, picked up the heavy steel cock and reappeared before them.

"How the fuck did you do that Alli!" Andy was amazed.

"I'll tell you later, get in the hot seat Gina." She was stripped and in the chair in seconds.

I rubbed oil over a different thing to put up Gina's bum.

"Strap her in Olli and push this little thing up her bum." He did it all really fast. I rubbed oil all over the metal cock and positioned it inside her, pointed the arm so it pressed her clit and clamped it to the bar between her legs. I squeezed the bottle over her nipples as the next thing I had to attach were the tiny clips to the eyelets through them.

I handed him the control box. "It's all yours Olli, be gentle with it." Gina giggled in anticipation as Olli knelt between her legs. He didn't do anything for a few minutes and we could all hear Gina's mind screaming for him to start. She changed before he even started, she wanted it so much.

He turned the dials a little at a time. The Oo's and Ah's, shrieks and Hmmms, flowed from her endlessly. He must have changed the sensation; running up the steel cock into her fanny.

"I like this. You could be fucking me Olli, it's so real. Give me a bit more please." He turned it up a little and she got louder as the power climbed. The noises were phenomenal pouring out of her mouth.

"Undo the waist strap I want it in further, ahhhhh, please." I unbuckled it and she pushed her body down so it was right in. "Turn the clit thing up; this is fucking amazing." Olli turned the dial a bit. She nearly took the roof off with the words in her mind and from her mouth. When she came she went rigid. Ollie turned things down slowly until she relaxed back in the chair. He undid the ankle straps. Jo and I unbuckled a wrist each and she pulled back off the steel cock. Olli lifted her up and kissed her. She covered him with kisses. "Don't ever worry Olli, it would never replace you. That was some fucking experience though."

I opened my eyes to Harvey stroking my face. "Morning my husband." Harvey picked me up for a cuddle and to kiss me.

We were on the floor and I was naked except for the chastity belt, the rings around my boobs and the red shoes on my feet.

"You've been busy." He giggled.

"It's early and I want to make love to your bump this morning. Turn over Alli and turn on whatever you like." He handed me the controls and his eyes flashed for a second.

I turned over and Harvey changed his position, lying on his back between my legs. He pushed his hands under my thighs and held my hips in his hands. He lifted me up and slowly he pulled my fanny over his face. I turned the dials and dropped the controls on to the floor to wait for Harvey to start.

He kept me in suspense for a while and my mind was screaming for him to begin. I changed before he touched my bump with his tongue. When he did, he took me to another place in my head. The sensations made me delirious with love for him. His tongue ball touched it and the heat was so intense, I babbled in my mind and from my mouth.

Don't stop, please don't stop. "This is fucking beautiful, I love it." *Put your tongue into my fanny.* Harvey took off the chastity belt and pushed it right in. "My god, don't let this stop." The balls heated up, pins and needles fired all over me. When Harvey ran his tongue ball round and around my bump again the thunderbolt hit my brain.

As soon as I was conscious again Harvey started with my bum. I was still on the floor, face down and he was between my legs. He took me to paradise with his tongue and then pushed his thumb inside, found my bump with his other hand. He had me screaming, in no time. I stopped myself from coming, thinking of something different for a moment, every time I got near it. Harvey knew what I was doing. *Have as much as you want Alli, I love pleasing you.*

This is beautiful, I don't want it to stop.

I started shaking and backed it off, again. This went on for ages and when the thunderbolt hit my brain I saw stars, before I blacked out. I woke up in Harvey's arms on the sofa. He was stroking my face with the back of his finger. "I know you enjoyed that Alli."

I giggled. "I was a bit greedy Mr Burgess, sorry."

"Don't be sorry. I've told you before that word is meaningless in this house. You give me what I want, you always have and I love doing the same for you."

"I probably woke everyone up."

Harvey giggled. "You forget Alli, only one of them would've been asleep and she'd have loved being woken up like that." We heard Gina giggle in our minds. "What did I tell you," Harvey added.

"Right you shaggers, tea?" Lucas came in carrying three mugs of tea with a huge grin on his face. Andy stayed by the door because I had nothing on.

"Get in here Andy and relax. You've got us for eternity."

He came in and sat beside Lucas. He grinned at me. "I was full of drink last night but it seems different this morning." I put my hand up to stop him.

"You'll get used to us Andy. None of us gives a shit if we're caught naked at any time of the day. We don't wear anything in the pool. What I want to know is how you got on with feeding?"

Andy grinned. "The best experience of my bloody life Alli and the sex afterwards was out of this world."

"That never changes Andy. You get the same thing every time you feed. You never get used to it and it's always that powerful. I should know I've been doing it for over a hundred years." Harvey forgot Andy didn't know that and wasn't surprised by the look on his face, he couldn't speak.

"I've been twenty-four for over a hundred years now. Remember, this is for eternity."

"You look fucking good on it," Andy blurted out and that set us all giggling.

"Thanks Alli, I enjoyed that alarm call." Gina stood before us grinning. "We've got loads to do today, don't forget. You boys will have to help? I'll never reach the top of that bloody tree in the pool room."

"I've got special lights for in there girls, you'll find them in the van. They have to be outdoor lights because of the moisture in the air. We don't want to be electrocuted."

"Speak for yourself, Harvey," Gina giggled at him.

"Two hundred and forty volts might be a bit strong don't you think Gina?"

"But not for me, eh." Olli strode in with a smile on his face.

Harvey laughed at him. "I think you may be the exception Olli."

"You two generated some fucking heat down here this morning, it got us bloody going, thanks." Jo and Hillary came in with their arms wrapped around each other.

"We're going Christmas shopping for real this time so we're going home early. We hope you don't mind?" Hillary asked.

"Of course we don't." I got up to give them a hug. "If we don't see you later we'll see you Jo, tomorrow morning. You're always welcome, you know that and don't go mad spending on us. It's the thought that counts."

They went on to hug everyone, I thought myself into my dressing room, got dressed and met them as they left to say goodbye.

"Do you want any toast Alli and I'm making tea if you want another cup?"

"Yes to both Gina, I'll give you a hand. Where are the boys?"

"They're bringing the boxes of decorations into the house to save us from having to keep going out. I think Harvey knows we'll use it all."

"He's not daft at all."

Gina giggled at me as the toast popped up. She handed me the slices. "Slap some butter on them please, Alli."

By the time we'd made nearly a loaf of toast, made tea for everyone and carried it into the pool room they had the lights on the tree in there. Olli was wiring it into a junction box so no moisture could get into a plug.

"Switch it back on Lucas!" Olli yelled. The lights came on and white lights shimmered over the whole tree.

"That looks stunning," fell out of my mouth.

Harvey's arms wrapped around me from behind. "You like it, then?"

"It's beautiful, thank you." I turned and kissed him.

"Come on you lot get this toast eaten. It'll be cold soon." Gina got them moving and they hurried to grab a seat.

The builder turned up at one o'clock. "Put a jacket on Alli and meet me out there please." He left to open the door. I ran upstairs, grabbed a jacket and left the house. Harvey was just going into Jenny's with the builder and he held the door for me.

"Alli, this is Ben Rogers. Ben this is my wife Alli," I shook his hand.

"Sorry we messed you around yesterday."

He smiled. "Harvey's explained you get called into work at a moment's notice. I wouldn't be able to cope with a job like yours. I take my hat off to you. Now Harvey, what do you need me for?"

"We live next door and Alli owns this cottage. We're buying the next one in the row and I'd like them all joined together. Is it possible?"

"Anything is possible Harvey. The next one down is a big as yours. I'm right about that, I think."

"Yes Ben, it's exactly the same size. What are you thinking of doing?"

"Knocking this one down and building a wider structure to join them all together."

"That would have to go to planning, wouldn't it? We had to wait ages for the plans to be passed for the pool."

"I remember seeing those at the planning office. It's a huge pool room, that's why Harvey. If you'd only wanted it open air, it would've been simple. I bet you use it in all weathers."

"We use it every day Ben. We'll take you in and show you, later. How long do you think they'd take to grant what we want?"

"The fact you own all three and there's already a house in the middle, you may get it passed in a few weeks. It's totally different from a new build. I'll put some feelers out. Have you got an Architect if you need one?"

"I'll use the same guy who did the pool."

"Right. Don't get him to do anything yet, I'll have a word with someone I know from the planning office. You may not need planning at all Harvey and then I'll draw up what I propose for you to look at. How does that sound?"

"Perfect." Harvey took a card from his wallet. "Get in touch with me on this number. It's my hot line for work so if I'm a bit abrupt, don't get annoyed. I'm usually only like that if we're having a good evening at home and some idiot decides to murder his best friend." Ben laughed at him.

"I'll keep that in mind Harvey and try not to ring you too late."

"My boss has copped it a few times, don't worry. He must

think twice before he rings. We'll take you next door and show you the pool."

If anyone is in the pool, get out we're bringing the builder in.

We locked Jenny's cottage and took him indoors. He looked around as we went into the sitting room. "You've made an excellent job with this house Harvey. Who did you get in?"

"No one Ben, I did it all. I had plenty of time on my hands before I worked for the police. I only joined up four years ago. I want the other two on a par with this one. Could you do that Ben?"

"I have an excellent team of tradesmen Harvey." He stepped into the kitchen. "You spared no expense in here, I can see that." Harvey opened the pool room doors and took Ben inside.

"All the arguing at the planning office was worth it Harvey. Beautiful."

"You know there should be another room beside what we use for the dining room. They're all the same down this street." Ben nodded. "I've used ours in a different way. It's best if I take you up to show you Ben, you'll get what I mean. Come upstairs." Harvey took him through the dining room to the stairs and I tagged along.

He opened the pool room door and put the light on.

"Bloody hell. I wasn't expecting this. Sorry for swearing Alli. Did you put this in Harvey?"

"Yes. Its twelve foot deep, right down into the cellar so I'm a bit concerned it doesn't get cracked if you dig for footings. I've had piles driven into the ground to take the weight of the water and marble."

"You've done the right thing there Harvey. Let me see if you need planning, first. If you don't the back wall of the middle bit, between the two houses could be laid behind this room altogether. I'd feel happier with that as this must have cost a fortune."

"Not far short. It's insured but I don't fancy this amount of water inside the house."

"I wouldn't fancy that either."

"The bathrooms I want in the other houses have to be like this one, I'll show you." Harvey opened his bathroom door.

"You like your marble Harvey, a man of taste."

"We like fine things Ben. I'll get the marble imported from

Italy where I bought this. I'd like to keep it the same, if you don't mind."

"I don't mind at all Harvey. Get whatever you want and I have the perfect man for this job. I get him down from London when I have jobs like this to do. He works in the fancy houses and he likes to get away from it all, calls it a rat race." We walked downstairs as they talked. I said goodbye to him and let them finish talking but I still heard their chat through the open sitting room door.

"I can understand that. I'd have hated working in the Met myself. It's alright to visit London but so nice to get home."

"Very true and on that note I'll leave you to the rest of your day off. I'll be in touch Harvey, this week, I should think."

"Thank you Ben. If you don't find out before Christmas don't worry I just want a good job done."

He shook Ben's hand, "You'll get that I promise you."

"Alli," Harvey came into the sitting room. "Would you come with me a minute please."

I got up. "What are you up to?" He put his hand out for me. "Come for a little walk with me please." I put my jacket back on and held his hand. He took me outside and walked me down the street.

"Where are we going Harvey?"

"I've brought you to see something Alli. I want your opinion on an idea I have. I think you'll agree with me." We turned the corner to our right and Harvey stopped.

"You see that house for sale across the road." I looked at it carefully. "I'm going to buy it for Jed and Abbey, what do you think?"

"The idea is great but would they accept it Harvey?"

"They rent and are waiting for the money from Abbey's mum's house to buy somewhere near us. That means they'd still be saddled with a mortgage. You know what the prices around here are like, Alli. They'd still be struggling and the baby's coming. They'll be paying for the next twenty-five years. That means nothing to us but it's up to their retirement."

"I'll buy it for them Harvey and get Lucas to hand them the deeds. They wouldn't refuse him. He's living with us now and it's the only way they'd accept it. I'm not being funny but I don't think he'd accept it from you. He's too proud Harvey."

"You're right Alli. We'll do it your way. It's not in a chain and the people have already moved out. If we get a move on they could have the deeds for a Christmas present."

"That quick?"

Harvey giggled. "Money talks Mrs Burgess. Wave enough at a solicitor and he'll get off his arse and do the searches himself."

Harvey pulled his phone out and keyed in a number. "Hello Nick, sorry to bother you on a Sunday but do you know of any conveyancing solicitors who'd pull their finger out if I gave them a backhander." He listened for a while. "Great, thanks Nick. How are the kids?" Harvey laughed into the phone. "We bloody loved it. Thanks Nick, see you soon."

"Well, did he faint when you said backhander."

"No Alli, he's got a friend who moves bloody quickly if he has to. He deals with people emigrating and has to get things sorted really fast. Nick's getting him to ring me first thing tomorrow." Harvey held his hand out. "Shall we go home, Ma'am."

"Watch it Harvey Burgess, you're not too big to put over my knee."

"I know and I'm so bloody pleased Mrs Burgess." I giggled at him as I took hold of his hand. "Home James and don't spare the horses. We've got decorations to put up."

"Where have you two been? I've looked all over for you." Gina was upset about something. "I need to know what colours to put where, it's your house."

"And you live in it Gina, it's your home, too," Harvey told her. She smiled at him and dived into a huge box, full of decorations.

"I'm making tea, do you want one Gina? I'll be helping you from now on."

She pulled her head out of the box. "Okay, but don't disappear again please."

In the sitting room Lucas and Andy were putting the lights on the tree. "Thanks for doing that, do you want tea?"

"Please," they said together.

"Where's Olli?" I asked them.

"Putting lights up in the pool room." Harvey followed me to

the kitchen and on into the pool room. "Come and look at this Alli."

I switched the kettle on and went to the door. "They look beautiful."

Olli was hanging lights, high on the walls down the pool room on both sides.

"I'll give him a hand Alli. Call us when the tea is ready."

Olli looked up. "I hope you don't mind me hanging these Harvey. I found two more boxes of them."

"They look good Olli and we might leave them up all year round. I'll give you a hand. Alli's making tea, she'll call us in a minute." Harvey moved the ladder for Olli. He didn't mind heights, he hardly looked at the ladder as he climbed it fiddling with wires in his hands.

"Are you okay Sis?"

"I'm fine. Just daydreaming Lucas. The builder seems a nice guy, he knows someone in the planning office. We might not have to submit plans at all."

"I heard you and Harvey down the road Sis. That's a huge thing you want to do for Jed and Abbey. Harvey is right about them having a mortgage. Her mum's house will only bring her sixty thousand and there are fees to pay out of that, when it's sold and if they buy but just because I heard you don't feel compelled to go ahead with it if you don't want to. If you do I'll make damn sure they accept it Sis."

"Thanks Lucas. Harvey's pushing to get the deeds by Christmas. If something goes wrong and it's held up it might be New Year, we'll have to see. Could you carry those three Lucas?" He picked them up. I called to Harvey before I carried ours into the sitting room.

"The lights look lovely now they're turned on."

"I'll shift the boxes in the hall after I've drunk this Alli and we'll put them on the tree in there." Andy sat down next to Gina. "What colours have you decided on Gina?"

"I don't think we should put anything on the tree in the pool room. It's perfect the way it is. What do you think Alli?"

"I think you're right. It would be really romantic, swimming with just the tree lights on and the ones Olli's hung."

Gina's head shot up. "What's he done? I'm going to have a

look."

Andy laughed at her. "She's got a bee in her bonnet today."

Harvey came in grinning. "She's telling Olli how to hang lights now. I think we'll get the chair up here and strap her in it." We were all giggling when she came in with Olli.

"I heard that Harvey. The intent was naughty but the idea very nice. I'm not sure if I'm annoyed with you or not. I'll let you know in about a year." Olli picked his tea up and sat down.

"I just give in gracefully. I'm slowly going deaf." Gina giggled at him. "You're not deaf when I'm lashing your bits with a whip. You know exactly what I'm saying when I ask if you want more."

Olli just grinned at her and said, "She's a demon with a bull whip."

Andy and Lucas were nearly crying and so was I.

"I've just remembered something Harvey. Ring the wine people."

"Christ, I forgot thanks." He pulled his phone out and headed for the cellar.

"We could have gone for a few bottles Alli," Gina offered.

"Harvey orders it from London Gina. We've still got plenty." Harvey came back in and picked up his tea. "Will you get it before Christmas?"

"Yes it's fine Alli. They're sending a lorry. It'll be here at seven tomorrow morning."

"Bloody hell. That's good service Harvey. You must be a bloody good customer, they wouldn't do that around here." Lucas was really surprised.

"I've bought the best wines from them for the last fifty years. They're probably wondering when I'm going to die… they've got a long wait! The guy who normally comes to see me has got as old as the hills and he's never said a thing. Some people must be oblivious to what's going on around them."

"I think I know why it is. Because you're pleasant and nice to people they don't care. If you were a pain in the ass they'd notice, I'm sure of it," Gina told him.

"I think you're right Gina; are we friends again?"

"I don't know if I ever had a brother. You'd be the kind of guy I'd like as a brother Harvey."

Harvey stood up and put his arms out to her. She gave him a hug. "I'd be honoured to be your brother Gina, you know that."

She went to sit next to Olli again. "Something has been bugging me Harvey. I've no idea who I am or what my name is. What are they calling me for my pay at work?"

"I've never asked Gina but you can take the surname Burgess as you're my sister now, if you want."

Gina looked at me. "Do you mind Alli?"

I smiled at her. "Why would I mind Gina? I already think of you all as family. Sister; sister-in-law; what's the difference?"

"Thank you Alli and you Harvey. I know I have Olli but it's felt very odd having no family I can remember. God knows what they did to me. You all remember your families good or bad. It's like I'm a nobody. I know I'm being daft."

"You're not being daft Gina. Hillary, Jo and me had families that didn't give a fuck about us, so in a way we've felt like you, a nobody. It took me a while to get used to Harvey and Jenny being so kind to me. I've told you that before Gina. I think you go through a grieving process, I know I did. Adey bore the brunt of it. We didn't have an intimate relationship, we were only friends but he was there for me and we're here for you and will be forever Gina. You are our sister."

Gina came over for a hug. "Thank you Alli, I've held up the decorating."

"This was important Gina," Harvey told her. "More important than trimming trees. This is your home as much as ours Gina, please remember that. That goes for all of you." Harvey looked at Olli and the boys.

"We already feel that Harvey," Lucas told him.

"So do I," Olli said.

"Do you feel any better about everything, Gina?"

She smiled at him. "Yes Harvey, thank you."

Chapter 17

We got on with the decorations and were finished around seven that evening. Gina was right. There wasn't much going back to the man. Harvey told us he'd pay for the lot. We could keep the excess so we can ring the changes next year, if we want. He loves everything we've done. I think because none of it looked tacky. Andy trimmed up the mirror over the fireplace in the dining room and asked if it was good enough.

He used glass blackberries, raspberries and all sorts of leaves and rose hips, which looked so realistic you'd think they were growing there.

"It's perfect Andy." He bent down and flicked a switch. The whole thing lit up. "Bloody hell it looks gorgeous." Harvey came in.

"Alli's right Andy. We could eat in here with that on and a few candles down the table." He turned the chandelier off and the room took on a subtle glow. Perfect for a candle lit dinner.

"I wasn't sure if I should do it but after what was said earlier I took the plunge."

"Good Andy, it's perfect." Harvey was really pleased, he felt comfortable enough here to make decisions about things, as I was.

"I'll order dinner and then we'll go for a swim. It's been a very good day today." I stayed with Harvey when he ordered and when we dived in we weren't the only ones shagging at the bottom of the pool. Lucas and Andy were down there having a bloody good time. They took no notice of us and we got on with what we wanted with everyone's thoughts turning us on, as ours were for them.

We got out earlier than they did to be ready for the delivery. I set the big table in the dining room at one end and turned off the chandelier. The glow from the candles and the decoration over the fireplace was really romantic.

Harvey's hands slipped under my arms from behind and he cuddled me close to him. "How are you feeling Mrs Burgess?" he asked next to my ear.

"Happy, Mr Burgess; very happy." I turned to kiss him and the doorbell rang. I giggled. "I think they must have a bloody camera in here, to make sure they pick the right moment."

Harvey grinned. "Don't go away."

He was back in seconds with the bags and plonked them on the side table.

"Where were we?" He kissed me until I was melting. "I think I better stop or we no one will eat. We'll carry on later Mrs Burgess, we need food," he laughed and opened the bags. I helped put all the food into dishes and laid them on the table.

"Call them in Harvey."

"You don't need to Harvey we're here."

The four of them came in laughing. "This looks lovely Sis." Lucas squeezed my shoulder.

"Thanks Lucas, the mirror is down to Andy, he's very clever."

Andy grinned at me. "Hidden talents."

Lucas grabbed hold of Andy. "It's going to be interesting finding out how many more you have." Andy laughed at him and pulled his chair out. The conversation carried on as we all helped ourselves to dinner and tucked in.

"When did you find out you could both hold your breath under water. Lucas?" Harvey asked, because it's news to us.

"After you left the pool last night we decided we'd like a swim. Andy was first diving to the bottom and stayed down there. I got a huge lung full of air and swam down. I was waiting to feel my lungs explode but it didn't happen and we stayed down for about half an hour."

"You'll end up staying down longer than us in the end Lucas. We started at fifteen minutes at first," I told him.

"I've seen you swim like crazy for forty minutes Sis. You must have been using up oxygen swimming so fast. I think you're wrong but we won't have a contest there's no point. I'm just pleased we both do it, it feels totally different down there. It's got to be due to water pressure, it heightens everything."

"Maybe we should try it Gina. I always wondered why you two shagged down there every day." Olli grinned at us.

"Well now you know Olli," Harvey giggled. "Bloody hell I was so engrossed kissing my misses I forgot the wine." He left the table and brought two bottles in with a corkscrew.

I started giggling. "What's tickled you Mrs Burgess?" Harvey asked.

"You haven't used that corkscrew for a very long time Harvey."

He looked at it and laughed. "I should have had it framed." He could hardly speak and was almost in hysterics holding his sides.

"Come on," Gina said. "You've got to tell us now." *I'm not telling them, you have to Harvey.*

They all heard my thoughts and looked at me, then at Harvey who was grinning. "Alright I'll tell them in a minute." He opened the two bottles. "Lucas, pour the wine please. If I start laughing again you'll be bathing in it." Lucas grinned, took the bottle and filled the glasses.

"Alli cooked a steak dinner for us after we'd been to see Ron. He wanted to meet her because we'd got engaged and she'd helped me in interviews a few times." His eyes started to sparkle.

"I played my guitar while she was cooking and I was called into the kitchen, I thought to get my dinner. Alli was stark naked but for a tiny white pinny. I couldn't take my eyes off her. She told me she was dessert and to go for the wine. When I came up with it she was playing with her nipples in the middle of the kitchen floor. My legs almost buckled; I nearly dropped the bloody bottle." The others started giggling.

"I told her she'd be the death of me. She put her finger between her legs and licked it. I had such a fucking hard on I could hardly move. She told me to open the wine and I couldn't see the corkscrew. She said it's over here, turned and bent over. It was between the cheeks of her bum. I never used that corkscrew again." Harvey looked at me and grinned.

The giggles got louder from the others.

"Did you get your dinner and dessert, Harvey?" Olli asked with such a straight face.

Harvey's eyes sparkled. "Oh yes. It was Fucking de Lux. We've had some bloody good fun in that kitchen." Harvey's eyes flashed at me. *If only they knew how fucking much.*

We fell apart laughing.

Lucas picked up his guitar when we went in to sit and relax.

He played some difficult music I'd never heard before and I know Harvey was surprised by his playing. He watched him in awe and so did we.

When he finished he put his guitar back on its stand and sat beside Andy.

"That was really good Lucas. I've not heard that before, what was it?"

"Thanks. It's on a CD at my bedsit. I've listened to it dozens of times but couldn't play it. I'm a bit shocked myself to be honest." He looked worried.

"Lucas, I wanted to learn the guitar for many years and one day I bought mine when a new shop opened. I looked at it for weeks but wouldn't touch it. When I did I was shocked, like you. Every note I played I remembered and could play anything I heard. Alli was the same.

"She wanted a piano when she was living with her parents but she never got one. I bought her the piano as a surprise. She sat there late one night and listened to the sound of every key down the keyboard.

"She worked out cords and what went with what to sound good. By the end of a couple of hours she was playing with both hands. It is scary at first; embrace it Lucas, you play really well."

"Thanks Harvey. I didn't know you'd learned like that. You both play like you've played all your lives."

"You had so much to think about the night Jed asked how long we've been playing, I'm not surprised you've forgotten. I've been playing for twenty months and Alli a year."

"Bloody hell, is that all!" Andy was surprised like Lucas.

"Before we forget to do this we've got a few things to practice before Lucas starts his new job. You can do the speed thing now but you have to learn how to think yourself to another place." Andy looked baffled. "I'll show you the speed thing Andy, the others learned it when we rescued you." He nodded to Harvey.

"When you want to think yourself to somewhere else you have to have the other place in your mind first. You can't just hope it'll happen to get you out of a tricky situation. I want each of you in turn to stand up and think yourselves to the landing upstairs and back here again. It's easy, don't worry. Olli and Lucas, you'll have to pick a specific place to do it to, where you work. Somewhere you wouldn't be seen. Now get up and try it Olli."

He got up, disappeared and stood in front of us giggling, two seconds later.

"It's fucking brilliant!" He sat down next to Gina. "You have a go next." She giggled and stood up.

Everyone did it and were elated afterwards. "Andy, when you want to do the speed thing you have to push with your mind as you're doing something. If you keep pushing the speed thing carries on and when you want to stop you stop pushing, it's that simple. Walk out to the pool room and push with your mind, don't forget to stop pushing before you hit the water."

Andy laughed at Harvey and got up. He took a couple of steps and sped out of the room in a blur. He came back fast and stopped in front of Lucas, laughing.

"Don't do either of them at work Andy, you'll have the team running for the fucking hills."

"They'd be shitting their pants Harvey. Don't you ever wish they knew though?"

"It would make life a bit simpler at work but the powers that be, The Home Office, won't have it Andy. They want to keep us a secret, more I think through embarrassment than anything else. They'd never get a handle on the crime that's committed now without us and they don't want to admit it to themselves let alone the public. The very fact they're making Hybrids proves that."

"They're what!"

Harvey smiled at Andy. "They made Gina into a Hybrid, she's had an outstanding brain but that wasn't enough for them."

"The fucking bastards, I understand why you turned me and I thank you for it Alli. To do that to someone when there's no dire reason is worse than rape in my books."

Gina smiled at him. "Thank you Andy."

"We feel the same as you Andy," Harvey told him. "They'll rue the day they started it because it'll backfire on them."

"I hope it fucking does!" Andy was outraged like the rest of us.

Harvey's phone rang before anyone could agree with him.

"Yes!" Harvey bellowed into the phone. He listened carefully for a few moments "We'll be there in twenty minutes." He closed his phone.

"Grab your coats we've got a murder scene to visit. This will help you Andy without the team there, to control your feelings. A woman's body has been dragged out of the river." Harvey stood up and headed for the door. We followed close behind, grabbed our jackets and hurried out for cars. Harvey locked up and joined me in ours, drove away from the house first and the others followed.

Because it was late on a Sunday night, the traffic was light and Harvey could put his foot down.

"Who rang you Harvey?"

He kept his eyes on the road. "Vice Alli. They've been watching a house for weeks. The woman they've been watching was pulled out of the river. They thought she was inside the house. Someone has cocked up somewhere, they're fucking useless."

"Sounds like a Hybrid's job coming up to run them."

He snatched a glance at me. "There speaks the truth. Olli or Lucas could run that shower one handed Alli. I might hint to Ron after all this is over."

Harvey turned into a field and drove to lights on the riverbank. Two squad cars were angled with their lights on to give Brian a chance to see the body properly.

We joined him just as the others pulled up beside our car.

"What's the verdict Brian?" Harvey asked him after he'd finished looking at the body.

"She's been in the water about an hour at most Harvey. Strangled, the bruises are just showing on her neck. Hillary will tell you more I'm afraid."

"Who rang you Brian?"

Brian looked pissed off. "Who do you think? Vice rang me covering their arses I think. I know it should have been you. They told me you were on your way and they knew you'd call me out. I was really pissed off when they phoned you from here."

"Thanks Brian. I'll sort those bastards out, don't worry."

"Thanks. I'll get her shipped to the morgue. Hillary can get her from there tomorrow. The van is on its way now, you needn't wait around."

"We're staying Brian. I want her taken straight to the path

lab. I don't want anyone touching the body, I'm sure you understand what I mean."

He glanced at the Vice Officers. "Understood Harvey, they've cocked up royally." Harvey pulled his phone and rang Hillary.

"Sorry to bother you Hillary, who's on call. I want a body taken straight to your lab." He listened for a minute then explained we had to wait for the van. He listened again. "Thanks Hillary. We'll meet you there with the body." He closed his phone, "Would you come in tomorrow to make a statement Brian? This looks fucking dodgy to me, it stinks."

"My pleasure Harvey. You always go by the book I should have known that."

"You could have hardly said no, Brian. I've got no beef with you." Harvey stared at the Vice Officers.

"Come with me Alli." *Make sure this bugger isn't lying, please.* Harvey walked us over to the officers from Vice.

"Hello Ian. What's been happening tonight?" He looked at Harvey.

"Hello, Sir. I've no idea. I wasn't on duty tonight. John and I were phoned and told to get here, and to phone you when the doctor arrived."

"A bit strange; don't you think, Ian?"

"We were surprised Uniform weren't here. She was already out of the water, Sir. God knows who pulled her out and we saw no one about. How anyone knew she was here has baffled us, Sir."

"This smells more like a cover up by the minute. I want statements from you both, tomorrow without fail Ian."

"Yes, Sir. We don't want to be dragged into this mess."

"I'm bloody sure you don't. The shit's going to hit the fan gentlemen. Stand well back." Ian grinned at Harvey.

"How's your wife, Sir. She had an accident last time we met."

"She's fine." Harvey held his hand out to me. "This is my wife Ian."

"So you're married to the psychic, Sir. I didn't know." Ian smiled at me.

"Her name is Alli and she's a DI now. You've got a good memory, that was months before we got married."

"It wasn't just your wife's accident that was memorable that night Sir. You banged up our DI. I won't forget his face in a hurry."

Harvey laughed at him. "He won't see the light of day again, not on the outside anyway." Harvey noticed a van approaching. "You get off, write your report as normal and give us that statement tomorrow."

"Okay, Sir. We'll be there. It was very nice to meet you Ma'am."

"It's Alli, Ian, not Ma'am." He grinned at me and walked off with John.

Harvey squeezed my hand and giggled.

"He's not lying at all. The crafty bastards, getting them out to this."

"They're idiots, Alli. This stinks to high heaven. Ron will have a field day with this case."

Harvey sent our lot, home because we were escorting the body.

Hillary got there with Jo, just after us and pulled her keys from her pocket.

"That bloody lot have the perfect name Harvey." He nodded to her as they both stood back for the guys to wheel the body through the double doors. They transferred it to one of the fridges and left us.

Hillary looked over the body. "Where was she found?"

"On the riverbank. Why Hillary?"

She smiled at him. "River water usually smells of mud, not perfume. Smell her." Harvey put his nose near her and Hillary moved her clothing up to her abdomen to leave her legs bare. We could see the bruises inside the top of her legs.

"A rape gone too far, I'd say. When I open her up her lungs will be full of bath water, I've no doubt."

Harvey rang the nick, asked Uniform to pick up the officers who'd been monitoring her and put a guard on the house, it was a crime scene.

"I'll do the PM tomorrow, Harvey."

"Ten thirty would be a good time for us Hillary. I've got a lot to sort out before we could come."

"I'll make it eleven. I know you've got a meeting with Ron,

first thing."

"Ron's at your house now, Harvey. He's having tea with the others," Jo told him.

"Hi Ron. I expect you got all that, from Gina?"

He looked at Harvey and laughed. "A running commentary Harvey, it amazes me. I've come over because Vice tried to get their story straight with me before you even got to the bloody body."

"Who rang you Ron?"

"Colin Spears. He was bloody agitated and kept saying, she must have gone out when they went for coffee on the High Street."

"Only one of them should have gone for that. Who was he with Ron?"

"Tommy Walsh's boy, Sam. He'll bloody kill him if he's mixed up in a murder. I've known Tommy for years, straight as a dye."

"They're getting picked up now Ron. We'll interview them first thing. I may need warrants for their houses. Our meeting may have to wait until later in the day."

"That's fine by me Harvey." He turned to Lucas. "Good luck with your interview. If they take you on keep in touch with Alli, Lucas and if you need to know anything from this end, she'll let you know."

"Okay Ron, thanks. I'm really looking forward to this."

"I can see you are. Olli I'm pleased with your progress as a spy, very 007."

Olli grinned at Ron. "I love it. I've got the biggest blabbermouth to get information from. A spy's dream, really. He hasn't got a clue he's put himself behind bars."

Ron chuckled at him. "I'll get off and see you tomorrow." Harvey saw him out and came back looking really pleased.

"I think wine is on the menu I'll get some up."

"There's a bottle open in the kitchen Harvey."

He grinned at Andy. "Well done, a man after my own heart. Do you want tea, Alli?"

"I'll have a small glass of wine Harvey please. Its hours since I had the last one, and I'll give you a hand."

I poured the wine and Harvey took it in. When he came back for ours I was looking into the pool room. The tree lights and the one's Olli put up were on. The whole room looked lovely as they shimmered on the water.

"Do you fancy a swim Alli?" He cuddled me from behind, looking at the spectacle before us.

"A bit later. I won't have the wine. I don't want to swim if I'm tipsy, it's like fairyland in there."

"I'll make you some tea Alli." He reached over and turned the kettle on.

"Changed your mind Sis?"

"I fancy a swim later and I remember the last time I had two glasses this far apart. I was walking on my knees I was so drunk."

Harvey giggled. "I remember it well Alli, I'll never forget it. I had to go in the Jacuzzi, I wanted to shag you that night." He looked around at the others. "I found it fucking difficult at times, before we became a couple."

"You loved her then Harvey, it must have been very hard for you."

Harvey looked at Gina. "You're right I did Gina. Hard no. I just wanted Alli near me, that was enough."

"None of you know this. I was raped when I was bitten and was so worried about being raped, I didn't know I'd been bitten. I didn't know that until I met Harvey and Jenny."

"Alli you were a toddler, I'm so sorry." Gina's eyes filled with tears.

Lucas changed and did the speed thing out to the pool room to cool off. Andy got up to follow him. "Leave him Andy, he's like me. I wanted to smash everything when I saw it in Alli's mind. It took me a while to sort my head out. He needs to do this by himself, sorry." Andy sat down.

"He thinks the world of you Alli, I'm not surprised he changed hearing that."

"I shouldn't have said anything about it Andy. I'm sorry I upset you Gina."

"Don't be sorry for anything, you've helped us through so much shit. You have an inner strength I admire Alli." Harvey cuddled me, he knew I'd be embarrassed by Gina's words, I was.

Lucas came back in with a towel around his waist and another being rubbed through his hair.

"I'm sorry I changed like that Sis. Your whole life crashed into my brain and I couldn't take it. I have another score to settle with those bastards in London for what they did to you two." Harvey was astounded.

"I saw it all Harvey. If they ever come near you two I'll fucking kill them all."

"I think they'd be scared of coming here now Lucas. Alli chose a good word for us, 'Worriers'. They know we're strong enough to overpower a Hybrid and contain it. They have no idea how strong we really are and will be worried about that. Alli can make them leave us alone just by talking to them. She's very persuasive when she wants to be and they don't stand a fucking chance. We'll do the job we love, get paid well for it and have a ball. The stronger we get the faster we solve the shit we deal with. They won't upset that Lucas, they can't afford to believe me."

"I hope you're right Harvey. What did you mean about Sis talking to them and they'd leave."

I told him. "Hypnosis, Lucas. You've seen how I used to feed. I only have to look at someone and they're under if I want them to be. That's how Josie is with Nick and Jess now. She sees the dead like Gina and me. Her parents were exactly like mine and beat her, calling her a liar. Her mother was having her certified. I couldn't let that happen. Nick and Jess asked if they could adopt her, many times before that day and they don't know how I made her change her mind but I'm not sorry I did it."

"Nor am I Sis, she's a lovely kid. What you went through was fucking horrendous. I'm so pleased you two met each other. It's a shame we didn't get to meet Jenny before she joined Charlie again. She was a lovely woman."

"Lucas, I'm actually shocked how much you've seen of Alli's life."

"And yours Harvey, you two are linked. You didn't have it so good before you met Jenny and Charlie."

"Bloody hell. I need another drink." Lucas laughed as Harvey went to the drinks cupboard and brought the brandy and glasses to the coffee table. He poured a drink for everyone.

Harvey lifted his glass. "To being gobsmacked."

"I'm changing that Harvey. Without you two we wouldn't be

here. I'm proud to call you my brother and sister."

Lucas stood up. "Here, here," called the others as they joined him on their feet.

"Alli and Harvey." They toasted us and tears filled my eyes. I could feel Harvey was gutted. Neither of us could speak, they knew that. Lucas picked up his guitar and played for the next half-hour until we weren't so emotional. Andy made coffee and we talked like all that had never happened. It will never be forgotten.

We went to feed an hour later. We both changed and Harvey took me into the pool and we floated together for a while in the twinkling lights, dancing on the water. Our minds mingled as we soaked up the feelings of the blood in our bodies.

"Come with me Mrs Burgess." I smiled as he pulled me to the edge of the pool. He hauled himself out and reached for my hands.

"I have a surprise for you in the cellar." I giggled, he picked me up and did the speed thing to our toy room door, tapped the numbers into the lock and took me inside.

He sat me on the weird chair and buckled straps on to my wrists and ankles. Next, he put a hood over my head and padlocked it on and then a gag in my mouth. *What have you got in store for me tonight, I wonder.*

He didn't touch me for ages, then all of a sudden the rings through my nipples and bump pulled together. I changed immediately and they kept pulling until my body was only held down by my wrists and ankles. *This is fucking beautiful Mr Burgess.*

Cold steel was pushed up my fanny and turned on. The electrical pulses made all the balls heat up and I was being shagged without moving.

My rings tingled and the power was turned up until pins and needles shot through my whole body. He turned it down so I wouldn't orgasm, yet.

Clever boy.

He rubbed oil up the insides of my legs right up to my fanny and over all the balls from my bum to pelvic bone. He knew I was excited about what was coming and left me alone with just the steel cock throbbing really low like his cock moving in and out of me slowly. The anticipation built to such a height I nearly came with his first touch and thought of something else for a split second.

Clever girl.

What touched me next flowed up the inside of my legs and all over the balls surrounding my fanny and bump. It was thrilling and I wanted more. Harvey turned whatever it is up until it pulsed. He turned the cock up and lined up the pulses. I was being fucked from my ankles to the top of my fanny and it was fucking gorgeous. I haven't a clue how he managed the next thing for me but he did. He pushed his cock up my bum but that was different too. Around it was something metal and when he turned that on we went mental. Every time we got near to coming we backed it off until it wasn't possible anymore and let it overwhelm us. I blacked out.

I woke up in Harvey's arms. His finger traced down my face. I looked around and knew we were in his new bed behind the pool.

"I think you liked that Mrs Burgess." He smiled at me. "I know I did."

"It was perfect for me but you missed out for so long."

He giggled at me. "I missed out on nothing. I had my own little party going on when I was seeing to you Alli. It's bloody fantastic that stuff no one gets left out of anything."

I grinned at him. "I'd like to know how you managed to shag me?"

He laughed, "That's easy. I have one of those ladders that folds into three parts. They're hinged together so you could stand on it, to do ceilings. I put it up under you and laid a board on the top."

I giggled. "Quite the little handyman." He tickled me to shut me up.

"Sleep wench."

"Good morning Mr Burgess. I had a dream about our little session last night."

Harvey kissed me before he spoke. "I heard your dream and had to sort myself out. I didn't want to wake you up. We played a lot longer than normal last night." He was giggling when he finished his little speech.

“I’m pleased you enjoyed it.” I grinned at him. “I know I did. I’ll change the sheets.”

“Not before I shag you again wench. Come here.” He picked me up and held me high, did the speed thing to stand up and lowered my fanny over his mouth. I shuddered when his tongue touched my bump and nearly passed out when he ran the ball in his tongue all around it.

He got me to nearly screaming pitch and did the speed thing again ramming his cock into me and laying me on the bed. As he pushed in his implanted balls at the base of his cock ground against my bump to give us both an extra thrill. We were babbling like idiots. Me yelling for him to push it in harder and him groaning, as he thrust his cock in moving me sideways so my bump hit every ball. I ended up shrieking it was so fucking good and we screamed each other’s names as we came together.

Harvey stroked me until the feelings passed and we cuddled each other.

“It’s still early, do you fancy a swim, Alli?” He asked as he rolled me up on to his chest. I put my hands either side of his face and kissed him.

“That’s a thank you for last night and this morning. I’d love to have a swim.”

As we got near the door into the pool room we could hear very loud splashes. “I wonder what those two buggers are doing.” Harvey grinned at me and opened the door. We couldn’t believe our eyes.

They were shooting out of the water in the middle of the pool, about twelve feet. Rolling into a ball and dropping back in, creating huge splashes. Harvey was giggling beside me. “How the fuck are they doing that?”

Lucas heard us and swam to the edge with a grin on his face. “We’ll mop up I promise.”

“Looks good Lucas.” Harvey watched Andy have another go. “How are you doing it?”

“You said turn the speed on. We were shagging on the bottom and then had a bit of rough and tumble. Andy turned it on to get away from me and shot up out of the water. We’ve been in here since you went to the cellar.” I laughed so much I nearly fell in. I sat on the side and watched Andy again.

"You've had a good time. I'm surprised you don't get shocks off things when you touch them."

Harvey was giggling at him. "Give it time Lucas. That might happen yet. You're going to enjoy yours I've no doubt. I'm having a go at that, it looks good." He dived in and I waited until he had his first go.

He shot out of the water waved at me and rolled into a ball. The splash was huge. I dived in and began swimming lengths near the side so that I didn't spoil their fun.

Lucas joined me and tried to swim as fast. He turned on the speed to keep up with me. I looked at him and grinned, turned on the speed and he disappeared behind me. I looked back and he'd stopped to stare.

We were ready for work and drinking tea in the sitting room. Harvey handed Lucas and Andy keys for the house.

"The alarm code is eighteen-eighty." Olli giggled and they both looked at him wondering why.

Harvey grinned at Olli. "I'll tell them; it's the year I was born. Olli seems to think it's funny for some reason."

"You've seen some changes Harvey." Andy was a bit baffled.

"Get your heads around it lads, this is forever. Alli said the other day she's glad she's a Hybrid and so am I. I'm dreading what this planet will be like in another hundred years."

"That's brought me down to earth with a fucking bang Harvey," Olli uttered. "I won't be so clever in future."

"It's alright Olli I know it's in fun. Alli's right we ride it out and enjoy ourselves in the process. We'll always have jobs; that's a fucking certainty. Are you ready in your head for your job interview Lucas?"

"As ready as I'll ever be Harvey. I have to say something. This weekend, has been the best in my life to date. I have a partner to enjoy for the rest of my life and a new family I'd happily die for. Jo and Hillary are included in that. Is there any more tea going?"

We all knew he was a bit choked and said nothing. He had to get it off his chest. I got up and made another round of tea.

"Not for me Alli I'm off." Olli held Gina's hand to the front door and said goodbye; we'll get updates from him during the day.

"Does anyone want toast, I'm starving." All hands shot up, "I'll give you a hand Alli." Gina found the bread and loaded the toaster.

Lucas came to work with us and will go for his interview from there. Andy came straight into our office to write down everything that happened to him from Friday night. Lucas sat beside him to give him moral support as it was a traumatic thing for him to remember.

He stopped a few times unable to carry on. Lucas spoke to him, couldn't put his arm around him but Andy relaxed and carried on. They spoke to each other in their heads and we truly understand what they feel for each other. When it came near the time for Lucas to leave they both went to the gents to say goodbye in one of the loos. Not the most romantic place but they didn't care.

"I'm off now Harvey. I'll keep in touch with Alli." Harvey shook his hand and he left the office.

When all that was going on, Harvey had a word with Jamie, about the interviews with the two officers from Vice. He was shocked when Harvey told him. Brian came into the office to give his statement while Harvey was still out talking to Jamie.

"Come into our office Brian. Jo, could you come in and take his statement please."

She was pleased to do it as most of her work had come to a halt now we knew about the two supposed doctors being once held at Rampton.

Colin Spears and Sam Walsh were in cells and Harvey would be interviewing them with me.

Once Jo was settled with Brian, and Gina waited for the first things to come from Lucas, we headed to interview room two to start with Colin Spears.

He looked uneasy when we he saw me with Harvey and not another detective. They all know what I see and sweat beaded on his forehead.

Harvey started the tape and we gave our names and ranks and he was a bit shaken I'm a DI now and I still kept psychic in my title so he was under no illusion why I was here.

"Colin, I'm asking you now if you want a solicitor present at this interview?" Harvey asked him.

"Why would I want a solicitor I've no idea why I'm here."

"Yes you do Colin. You know exactly why you're here." He stared at me and then at the table.

"All right I do but I've done nothing wrong." *He's lying Harvey but he's going to dig his own hole; shall we let him?*

That's fine by me.

"Why did you both go for coffee on Sunday night when you know only one of you should have gone?" He smiled at me. *The cheeky bastard thinks I can't read him.*

This is going to be interesting.

"We watched her go past the window on her stairs and the bedroom light go off so we thought she'd gone to bed."

"Still not a good enough reason to both go. Try again. You've got three chances to get it right and then I'll tell you." His hands on the table balled up tight.

"I'll tell you the truth. I didn't want to drop him in it but I need to save my own neck. I went for the coffee and Sam needed a piss so he went into one of the gardens to have one."

"Try again." He glared at me. Harvey looked at me and smiled. Spears noticed and sat back in his seat.

"I want a solicitor."

Harvey grinned. "Fine; interview terminated at nine-forty-five." *Jo, ask Jamie to get in here please.*

We watched him for two minutes while we waited. He wouldn't make eye contact at all.

Jamie came in. "Jamie, could you take Colin back to his cell please and let me know when Nick gets here. We'll interview Sam next."

"Yes, Sir. You know the drill Colin, do I need to handcuff you."

"No, Jamie you don't." He got up and stared at me as he passed the table.

Harvey pulled the two tapes from the machine and put new ones in. He wrote Colin's name on the tapes and put them to one side in full view where Sam could see them. He'd be in no doubt we'd interviewed him first.

Harvey pulled his phone and rang Hillary saying we'd be late and to go ahead. She told him she'd wait for us. A job had arrived from the coroner and she had to deal with it first.

Harvey was relieved. He doesn't like being late for anything. While we waited for Sam I asked Harvey a question.

"Ron was really upset about Sam being involved in this, why?"

"Tommy Walsh turned down his promotion to Commissioner because he didn't want to move away from his kids. He's got three boys, two of them in the Force. Ron's been mates with him for years."

"Bloody hell. Now I understand." We stopped talking when the door opened.

Jamie brought Sam in and asked him to sit opposite us. He was very nervous from the word go.

Jamie gave Harvey a note as he left. He looked at it and pushed it in his pocket, turned the machine on and went through the rigmarole of names, etc.

"Sam, do you want a solicitor present?"

"Dad'll fucking kill me for being involved in this, Sir." He looked Harvey in the face. *He's got nothing to do with this Harvey.*

"Involved in what Sam?"

"I went for coffee on the high street and got chatting to a couple of girls I know, Sir. When I got back to the car I realized I'd been gone for half an hour. My watch needs a new battery and I was relying on the clock in the car for time. Colin was really snotty with me; unusual for him as we've been mates since basic training. I let it go and glanced up at the house until we were pulled off the job before the end of our shift.

"That's all I know, Sir. When I heard what happened to her I had a blazing row with Colin in the back of the squad car. He told me he'd gone for a piss and she must have slipped out then. Sorry for swearing Ma'am."

"That's alright Sam you've told the truth. Thank you."

"Have you got any ideas about what happened?" Harvey asked him.

"How she got from the house and drowned in the river seems odd to me, Sir. She must have had transport and she doesn't own a car and he would've been pushed to get there and back in half an hour.”

“He’s in it up to his neck Sam. I expect you know I read minds.”

“Half the bloody town knows that Ma’am.” He grinned at me. “If he’s lied to you then he’s an idiot.”

“He wasn’t pleased I was here, that’s for sure. I know exactly what happened but we must get it on tape from him. Does he hang around with anyone else apart from you Sam?”

“We haven’t hung around as much lately Ma’am. He’s made excuses about going for a pint more often over the last few months. Remember the bloke who grabbed your arm in the pub and got a medical diagnosis from you.”

I smiled. “I remember him Sam.”

“He’s been knocking about with him and another guy down from the met. He joined us about two months ago, Darren Hicks. Been in the force about a year I think. Moved here because of family connections in the area Ma’am.” Harvey glanced at me. I knew why.

“You’ve been very helpful Sam. You can go home after you’ve given a statement. Wait here and Craig will take it from you.”

“Thank you, Sir; Ma’am.” Harvey switched off the tape machine pulled them both out and we left the room.

“That note was a solicitor’s number about the house for Jed and Abbey. I’ll ring him from our office.”

Chapter 18

"Jamie, pick up Darren Hicks from Vice and your friend from the pub that night. They're in this up to their necks."

"He's no friend of mine, Sir," Jamie said forcefully.

"I know that Jamie, you missed my sarcasm." Jamie grinned.

"Sorry, Sir. It would be a pleasure to pick him up. His wife still goes through hell. She'd be pleased if he was locked up."

"Let's see if we can give her an early Christmas present."

"I'm on it, Sir." He picked up the phone.

I left Harvey to make some tea while he spoke to Craig. I passed Andy's desk. "Are you okay Andy?"

He grinned. "I don't know why I was worried. It's a doddle." I smiled at him and carried on to the kitchen.

Harvey was on the phone when I took the tea in. I gave him his and took some over to Gina.

"Thanks Alli. Lucas has got the job; he gave them some bullshit about helping out sometimes as a bit of a dogsbody with a firm in Wales. He told them they'd have to show him the ropes as everyone works in a different way and he'd been up Everest, twice since then."

"I bet he's pleased he's in." *I am Sis, dead chuffed. Excuse the pun.*

We both heard him laugh. *Drink your tea and get on the computer. I'm going to find out what they call all these buggers. The boss had something to do and he's going to introduce me to everyone after their tea break. You'll need to type it. They've got quite a few working here. Let me know when you're ready.*

"Okay Lucas I won't be long."

"I'm glad he got the job." I jumped. "Sorry Alli. I didn't mean to startle you." Harvey cuddled me. "I've put the solicitor in charge of buying the house next to the cottage. He's told me to offer about five thousand more if they'd complete in a couple of days. I told him to go ahead and he's ringing Australia this morning. Regarding the house for Jed and Abbey; he's sending a clerk to do the searches this afternoon."

"Bloody hell. He wasted no time."

"He's geared up for it Alli and has been for years. If nothing jumps out of the woodwork we'll sign in a couple of days. The deeds will be in your name at first but he'll start the process, to change them to theirs by New Year. We'd have to do it that way or it wouldn't be a surprise for Christmas. They'd never sign the paperwork."

"Why don't we put it in Lucas's name? He could give it to them from everyone in the house. They'd know it was from us but wouldn't refuse to sign for him when the names were changed on the deeds."

"That's a good idea Alli. We'll need to know Lucas's surname."

Believe it or not it's Smith, no middle name and that idea is great. Harvey laughed at him. "Thanks Lucas. I'll ring the solicitor back with the details."

Harvey got back on the phone and I took my tea to my desk opened up my computer and got a word document on the screen ready to start.

I finished my tea. "I'll take over Gina. Lucas I'm ready to start."

Thanks Sis. They're not very organised in here. You may have to wait a few minutes.

"Open your mind to me completely then I can just type anything you hear, or say. Tell me anything else you think is relevant Lucas."

Okay, get ready. The boss has just walked in. He's talking to one of the other men. He's coming over now.

Lucas, let me show you around. I'll take you into the front office. The women in here do all the paperwork and deal with some of the bereaved families. Sarah, this is Lucas, he's just starting today.

Hello Lucas. [She's shaking my hand.]

I'm pleased to meet you.

Gwen has been with us for quite a few years.

I'm pleased to meet you, Gwen.

Lucas has been a bit of an adventurer, climbs mountains. [They're both smiling.] We won't hold you up.

[He's taking me out through the chapel of rest to a door

behind a curtain.

Bloody hell. Bodies in here on tables and the smell is putrid.]

Lucas, this is Jimmy Dixon.

I won't shake your hand Lucas, you wouldn't want this all over you, on your first day. [I grinned at him.]

No I wouldn't. [He's laughing. This place is fucking disgusting.]

Brian here works on the bodies but helps with the bereaved out front. Brian, Lucas has come to work with us. He's done a bit of this work, a few years ago. You'll have to show him the ropes as things might have changed since then. [A happy face at last. I was going to shake his hand; he's covered in, Christ!]

I wouldn't if I were you, I think hello will do, don't you? [Lucas laughed.]

Absolutely, you're up to your elbows, in it. [Brian belly laughed.]

Someone, with a sense of humour, at last. Sorry Boss, better crack on Lucas, big funerals tomorrow.

I'm very pleased to meet you Brian. [The boss was pissed at him.]

Now we get to our friend from the Emerald Isles, Pete O'Brian. Not quite tall enough, for a Pall Bearer but his arms are strong so we shove him in the middle.

Hi, I'm Lucas.

Hello, I won't shake your hand.

Fine by me. [He's grinning.]

Where are you off to Jason? I told you to finish that job, before you go and sign on. Bloody kids these days. Meet Lucas before you leave. If you didn't spend half your life smoking, jobs would get finished. Lucas, this is Jason Hicks, nephew to our Doctor, that's why I put up with him. He's useful sometimes as a Pall Bearer; not for much else. [He just nodded to me.]

Hi. [He hates the boss.]

Rickie before you go back in, with our eminent doctor. [Jesus Christ, he looks just like Olli]

This is Lucas, Rickie. [He's just staring at me.]

Hello. [He's not answering.]

Come with me, to meet the doctor? [He even fucking sounds like him. The boss looks pissed. He's holding the door open for me, I'll have to go.]

What the fuck's wrong with you mate! [He grabbed me from behind, cheeky bastard.]

Don't fucking like that do you! [The doctor is at a desk and I've got my arm around the big guy's throat.]

He wasn't going to hurt you.

Doesn't look like that to me; some fucking welcome! I've only come for a job.

You're a Hybrid.

I'm a what!

You've been bitten.

How would you know that?

Because I have.

What! I thought I was the only one.

Come and sit down. Rickie leave us please. [I let him go; if looks could fucking kill. He's gone.]

Why did you think you're the only one?

Because you're the first person I've met who's been bitten, that's why.

What happened to you? [He actually looks concerned.]

The last time I climbed Everest, I got frostbite so bad, I'd have lost both legs. One of the hospital staff told me I'd be whole again, if he turned me. He told me I'd be fine afterwards. He was right about that but when I craved blood, I couldn't fucking believe what he'd turned me into. I've been too ashamed to look for work in case anyone found out. I was having a drink in one of the pubs in town and heard someone talk about a job here.

You're among friends here. What's your name?

Lucas Smith. I promise you, I really am a Smith. [He's laughing.]

I wish Anthony was here to meet you. He's probably golfing. They must think he's an idiot golfing in this cold weather, but we don't feel it.

[Lucas is laughing.]

That Rickie is he one? [He smiled at me.]

No, he spent a long holiday with me quite a few years ago. He's quite a nice chap when you get to know him. Then he did a stint at the hospital with me. I was doing a surgical rotation there at the time.

If he tries that again he'll be bloody sorry.

He can spot a Hybrid a mile away and he should have known better, Lucas.

Is that what I'm called, a Hybrid? [I look astonished.]

Don't let it bother you. It's just a label, they've put on us.

Who's they?

The government. They're scared of us because we never age.

What the hell are you saying! [I looked mystified.]

That idiot didn't tell you anything when he turned you. You'll never age from the day you were bitten.

How come, you look around sixty if that's the truth? [He's laughing.]

Anthony was bitten about ten years ago. I asked him to turn me just over four years now.

You fucking asked him. Are you nuts! [He's laughing again.]

Some would say that, I've no doubt. I tend to think I'm quite sane.

That's debatable! Sorry, I shouldn't have said that.

We say what we think, Lucas. I'm going to keep you for special jobs. You don't want to be getting your hands dirty with all that out there. You can do the odd coffin carrying but you're destined for better things, Lucas.

What the hell do you mean?

Dr Lewis and I hold a special surgery for people who need our help. The poor souls, born in the wrong body and we like to keep our hand in, with all the new surgical procedures. I'd like you to join me tomorrow morning at the surgery, so you can see the good work we do.

I've had no training in anything like that.

That doesn't matter at all. You'll be helping with things like bandaging. Someone will show you the ropes, don't let it worry you Lucas. You're strong, that's the main thing.

If you're sure? [He's smiling and pressed a button on his desk.]

Rickie, bring William with you please. [They're coming in.]

There you are William. I'm keeping Lucas. He's helping me at the clinic tomorrow. Give him a map on how to get there and he can go home now.

[They're really fucking pissed off.]

What time do I have to be there?

Ten o'clock, on the dot. I'm a stickler for time keeping, Lucas.

So am I. Sorry, I don't know your name?

Dr. Gerard Withers. Just call me Gerard, as we're friends. [He gave me a knowing smile and I smiled back.] Show Lucas out. You'll get a petrol allowance Lucas. I'll see you tomorrow; I'm looking forward to it already.

So am I Gerard, thank you.

[The boss and Rickie are really annoyed. They handed me a map and got me off the premises really fast. I'm coming back to you.]

"Okay Lucas, see you soon."

I sat back in my chair and looked over to Harvey. "Well done Alli. Send it to the printer and we'll go for some lunch. Lucas will find us up there."

Get the tea in. I can't get that smell out of my bloody head.

We'd just started eating when Lucas joined us. He sat beside Andy and had their backs to everyone.

A few of the women looked over and smiled. They knew Andy had a partner now. They hadn't a clue who he was, but were pleased about it. Harvey caught my eye and smiled, he was happy they knew.

"That went very well Lucas. It seemed bloody awful in there."

"I couldn't tell you now what it was like Jo, you're eating. I don't think I could face anything yet, except this." He picked up the tea and downed the whole cup. "Did you get it all down Sis?"

"Every last word Lucas." He pulled some paperwork from his pocket and handed it to Harvey.

"The map for the clinic is in there and the bumf about what they do. He's fucking insane."

"That big bastard sounded a handful?" Lucas elbowed Andy and grinned.

"You heard it all then."

Andy giggled. "Every word, and Jo kept looking at me because we couldn't believe how much he told you."

"Nor could I. It was difficult keeping a straight face at times."

"I thought the bit when you called him nuts was the high point."

Jo was grinning at Lucas who burst out with, "It just came out, I couldn't stop it." We all giggled at him.

When Harvey could speak: "We've all been there Lucas. It actually made it more convincing. Ron will be wetting his pants reading the transcript. I'll give him a copy to read before we go to the PM this afternoon. I take it you don't want to come with us?" Harvey asked with a straight face.

"Not fucking likely Harvey, sorry. If I never see another dead body in that state again it would be too soon for me. How you and Gina deal with that Sis, I don't know. You deserve a bloody medal. I'm sure every funeral place doesn't deal with the dead like that. I couldn't believe my own eyes. Two guys were up to their elbows in shit. Sorry, I wasn't going to say anything."

"It's alright Lucas you need to get it off your chest. While we're away could you write down everything you saw in there. I'll show it to another Funeral Directors and see what they say about it. If it's not right we could get the buggers shut right down. As it stands they wouldn't have many staff left to run the place, once we've finished."

"The money they charge for funerals is bad enough. I bet the families wouldn't use that place if they knew how their loved ones were man-handled and abused, there'd be uproar. I expected the smell of chemicals and a bit of a hum but it bloody shocked me and I've seen a few frozen dead bodies before. It can't be fucking right what they were doing. I'll be as descriptive as I can and won't bullshit Harvey. A good place to get that little bastard Hicks is at the dole office. He could be done for fraud as well."

"We can find out where he's living from them Lucas. The computers may be at that address. You could do that Andy."

"I'll get on to the dole as soon as we go down Harvey."

"Thanks Andy. When we get the nod from Ron you can find out the address of that site Lucas."

Lucas lowered his voice. "Couldn't I think myself inside his house and take a look?"

Harvey grinned. "You wouldn't be breaking and entering. Ron needs to see all we have and he'll formulate the plan. I'll tell him what you said. He doesn't know we could do that, he might agree to it." Lucas smiled at Harvey. "I'll give Ron the transcript to read and we'll see him later after the PM. We'll have to go girls. Do you want to come, Jo?"

"Not really Harvey. I've still got to finish a report and chase up who the two guys that were talking over the fence in Milton crescent. Hillary might want DNA swabs from the relatives."

"Right. We'll leave that with you. Try and get everything we need by the time we get back. Andy, chase up all the reports from the team. We need everything finished if we have to move fast. I don't think it would be today, it's too late to organise it."

"I'm on it Harvey. I'll tell Jamie and he'll crack the whip."

We got up to leave. "Get something on your stomach Lucas, you need to eat. You won't feel so sick. That's what I do."

"Okay Sis; I'll take a sandwich down when I write that report."

We left Jo and the two boys. Harvey ran up with the transcript for Ron and met us at his car.

"That must have been bloody rough in there."

"You keep forgetting Harvey, Gina and I saw it. They didn't just have shit up to their elbows it was all over the floor where they were working and they throw the bodies about like carcasses. I'm surprised they don't hang them from bloody meat hooks."

"Fucking Hell. We have to shut those bastards down."

"Lucas must have seen some sights to have been able to stomach it Harvey," Gina added.

"I was wondering if he should go to that clinic."

"It's probably not a clinic. The man's deranged. In his head it's a posh hospital. He talked about a surgical rotation at the hospital; he worked in the bloody morgue cutting bits off bodies. Did you look at the address of the clinic?"

Harvey pulled the paperwork from his pocket as he was driving. "Look Alli, see where it is."

"It's where we rescued Andy from."

"Fuck; we have to repair that bloody wall and tow the car. Get your phone out Alli please."

Harvey gave me a number to ring and I had to ask for a brickie for an emergency job tonight. Whoever I rang was very obliging and said he'd meet us there at six with sand, cement, water and a mixer. I also had to ring our boys and get the car taken away on a tow truck before dark. The next phone call was for the hire of lights and a petrol generator, full of fuel to be delivered to the nick by four thirty. I finished all that five minutes before we got to the lab.

"How do you know a brickie you could call on that quickly Harvey?"

"He's a registered snout Alli. An informant but a bloody good brickie."

"Oh." We pulled into the car park.

"We have to get information from wherever we can. He's helped us on a lot of building site thefts when the new estates were being built. He gave me a hand when I was doing some work on the cottage a couple of years ago. The back wall had to be underpinned, subsidence. Jenny had a good laugh with him. He's funny, a bit like Olli."

"That's alright then." Harvey grinned at me as we hurried into the lab.

"Hi; you've been bloody busy today," Hillary said with a smile. We bumped into her outside the pathology room.

"Hello Hillary. We've met ourselves coming back this morning. Did you get any of Lucas's visit to the Funeral Directors."

"Yes Harvey. I picked it up through Jo. That bugger should be back in Rampton."

"He'll be going to London Hillary. That reminds me Alli, we'll have to get more of that Bungee strapping pretty damn quick."

"Don't worry we've got plenty at home. Just order some for us and take ours. Jo could take it to work tomorrow, along with manacles and handcuffs."

"Thanks Hillary. That would save us some time."

"I ought to get on with this PM. You need to get back as you're so busy."

We followed her to the table and she started. She had definitely been raped and no condom had been used so Hillary got plenty of samples. Whoever raped her was really violent. The membrane between her bum and fanny was ripped wide open. It was bloody shocking for me.

A Hybrid's done this. We all looked at Harvey and he looked distraught.

I've told you before, she didn't blame you. They knew what I meant but didn't comment about it.

Her lungs were filled with bath water like Hillary predicted they'd be. When we left there Harvey was very quiet as we drove to the nick. When we pulled into the car park and we were ready to get out. "You go in Gina, we won't be long." Harvey turned to me as she got out and waited to hear what I had to say to him.

I put my arms out to him for a cuddle. "Come here." I held him for a few moments before I spoke.

"You know she doesn't blame you Harvey. Please stop persecuting yourself over it. I understand it was a shock for you and I know you haven't got a bad bone in your body. Save the shit you're thinking about yourself, for the bastard that did that to her."

"It was a bloody shock seeing it Alli. It just brought it all back. I'm alright now."

"If one of those two is a Hybrid you'd have to tell Ron. They'll need to come for him. Can you tell by looking at him?"

"No Alli. That's the difficult part. I think it must be Hicks because Jimmy's wife would've been like her if it was him."

"Put him in front of us. I'll read his mind. Have Jo and Lucas at the back of the room and Andy can tell Ron if he is."

"It's a pity you have to be that close to him."

"I can hypnotise him Harvey in an instant. Don't worry about me. He can be banged up until they get here."

"Come on then Mrs Burgess, do your stuff." He smiled.

"That's better." I opened the car door.

On the way in I asked Harvey how they picked him up without us if he was that dangerous.

He laughed and said he was told Traffic needed a word with him for doing sixty in a built up area.

As we passed Andy's desk: "I need you for a minute Andy and you Jo." They followed us into our office.

"That woman was raped by a Hybrid and I think it was Hicks from Vice. Alli would have to read his mind to make sure. I want you Lucas, and Jo at the back of the interview room. Andy, you stay outside in case we need you to do something. Alli can hypnotise him and he could wait in a cell until they collect him.

"Lucas, you and I will get him up from the cells. If he kicks off we'd be able to hold him until Alli arrived. We'll have to do this now as we have a job to do tonight, at six. Gina, go up and tell Ron everything I've just told you please and stay up there. Relay everything that's going on down here. Lucas, come with me."

Gina headed for the stairs while Jo, Andy and I waited to be called.

We didn't wait long and followed them into the interview room. Harvey asked him to sit down and I sat beside Harvey as he switched the machine on.

"I thought Traffic wanted to see me. What am I here for?"

Harvey said his name and rank into the machine and I followed. Hicks sat there listening to all this and was surprised two Detective Inspectors were interviewing him with two other Detectives at the back of the room.

"Could you state your full name please?" Harvey asked him.

"Not until you tell me why I'm here." I looked into his mind.

"How do you get on with your cousin Jason, Darren?" He shifted in his seat.

"Why do you want to know that, what's he been up to now?" He was passing it off as a joke.

"I think you know Darren and I think you've been helping him. Gay, aren't you?"

"Don't talk wet, I only shag women me."

"That's what gay men do when they're in denial. You help him with the gay websites."

"I just wind them up, that's what Jason told me to do."

Can I ask him something Harvey?

Go ahead Lucas.

"I bet you'd let me shag you Darren. I saw that look in your eye when Harvey wasn't looking." Hicks stared at Lucas and truth flashed for a moment. "You really want me to, I can see it."

"That's bullshit and you know it." Lucas came to the table and sat on the end beside me, in front of him. Hicks couldn't take his eyes off him. He forgot we even existed.

Lucas ran his finger down Darren's face and he went all gooey eyed.

"Where are the computers, Darren?"

"In my house, and at Jason's girlfriend's."

“Where does she live, Darren?” Lucas ran his finger down his face again.

“Seven Milton Crescent.” *Andy, get Jamie and Craig on to it now, you’ll need a warrant for Milton Crescent.*

Okay Harvey.

“Why do you deny what you are? I think we could become really good friends you and I.”

“I didn’t want to be called a poof and if I only shag women then no one would find out.”

“You lost your head last night and killed that woman, Darren.” I thought he’d kick off. He let Lucas stroke his face again.

“I was drunk; you’ve made mistakes I’m sure?” Lucas picked his hand up and held it and we could see it thrilled Hicks.

“She would have bled to death if you hadn’t drowned her Darren. Why didn’t you come to me for help, Colin hasn’t a clue what we need.”

“He said she was fair game, only a bloody tom and I hadn’t had a shag for weeks.”

“I would have shagged you Darren, you only had to ask.”

“I told you I’m not gay.”

“Oh but you are and you’re a Hybrid. We could have been so good together. We are the same as your uncle. I met him today, such a lovely man. He’s given me a job, didn’t I tell you. I’m helping him at his clinic tomorrow.”

“I wouldn’t have a job with him if you paid me to.”

“Why’s that, Darren?” Lucas kept playing with his hand between his. We could see Hicks loved it and stared into Lucas’s eyes.

“He turned me a few months ago when he found out I’d moved back here. He wanted me to leave my job and work with him. I told him to fuck off.”

“He was very naughty, Darren. I wouldn’t be like that with you. How many lovely boys did you arrange for him, Darren?” I could see he was adding up in his head.

“Seven or eight. They are lovely.” *Ask him where they are Lucas, we’ve only found one, recent one.* Lucas stroked his face again and got closer.

“Where are they Darren? I’d like one and I know you would

after I've shagged you." Hicks looked eager now.

"Uncle would be cross with me but I don't care, I could take you to them."

"I'll bring one back for you, I'll shag you before I leave, don't worry."

"Would you please?" He was bloody gagging for it.

"Tell me, I want you so much." Lucas kissed his hand. "You're what I really want. I have such a huge sex drive, I'd need another one, too. Don't forget I'll bring one back for you to play with. We could shag them together, you'd like that. We could even swap afterwards. I believe in sharing." Hicks' eyes lit up.

"They're in the cellar at the clinic only he's operating tomorrow, all day. They wouldn't be any good for us, after he's touched them."

"Why is that, Darren?"

"He cuts their dicks off. Shag me now please?" Lucas ran his finger down his face again. *Hypnotise him now Sis?* Lucas spoke to him one more time.

"I'll have to make myself ready for you Darren. You want me at my best."

"Don't leave me for long please?" Lucas smiled at him and got up.

"Darren, look at me." He turned his face.

"You will go with Harvey and sit quietly. You're going on holiday. Lucas will be waiting for you when you get there. He won't come if you're naughty. Are you going to be good?"

"Oh yes, I'll be very good for him. Thank you."

"You're welcome. Now run along with Harvey." Harvey got up and quietly walked over to Hicks.

Hicks stood up eagerly from his chair and ambled along beside Harvey, out of the room, as meek as any lamb.

"I'm going to be sick." Lucas ran from the room and headed for the loos.

Lucas came back into our office and looked very pale.

"I couldn't thank you enough for that, Lucas," Harvey put his hand out to him.

Lucas shook it. "I admit, I wanted to vomit most of the way through it." I stood up and gave him a hug.

"You took that to another level Lucas. Thank you."

"Christ knows what Andy thought, Sis."

"I think you're a fucking hero Lucas," Andy told him as he closed the office door. He gave Lucas a hug.

Ron came in. A broad smile filled his face. He put his hand out to Lucas.

"Well done Lucas. He was like putty in your hands. Gina relayed it all to me. I can honestly say I've never heard anything like that before."

"You're as straight as a die Ron. I'm bloody sure you haven't." Ron laughed at him.

"Well Harvey we've got a rescue mission on our hands, as well as repairing that bloody wall. Gina told me how you ran through it when you rescued Andy. I'm bloody shocked by that. I still can't get my head around it," he looked flummoxed.

Harvey grinned at him. "Prepare to be shocked again Ron. We can think ourselves to another place, if we wanted to. Lucas proposed he'd try it into Jason Hicks' house, but that may not be necessary now, if you've got the warrant."

"This gets better by the bloody minute Harvey. I had to have enough evidence from the interview and I've only just put the application through by fax. The Judge I usually use is away. I'm in no-man's land at the minute." Harvey was elated.

"Could you let us try it Ron? We wouldn't technically be breaking and entering."

Ron smiled, "I see that Harvey. There are plans for Milton Crescent in my office. I took the liberty and rang the Council for them when this started."

Harvey disappeared and stood before Ron seconds later with the plans in his hand.

Ron burst out laughing. "Christ, I wish I could do that. You lot will be bloody unstoppable from now on."

Harvey unrolled the plans on his desk and Lucas studied them with him.

"Ron, get Uniform to watch his house. We have a lot to do tonight and we need to know when he's out."

Ron picked up the land line and spoke to someone for a few minutes. He was adamant there'd be no cock-ups or heads would roll.

"That's sorted Harvey. You'll need ambulances tonight."

“We couldn’t have them parked in the old hospital grounds Ron. We’d carry them away from there, so fast, your eyes wouldn’t see us.”

Ron’s smile got wider by the second.

“What you did to him was shocking in its own right Alli. They should be bloody worried by you lot in future and think twice about messing with any of you from now on.”

“I’ve been worried about them taking Alli, Ron.” Harvey glanced at me and smiled. *I know you have.*

Ron laughed. “She’d hypnotise them and get away Harvey. They wouldn’t try it. Believe me, they will be shocked rigid, when they pick Hicks up.”

“That slipped my mind Ron. We’ll have to deal with Withers the same way tomorrow. What with him using that old hospital it’s made it easier to deal with them. I wasn’t relishing raiding that funeral place with two Hybrids inside to deal with.”

“That would’ve been tricky, I can see that. Those bastards sound fucking terrible. Gina told me what you three saw. I think we should close them down, as soon as Withers is picked up. I feel so sorry for the families whose bodies they’ve had through there. We couldn’t let them carry on like that, taking in more bodies. It just wouldn’t be right.”

“I’ll pay for them to be buried from the same Funeral Directors we used for Adey. The families may have paid up front and would never get their money back Ron. It’s distressing enough for them, without going through all that.”

“You’ve got a good heart Harvey. Thank you. When we go in I’ll get the families names and contact them all myself.”

They have a big funeral tomorrow Ron. I dread to think what those bodies look like, inside the coffins.”

“Don’t worry Lucas, we’ll stop them before they’re buried. I’ll arrange for extra troops for tomorrow; cancel all leave if I have to. I’ll also have Withers’ house watched, properly this time, to make sure he doesn’t go near the business before he goes to the hospital. I’ll have Traffic hold him up so long, he’d be late if he didn’t go straight there.”

“Thanks Ron. It was like a fucking slaughter house in there. I don’t expect the families were allowed to view their loved ones. The bodies they were doing today are for burial tomorrow.”

"They should be pleased we stepped in Lucas. I think you could leave the other interview until tomorrow. We have enough on tape to convict him. You need to get off soon and I'll be here until you've finished tonight after they've collected Hicks. Ring me as soon as you know how many ambulances you need Harvey."

"I'll let you know as soon as I can, Ron."

"You've worked extremely well today. I'm bloody proud of you all. Andy, I'm just about to tell Jamie about his promotion. You'll be in his job from next Monday. Congratulations."

He shook Andy's hand. "Thank you Ron. I'll be sorry to see him go. He's been a good friend to me."

"I know he has Andy. He's going to Thames Valley based in Reading."

"He'd be pleased with that. Gina's mum lives there and she's offered to help, if they have kids."

"That's made me feel better about moving him on, thanks Andy."

The door knocked and Jamie came in. "Sorry to interrupt, Sir. A generator and lights have been delivered here for you. What would you like me to do with them?"

"I'm pleased you've come in Jamie." Ron stepped towards him.

"I've just been telling Andy about his new job. You've been promoted lad. You'll be the new DI at Reading for Thames Valley. Congratulations Jamie. You've worked bloody hard here you deserve it." Ron shook his hand.

"Thank you, Sir. The credit for that goes to the boss." He put his hand out to Harvey.

He shook it with a huge grin on his face. "Well done Jamie you get to call me Harvey from now on."

Jamie grinned at him. "That's going to seem weird but I'll get used to it Harvey."

"Andy's stepping into your shoes Jamie. He's had a bloody good tutor, thank you." Jamie glanced at Andy and smiled.

"He knows the job inside and out already. I shouldn't have to leave him any tips. We have to have that drink before I leave Andy." Andy nodded to him.

"Jamie, tell everyone they can go home early tonight." Ron

broke up the chat, thank God.

"We haven't quite finished the reports, Sir."

"They'll get finished in the morning. There's no rush for them tonight."

"Okay, Sir. Thank you. Goodnight everyone." We all said goodnight to him and he left the office.

"Right. We better get moving. Lucas, could you drop the back seats in your car, the lights will have to go in yours." Lucas picked up his jacket. "You go with him Andy." They left the office quickly.

"Are you going to be okay here, Ron? I'll hang around until they collect him if you like, just in case he's any bother." Harvey looked at me.

"You should stay Alli but I insist Jo stays with you. You need one of us with you, if he kicks off, and Jo could easily handle him."

I looked at Jo. "You don't get rid of me that easily Alli, I'm staying."

"I'll stay, too. I'm sure Olli wouldn't mind if he had to picked me up from here, and could be extra muscle, if he hasn't gone by then."

"All that was organised, without me opening my mouth." Ron laughed at us.

Harvey gave me a kiss and left us to join Lucas and Andy.

"I'll get the kettle on. They'll be like pigs in shit, playing at builders. Let's face it we'd only be watching. Boys and their toys." Ron laughed at me and pulled a chair out.

I listened to the girls talking to Ron when I made the tea.

Are you any good at chess, Ron? That was Gina.

I haven't played for years, why?

They've got chess, on computers these days. Come over to my desk and we'll get you playing with a machine. Ron giggled.

When I walked back in, they were watching him play. He was very good and I sat down to drink my tea.

"They're just leaving the car park, Alli."

"Thanks Jo. It's daft but I've always felt lost if I'm not with him."

"I was going to say, it's because you work with, him but it's more than that. He's the same if you're not there, and I don't think it has anything to do with love. It's like you were meant to be joined. I know there's all that time between your births but you were both on a path to meet each other. He truly waited for you."

"You'll have me balling in a minute Jo."

"Sorry Alli. I've always thought that about you two. I'll stop there, Hillary's on her way up."

We waited for another hour before they arrived. Two huge men came into the office looking for Ron.

"Follow me gentlemen. Alli, Jo. This will only take a minute."

We went down to the cells with Ron. The men were surprised we were with him. They were in for a bloody shock. Ron asked the Custody Sergeant to unlock his cell. I went in there by myself and took hold of his hand. "Come with me Darren, these two lovely men have come to take you to Lucas." He smiled at me and stood up. I looked at their faces as we passed them. I wish I had a camera. I could hear Ron giggling in his head as we walked quite casually through the building and out to the waiting truck.

The back door was already open. "Get in Darren and remember to be good. Lucas will be waiting for you." He climbed the steps and found a seat in the truck. I stepped back just as the door slammed shut, to lock him in.

He kicked off as soon as he heard the bang. The whole truck shifted when he kicked against the side.

"Get that bloody charge on, now!" one of the men yelled. We heard him scream from inside the truck and then silence.

"How the fuck did you do that!" the nearest one yelled to me.

I smiled at him. "Night boys," and we left them scratching their heads. Once we were out of earshot, Ron doubled up laughing.

"I'm sure Harvey would be annoyed with me, but I couldn't resist it. Their bloody faces!" Jo couldn't speak for giggling. Gina and Hillary brought our stuff down in fits of laughter.

"That'll bloody show the bastards who they're playing with if they ever come here to cause trouble," Ron said to us still grinning.

"Have I missed all the fun?" Olli's head was out of his car window.

Gina hurried over to him. "I'll give you an action replay later,

Olli."

"Can't bloody wait Gina."

"They haven't rung for ambulances yet. We better get over there. They may be having problems, Ron."

Chapter 19

Hillary left her car at the nick and we drove over in Jo's car trailed by Olli and Gina. When we got there the floodlights were trained on to the builder closing the massive hole in the wall. Andy helped him but there was no sign of Harvey and Lucas.

"Where are they, Andy?"

"It's like a bloody rabbit warren under the whole hospital. I'm pleased you've come, Alli. They need you to sense where they are?" The builder guy glanced across at us. Andy told him: "Alli's a psychic and she finds dead bodies for us Marty." He just nodded and carried on with his job.

Harvey and Lucas walked towards us from the main entrance.

"Before you confess anything Alli, Lucas has told me what happened. I think it's fucking brilliant." He gave me a hug. "We need your help with this, and you Gina."

"What can we do to help Harvey?" Jo asked.

"You hate the smell of bodies, so you'll pick up the smell better than any of us Jo. With three teams, we should be able to find them. Gina, you go with Lucas. Olli, would you go with Jo and Hillary."

"Eye, eye captain, let's get going. Have you got torches?"

"Over there against the main door."

We spent the next half-hour searching the long underground corridors that joined the scattered buildings across acres of ground and found nothing.

"Something isn't fucking right, Harvey. They wouldn't have them, this far from where he'd operate. Take me back to the main entrance please? I've lost my bearings down here."

When we got to the steps outside I sat down, closed my eyes and concentrated with my head in my hands. Harvey waited patiently beside me and kept his thoughts to himself.

I stood up with my eyes closed and put my hand out for Harvey's. He took hold of it and let me lead him, and told me whenever I came to an obstacle. I'd no idea where I was but didn't care. I was pulled by some unknown force and had to follow it. When I stopped Harvey asked me to open my eyes. In front of me was a stone building, not very big. The sign on the door said 'Water'.

"They're in there Harvey, is it locked?"

Harvey tried the handle and it didn't budge. "Stand back Alli." I moved away from him.

He put his shoulder against it and turned on the pressure. The wood split and groaned until he pushed his way inside.

"Hand me the torch, Alli." I gave it to him, stepped inside and Harvey turned it on.

Stacked on both sides of the small room were bodies of young men. Naked and piled on top of one another like rubbish.

"I can hear their hearts, Alli, they're drugged." He bent down and did a head count. "Fuck, there's twelve here." He pulled his phone out and called Ron. By the time the call ended the others were waiting outside for us.

We went back to where the wall was two thirds done to wait for the ambulances. There was nothing we could do for them as it was too cold for humans outside and they were better off left where they are until medical help arrived.

When Harvey phoned Ron he told him they could come straight to the hospital. He wasn't worried about us being seen anymore as Ron had a team watching Withers' house.

The first of them came twenty minutes later. The paramedics were horrified and rang their Control Room to hurry the rest up. This is bloody vital. Four turned up a few minutes later apologising for the delay. They were still on shouts when they got the call for us.

The brickie was pointing, when the last of them left for the hospital. "That looks excellent. Thanks Marty."

"A pleasure Harvey." He brushed the pointing and you wouldn't know it was a repair. "Do you want it rendering inside?"

"He wouldn't get that far, to see it Marty." Harvey handed him a wad of notes.

"Thanks Harvey. Has the genny come from the tool hire place?"

Harvey nodded. "And the lights."

Marty smiled. "I'll return them for you. The mixer should go back tomorrow."

"Tell them to put it on my account and they can ring me if they want." Marty put his thumb up and gathered his gear together. Andy gave him a hand and Harvey rang Ron again. He told him everything was done and should go home, as we have another heavy day tomorrow.

After having a swim to wash the vile day from our bodies we ate and talked about everything. Andy confessed to us he couldn't have stepped foot in that building and didn't know if he could tomorrow, if it came to it.

Lucas put his arm around him. "Andy we've all read what he did to you before he cut your dick off. No one here would expect you to go anywhere near him."

"I second that Andy," Harvey stated. "If you'd prefer to help Ron at his end, that's fine by me. He would need at least one Hybrid with him anyway. The job's yours."

"That Rickie is your double Olli, so you should be with us," Lucas threw in again.

He still looked puzzled about something, "Spit it out Lucas."

"Okay Sis. I made a point of asking that maniac if Rickie was a Hybrid. Olli was turned by the other one and he knew Rickie wasn't one. I would've thought he'd find that strange."

"Maybe after he saw he wasn't turned he thought the other one got it wrong. He's so fucking insane Lucas, who would know if he thought anything rational."

"It bloody amazes me how all three were let out of Rampton in the first place. He should be put down."

"We all agree with that Lucas." Harvey pushed in. "They wouldn't do it. They'll study him for years and something will go wrong somewhere and he'll escape. I bet we have to deal with him in the future. Watch this bloody space."

"He's never going to age like us so that's highly fucking likely," Jo added.

"I've got to say this Alli. What you did with Hicks was fucking genius. The look on those bugger's faces, made my bloody day. When he kicked off inside that truck it moved sideways about a foot and one of them screamed for the charge to be turned on. He bloody howled when they did it. He soon fucking shut up." Jo's face was lit up.

Harvey giggled. "I wish we'd seen it. They won't come near

us after that."

"I think what you did Lucas, topped that. I could feel the revulsion you felt for him. To hold his hand and coax all that from him was above and beyond for me."

Lucas just smiled at me. "I've just thought of something. The computers, what's happened with them?"

"You were on your way to us when Ron rang. The warrant was granted and the night shift and some Uniform raided both places. Ron has them and he was a very happy man tonight."

"I was looking forward to that." Lucas put on a sad face.

"Now Ron knows we do that he won't forget, I promise you Lucas." Harvey grinned at him. "And he'd use any trick in the book to solve a case." Lucas rubbed his hands together.

"What time are we starting tomorrow, Harvey?"

"You and Gina will have to have an early night Mrs Burgess. We have to meet Ron at the nick at six."

I giggled at him. "No nookie tonight then. We need a clear head for tomorrow."

"I suggest everyone just rests tonight. It won't kill us." Smiles touched everyone's face.

Ron's face was serious when we arrived in his office. He concentrated, to make sure everything ran smoothly, with no cock-ups. Hillary travelled in with us that morning to pick her car up and dash for home. She insisted she would collect all the Bungee things we needed to contain him as we wouldn't have cells to put him in and we should all be at the meeting with Ron.

I helped Ron make the drinks and he sat down with his, thinking, and stirred his tea longer than usual. A heavy weight on his shoulders.

"You already know I have Traffic covering every possible route from his house. They've been warned I'd bloody lynch them if they cock this up."

"Ron. Andy couldn't go in that hospital with us and I don't blame him. He's staying with you. You need one of us with you and it shouldn't be Olli. You might arrest the wrong body."

Ron grinned. "I don't suppose you'd like a night in the cells?"

"I wouldn't be in there long, you know that. Rickie could get away in the confusion, though."

“Agreed Olli, good plan. How are you going to contain him at the hospital; hypnosis?”

“No Ron. We have no cells to put him in and if there was too much to distract him, Alli might have a problem keeping him in that state. Hicks kicked off when he was enclosed in that truck. The noise when the door slammed shut, broke into the hypnosis and we couldn’t take that chance. Hillary has gone home to bring more Bungee strapping and the special manacles and handcuffs, I can’t break out of; he fucking won’t.”

Ron nearly sprayed his tea all over us as that last sentence left Harvey’s mouth. He couldn’t help laughing with us.

“You certainly have a good time,” he giggled

“We try very hard Ron. It’s not difficult and we need to, after the shit we deal with.” Harvey was deadly serious.

“I understand that fully.” Hillary came into his office carrying a huge bag. Harvey got up and took it from her.

“Do you want tea, Hillary?”

She smiled at Ron. “I’d love one thanks and then I’ll have to get off. No peace for the wicked. I’ve got a mountain of paperwork to deal with regarding the DNA for those fifty-two bodies. You’re going to need it for your records.”

“Paperwork is the bane of my life Hillary. It slows everything down.” He handed her the tea.

“Thanks for getting that Hillary.”

“Glad to help Harvey. I’ve been listening to all the chat on the way back. I don’t relish your day.”

We left Ron at eight as we had an hour’s journey. It was rush hour and we needed to hide our cars and find a hiding place to catch him.

Lucas would be in his car near the hospital entrance to wait for his arrival.

On the way over with Jo, we talked about what was about to happen.

“I have a feeling he will be harder to catch than the other bastard, Harvey. He wouldn’t be preoccupied like him.”

“I know that Alli, but we have enough muscle with us to keep hold of him until the Home Office get there, if necessary. Don’t worry.”

We had to put the sirens on once, to open up the outside lane for us. A car had broken down on the inside lane and wasn't pulled off the road properly, causing chaos.

"You're quiet Jo, are you okay?"

"I'm fine Alli. Just wondering what to get for two other people for Christmas, that's all. Jed and Abbey, to be exact. They'd have to have normal things." We both giggled.

"Now that's tricky, Jo," Harvey said to her and she giggled. "I'll give you a clue. We're buying them a house, they know nothing about, Jo."

"Fuck, you kept that bloody quiet. Now I have loads of ideas, thanks. Where is it?"

"Quite near us. We don't want them saddled with a mortgage and struggle for the rest of their lives. We want them to enjoy life. It'll be short enough for them anyway."

"That's the awful thing, leaving people behind. You must have found that hard with Jenny. I know we miss her."

"It's certainly made me think differently, Jo."

The chat stopped as we neared the hospital. Serious heads were screwed on for the task ahead.

Lucas parked his car outside the front entrance and we parked down a lane, well away from the hospital. We did the speed thing and had a look round, to make sure we'd left nothing the night before and found hiding places. We could hear Lucas had the radio on, at least we weren't bored. I know we had get here early so we weren't anywhere to be seen when he arrived but the time dragged like hell. Harvey kept looking at his watch.

"Don't Harvey, it just makes the time pass slowly."

"I'd be no good on surveillance, that's for sure Alli." We listened to the radio for a while and I could feel Lucas getting anxious.

Are you okay, Lucas?

I'm fine but it's gone ten.

Fuck!

Harvey pulled his phone out and rang Ron, to tell him he hadn't turned up. He told Harvey they'd been counting heads as everyone arrived to work and he thought he was there and that Rickie definitely was. Ron said he'd contact Traffic and get them to go to his house. He'd phone back. *This is all we bloody need.*

"The worst scenario fucking possible, Alli." Harvey got to his feet and I followed him to the entrance. Olli and Gina heard us and were at Lucas's car when we arrived.

"This has gone tits up. Gina, could you tune in to Andy? Let's see what's going on back there."

She closed her eyes and we started to pick up the chat around Andy. He must have been right away from Ron. *Stand next to Ron, Andy, please.*

Okay, Gina. We could hear Ron much clearer as Andy got closer to him.

He was yelling into a phone, blasting Traffic for letting him get away. They're on their way to his front door and his car was still there. No one was answered the door. One of them shouldered it under Ron's suggestion and they searched the house. Zilch.

Tell Ron we're coming there, Andy.

Will do, Harvey.

We had sirens and lights flashing the whole way back and it took thirty minutes.

Harvey pulled Ron out of earshot of anyone human.

"Ron, you have to let them take the bodies away to start the funerals. That way, we wouldn't have as many people to deal with.

"Olli will have to think himself in there to look through their diary and find out where they're headed; fucking dodgy Ron, but it has to be done.

"I just hope Withers is in his office. If we hear Olli's in trouble, we go straight in but I'd rather play it like that than Withers gets spooked. God knows what would happen. He must have thought his way past the cops."

"I agree with that Harvey, go ahead."

Harvey took Gina and Olli to one side. "Gina, could you show Olli the layout of their offices. Olli will have to think himself in there to look in the diary. We need to know which churches the funerals are going to."

Gina held his hands and closed her eyes. Olli disappeared seconds later.

What are you looking for, Rickie. I thought you had all the instructions?

What's it got to do with you, I'm just making sure I've got it right.

There's no need to take that attitude.

Don't poke your bloody nose in then. [She's pissed off.]

[Got it. St Andrews, eleven o'clock. Bottom of the High Street. Name Harrison. The Crematorium at eleven o'clock. Name Pierce. I'm getting out of here.]

Olli appeared before us. "Thanks Olli;, couldn't have done that without you." Olli just smiled.

Harvey told Ron the two venues and he rang Uniform. They had to stop the cars before they got near the venues and had to confiscate all mobile phones from anyone that worked for the business. Ron left in a squad car to tell the two families why they had to be stopped and what would happen with their loved ones.

We waited for him to come back, before we made our next move.

"Lucas, when Ron gets back I want us to appear in his office together. Alli will show me the layout in a minute. I want you to take this hood and appear behind his office chair. I'll appear in front of him. He'll be shocked when he sees me. The hood must go on then. He couldn't think himself away, once that's on. I've tried it at home so I know it works." Harvey grinned at me.

Watch it, Mr Burgess.

Harvey got straight back to the job in hand. "We'll be able to hold him until the bag of strapping gets to us. Olli could carry that in as Rickie is on the funeral. He can manacle and handcuff him for us."

"That's a good plan, Harvey. Do you think Ron's going to be long?"

"No. He's got councillors to talk to the families. Alli could you show me what the office looks like please?"

"Of course. Give me your hands and close your eyes." It was done in seconds and waited for Ron.

Ten minutes later he arrived back in the squad car.

"We've got everything organised Ron. Can we just go ahead? Andy will tell you what we're doing."

"That's fine Harvey, carry on."

Lucas and Harvey disappeared before his eyes. All he could do was smile.

What the fuck are you doing here! Who are... He didn't get another word out. The hood was on and padlocked.

Ron stormed the building with Uniform who arrested everyone in their wake. Shouting and swearing accompanied every arrest apart from the two women. They made no sound at all. Perhaps they knew this day would come.

I appeared in the office. Harvey had him around his chest with his arms trapped and Lucas held his legs. Olli came in with the bag of Bungee and tipped it all out on the floor. He manacled his ankles and handcuffed him. They both let him go. He hit the floor and squirmed but not for long. Harvey turned on the speed and he was swaddled in Bungee, up to his neck in seconds.

Lucas brought his office chair to the front of his desk and they lifted him on to it.

Harvey took his hood off just as Jo and Gina came in to see what had happened. It would be futile if he thought himself anywhere with all that on him; he still wouldn't be able to escape the strapping.

"Oh Sarah! I never thought I'd see you again, I'm so pleased." Jo looked mystified but Gina was worried and confused. Olli held her as she stared at Withers.

"You looked after me perfectly at HQ. How are you now dear?"

Gina still stared at him and then found her voice. "What are you talking about!" she suddenly screamed at him.

"Don't you remember being a junior doctor and looking after me?"

"No I bloody don't, you're insane!"

Harvey didn't stop it. Gina needed to know her roots, good or bad.

"You looked after me for two years Sarah. Such a happy time for me."

"I'm not Sarah!" Gina screamed at him.

"Oh. Have you changed your name, you were Sarah then. I didn't want to do it. They cut my privileges for weeks."

"What the fuck are you saying!" Gina's really angry and near to changing.

"They held you down so I could bite you. I did..." He couldn't speak because Gina changed and launched at him, biting his face and twisting his head around. She sunk her teeth in again, right across his face. "You fucking turned me, you bastard! I'll kill you all!"

I grabbed her off him. "Gina don't! He's not worth it! You've got Olli now!" She changed back and spat at him before Olli cuddled her.

Ron came in, having heard all the commotion. He looked at Withers with disdain and consoled Gina.

Withers goaded Gina one more time. "You know you liked it Sarah! You're my dau…" Harvey changed and hit him across his head, so hard we all heard the crack when his neck broke. His head lay on his right shoulder.

About ten seconds later it came up straight again and he grinned insanely at Harvey. Harvey swung at him again as his mouth opened to finish his last words.

Lucas quickly pushed the hood over his head and pulled him back. I padlocked it on and Lucas hurried to stop Harvey.

"Don't Harvey! We all want to kill him! You're only getting yourself upset and he'll get his comeuppance in London! He should be fucking put down, like an animal!"

"I'd like to chop him up and bury the bits from here to kingdom fucking come!" Harvey screamed at Withers.

Lucas cuddled him. "Let it go Harvey, remember Ron is here!"

Harvey changed back. "Sorry."

"Don't be sorry Harvey. I'd like to do the fucking same to him. Come on lad, you've all pulled off something very complex today. I'm proud of all of you." Ron put his hand on Harvey's shoulder and squeezed it. "Let's get out of here, this place stinks."

We waited outside for the Home Office truck to arrive. The men that drove it were bloody wary of us all. They'd only speak to Ron and kept their eyes fixed on us when they were near.

When they'd gone we drove back to the nick. Harvey headed up to see Ron, to apologise for his outburst. He was thoroughly ashamed he'd done it. Ron asked him what outburst as he hadn't see anything and if Harvey thought he'd done anything wrong, Withers deserved all he got for changing Gina.

Harvey came down a lot happier and sat with us drinking tea.

Jamie knocked and came in with a grin on his face.

"You've had a bloody good day. The Custody Sergeant is

doing his ends, down there. Every cell is bursting at the seams. We might have to shift some of them to another nick."

Harvey laughed at him. "Make sure they keep Jason Hicks here. I'm interviewing him, the little bastard. And the one that's Olli's double. I think you'd like to be in on that Olli."

"Agreed Harvey and the little twat from the hospital."

"He's on his way here now Olli. The Commissioner threatened them all, today. I heard him go to town on the phone before he left here," Jamie informed us.

"What did Gina think of your promotion?" Harvey asked him before he asked why they weren't involved.

"She's made up. We want kids and couldn't have managed as she had to work. Her mum will help us."

"It's about time you got married Jamie."

Jamie smiled at Harvey. "Seeing you two so happy has made me think of it Harvey, and I know Gina wants to. Now I'll have more money coming in we'll bite the bullet, before she gets pregnant. Her mum would be thrilled she's hinted so many times."

"I highly recommend it Jamie. I'm waiting for these buggers to pop the question." He looked at Olli and Gina.

"Us?" Gina asked.

"That's who I'm looking at Gina." She went all coy and giggled. Olli just smiled at Harvey. Something passed between them and I couldn't catch it.

"I better get on and tell the Custody Sergeant not to let them go. Don't want to spoil your fun." Harvey laughed at him as he left.

"We've got Jimmy Thompson to interview Alli, I'm sure you'd like to get your hands on him."

"I've touched him once and that was enough, slimy little bugger. I want to dig around in his head, much more interesting." Harvey laughed at me.

"Do you want to stand at the back of the room Lucas to see how Alli really operates?"

Lucas stood up. "I'm already there Harvey."

Andy got him from the cells and stood in the room until we got there.

Stay Andy, Harvey told him as we trooped in. Lucas stood

beside him, to listen.

"What's all this then, armed guard." Harvey ignored him, turned on the machine and we stated our names and ranks.

Jimmy sat up when he heard I was a DI. He looked worried. I kept the word psychic in my title to remind him of last time and rub it in. He shifted in his seat.

"How long have you been knocking around with Darren Hicks," Harvey asked.

He sneered at Harvey. "Is that why I'm here because I'm friends with him?"

"How much did Darren pay you to find someone he could shag?" He pulled back in his seat.

How the fuck did she know that. I just smiled and carried on.

"You got someone for his uncle as well. A young guy because he said he was gay and needed a shag. What are you the local pimp? We've got twelve more boys in hospital right now."

Shit.

"Shit indeed." His hands were shaking on the table. "You're up shit creek, Jimmy. They will have interesting interviews, and you collected them from pubs around here," I leaned closer to him. "Not a good move on your part and shows how thick you are Jimmy. We have a charge sheet as long as my bloody arm.

"A few weeks back Jason put you on to another lad for a blind date. I'll give him his due, he knew how to coax the poor bastards into a meeting. I look forward to his interview. We watched his site online." Jimmy's eyes nearly popped out of his head.

"The lad was a bit reluctant to go with you. Rohypnol works wonders, doesn't it? You don't know this but your friends at the hospital, have all been clocked." He looked to the ceiling.

"It's no good praying to him up there as he won't get you out of this. That bastard doctor chopped his cock off. You don't even know his name, do you? I'll tell you. Jay Henderson. He spoke to us at his post-mortem. I hope this hits home, you're up for his murder, for taking him there. You'd do anything for money. A pity your kids didn't see any of it.

"You would have been next, if you hadn't bottled the last little job. You took a grand for that one. You've no idea who you were dealing with.

"How did it go at the clinic? Sorry, you're still going. Genital warts are tricky little fuckers to get rid of. Painful, I've heard you cry. Not as much as your poor wife, though.

"She can't have any more kids because of you. You've really fucked her up. Had to have a Hysterectomy because of the things you shoved up her. I don't know why, but she defended you when she had to be re-stitched after her op.

"Oh. Silly me, I got that wrong. You threatened to kill her if she told the truth. You couldn't even let her heal.

"A few of the toms have come off badly at your hands. The last one you and Colin teamed up with Darren, was ripped wide open, by him. That's two murders and grievous bodily harm. Add to that trying to run rings around us and the twelve boys you rounded up last week. What's next?" I sat looking at him.

"Don't look for anything else, please?" He had tears in his eyes.

"Scared aren't you, because there's plenty more where that came from. Have you got enough Harvey or could I have another dig around inside his head." I leaned closer across the table.

"I'll tell you one thing, your wife and kids are getting the best Christmas present they've ever had. You'll be gone for good now." I sat back in my seat.

"Interview terminated at three forty-two." Harvey switched the machine off.

"Andy, would you take him back to a cell please, and put him in with Rickie."

"It would be a pleasure, Sir." Andy handcuffed him and dragged him out.

Lucas sat in the chair he just vacated and laughed.

"Fucking hell, Sis. You made mincemeat out of him."

"She's very dangerous when she wears black." Harvey giggled. I looked at my clothes and laughed with him. I didn't realize that's what I was wearing.

We walked into the office to clapping from our lot. Jo had tea ready, thank God.

"Thanks Jo. Harvey is there anywhere we could get a Christmas hamper made up. I'd like his wife and kids to have one. She could do with a bloody nurse, as well."

"I think I could organise that, Alli. I'll find out from Jamie how old the kids are and get them something. When Jamie said she was still going through hell, I had no idea it was that bad."

"I bet they've got fuck all. I wish I hadn't told him what was wrong with him, that time. He might've dropped dead before now."

"I'll be back in a minute Alli." Harvey talked to Jamie for quite a time and when he came back in he sat beside me.

"I've spoken to Jamie. You're right, they live from hand to mouth and have nothing in the house that's decent for the kids and that goes for food and clothes. I've told Jamie to take the day off tomorrow; find out what they need in the whole house and he's buying the lot from everyone at the station. He worked for us. She must think we're all like him.

"She deserves to have a life now he's gone. Perhaps she might meet someone who would be good to her and the kids."

I flung my arms around his neck and cried.

He let me cry for a while and gave me one of his lovely white hankies, which I got make-up on, straight away.

"Thank you Harvey. I couldn't bear to think of those kids with nothing."

Andy came over to us when I was alright again. "Sorry Harvey. Debbie thought we should draw the raffle and give his wife the charity money. She visited her when she was in hospital."

"That's a good idea Andy. Tell them we'll be out in a minute."

"I'm alright now Harvey. I better check my face. Half of it's on your hanky." He giggled and passed my bag.

Ron came in just as I was finishing the repair job.

"I've just come to tell you the families of the deceased are very grateful we stopped the funerals. They want to thank you Harvey. They had no chance to say goodbye in a chapel of rest and the new Funeral Directors have picked up the bodies and are getting them ready, properly. I have to say they were horrified at the state of them. They'd never seen anything like it when they opened the coffins. Thank you for making it obvious about what went on in there, Lucas. I feel sorry for anyone who's had a funeral from them. You've all worked extremely well on this case and I couldn't have asked for more."

"I have to ask you something, Ron. Would you drawer the raffle in the big office? The charity money is going to Jimmy Thompson's wife and kids."

"I certainly will. I've just listened to his interview, that poor woman." Ron got a bit choked and had to turn away for a moment. He coughed and stood tall. "I'm okay now."

Harvey put his hand on his shoulder. "They're going to be okay Ron. Come and drawer the raffle."

A cheer went up when we flowed out of the office. The raffle tickets were in a waste paper basket, all folded carefully.

"Come on Debbie, you hold it up. We wouldn't be doing this if it wasn't for you!" Jamie called. She came forward and picked the bin up.

"Would you do us the honour of drawing the first raffle, Sir?" Ron stepped forward and reached into the bin. He gave the ticket to Debbie to unfold.

"Number seventy-four, pink ticket," she called. There was lots of mumbling and dull noise but eventually there was a voice from the back of the room and a hand in the air. The hand made its way forward through the desks and onlookers. She came out of the huddle at the front with a huge smile.

"Put it with the money for Tess. My friend's kids play with hers. They haven't got much."

"That's very good of you Clare. Thank you." Ron shook her hand.

"How much have you raised Debbie, just out of interest?" Ron asked.

"I don't know if you know this, Sir. They've given the price of a drink for a raffle ticket. The money is at the pub and with the hundred pounds Clare's put in, there's about fifteen hundred in their safe. It was started to get this lot drinking less but they've put money into a jar on the bar, as well, so I'm very proud of them."

"So am I, Debbie."

Ron gave her forty quid to add to it. "Thank you, Sir. It's going to a good cause." He just patted her hand. I don't think he could actually speak, he was that emotional.

"Debbie."

"Yes, Sir." Harvey asked her into our office.

"Have you got anything planned tonight?"
"No, Sir."
"I think we should go to the pub with you, to get the money out and take it to her. She doesn't know me and I need to tell her what happened here today. Also what Jamie's doing tomorrow?"
Debbie smiled. "I'd like that, Sir. I'll ring the pub and ask them to get it ready to pick up and could I ring Martin to say I'll be late home?"
"Of course you can. Thanks Debbie."
She left and our lot came in. "Jo, do you fancy doing a huge shop, at the local supermarket. You can take Andy and Lucas with you."
She grinned at him. "Why not. Come on you buggers; there's no slacking here." Harvey gave her a wad of notes which she stuffed into her jeans pocket. "Thanks Harvey. You two are my bodyguards." They laughed at her and went willingly.

Three cars pulled up outside the house, Debbie's, ours and Jo's.
Debbie went in to speak to her first, to tell her Harvey had to talk to her. She came out again and invited us in. Tess was huddled on the end of an old-fashioned sofa and asked us to sit down.
The place was clean but they had nothing to speak of. Harvey sat next to her and he introduced me. Debbie sat the other side of her in a chair that didn't match the sofa. We could tell she'd tried to hold it together for the sake of the kids.
"Tess, you can call me Harvey. I arrested Jimmy yesterday and he's seriously implicated in two murders." She started crying. Harvey wasn't sure if he should carry on.
"Tess isn't upset for him Harvey, its relief." She looked at me and nodded through her tears. She composed herself and spoke to Harvey.
"Thank God you've got him on something like that. I never want to see him again. You have to excuse the state of the place." She was going to carry on and Harvey stopped her.
"Don't apologise Tess. We know now, what you've been going through. Debbie organised a raffle at work and she's here to give you something."

"There's fifteen hundred and forty-five pounds here Tess. We couldn't think of anyone more deserving than you, after all you've been through and that's not all. Sir?" Tess sat there stunned.

"Tomorrow, Jamie is coming to see what furniture, clothes and anything else you need, to make this house comfortable for you and your kids. It's from everyone at the station. Just tell him what you want and go mad if you like. Have a bit of fun. There's a car outside full of food and Jamie's told me the ages of your kids. They'll have a good Christmas, I promise you that."

She broke down and sobbed. I stood up and Harvey moved along so I could sit beside her.

I cuddled her until she stopped crying. "Tess, you've been through hell with him, I feel it. You'll never have him on your doorstep again. We'll hear if they ever consider letting him out and I know enough to convict him of other crimes. Believe me, he'll never get out."

"Alli reads minds Tess. She's telling the absolute truth. I listened to the tapes and he begged her to stop looking inside his head."

Tess looked at me and grinned. "He's finally met his match, I like it."

"Are you medically fit Tess, or could you use a hand with the kids." She looked worried and Social Services flashed into her head. "You've got it wrong, I'm not thinking that. I'll organise a nurse to come every day to help you until you've got over your op, properly. You shouldn't be lifting anything and kids are a handful. This is my Christmas present to you."

She held my hand. "Thank you. I get very tired."

I smiled at her. "I know you do. Get plenty of rest and we'll come and see how you're doing, after Christmas."

"I'll get the shopping in with Jo." Harvey left the room.

"You won't have to lift a finger. We'll organise a few lads from work, to move all the new stuff in and take away what you don't want anymore. I wish I'd known about you sooner. I'd have tried to get the little bastard, before now. Sorry, that's what I think of him."

"Fill your boots Alli. I've wished him dead for years."

Debbie got up and showed Harvey the kitchen and Jo smiled at Tess when she carried things through.

When they'd finished Debbie said, "I'll stay with Tess for a while and put all that away."

Tess tried to get up. "Don't Tess." I gave her a hug and Harvey held her hand to say goodbye. Jo just smiled and we left the house.

"She's well shot of him," Jo uttered as we got to the cars.

"Agreed. Are you coming to ours Jo, or have you got other plans?"

"I'm going home for a shag, Harvey. This abstinence, for even one night is not good for you. A shag a day keeps the doctor away, didn't you know."

"I'll have to remember that Jo, see you tomorrow." He grinned as she got in her car. Harvey took his phone out after we were in ours. He rang an agency in London and hired a nurse to help Tess, every day for three months. Next, he booked her into The Carlton and hired a car for her to run around in for the duration. We pick her up from the station at nine in the morning.

On the way home I said to Harvey, "I've got an early Christmas present, for you. You've been a very naughty boy today, and naughty boys get presents."

Harvey glanced at me, flashing his eyes. "Give me a clue please Mrs Burgess."

"It's not electrical."

"Now that's interesting, a new whip?"

"No. Try again."

He tried to read my mind so I let him in.

"Hmmmmm; you little minx, let's hurry home." He turned the siren on and we got home in record time and headed straight for my dressing room.

Harvey stood there, stark naked with his hands above him on the arch, going nuts in his head.

"Take a deep breath Mr Burgess."

When I screwed it in he felt me pull back, just a little, and looked down and smiled.

Clever girl.